1987

12 JUN 1988

-6 MAR 19

29. SEP. 1988
28. JUN. 1989

28 MAY

-3 MAR 1995

WITHDRAWN

C 08 0313619

The Dawlish Season

The Dawlish Season

DESMOND RAYNER

HODDER AND STOUGHTON
LONDON SYDNEY AUCKLAND TORONTO

The author would like to thank the following for their help with research: British Actors Equity Association, The Management of Her Majesty's Theatre, London Weekend Television, Anvil Film & Recording Group Ltd, Moroccan Tourist Office, Raymond Mander and Jo Mitchenson, theatrical historians, Automobile Association.

Apart from the household names of the theatre, the characters and events depicted in this book are entirely fictitious; any similarity to real people, living or dead, and actual happenings is purely coincidental.

British Library Cataloguing in Publication Data
Rayner, Desmond
  The dawlish season.
  I. Title
  823'.914[F]   PR6068.A949/

  ISBN 0 340 35463 1

Copyright © 1984 by Desmond Rayner. First printed 1984. All rights reserved. No part of this publication may be reproduced or transmitted in any form or by any means, electronic or mechanical, including photocopy, recording, or any information storage and retrieval system, without permission in writing from the publisher. Printed in Great Britain for Hodder and Stoughton Limited, Mill Road, Dunton Green, Sevenoaks, Kent by Biddles Limited, Guildford and King's Lynn. Typeset by Hewer Text Composition Services, Edinburgh.

Hodder and Stoughton Editorial Office: 47 Bedford Square, London WC1B 3DP.

For
my pseudonymous wives
Ada – Ann – Helen – Ida
Johnny – Ruth – Sheila
but quintessentially
their joint and understanding begetter
CLAIRE

Entrances

First Entrance

"Christ! This is no job for a grown man." The thought murmured its way from Mitchell Dawlish as he strode towards Her Majesty's Theatre for his opening night. He couldn't recall who had first laid claim to the sentiment, Larry or John, but it was one to which he subscribed as every first night drew closer. The dry sensation of nausea crept into his throat as it always did on these occasions. His fingers were numb, and his hands clammy as first night nerves edged their way through his body.

Mitch had decided to arrive at the theatre with time to spare; it was a pattern he always followed on these occasions. He needed time to unwind. He needed time to contemplate what lay ahead of him, and fully appreciate the significance of this particular production. He wanted to drink deeply of the uniquely heady atmosphere that is theatre. He wanted to immerse himself in the classically unplayable role of King Lear.

The abstracted stroll down the Haymarket might have been taking place in midsummer for all the effect the inclement February weather had upon him. For a brief moment he looked up at the rain soaked sky, and reflected upon the appositeness of the wind and the driving dampness. A half-smile fought across his face as he pondered removing his clothes and performing the heath scene. What a great publicity stunt! The idea remained stillborn.

As he approached the theatre he could see a sign hanging from below the glass awning. The lettering proudly proclaimed the fact that the entire Dawlish family were appearing together for the very first time, *all six of them*. The public relations machine had revved into action to make great play of this point, their handouts had carefully avoided any mention of the real reason for this unexpected united front.

"A great theatrical event – not to be missed", informed a large poster alongside the main entrance. Darkly atmospheric photographs were displayed. The season was widely announced as being limited to a twelve week period. The management fully anticipated a further twelve week tour of the provinces, and then a number of prestigious bookings to carefully selected European capitals.

Mitch turned into Charles II Street and spurted across the road to seek refuge under the covered side entrance. People were already tightly clustered around the stage door. A few leaned against the wall as though they had been rooted there for hours. They were the true devotees, now concentrated in little huddles of mutual protection against the driving wind. They were not all teenage fans, not all eager drama students keen to be near a living legend. Many of them were theatre-goers of long standing, people who recalled the many stimulating evenings they had spent under the spell of Mitch's magnetic personality. They had turned out because they knew he needed their support.

He looked up from the anonymous confines of his coat collar, grateful for the reassurance afforded by the sight of these dedicated fans. His wavering self-confidence urgently needed all the moral boost it could get.

As the light fell on Mitch's face one could see that he looked slightly older than his early fifties. There was still no escaping the strong square jaw that had helped him through his early years of endless romantic leads. His eyes had always been a little larger than life, and although they were now sunken and red-rimmed, it was impossible to deny the alertness that still shot from them. His hair had remained thick and healthy, changing from a dense black to an attractive iron grey, full and heavy around his ears. His nose had always been his most remarkable feature, carved from pure granite and as straight as a set square. There were times when critics had accused him of playing in profile in order to capitalise on this outstanding feature. With a commanding height of six foot three inches there was never any doubt about his star status once he stepped on to a stage. He held his lean body erect, walking with a steady swing of his long legs directed from still narrow hips.

His smile slithered into place as he switched on his faded matinee charm at the approaches to the stage door. Hands thrust towards him with autograph books, or the backs of torn envelopes. It was a traditionally cliché situation, handled in the cliché manner.

"Good luck, Mitchell," called a faithful supporter edging her way towards the front of the little knot of people. Her eyes were alive with excitement at the proximity of this great man of the theatre. The cry was echoed by others, and accompanied by pats on the back. Ball-point pens and the ends of chewed pencils were thrust under his nose, and just as keenly retrieved.

The happening lasted no more than a few seconds, but it helped. The momentary feeling of well-being was rekindled within his belly. It allowed him to think that perhaps he really was about to climb back to where he belonged after having been in the theatrical wilderness for the past six years.

"Evening, Mr Dawlish," said Joe, from within his confined cubby-hole. "There's been a pile an' 'alf messages for you. I've put 'em in your dressing room."

"Oh! How nice. Thank you." He flicked down his coat collar and stamped his feet. The dressing room key was offered with great propriety. The exchange was brief, but it served to cement the relationship. Mitch hurried on upstairs towards the welcome silence of his dressing room, and the relaxing warmth of the central heating.

The management had allocated to him the star suite consisting of a dressing room that doubled as a reception area for friends, a small make-up room, and a complete bathroom. It all sounded terribly grand. The facilities were welcome even though they were tatty around the edges. The indigo carpet only just matched the curtains, while the furniture was lumpy and cumbersome; there was certainly no star quality about the decor.

Once inside Mitch decided to get out of his damp clothes and change into part of his costume. He was still sufficiently conceited about his youthful physique to stand sideways on to the enormous wall mirror in order to admire his flat stomach, and the general firmness of his naked body. His hands splayed over his abdomen as he nodded to himself with an unmistakable smugness that would have puzzled a fly on the wall. He pulled on his jock strap, arranging himself comfortably as a prelude to clambering into the thick tights already laid out on the wicker chair.

Mitch lay down, shifting his position several times until he finally managed to escape the worst of the lumps in the upholstery. His eyes closed as he began to think back over the past few years. He had never been out of work, but as a result of a number of unfortunate productions in which he always seemed to be badly cast, he had not appeared in the West End. The intervening period had been spent with prolonged tours abroad, particularly in Australia and South Africa. There had been several special guest appearances in other stars' films, one seven part epic for TV, a Broadway appearance that folded within a month, and a few provincial dates that really amounted to nothing more than personal appearances. There had been nothing to stretch his talents, nothing to challenge his undoubted ability.

The current show had been grafted around him, constructed by a management to whom he owed his services for a single production. This was the final vehicle at the end of a long deferred three-play contract. The project had been left in abeyance for a number of years, and although Mitch had often asked to be released from his commitment, Maggie Roxborough had held on very tightly.

Second Entrance

Elizabeth had been married to Mitch long enough to know exactly what he was going through. It was because of this that she had encouraged him to leave even earlier than usual for the theatre. No matter how many first nights an actor had experienced, the next one was always the worst. They had spent the previous night discussing every aspect of the production. They talked until the early hours, going over motivations, characterisations, climaxes and stage business until every detail had been thoroughly explored.

The previous weeks of mounting concentration had been a great testing time of patience, of nerves, of true love and deep devotion, and all essentially one-sided, coming as it did from Elizabeth. This was nothing new. Over the years she had learned to sacrifice her personal needs, together with a great many of her career opportunities, to those of Mitch.

They had met when cast opposite each other in a frothy comedy at the St Martin's theatre. Elizabeth was twenty-two when they married and already well on the way to a successful future, but she had to retire the following year to produce their first child, now twenty-eight. Although this had been her first marriage, it was Mitch's second. His first, succumbed to at the youthful age of twenty-one, had ended in divorce within a very few years, leaving his daughter, Fiona, with her mother. During the succeeding few years Elizabeth's career had been punctuated by pregnancies. After Bruce there was Susanna, now twenty-five, and then Robin, twenty-one. The last time round there had been a half-hearted suggestion of abortion, but Elizabeth refused to consider it. The breaks in her career had prevented her from making it to the very top flight of international stardom. So though they had often appeared together, the productions had invariably been carefully selected vehicles designed to show Mitch to greater advantage. At most they had allowed Elizabeth a cosy, very occasionally showy, supporting role, but with few theatrical fireworks. So it had remained, both on and off the stage.

There had been a time, way back, when justifiable resentment began to thrust its way to the surface. But then, small incidents were revealed that made Elizabeth appreciate the extent to which Mitch needed his personal glory. They emphasised the conceit of self-awareness, and the universal loneliness that accompanies both rapturous applause and silent rejection. Elizabeth had reluctantly accepted that her husband's first love was for his craft. She had learned that he could only be truly alive within the prescribed emotions of a shadowy third party. She knew that when he was away from the theatre he was never more than half a person, silently nursing his secret miseries, his self-doubt and his self-loathing. Her love for him was unequivocal. She admired him, was a true friend to him, and blatantly lied for him to the entire world. Rightly or wrongly, this was the major role she had elected to portray. It was a role she carried off with more artistry than any she would ever play before a paying audience.

They supported each other like stooks of corn yellowing in a newly mown field. Mitch leaned more heavily as the years progressed, and Elizabeth grew more supportive. There had been occasional hints of scandal in some of the lighter Sunday newspapers, particularly during the annual August silly season, but no one had ever managed to penetrate the barrier of privacy erected by family solidarity.

On this occasion Elizabeth had agreed to appear as Goneril, thus adding yet another strut to support her husband's failing career. There had been a number of wry comments relating to the fact that her looks still allowed her to appear as her own husband's daughter. These had been penned by ill-informed tabloid gossip writers who were almost illiterate when it came to the theatre, and who couldn't even begin to appreciate that Lear's age was eighty.

In spite of the three children, Elizabeth's figure remained remarkably trim. Her tall willowy frame still held a firm bust-line and clearly defined waist. Her slender neck was still smooth, and served to support elegantly her pointed chin angled from wide cheekbones excitingly high below her dark eyes. Whatever she wore was never less than striking. Her taste had matured to favour superbly cut suits and well-fitting trousers, all uncluttered by fripperies and frills. Her clothes clearly reflected her personality, at once warm and receptive, yet quite private and clearly defined within its own boundaries.

Their home in Highgate had a commanding view of Hampstead Heath. It was well away from the middle of London, yet still within easy reach of the West End and their small circle of close friends. The walls were hung with theatrical posters and numerous signed photographs of instantly recognisable faces. There was an eclectic collection of paintings bought for their appeal rather than intrinsic value. The furniture was slightly battered, yet well cared for, comfortable rather than contemporary, colourful without being over-bright. It was a warm home that offered an immediate welcome. It was a relaxed retreat from the exaggerated hyperbole and false glamour associated with the world of theatre. Odds and ends of mementoes gathered from all over the world were spread around the rooms, each having its own, long forgotten association.

An Oscar stood on the mantelpiece in the living room, shyly concealing itself behind a large clock. This was an award bestowed upon Mitch some ten years previously for his performance in an American movie dealing with the British and the Boston Tea Party. Nearby was an *Evening Standard* trophy awarded to Elizabeth for the Best Supporting Actress when she had appeared as Volumnia in a revival of *Coriolanus*. The critics had universally acknowledged her performance as being a remarkable achievement, not least because she had played against type. This had culminated in a highly charged, yet delicately restrained performance in the great pleading scene, until the inner strength of Volumnia had gripped the audience in the final emotional speech to her son. Elizabeth was too honest to have denied the personal satisfaction this acclaim had afforded her, yet she rapidly returned to her allotted place as supporting player to Mitch.

Once Mitch had left she roamed through the house aimlessly looking at the collection of memorabilia, running her fingers over several items, wondering whether this evening would result in a further trophy. She decided to take a long slow bath as an aid to relaxation. Once the hot water was flowing she scattered her favourite rose-scented bath oil through the steaming vapour, allowing its perfume to float around the room and hang in the air. The heat met her as she lowered her porcelain body towards the embrace of the tingling warm bubbles. She always enjoyed these moments of private anticipation before an opening night. These were the final hours before the precise time when the curtain would drift away to expose tense nerves, and a mind stretched to meet the new demands being placed upon her ability. She almost relished the sense of uncertain outcome. There was a challenge to control her entire being that had to operate at a subconscious level if there was to be any truth in the performance.

Once this sybaritic pleasure was over she enveloped herself in a thick yellow towelling bathrobe, and made herself a pot of china tea. The delicate flavour was an acquired taste that had the effect of calming her nerves. The usual first night party was planned, and so she had to select her clothes with great care. She needed something that was not too ostentatious for that hour of the day, yet a combination that would look right much later. She finally settled upon a black velvet trouser suit with a simple pearl-grey silk blouse.

Elizabeth drove herself down Highgate West Hill, through the swirling rain in Kentish Town and on to Camden Town, encountering the mounting traffic that was just beginning to fight towards the outskirts of London. She parked her little Triumph at the garage behind Cinecentre off Panton Street, and took herself along to Hatchards, the famous bookshop in Piccadilly from whom she had ordered a book for Mitch as an opening night present. It was an illustrated volume of the humorous verse of Edward Lear. She thought the juxtaposition of humour and horror would appeal to Mitch's sense of the absurd. No sooner had she stepped outside the shop than she was stopped for her autograph. A tiny incident, yet it served to reassure her of her own status with the public.

She tugged at the belt of her black trench-coat and swiftly opened her umbrella against the rain, stepping out towards the theatre with the book safely locked under one arm and both hands tightly clenched around the ebony shaft in front of her. She made her way down the narrow alleyway alongside Simpsons, and turned into Jermyn Street. At the end she turned right into Lower Regent Street hurriedly crossing the bustling road to then turn into Charles II Street where the crowds outside the stage door had now increased.

Third Entrance

Susanna was decidedly edgy. She was still not totally convinced that appearing with the family was right, either as a means of enhancing her father's reputation, or for their collective relationship. She sat gazing from a window watching the rain trickle down the glass, occasionally obliterating the view, only to be brought back into focus by the driving wind. She was looking, but not seeing, trying to assuage her mounting misgivings by nervously drawing on a cigarette.

"Matthew, darling, will you be long?" she called, without moving her head.

"Just zipping up," he replied. "Perhaps we ought to hang on until the rain gives over a little."

"No, I'd rather not. Taxis will be impossible to get. The last thing I want to do is finish up rushing through my make-up."

Matthew appeared at the bedroom door, hurriedly combing back his thick curls, hanging like assorted corkscrews to frame his youthful face. He had obviously made as much of a sartorial effort as could ever be expected of him. This extended as far as a reasonably well-pressed pair of dark-blue trousers, a cheesecloth shirt and a tweed blouson jacket. A silk scarf was loosely knotted into the neck of his shirt, and a silver chain held a chunk of heavy ceramic against his chest.

"Will I do?" He assumed an exaggerated pose, smiling broadly, arms extended as he slowly rotated on one foot.

"You will as far as I'm concerned."

"Good! Sod the rest of the world." He moved towards her, fully aware of the untold agonies through which she was going.

As an up and coming director he had often found himself soothing the nerves of many performers on opening nights. He was sympathetic to their needs, yet remained firm enough to instil the self-confidence demanded of the occasion. It was this same firmness that had helped to make the critics aware of his potential, and to get them to visit the fringe theatres where he had directed. Not for Matthew the hard and tried commercialism of money conscious West End managements. He insisted on subjects that had a point to make, a comment on current situations. He was only interested in works that spread their guts before an audience, shocking it into awareness. He had been fortunate in his choice of plays. There had been at least three such vehicles in a row, and each had served to reinforce further his early promise. They had also served to bring his work to the attention of those in a position to help him on the next rung up the ladder of uncertain success.

He and Susanna had been married for just over a year, having first met at an Equity meeting some eighteen months earlier. They had got up to speak simultaneously, each opposing a point being made by Fiona, Susanna's half-sister. There had been a minor uproar at the time, not an unusual occurrence whenever Fiona got up to address such a meeting. The result was that Fiona had been shouted down, while Susanna was accidentally pushed out into the aisle, almost falling flat on her face. Matthew had gallantly leapt from the far side, managing to catch her just before she hit the floor. They had finished up laughing about the stupidity of the situation, and gone out for a cup of coffee.

There had been many gallons of coffee subsequently, neither being able to afford much more. Although Susanna was a Dawlish, and too honest totally to deny the advantages that accompanied the family name, she refused to trade on it. It had taken a great deal of gentle persuading from Matthew before she agreed to play the role of Cordelia and ignore its lineage.

She had certainly enjoyed her share of supporting roles in the West End, but nothing important enough to enable her to make the really big leap towards total independence. It was with this in mind that she had finally relented, and agreed to join with the rest of her siblings for the current production.

She and Matthew were currently living in a small rented flat just off Gloucester Road. The living room doubled as a dining room, and they had lightened it by the application of soft creams and pale greens. Dark-brown sag bags were flopped around the walls, and second-hand scrubbed pine furniture, plus odd items of renovated bamboo, filled their main needs. The look was relaxed. If not exactly High Tech, it was certainly functional and welcoming.

"Christ! But I hope this works. I'm beginning to shake all over." Susanna's voice was suddenly quite childlike. She turned to Matthew, trying desperately to hold back her nervous tears.

His arms found their way around her shoulders as he gently kissed her soft hair tightly pulled back from her face. "There's nothing to worry about, love. It's just another opening night. Another part to get through – "

"There's that bloody great chunk in the middle when I'm not on. That's the worst bit of all. Sitting in that bloody dressing room, just waiting to be called."

"Don't panic so. They won't forget you." He kissed her again. "Now, come on, Sue, you know you can do it."

"You just don't seem to understand. I'm not concerned for *me*, it's *him*. If this one doesn't work he could be finished. He can't spend the rest of his life touring the outposts of the Empire."

"Stop being so fucking concerned about your old man, and start thinking about yourself. When he steps on to that stage tonight, his future will be in his own hands. You can't go out there and do it for him. Mind you, it would be different." He held her at arm's length and laughed.

This served to break the mounting tension, causing both of them to giggle and to fall into each other's arms. Susanna hung on tightly as she slowly regained her composure, sniffing back another tear as she took a deep breath.

"That's better," said Matthew. "Now let's make a run for it before you start up again." He didn't wait for her reply, but dashed into the bedroom to collect her heavy swing-back coat, almost pushing her into it before she could object.

"I've left something at the theatre to wear after the show. I didn't want to arrive all tarted up."

"I had noticed." He slid his arms around her waist, cupping her breasts in his hands as he kissed the side of her turned face.

"I feel better already. As you so rightly said, sod the rest of the world."

Once outside they found it impossible to hail a taxi. The rain had ensured that any cruisers were snapped up immediately. They stood on the kerbside, waving their arms like windmills, as Susanna's tension began to show in anger.

"Listen, Sue, before you explode in all directions, let's go by underground. It's only about five stops and we can be at Piccadilly Circus in no time. If we do manage to get a cab it could well take longer in this weather."

She grudgingly agreed and they arrived outside the stage door in Charles II Street within half an hour. Both were breathless as a result of their brisk walk from the station, but both were in a better frame of mind.

Fourth Entrance

To be Robin Dawlish, the youngest of an acknowledged talented family, had more than its fair share of drawbacks. Inevitably, he was not only compared to his brilliant parents, but also to his siblings. He had long ago decided that everyone expected too much of him, with the result that he had developed a wide stubborn streak that blossomed with his years. As a youngster there had been accusations of deliberate attempts to deny the family link, but whatever the truth of this the fact was impossible to conceal. The name, the likeness, the pressing need to be bang in the centre of the action, were all part of the personality of such a family. Exhibitionism was firmly entrenched in his genes. There had been a brief period when he had tried to do something outside the theatre, but it had proved impossible to keep away from the grease paint for long.

Robin had been to a theatrical school and managed to make a passable success of the training, but no one ever pretended he was as gifted as his father. Robin was the first to admit this, and although he held his father in great esteem there was a calm animosity between them.

Mitchell had once been at great pains to apologise to his son for his own success, explaining that he was unable to withhold his own ability, and taking some time to explain that no one ever expected Robin to set himself alongside his father's achievements. Instead of helping to solve the problem, it had merely served to highlight further the artistic chasm between them.

Robin was definitely lightweight, in stature, in emotional stability and in histrionics. There had been successes when he was younger, but these had inevitably led people to anticipate even greater triumphs in later years. A revival of *The Winslow Boy* had brought him a clutch of good notices, particularly for the cross-examination scene. There had followed parts in a number of children's television programmes, and an interesting role in a science fiction film in which children remained eternally young while slowly assuming control of the world. *The Tomorrow Game* supplied him with another batch of good reviews, but it was always in the shadow of his father that he was commented upon.

The family had been quite shaken when Robin calmly announced, at the age of eighteen, that he was moving in with a theatrical designer friend called Jake Lawrence, a forceful American of Japanese descent, and ten years older than himself.

To say that Jake was flamboyant would have been an understatement. To add that Robin adored him, and aped him, would be equally to understate the case.

Jake was gay. Jake had great style, tremendous self-awareness and more than his share of *amour propre*. Robin had at first attempted to conceal his own homosexuality, but he wasn't a sufficiently good actor to succeed even in this. In any case, to announce the fact by simply living with Jake was sufficient confirmation of what most people had long suspected.

It was Jake's flat they shared. It was Jake who supported Robin when he was resting. It was Jake who called the tune all down the line. Jake's money came from family investments spread throughout the United States, and Jake unashamedly requested large sums whenever the need arose.

They lived in splendid style just off Redcliffe Square, Kensington, in one of those large Victorian houses that had long since been divided into self-contained flats with exorbitant rents. The carpets were thick, the upholstery deep, the rosewood furniture was dazzlingly polished, and the chrome and smoked glass gleamed even on the dullest day. Jake had designed everything himself, but his pride was the bedroom. It proudly proclaimed his total lack of concern for the comments of others. The ceiling was hung like a Bedouin tent, with gathered silk of deep Prussian blue pulled out from the centre towards the walls. The vast bed had been designed to appear as a four-poster by having a false canopy suspended from the ceiling and covered in peacock-blue. The underside of the canopy reflected the expanse of counterpane piled high with shaped cushions in an amazing array of blues and greens. The walls were hung from ceiling to floor with a finely gathered dragon printed chintz on a sky-blue ground. One side held fitted wardrobes faced with mirror to create an enlarging effect, and to reflect activity. The floor was a forest of bottle-green shag-pile carpet, additionally covered with rich skin rugs. The effect was quite stunning, and so were some of the athletics silently viewed by the mirrors.

Robin lay back in Jake's arms, looking up at their nakedness. "They'll be gunning for me, you know."

"Aw! Come on! You're too sensitive. Relax, Robby, no

one's gonna give a damn about you. It's your father they'll be after."

"I wish I could believe that." He rolled over and lifted himself to look down on Jake. "Shit! But you're a handsome bastard. Tell you what. Let's forget the first night and start all over again."

Jake laughed, his wide oriental cheeks flattening his eyes into tiny slits of light. He reached up and stroked Robin's downy belly. "Save it up, sonny. Treat it like medicine. Once before, and once after. And stop twitching your arse at me. You need your strength for your performance." He suddenly pulled away Robin's supporting arm, causing him to fall flat on top of him.

They rolled around for a few seconds, acting like playful puppies, buffooning and tickling each other affectionately. They laughed aloud until they slowly relaxed to lie side by side, breathing heavily. They looked up at themselves, now deeply wedged between the cushions, their pale bodies sharply outlined against the dark counterpane.

"I suppose I ought to get ready. Have a quick shower and prepare to meet my doom. At least in this little number I get to die on stage. That ought to be worth a few grunts and groans."

"Are you still determined to take your motorbike?"

"Yes, of course."

"I'd rather you didn't. You're a bit strung up about tonight."

"Oh! Sod that! I'm a big boy. Haven't I just proved it?"

"You know exactly what I mean. Well, please yourself. But, for Christ's sake, don't be a goddamn fool and chance your luck."

"Yes, Daddyo." Robin blew a resounding raspberry and promptly disappeared to take a shower.

The bathroom was even more mirrored than the bedroom. The essential difference being that it was so small it made a user feel as though he were sharing the room with his own alter ego – a disconcerting experience to the uninitiated. An amazing range of toiletries sat upon a glass shelf. Robin selected one with a rough musky tang that exuded male sexiness. He waved talcum powder in all directions, and eventually reappeared as though dusted ready for baking. Jake had carefully laid out what he thought Robin should wear. There was a pair of deep maroon trousers to be worn with a white collarless ruffled shirt and a subtly coloured brocade jacket. Robin looked slim and interesting, he smelled butch and felt great. His adrenalin began to work towards the evening's performance. He felt right about his characterisation. He ought to, he was playing most of it off his own personality.

Robin looked more than a little incongruous as he pulled on a pair of yellow oilskins against the continuing rain. He had flatly refused to be talked out of using his motorbike. Even though the weather had taken a sudden turn for the worse, it had now become a matter of personal pride not to succumb to Jake's pleas.

Although Jake was going to be out front, he saw little point in going to the theatre as early as Robin. He drew back the living room curtain and watched as the motorbike pulled away from the kerb. He shook his head in dismay as the white skid-lid vanished, muttering to himself, "Fucking schmuck."

Robin zig-zagged his way up the Fulham Road towards Knightsbridge, narrowly missing a befurred pedestrian outside Harrods as the motorbike swerved towards the centre of the road. There was a space outside the theatre in Charles II Street where he lost no time in kicking down the wheel support before sprinting towards the stage door.

"Bet he's a messenger boy," said a knowing youth to his girlfriend.

"Up yours," shouted Robin, removing his skid-lid as he vanished from sight.

Fifth Entrance

Tracy was washing up two sherry glasses in the kitchen. "Are you sure you've got everything you need?" she called.

"Yes, I think so. I've been over the list at least half a dozen times," said Bruce.

Lists were a long standing feature of Bruce's life. Whatever he did, wherever he went, there was always a checklist to ensure that nothing was overlooked. Some of his gear had been taken to his dressing room a couple of days before, but there were still enough items to fill another small holdall. There was his heavy white robe, a spare towel and some soap, spare make-up, a large bottle of Paracetamol, always – just in case – gargle for the same reason, tissues, a bottle of sherry and a couple of glasses. Make-up, slippers, hand mirror, aftershave and a spare razor were already there together with some spare clothes. He ticked off the last few items and put the sheet of paper neatly on top of the pile as he zipped closed the bag.

"I seem to have done this so many times before," he said, throwing the holdall on to the floor.

"Don't complain." Tracy smiled across the room towards him, trying not to reveal her own nervousness.

They had lived together for the past three years, accepting each other as spouse in all but the public piece of paper still demanded by more conventional society. Tracy enjoyed the freedom the arrangement gave her. She felt she still needed to be her own person, but could share herself as she was so inclined. Bruce on the other hand was far more conventional, having asked her to marry him on at least three occasions. He had now reached the point where he had decided not to pose the question any more but, hopefully, allow the relationship to steer its own natural course in that direction.

Tracy's work as a fashion model often took her abroad; there was nothing sensational about her looks, but she had the knack of being able to spring into animation the moment the camera was on her. She assumed a warmth and a vitality that was needed to sell certain types of products to young mothers; they were able to relate to her. She looked her best in sloppy sweaters and faded jeans, and only ever dressed to kill when the job demanded it of her.

Bruce had tried to encourage her to try her hand at acting, but she had been with him far too long to chance the uncertainties of the theatre. She knew about the large percentage of actors who were always unemployed, hopefully sitting it out near their telephones waiting to be summoned for an audition along with the rest of London. She had decided that that was definitely not for her.

But now Bruce was reasonably well-established within the profession, able to select what he wanted to play from a restricted range of parts. Like the rest of the family, he too was for ever in the shadow of his father, often being compared to him at the same age. He now felt he had reached a vital period in his career when he had to decide whether he was going to try to make it to the dizzy heights in classical drama, or settle for the often less demanding roles in modern plays that were well within his grasp. When he was first offered the role of the Fool, there had been a lot of personal misgivings. He had not cherished the idea of working so closely alongside his father, inevitably inviting more comparisons. It was Elizabeth who had finally prevailed upon him to accept, assuring him that the role was well within his range, and emphasising how much the family needed to present a united front in order to squash the gossip about Mitch being on the skids. It was pure emotional blackmail of the sort that Bruce had been unable to resist.

Of all the family it was Bruce alone who constantly doubted himself. It was he who questioned his own ability to continue to earn a living from the theatre. It was he who questioned the sense of constantly being in a position of looking for work. He wasn't sure whether he really had the stamina demanded by a profession that saw its exponents back in the dole queue after every last night. He didn't think he could hang on to the end of the telephone making small talk with people he disliked, or chatting up managements and agents.

"I still think the opening scene's too dark. You saw last night's preview, what do you think, Tracy?"

"I think you're just looking for problems. It's a fantastic opening. What the hell do you want, a rainbow across the backcloth as the curtain goes up?" She knew how to handle him by now, and chose to make light of his doubts and fears. "You've got a smashing first entrance, concentrate on that."

"You're right! You're right! You usually are." He put his arms around her, gripping her buttocks with his hands and pulling her towards him.

"Not now, there's a dear. Keep your mind above your cod-piece, otherwise you might fluff your lines."

"Sex hasn't weakened my brain yet."

"No, but it could sap your strength. You've got a lot of leaping about to do. I'd hate to see you collapse in a little heap in the middle of the blasted heath."

"That would steal some of the old man's thunder." He laughed and pecked at her retroussé nose. "Oh, well, off to the slaughter."

"Why do you go on with it if you hate it so much?"

"Buggered if I know. I suppose it's a bit like a drug. Once you're hooked, that's it. That is bloody well it!" He shrugged his shoulders as he looked about the room.

It was small, it was neat, but it lacked any real signs of permanency. They shared rented rooms in a large house in Maida Vale. There was no private front door and other residents' noises came through the walls, cooking smells permeated through the floorboards. Bruce ached for a place of his own, somewhere he could really feel he had a right to be, a retreat from the stupidity of the theatrical roundabout, but there was no chance of that for the time being.

His face was quite pale, throwing his dark eyes into contrast with his clean-shaven skin. His jaw wasn't quite as square as his father's, but on Bruce the same degree of firmness would have been out of character. Unlike his father, his hair had already begun to recede causing him to appear somewhat older than his years. Not such a bad thing when it came to casting.

"Bloody rain! Could have done without that. Good thing the house is already sold out."

"Here's your brolly. Try not to get too wet. Shall I come round before the curtain?"

"I'd rather you didn't. I'll have more than enough to contend with having to share the dressing room with brother Robby. If that boyfriend of his comes poncing in I shall probably kick him in the balls."

"Yes, dear, if it will make you feel any better." She kissed her fingers and delicately placed them over his lips. "Good luck, my darling."

He pulled back, searching her face in silence. "Thanks. Make notes."

Bruce didn't wait for a further response. He simply turned and went out on to the landing. He hovered on the top step just beyond the front door, the rain finding its way down his cheeks and inside his collar. The umbrella didn't want to meet the howling wind, but he managed to struggle to success and then fought his way against the weather to Maida Vale station.

He sat at the far end of the carriage breathing deeply and going through his lines while mentally checking his moves. He then slowly began to relax his toes, then his calves and his thighs, followed by his stomach muscles and those very knotted areas at the back of his neck and across his shoulders. He arrived at Piccadilly Circus before he realised it, and made his way through the long subway into the Haymarket.

"That's Bruce Dawlish," screamed one of the crowd outside the stage door.

"Don't look much like 'is father, do 'e?" said another.

Bruce had heard it all before, so many times. He was in no mood to encourage autograph hunters, and bustled into the theatre before anyone was able to approach him.

Sixth Entrance

The monotonous plunk, plunk, plunk of amplified guitar music filled the house, throbbing through every floorboard and into every room. It wasn't always quite as noisy as this, but for some reason Andy had decided that today it would be all systems go. Perhaps this was intended as his unspoken comment on Fiona's agreement to appear with the rest of the family. He had a perverted knack of doing exactly the wrong thing at the right time – and this was the right time.

There had been several occasions in the recent past when Fiona had decided to call it a day and invite Andy to leave, but he had always managed to get round her. He always managed to convince her that she needed him – really needed him!

She had been through two unsuccessful marriages, the legacy of the first being a nine-year-old daughter, Kate. The second marriage still screamed in her ears reminding her of the constant fights and arguments. She was determined not to marry again, but simply to take from any man precisely what she wanted, when she wanted it. Andy and she met at a pop concert sponsored by a left-wing political party for which she worked whenever she could. He had a certain animal charm that she found attractive and that suited her current requirements. He'd been invited to move in to satisfy those requirements. They had now been together for nearly a year, living in her St John's Wood house in a state of armed connubial truce. The fact that he was a mere twenty-two appealed to her. It made her feel both mother and mistress in a confused way.

Of all the Dawlish offspring, Fiona was undoubtedly the most successful. Although she had always kept in touch with her father, they had never appeared together until now. It was he who had paid for her years at drama school, and it was he who had helped to get her first job with Birmingham Rep. The very last thing she wanted now was to spend time in a production of *King Lear*, a production that she knew would force them all to act, metaphorically, downstage. Her string of successes was considerable, ranging as it did from an early Juliet, Ophelia and Desdemona, through roles in Ibsen, Shaw and a number of modern works. Her most recent success was a revival of *A Streetcar Named Desire* in which she had brought new depths to Blanche Dubois. Her list of screen successes was no less imposing. There had been two nominations for Oscars, but she had never quite made it up to the dais. Nevertheless she had more than her share of assorted trophies, none of which held any great significance for her. There was no doubt that she was now in a position to call her own tune and need never be in search of her next shop, but she had been known to overstep the mark on several occasions in an effort to bring her political mores into the theatre. Antagonism was the name of the game, and Fiona had managed to ensure that at least two West End managements would never offer her another engagement.

Her resistance to the present production had been quite prolonged, with her final acceptance only being assured on the understanding that she did not have to go on the provincial tour, or join the company in Europe.

Fiona's current preoccupation was directed towards getting her own company together to present plays about social problems, works that could hammer home the sharp political dogma she wished to voice. Most of these were left of left. The very name of her company was designed to spell it out to those with any doubts about her intentions, CHASE – being "Community

Harmony And Social Education". There were sufficient actors who shared her beliefs, but few could afford to support this by working for principles alone. Her latest venture was to get together a company to present works about the General Strike, the Luddites and the Jarrow Marchers to highlight contemporary problems.

"Andrew, for Christ's sake! Will you turn that bloody noise down?" She stood in the doorway, holding on to the door with a tight fist that caused her knuckles to whiten through her controlled rage.

"What's up, doll? Don't you dig the music all of a sudden?"

"You bastard. You lousy, rotten bastard. You're doing this on purpose. If you don't turn that damn thing down, I'll throw you, and all your bloody gear, out on to the pavement."

"OK! OK! No need to go all ladylike on me. I'll turn it down. You've only got to ask." Andy laid down his guitar with deliberate ceremony, and then crossed to the amplifier, carefully pointing his finger and thumb to encompass the dial as delicately as possible. "There we are, doll. Soft and gentle. Like I said, you've only got to ask." He turned back to her, smiling as only he could, showing his cigarette stained teeth through his fair beard and ragged moustache.

"Thank you!" She turned to leave, still angry that he had forced her into the stance of reprimanding mother. She felt his hand tighten over hers as she tried to release the door. He was standing next to her, pulling her back towards him.

"Please, Andy, I've still got things to do."

He ignored her plea and continued to draw her close. "They can wait." Her head was pulled back as he closed his lips over hers, pushing her mouth open with his tongue until she had to respond.

Her arms flayed around his slim shoulders; her nails digging into the rough cloth of his denim shirt. She caught her breath, sighing deeply as her face came to rest in the crook of his neck. "You bastard. You lousy, rotten, stinking bastard. Why do you do this to me?"

"It makes life interesting. Anyone can have roses, roses all the way. You wouldn't be happy with that. That's why I'm here. We need each other, doll."

Fiona finally managed to regain her composure as she pulled herself away, secretly ashamed that she had allowed the moment to happen. "I ought to be going. Will you be at the party?"

"Do you want me there?"

"You know I do."

"Great, doll! Then I'll be there."

If only the theatre-going public knew. If only they had any idea what went on before an opening night. But that's not part of the glamour. It's not part of the razzle-dazzle and the excitement. It's all too mundane, too ordinary, too *unlikely*.

There was a ring at the front door, and Fiona knew that it would be the car she'd ordered. She wasn't in the mood to get to the theatre under her own steam, and the rain had served to arouse in her a strange sense of foreboding. The best plan was to allow someone else to drive her there so that she could relax for twenty minutes or so before her first night nerves took over.

The driver took her through Regent's Park and down past the BBC into Regent Street and then on into the Haymarket, finally turning right into Charles II Street. The car pulled over to the kerb outside the stage door. As the driver made his way around the car to help Fiona out a small group of fans clustered about the door. Fiona, ever impatient, was halfway out by the time the driver got to her.

She managed to draw the small crowd out of the rain below the shelter of the awning, and signed their autograph books. She was professional enough to know how much it meant to keep faith with the public. At the very first opportunity she made her excuses and sought the protection of the theatre.

1

The narrow foyer was beginning to shrink as the fashionable first night audience insisted upon milling about, playing the eternal game of see and be seen. There was a time when a theatrical event of this importance would have been heavily patronised with genuine old-fashioned glamour. Furs and jewels would have been dusted off and paraded. High society chat, and the jostle for prime positions in front of the flashing lightbulbs, would have been the order of the day. Now it was reduced to a preponderance of jeans and bulky knit sweaters and long cardigans, all combined with intense concentration on ignoring the famous. Those who still insisted on evening dress looked slightly out of place and self-consciously aware of their avowed determination to make an occasion of the event.

There was an abundance of vaguely recognisable faces, pseudo personalities, mainly from the small screen. Many of them were there simply to endorse a previous public statement about their sincere support for the live theatre; as ever, in a state of imminent mortification. In spite of the bubble of excited voices there was an undeniably tense atmosphere, an air of expectation conjured as much by the media as by the magic name of Dawlish. The full-length portrait of Herbert Tree as King John looked down on the scene enigmatically, perhaps with a sense of wry amusement.

Programmes were being handed out to the press by a blackbow-tied body of undistinguished proportions and sallow complexion, a minion of the management who was being just a little overcautious in his duties. *The Guardian* critic was vociferously annoyed at actually having to ask for his programme. The BBC had hedged its bets for this one, requesting tickets for an army of presenters and assistants from both sound and vision. They had refused to commit themselves, merely suggesting that schedules would be looked at for a suitable slot in whichever section of their media they felt most suitable for the occasion. The management were forced to accept this arrangement in order to ensure that good public relations were maintained with that august body.

"Will you please pass through to the theatre. Please leave the foyer clear," called the black-bow-tie. The request made little impact on the nodding crowd, now fast clogging to a halt. The rain had served no good purpose either, as the arriving audience spent longer trying to remove damp coats without causing too much inconvenience to those tightly clustered around them. The black and white marble floor had become dangerously slippery and several people had inelegant narrow escapes, only being saved from falling by the push of bodies. Cars had been delayed, parking was proving to be extremely difficult, and the curtain would have to be held until everyone was seated.

Necks were craned and heads turned towards the difficult centre doors as yet another vaguely familiar face entered. The wide wooden staircase leading up to the circle had its share of sightseers festooned over the polished parapet. Fingers were pointed, arms anxiously waved to short-sighted friends who wished to be sought out more obviously. Hissing and cooing overlapped for attention. An unexpected flashlight suddenly brightened the foyer as a popular knight of the theatre arrived, waving to fans in an attempt to substitute the general greeting for the particular one of personal autographs. A way opened up through the entangled bodies as though God himself had once again worked upon the Red Sea.

Many thousands of words had already been written surrounding the politics behind the project. The *Daily Express* had carried a full page, complete with some very early photographs, detailing the many milestones in the career of Mitch over the past quarter century. The article had been at some pains to mention the period in Mitch's life when his whereabouts were totally unaccounted for. There had been hints of a nervous breakdown, of alcoholism, of strange goings-on in his love life, but there had been no categorical statements of fact. Half-truths and bizarre speculation were about as far as anyone would venture. The charisma that was Mitch's stock-in-trade still meant a lot to the diminished loyal band of theatre-goers, a demi-god not to be tampered with.

"Will you *please* take your seats. The curtain will rise in five minutes." Of course such threats were seldom carried out on these occasions, but the point had to be made.

The bustle backstage was no less tense than anywhere else in the building. Although a delayed curtain on opening night was always expected, it never failed to add to the nervous energy expended by all concerned. The stage manager was trying to keep as calm as his position of authority demanded, issuing final instructions to his three assistants. They had to double check that there was sufficient room for the large cast to move behind the set without breaking a limb. Someone was despatched to inspect the small props room and to make sure that everything was laid out scene by scene as required. Nerves were tensing amongst the scene shifters who had taken too long over certain transitional scenes during the final preview the previous night. The complicated lighting plot was being double checked in the glass-fronted console box in the auditorium. Nothing was going to be easy. Everyone had been made aware of the importance of the occasion. Not in so many words, not simply because it was the entire family, not by virtue of the play alone, but because it was Mitchell Dawlish playing the lead. There was no doubt left in anyone's mind as to how much depended on the success of the evening.

Elizabeth was ready well in advance; she never left anything to chance. She needed time to peruse her final appearance, time to settle into her heavy costume and to assume the personality of the character she was about to portray. Having poured some whitening on to her hands she now sat idly massaging them together. There was no obvious concentration on the small movements of her wrists; her thoughts were elsewhere. Her composure was broken by a faint tap on her dressing room door.

"Come in," she said. Her voice was already acquiring an edge to its fulsome tones.

The door opened slowly as Victor Aldiss put his head into the small room, seeking out Elizabeth with his eyes. To be backstage was a great adventure for him, and he never failed to experience a sense of shock at the sight of an actor in make-up. He was rather like a small boy opening his Christmas presents; there was an air of suppressed excitement mingled with nervous curiosity. The caution now expressed was just another of his endearing characteristics, a natural diffidence that Elizabeth found so warming and real.

They had known each other for almost two years, during which time their emotional involvement had grown steadily. It was a gentle lovingness fanned by their maturity, and allowed to simmer quietly without ever bursting into a flaming passion. Victor's wife had died several years earlier, leaving him isolated and with a sense of permanent grief. It wasn't until he had met Elizabeth at a dinner party that he began to return to anything approaching a normal life. Their relationship was always discreet. It slowly assumed greater importance to them as they came to appreciate that they were able to offer the other what their own life seemed to lack. Elizabeth's overdeveloped sense of duty towards Mitch had held her back from accepting the care and devotion that Victor wanted to give her. She ached for a full life of her own, she ached for the emotional freedom to accept the undemanding love waiting for her.

It would be too easy to miss him in a crowd; short, slightly balding, softly spoken, perhaps a little less than lithe. Yet behind all this was a rich intelligence, someone who was widely read and who loved music. He was a truly sincere man, a *gentle* man in every sense.

"Is this a good moment?" His voice was warm and hesitant.

"Of course. I was beginning to think you weren't going to make it." She moved towards him, her costume dragging around her feet, her face growing falsely stiff with Goneril's cruelty, and with a mean mouth that belied her own capacity for affection.

There was a silence broken only by the muffled sounds of swishing costumes echoing down the narrow corridor outside. Victor continued to look at her as though she were a stranger, studying her features, noting the hard lines and sneering curl to her lips.

"Do I frighten you?"

"Fascinating. I wouldn't have thought you could ever look like that. Oh! Some flowers. Flowers are all right, aren't they?"

"They're beautiful. I adore spring flowers. I'll get them put in water."

"I suddenly remembered hearing someone once say they were unlucky – "

"Only *on* stage, but not here, not in my dressing room." She kissed his cheek, and then pulled back to brush away the traces of powder she had left on the sleeve of his dinner jacket.

"Seems to be quite a hubbub going on everywhere." He was unaccountably subdued, as though thinking one thing, yet saying something quite different. Almost as though he were making small talk at a first encounter.

"It is an important night. There's a lot to attend to. A lot that can go wrong." The feeling was contagious; she could sense herself slipping into the same attitude.

"I – I hope it all goes well."

"Why do you say it like that?"

"Like what?"

"What is it, Victor? What are you trying to say?"

He shook his head, turning away as though about to go.

"Please – ?" she said, holding on to him.

"I'm sorry. It's unfair of me to come to you like this on an opening night. I can't help it, Elizabeth. I know how much the success of this evening means to you – to Mitchell. I hope it will mean as much to – to us."

"Us?" Her concern was beginning to break through the mask she was wearing. Her apparent lack of understanding needed an answer.

"You've always said that when he gets back on top, when he no longer needs your support, you'll consider marrying me. If this evening gives him back his self-confidence – if he does climb back on top, will you keep your word?"

"Darling, darling, Victor, will you never give up? I can't possibly answer that now. Not yet. Mitch needs to be loved. If I withdraw from him even a moment too soon he'll go to pieces overnight. Please, darling, let's wait and see. Let's get this evening over before we make any rash promises, either of us."

She knew she was hurting him, but it was no greater than the hurt she was inflicting upon herself. For once she was grateful for the refuge afforded by her make-up, for the camouflage of grease paint and powder.

"Good luck. I'll be cheering for you. For *all* of you." He turned and eased his way around the door as silently as he had come in a few moments earlier.

The only evidence that she had not imagined the short scene lay in the small bunch of yellow flowers still clutched in her hand. For a moment she wanted to cry, to let everyone know exactly what she was feeling, what she had felt for so many years, but she fought it back through a conscious tightening of her muscles, through sheer willpower and applied theatrical technique.

Next-door Mitchell was adding the final touches to his delicate make-up. His face had retained some of its youth, but there was a flabbiness behind the sharp angle of his jaw that made him appear too well fed. It was a feature he managed to conceal with shading and highlights. A creeping sadness had spread across his face as he slowly dealt with each section of the representation: furrowed brows, sunken eyes, lined cheeks, the corners of his mouth turned down in sorrow, and an overall grey pallor that betokened unhealthy age. As the character of King Lear slowly breathed into life, so the life that was Mitch melted into the bright lights of the dressing table mirror. The final touch was a delicately combed wig of flaxen grey hair supported by thin side plaits that framed his face, and then fell into a wisp of toning beard.

Mitch leaned back to admire the finished picture as Mrs Grace, his dresser, opened the door of the outer room to admit a visitor.

"Hullo, Mrs Grace. How's it going?" Maggie Roxborough's voice was controlled, but there was more than a hint of concern behind the falsely casual enquiry.

Mrs Grace had been a dresser to the stars for years. She knew everyone, and they all knew her for her will of iron, her unflappability, and her knowing nature. She nodded towards the next room, and stood aside to let Maggie through.

"Come in! Come in! What's the house like?" asked Mitch,

still tapping in an odd highlight on the canvas that was his face.

"Need you ask? It's full of excitement. You look fantastic, darling. You've softened it since last night. It's better." She was very business-like, very direct.

"If it only depended on looks, I wouldn't worry." He smiled at her through the mirror, not seeing her expression clearly, just her shape between the glare of the lights. "I wish last night had gone better."

"The opening was a little rushed. Don't worry, you'll get the feel of it."

"What's the matter, Maggie? You've suddenly got misgivings, haven't you?"

Mrs Grace knew enough to know when she wasn't wanted, and this was one of those moments. "I'll just be outside if you need me. I think you look lovely." The outer door closed behind her with a firm click.

Maggie said nothing, her fingers remaining intertwined in front of her, nervously twitching, speaking all there was to say. "I'm – I'm always worried on opening nights. You should know that by now."

"Whatever else happens tonight, I'll always be grateful to you for what you've done." He looked into her face, trying desperately to read whatever it was she wasn't saying.

"Don't rush it, Mitch. Take your time. Ease your way into it. You can do it."

"Oh, Christ! I wish I hadn't let you talk me into this. I should have tried Othello again. At least I know the dangers of that play. I've been in this business for thirty-five years, and I've never felt like this in my entire life. It's as though I've just come out of drama school. What the hell's wrong with me? Do you think the pundits are right, Maggie? Is this whole production a terrible mistake?"

"Mitch, you ought to know better than that. I've been in this lousy business a long time as well. I haven't got to be a queen bee in the West End by making wrong judgments."

The intercom gurgled a noisy summons. "Fifteen minutes, please. Fifteen minutes."

The door opened without ceremony. "I just wanted to give

you – " Elizabeth's voice trailed away as she caught sight of Maggie. "Hullo! I thought you'd be settled out front by now."

"Just on my way. Good luck – both of you." She reached the door with two purposeful strides, and then turned back to look at Mitch. He was now magnificently regal yet old and senile, lost yet oddly composed. "We're all with you, Mitch." She left them together, simply looking at each other as though they were strangers, neither husband and wife, nor yet father and daughter.

"I just wanted to give you this. It's a collection of the nonsense poems of Edward Lear. I thought there was room for another Lear in your life." Elizabeth put down the book on his dressing table alongside a tumbler of whisky. "Not too much, there's a lamb. If the going gets tough, just think of this Lear for a few seconds, it might help."

Mitchell put his hand over hers as she lifted it from the book. "Thanks. Sorry if I've been difficult lately. I've had quite a lot on my mind, one way and another."

"I know. I do understand. I live with you, remember?" She kissed him delicately, enough to let him know she cared, but with the skill of an actress aware of make-up.

The main door opened once again, but this time with a lot less concern for those on the other side. Tony Shaw was doing his final rounds to instil self-confidence into his cast. The consummate skill he demonstrated as a director was wildly acknowledged on Broadway and in the West End alike. He never considered a production completely finished until the final curtain fell on the final performance. Although he may well have several productions running simultaneously in the far corners of the world, no one was ever surprised when he turned up unexpectedly with new ideas, new bits of business. It was this tireless energy that kept his productions running, and kept the cast for ever on their toes.

"Hi, Liz! Mitch, you were great last night. Spread your first entrance by just a fraction more, that's all. Just a fraction. There's a hell of a lot for the audience to take in before you enter. They're expecting the usual thrones, and all that crap. Let it sink in. Believe me, those first few moments can take it."

"I thought you'd taken Concorde to Australia. I certainly

would in your shoes." Mitch gave a false laugh, causing his beard to puff up.

"If they're not emotionally drained after this, then I'll eat my notepad."

"You may have to." Mitch extended his hand, nodding in gratitude. "Thanks, Tony, for all you've done. I suppose I'm as ready as I'll ever be."

"I know you're worried. *I'd* be worried if you weren't." He laughed loudly, looking from Mitch to Elizabeth. "You're going to be just great. Relax, let it roll over them." He vanished just as suddenly as he had arrived. But then he always did.

Bruce and Robin were sharing the dressing room off the half-landing at the top of the stairs, not essentially because of their relationship, but because space was limited with such a large company, and it was decided that these two might as well share as two total strangers. The room should have gone to Elizabeth, but she had volunteered to use the smaller room alongside Mitchell so that she could be close to him if he needed her for anything. Bruce would almost certainly rather have been sharing with someone else, but once the arrangement had been made, and Robin expressed his pleasure at being with his brother, Bruce had decided to let it ride.

"Robby, you were over the top last night. Smooth it out a bit. And don't make too much of a Henry Irving out of your death scene."

"You can bloody well talk. Leaping around on the blasted heath like a lame gazelle."

"Sorry I spoke." Bruce snatched up his script to consult a particular scene once more, and moved away towards the window.

"If you don't know your lines by now, I shouldn't bother if I were you. Two thirds of the audience hasn't a clue what it's all about anyway."

"And they'll know a damn sight less by the time you're through with them."

Jake knocked and entered at one and the same time. He was wearing an off-white tunic suit with the trousers tucked into high boots, and a shirt that was almost open down to his waist.

The effect against his tanned skin was quite stunning, if a little out of place in the present setting.

"Oh! What a wondrous change is here." Jake allowed the door to swing away from him as he extended his arms in mock applause towards Robin. "Hullo, Bruce, looking after little brother?"

"I'm not my brother's keeper. I'm sure you're much better at that than I could ever be."

"That's what I like about you, Bruce. Always ready with a warm response." The moment of tension was broken as the intercom announced, "Five minutes, please. Five minutes." Jake moved behind Robin to glance at his own reflection above Robin's head. "I ought to have worn something in the neck of this shirt."

"Try a noose next time." Bruce had long ago stopped trying to conceal his dislike of Jake.

"Not funny," said Robin. "Jake, it's nice of you to come round, but they've just called the five. You'd better get back out front."

"I'm going! I'm going! Good luck, dear heart." He swaggered out, full of his own good looks, unaware that his skin tight trousers revealed the edge of his briefs and created a slight indentation around his hips drawing attention to his heavy appearance.

"Listen, Robby. What you do with your life, in your own time, is entirely your own affair. But I'm telling you here and now, keep that stupid bitch out of this dressing room!"

"As I recall, *both* our names are on the dressing room door. That gives us equal privileges. I'm not putting any restrictions on you. You lay off me." Robin rose in a fitful sulk, turning to the long mirror to check his appearance. He was enough of a professional to know that he had to look right.

"Beginners, please. On stage, beginners, please." The disembodied voice called the cast to attention.

2

The darkened acting area was pierced by tiny pinheads of light as the stage crew made last minute adjustments. The cast began to assemble in their opening positions. There was a hiss of "House lights" from the prompt corner down left. The familiar rumble of anticipation from the auditorium settled into a dull murmur as the small central light high in the ornate ceiling began to dim, followed by the smaller lights throughout the cavernous hollow, until there remained only a glimmer in the darkness. As the final vestige of light faded the settling audience was startled into renewed murmurs by the resounding throb of a gong; it settled into a heavy rhythmic echo beaten several times in slow succession. Halfway through the fading sea of sound there was the unmistakable swish of the heavy front curtain being swept up high above the action.

The only illumination visible appeared to be coming from a flaming hole set into the top of a high rock. Immediately behind this glow was a near-naked servant wielding a heavy hammer on to a shimmering metallic surface. As the enveloping clang rolled away it was taken up by several woodwind instruments emitting long drawn out notes in the distance. What appeared to be an undefined animal emerged from a section of the rock upstage centre right, and revealed itself to be the characters of Kent, Gloucester and Edmund clad in heavy fabrics and weighty skins of deep browns and rich reds.

Tony had conceived the production with a strange timelessness, setting it against a series of darkly atmospheric caves, sinister in their shades of slimy greens and greys. The cyclorama had been designed to spread as wide and as high as possible in order to reduce the action into shadowy masses. Much of the lighting was plotted to come in at odd angles. It cast long menacing shadows and weird formations within groups of actors. The production had been planned to give the sensation of nature being the prime mover within the structure of events, all pushing towards a doom-laden inevitability from which there was no escape.

Kent uttered his opening lines with attention-seeking force. The action had begun.

The audience settled into alert silence, listening to the short three-handed scene while scanning the expanse of stage as their eyes grew accustomed to the uneven light patterns. From behind a massive rock formation there appeared flickering flambeaux, each held high by attendants clad only in leather codpieces and jewelled amulets. Following these came four magnificently tall litter-bearers carrying King Lear high above their heads, dramatically caught in the crimson glow of the torches leading the impressive procession. The entrance had the desired effect of creating an atmosphere charged with raw emotion, yet tightly contained within the craggy setting and drafted into perspective by the added height of the stage.

There was a spontaneous burst of applause as Mitch came into view, majestic yet bowed, regal yet lacking authority. His huge figure dominated the entire scene.

Mitch was remembering what Tony had so recently suggested. He waited for the litter to be set down, and the bearers to move away, before he stirred as much as a little finger. He slowly pulled up his weight, eyeing out his three daughters as he did so, and then took small uneven steps towards a carved out section of the rocks, allowing his bulk to drop on to a roughly hewn throne. His commanding personality was tremendous as he continued to hold the breathless silence, looking from one character to another until issuing his first line to Gloucester and Edmund.

There was no doubt that the audience had been stunned by the unorthodox opening of the play. They were now willing to be swept along with whatever outpourings of emotion and passion were about to be presented to them.

Elizabeth spoke Goneril's first line.

"Sir, I love you more than words can wield the matter."

Their eyes met across the flickering stage, yet they denied their true feelings. They were now alive with the sensations and cunning of those they were portraying. The unreal had taken over; it was the play speaking with the undercurrent of reality.

Mitch's voice seemed to be pitched rather low, almost as though he were saving his energy for the mighty scenes that were to follow. There was a little unrest in parts of the house as difficulty was experienced in hearing some of the lines. This was exacerbated by a sudden outbreak of coughing from just below the dress circle, a sure sign of straying attention. It only ever needed a single cough to breed others, and as though now given permission to hack away, a volley of spluttering echoed in scattered areas.

One half of Mitch's awareness was fully alive to what was happening, causing his confidence to waver for a fraction of a second, but it was long enough. He was at the point of striking Oswald with the line, "Do you bandy looks with me, you rascal?" which he uttered with such personal rage that the action following carried greater impact than planned. Mitch aimed his blow with uncontrolled force, catching Robin so unawares that the boy was thrown off balance and toppled over. Robin staggered to his feet, so dazed that his own next line was given a timid delivery. What followed should have served to relax the tension within the audience, and so prepare them for the next small climax. The unfortunate imbalance had only served to tighten the drama without the required easing of pressure, and so the passage was flawed in its outcome.

Bruce had been waiting for his first entrance, noting the mistake in timing, sweating into the palms of his hands as the mood changed towards the wrong direction. His first entrance took the form of tumbling down a rock face, a movement that required skill if he was to avoid hurting himself. This had been thoroughly rehearsed, and he knew that as long as he started off with his right foot firmly planted on the edge of the scenery all would be well. Unfortunately the preceding action had taken him unawares, with the result that his entrance was upon him before he realised the moment had arrived. Hearing his cue, he instinctively leapt on to the rock with his *left* foot, managing to catch his toes and ungainly bounding down to land in front of

Lear. The audience was totally unaware of the error of judgment, and took it for a clever bit of acrobatics, rising to the occasion with a small burst of applause. Gratified though he was, Bruce had felt his knee pull as he landed, and a stabbing pain shot around his leg. He stood up, only to discover that he was now unable to put much weight on to the leg. He was forced to play off his lines, using his disability to enable him to limp from one position to another.

Out front Maggie knew that something had gone wrong. She sensed concern from Tony as her hand closed over his. She had been making mental notes from the moment the curtain had risen. Tony, on the other hand, had relaxed into his seat, accepting what was being given to him, while occasionally wondering what had happened to the detailed directions he had so carefully worked out.

By the end of the scene Mitch had brought all his technique into play, slowly picking up the scattered fragments and gathering the play around him once more. By the time he returned on stage for his final speech in that scene, he was ready to shed the tears demanded of the action. With his growing anguish he carried the audience in the palm of his hand, tightening their preformed constraints of parenthood, and holding captive every pair of eyes.

The only sure performance was Fiona's. Her Regan was a creation of spite and self-concern, of singleness of purpose that seemed to bite on every word and spit it out on to whoever was within easy reach. To watch her build her character was, by general consent, the small wonder of the evening. She was a woman with green blood in her veins, and only lacking several heads.

As for Susanna, she presented a picture of almost too much goodness, of someone who couldn't possibly be related to the other two. In many ways she was presenting more of her own personality than she realised. She had found some difficulty in getting the slight edge to the character of Cordelia, a facet that would have made her more acceptable. She should have been more three dimensional, while still underlining the self-justification for refusing to rescue her rightful inheritance.

By the time they had arrived at the scene in which Oswald is set upon for the second time, Robin had still not fully recovered from the earlier blow and, being ever on the defensive, remained too distant from Kent, causing him almost to miss striking him across the face. The lines that followed sank into a meaningless jumble as he stumbled off stage crying, "Help, ho! murder! murder!" there being no impetus to warrant the cry.

The most telling moment came with Mitch's superbly controlled rendering of the lines,
> "I have full cause of weeping, but this heart
> Shall break into a hundred thousand flaws
> Or ere I'll weep. *O fool, I shall go mad!*"

By this time Mitch had shed part of his costume, appearing gaunt, trembling with age, and quite helpless. There was a long pause after "ere I'll weep". He looked from one character to another, arms half-extended, mouthing non-existent lines, shaking his head in total bewilderment. No one moved. There was no sound on stage. There was a magical holding of breath in the auditorium. The words, "*O fool*", came as a prolonged moan, pulled from the depths of his soul, to be capped by the last four words uttered with a mixture of disbelief and hope that in the fulfilment of madness he might find some comfort.

Regan's hate for her father was further emphasised with her entreaty to her sister to join with her in turning a united back upon him. The curtain fell on the first half as they moved sharply upstage, hands extended in unity and combined truce. The stage unexpectedly burst into brightness low behind the huge rocks, heralding the pending storm, showing both of them dwarfed in silhouette against the clouding cyclorama.

The instant applause was thunderous, and only quelled when the house lights brought the audience back to the reality around them. Maggie and Tony, deciding it would be better not to go backstage, disappeared into the bar to mingle with the audience. Voices were loud, knowledgeable, perceptive. Motivations were being expounded, the production dissected, costumes and scenery questioned. There were always those, particularly the least qualified, who knew all the whys and wherefores.

If it wasn't so serious it would have been funny, but both Robin and Bruce had to be given emergency treatment as a result of their respective misfortunes. Robin's mouth had been cut on the inside of his cheek when the first blow had landed, and it was now beginning to swell, with the result that he was finding it difficult to enunciate his lines clearly. Bruce had to have his knee tightly bandaged under his costume in order to try to take some of the weight, and to relieve the increasing pain.

Fiona had gone straight back to her dressing room to repair her make-up, saying little or nothing to anyone around her. She was one of those actresses who preferred not to break her concentration in the middle of a performance, particularly when playing this type of dramatic role. Susanna was already seated as she was not on just before the curtain fell.

"How do you think it's going?"

"Difficult to tell. I don't think Mitch is concentrating as much as he might," said Fiona.

"I wouldn't say that. He's carrying a hell of a load, in more ways than one." Susanna was on the defensive.

"I'd really rather not discuss it," said Fiona. There was a finality in her clipped tone that seemed to belong to Regan. Fiona was doing everything she could to bring her character to life, and if it meant being out of step with the rest of the cast, so be it.

"Oh! You 'ad me in tears at one point," said Mrs Grace. "Lovely it was." She was helping Mitch to change into a tattered loincloth in readiness for the second part of the play, powdering down his perspiring back and chest. Under his instructions she painted in a few uneven lines across his back to represent the marks of briars that had clawed at him.

The rest of the cast were trying to assess the evening so far, but as with all first nights it was impossible to gauge true reactions either from each other, or from the audience. It represented a many-faceted critic whose faculties were seldom overstretched, and whose voice only mattered if it could be heard two rows back.

"Act two, beginners, please. Act two. Act two, please."

In the wings Mitch was standing apart from his fellow actors, trembling more than he could ever remember doing in the past. Perhaps he had absorbed more of Lear's character than he realised, and his nervousness was being used to advantage. He had no way of knowing. He suddenly felt the pit of his stomach tighten and he turned to a sand-filled fire bucket to retch as privately as he could.

"Mr Dawlish! Mr Dawlish! You all right?" A timid stage hand hovered nearby.

"I'll do," was all that Mitch could say. "I feel better for getting rid of that." He turned back towards the stage as he heard the audience settling down.

Thunder clapped several times before the curtain rose. This time there was no tell-tale sound to announce the disappearance of the front barrier. The stage revealed dark clouds scudding their way across a high grey sky accompanied by the sound of wind screeching through the hollows of the heath. All was stark and bleak, and cruelly barren of any semblance of shelter. The opening characters were braced against the weather, bundled in their thick cloaks of fur, and wearing heavy-brimmed hats that outlined their faces. This was followed by Lear's first scene in which he appeared deranged, making his entrance by clambering over a large rock, first revealing his hands scratching at the craggy surface as he pulled himself into view followed by the Fool, now taken to limping on a makeshift crutch.

"Blow, winds, and crack your cheeks! Rage! Blow!"

Lines that have so often been uttered with wild fury, with flaying arms and deep anger in the voice; but not on this occasion. Mitch had decided to play off the character's age. To utter the lines with a failing voice, and an uncertain stance. To make the entire transformation one of rapidly degenerating senility. Unfortunately the sound effects ran away with themselves, causing most of the subtle inflections that Mitch had so counted upon to be utterly meaningless to those of the audience beyond the first few rows.

Even the ghastly scene in which Gloucester's eyes were plucked out lost some of its horror due to a slow lighting cue at the crucial moment of the action. The actor playing Gloucester had been stripped down to his waist, with the scene taking place in the depths of a cavern. Instead of the fire being rattled into life at the vital moment of torture, it was suddenly extinguished only to shoot back into brightness as Gloucester uttered a tremendous cry of pain.

The evening played through its tragedy in an uneven symphony of greatness and misfortune, but the few notes of high emotion lacked the essential cohesion for a totally unqualified success.

As Oswald, Robin failed to make anything of his death scene. Being aware how easy it would be to overdo the situation, he simply seemed to apologise for dying and let it go at that.

The dead bodies of Goneril and Regan were finally dragged in, lashed to biers, their limbs stained with blood, their hair in matted disarray. They were lowered over the rocks and left in an upright position with flickering torches on either side, propped up as though waxen images waiting for a further fate. This was soon followed by the final entrance of Lear with the dead Cordelia in his arms, silhouetted on top of a rock above the bodies of the other two. The repetition of the word, "Howl", arose softly until the fourth repeat seemed to fill the entire theatre like the baying of an animal in dire pain. Mitch slowly descended on to the general level of the stage, searching faces for understanding as he lowered Cordelia on to a pile of straw that supported her in a sitting position. He knelt at her side, swaying to and fro in mental torment. Again there was a repeated word, "Never", uttered five times, with all the modulation that human suffering could imagine. When he died it was as though the final vestige of life had been pulled from within him, as though his physical being had shrunk out of existence.

The near-naked body was lifted and placed upon a litter of crossed spears covered with furs. Four servants elevated this above their shoulders, allowing Lear's head to fall back and his arms to flop over the sides. Once again flaming torches led the way to the accompaniment of keening from the rest of the cast. The procession moved away, taking the light source with it and so allowing the stage to be cast in long shadows, leaving the three sisters in tiny pools of changing light as the curtain descended.

For a moment there was a stunned silence in the auditorium. The staging had hung together as a complete unity, the true tragedy had been pinpointed and carefully built into a great final curtain. Mitch's dying moments were undoubtedly among the most moving ever seen on any stage, and they had left the audience drained of emotion. The silence was uncanny. No one backstage could ever recall such a moment before.

It wasn't until the curtain rose to reveal the cast lined up that the hurricane of cheers broke around them. One by one the leading members of the company came on to an increasing appreciation that must have been heard all the way to Shaftesbury Avenue. Mitch had enveloped his near-nakedness in a rich purple cloak, and slowly paced down stage to acknowledge the enthusiasm that broke around him, both on stage and out front. The first few rows were on their feet, shouting and clapping until the swell of sound was deafening. The rest of the house followed suit. Mitch came out between the heavy front curtains for a solo call, a rare occurrence in these days of hurried line-ups. The cheering broke out with renewed vigour. There were at least fifteen curtain calls, with the Dawlish family stepping forward, hands clenched together in a united acknowledgment of the audience approval.

Tears were streaming down Elizabeth's cheeks as the final curtain fell, and the audience began to disperse. She edged her way to Mitch's side, to where he was now receiving the approbation of his peers.

"I'm so very, very happy for you, my darling. You deserve it. You deserve it all." What more could she say? What more was there to say?

3

The entrance to the stage door rapidly clogged to a standstill as individuals tried to force their way through to pay homage to all and sundry. The audience spilled out from the side entrances in a solid phalanx of bodies that blocked both pavement and road alike, while the police tried to maintain a clear way for cars attempting to cut through into Regent Street, and fought a losing battle to persuade pedestrians out of the road.

Joe had to search back a long way into his memory to recall the last time there had been as much enthusiasm for a straight play at this theatre. Personalities were calling out their names to him in exchange for dressing room numbers. Messages of congratulations were scribbled on scraps of paper and left for distribution. All was burble and noise mingled with the unmistakable smell of success.

There were very few critics among the visitors. They had mostly hurried away to scratch out their hastily considered opinions for the morning editions. It was only the Sundays that had the enviable luxury of contemplation. The ridiculous speed demanded by press deadlines led many actors to discount reviews, preferring to rely upon the more tangible public acceptance reflected in box office returns.

Mitch's dressing room soon bulged with well-wishers, people whom he had not seen for years, and was quite certain he would never see again. The full length of the corridor outside was a mass of movement. Bodies edged between bodies, smiling and greeting each other loudly, talking excitedly in high-pitched voices. His morale was being given a tremendous charge. Those who were on intimate terms with the balance of theatrical success and failure were already predicting that managements would again be queuing to offer Mitch an open cheque-book on his own terms, and with a choice of roles.

But though Mitch appeared to be in high spirits, deep down he harboured doubts. He was no fool, and he was the last person to allow himself to be beguiled by a slightly hysterical first night ovation. He was only too well aware that there had been sections of the action in which he had been in less than full control of his own performance.

Tony had managed to slip backstage through the pass door from the auditorium, ahead of the crowd, calling his thanks to the stage crew as he scurried on towards the dressing rooms. He always made a point of thanking every member of his cast, while at the same time qualifying his thanks by pointing out some of the errors he had noted. Not for him the unqualified pat on the back for a job well done; there were always reservations. Any production of his was just another job of work, something that had to be honed to perfection, and he insisted upon just that. If the public were prepared to pay to see actors strutting on a stage, then the strutting had to be precise and well presented.

By the time the masses had begun to leave, Maggie was able to settle in Mitch's dressing room to discuss the evening from her point of view.

"I was a little worried about the opening."

"Me too. Especially when that bloody coughing started. At one point I thought I was giving a benefit performance in a geriatric ward." He proceeded to clean off his make-up, now streaked with perspiration. His cream-laden face vanished in the fierce lights as false features smudged together, causing him to lose all semblance of character, either his own or that of King Lear. The process of "cleaning off" always had a momentary depersonalising effect.

Maggie lit a cigarette. "Do you mind?"

"No, help yourself. Well, now that we're over the first hurdle, tell me, Maggie. Why did you do it?"

If the unexpected question took her by surprise, she certainly showed no sign of it. "Do what?"

"I'm not that much of a fool," said Mitch. "You didn't have to mount a production quite as lavish as this."

"You *owed* me a performance, remember?" She tossed the answer aside as casually as she knew how.

"I signed that contract seven years ago. Things were quite different then. I was on top. I was in constant demand. Three productions seemed a fair exchange for the support you'd given me in the past. We both know that the second show only just about broke even. Beckett never was my cup of tea. A bit like James Joyce in that respect. You could have written off the third production against any one of the Australian tours. You didn't have to honour the contract to the letter."

"But *you* did. You're really very naive, Mitch."

His face was now cleaned and glowing. The area around his eyes had that slightly dewy look left after the residue of removing cream is wiped away. He poured some astringent lotion on to a pad of cotton wool. Maggie's remark caught him in mid-action. He turned away from the mirror to face her.

"How do you mean, naive?"

"This was as much for me, as for you. Roxborough Productions have been on a winning streak for the past few years. I've got five successful shows running in the West End right now. Three in my own theatres. There are two companies touring Australia, one in South Africa, and another in Canada. Too much success can be almost as damaging as a series of flops. The mass media take it all for granted, and treat one less seriously. Some label it flair, others call it commercialism; commercialism being the greatest crime, of course. Anyway, I thought the time had come to change my direction. I need something to make the right people sit up and take notice. The money invested in this production was partly this year's tax reserve, and partly Arts Council subsidy. If we succeed, it all goes back with a profit, and everyone's happy. If it fails, it gets written off. The Arts Council are more than used to that. Either way, Mitch, I come out with a reputation for not doing only the more obvious commerical properties. I've reached a point when I want the big boys to feel that I have a sense of responsibility towards my 'art'." The last word slithered from her. She smiled, full of self-congratulation. Cigarette smoke drifted across her perfectly painted features.

"So much for the milk of human kindness."

"I'm sorry, Mitch. I need recognition in the right quarters, just as much as you do. I want the Arts Council to fund a production for a prestige tour. Tonight could well be the first step in that direction. I also want in on the video scene. There's a consortium about to get off the ground and I want a share."

"And I've been used as the bait?"

"I wouldn't have put it quite as bluntly as that."

Mitch turned back to the mirror, patting the lotion on to his cheeks, wincing slightly, yet enjoying the cooling sensation with masochistic pleasure.

Mrs Grace popped her head back into the room. "Is it all right to finish off in 'ere now?" She had just returned Mitch's costumes to the wardrobe on the fourth floor, and was still puffing from the effort. She always insisted that every item be inspected before each performance. She knew the dangers of falling hems and loose fastenings.

"Yes, almost through. Sorry to be so long. I didn't anticipate so many visitors."

"Oh! Don't apologise! Time enough to worry when they makes excuses, and don't bother to come round. Like working in a morgue, that is." She toddled from one room to another, collecting together the small items of costume, belts, shoes, head-dresses. All had a special place, and each was lovingly laid to rest for the night.

The other dressing rooms had been no less congested, but they too were now beginning to thin out, leaving their occupants with a few family and some close friends.

Tracy was showing concern for Bruce's injured knee as he was finding it more and more difficult to put any weight upon it without experiencing considerable pain. "You'd better see someone first thing in the morning." She crouched beside him, helping him to rewind the bandage on his outstretched leg. She didn't really know what she was doing, but the concerted effort made both of them feel better.

"If I've damaged the cartilage again, there's not much anyone can do."

This had first happened years earlier, when he used to play rugby. Although there had been some talk of an operation, he had been strongly advised against it. Now, in an unguarded moment, there was always the possibility of a recurrence of the problem.

"Will you be able to appear tomorrow if you're still in this much pain?"

"Let's wait and see."

Robin was almost changed. He never did take long to climb out of costume or to clean off his make-up. There had been occasions in the past, when he was playing a straight juvenile lead, when he had allowed himself to be tempted to leave on the residue of his make-up and go home in war paint. It was generally considered very unprofessional, and he'd decided that as he was currently playing alongside the rest of the family he ought to conform.

"Will you be coming to the party?" said Robin.

"No, I really don't think you should, Bruce," cut in Tracy before he had a chance to say anything.

"Yes, of course I will." He caught Tracy's eye. "But I won't stay long."

Jake was hovering in the background, like a spectre at the feast, noting the silent animosity between the two brothers, but saying nothing. He called over to Robin, "I suppose you'll be going on that clapped out motorbike?"

"Well, of course. I can hardly fold it up and put it in my pocket."

"Then, for God's sake, don't have too much to drink. Anyway, I'll see you there. No point in me waiting here."

"Hang on. I'll give you a lift on the pillion."

"No, thank you. I'd rather crawl." He rose from his chair, pulling the creases from his tunic, and smoothing his trousers around the crotch. "Try not to be too long. I hate being alone with a bunch of butch actors, they're so boring. I'll test the temperature of the wine while I'm waiting." Bruce chose to ignore the remark while continuing to get changed.

Susanna and Fiona had said very little to each other throughout the entire evening. Instinct told Fiona she had come out of the venture with flying colours. Her entire performance had been delicately modulated, tightened like a piano wire until it reached the right pitch. Whatever else had gone wrong, she had insisted upon sticking to her own harmonics to ensure that her characterisation fitted into her preconceived idea of how it should evolve. The fact that certain scenes had been unbalanced by her selfishness hadn't bothered her; she knew what she knew, and was only concerned with self-preservation.

"I think you should have played down towards the final curtain," said Susanna.

"I saw no reason for all of us to make fools of ourselves."

"It would have been more helpful towards Father."

"He didn't need my help."

"He needed *everyone's* help. That's why we're doing this bloody production." She felt protective towards Mitch, she felt she had to say something about Fiona's attitude. There had been many comments about the lack of co-operation she'd shown during rehearsals, and her performance had reinforced this.

"Having agreed to appear doesn't mean that *I* have to drop my own standards." She snapped on her words, making a point that couldn't be ignored, or misconstrued.

Susanna picked up the jibe immediately. "If you're implying that I wasn't good enough, it was only because of the way you played tonight. You threw the production totally out of balance."

"I'd have given the same performance whoever was playing the lead. I've still got my own reputation to think about. Believe me, the long knives will be out in force tomorrow morning." She switched off the lights around her dressing table, and dragged a torn piece of towelling over her make-up tray. "You can go to hell your own way." She didn't wait for an answer, but pushed past Susanna and out into the corridor.

"Bloody hell!" Matthew's voice echoed outside as Fiona almost knocked him over.

Susanna jumped at the sound of his unexpected expletive. She had anticipated seeing him sooner, and was beginning to wonder what had happened to him. "Matthew, what kept you?"

"Sorry, love. Stopped off up the corridor to see Mitch and your mother. Had to make the right noises."

"Well?" Her eyes opened wide, awaiting his comments.

He paced around, pushing his hands into his trouser pockets while trying not to look at her.

"Well?" She repeated the question, now less forcefully and expecting the worst.

"Patchy, love. It was all very patchy. It should have toured for a few weeks before coming in."

"Fiona wouldn't agree to that. Tony and Maggie were all for smoothing off the edges out of town, but she refused. She's trying to get together another of her own companies. She's done it before. She said it would be impossible to get on with her own plans if she was out of town."

He drew in his breath thoughtfully, contemplating what to say next. "There were some good moments. Some very fine moments, in fact – "

"Don't overdo it," said Susanna, now beginning to allow her irritation to show.

"Listen, Sue. If all you're after is unstinting praise, then don't invite my comments. You'll only ever get the truth from me. You ought to know that by now."

"What about my own performance, then? You haven't said anything about that." She so desperately wanted his approval, to feel that she had acquitted herself well alongside the rest of the family.

"Needs a bit more light and shade. A little too saccharine sweet right at the beginning, and not quite enough bitterness towards the end. It's a common trap with that part. You'll feel its measure by the end of the week."

"Christ, but you're bloody grudging." She pulled herself away from him, hanging on to the back of her chair. The evening had been a battle of nerves, not solely because of the occasion but because of Fiona as well. Now, to have met with faint praise from Matthew was just that little more than she could take. Tears welled into her eyes, forcing their way down her flushed cheeks, and as much as she tried to control her emotions, there was no holding back. She began to sob bitterly, her still bare shoulders shaking.

Matthew stood his ground until he felt compelled to comfort her. "Hey, come on, love. It wasn't that bad." He put his arms around her, cradling her breasts in his hands and kissing the back of her neck. "This is a bit over the top." He gently pulled her round to face him, making her lift her chin so that he could kiss her.

Her arms reached up and clasped behind his neck, pulling his face closer to hers. "Sorry! It all seemed such a mess."

"Nothing that can't be straightened out. Tony will be on to it before you can say Shakespeare."

"I do love you. I wanted you to be proud of me tonight."

"I was. I was thrilled to little bits to see you up there with the rest of them." He smoothed away her hair, now sticking to her damp face. "Come on, sit down for a minute." He led her to a divan, covered by a tatty patchwork spread. "Now then. Deep breath. And again."

His instructions were willingly obeyed. Faltering a little as she tried to contain the last of her tears and throwing back her head against the cushions. "I'm suddenly so tired. I hadn't realised just how exhausting it's all been." He bent forward, lifting her feet from the floor as she gasped another small breath. "Oh, that's good! I'm sorry, Matthew. I know you're right. You always are."

Matthew was sitting on the edge of the divan, gently kissing her lips, her hot eyes, her moist cheeks, her cool neck. His hands pushed back her hair once again, and then found their way down on to her shivering body.

"Matthew, turn the key in the lock. It'll be ages before anyone comes round for a final check."

He said nothing, crossing to the door, and then returning to her side. He allowed his jacket to fall to the floor as she extended her arms towards him, smiling through her tiredness, wanting him so badly. She needed the comforting weight of his body, the assurance of his unstinting acceptance of her. Matthew lay down beside her on the narrow divan, enfolding her in his arms until they were both anxious to express their love. The setting added an unexpected dimension as they caught sight of themselves in the long mirror at the far end of the room. A heightened sensation of viewing and being viewed. There was a breathless gasp as they relaxed, happy in their renewed expression of love, of caring for each other.

"Do you think anyone's done that in here before?" asked Susanna, laughing, now quite relaxed.

"More times than you can imagine. There's very little that's original, believe me. Mind you, the staging might have been better."

"I wish you weren't quite so practical."

Elizabeth had had her share of visitors. Most of them had already seen Mitch, or were on their way to him. The congratulations and the praises were universal. She found this part of the evening almost as unnerving as the entire performance had been. Whenever a new face appeared in the small room she cast a furtive glance to where Victor was standing, trying to appear invisible and not being very good at it.

He had managed to be among the first to see her and he was determined to stay to the last. For him, the evening's success meant something other than a return to the top for Mitch. It signalled the possibility of a settled future with Elizabeth. He mentally discarded the reservations that had been part of her promise. He saw his life with Elizabeth as one that would stretch into the future to embrace all the relaxed contentment and complete fulfilment that they could ever need or want.

"Maggie seemed a little remote," said Victor, when the final visitor had departed.

"That's to be expected. Reserved judgment is part of her stock-in-trade." She looked at him through the mirror, observing the way his eyes followed her every movement. She knew precisely what he was thinking, and was afraid that he would try to rush her into a divorce before she was really ready, or before Mitch could accept the idea.

"He was brilliant, wasn't he?" Victor seemed to be trying to work towards the same conversation he had started before the curtain went up just over three hours earlier. It was almost as though the play had merely served as the interval within their own private performance.

"Yes. Splendid. I've never heard an audience cheer quite like that before."

"He should be feeling full of confidence again."

"It takes more than a single performance."

"Yes, but it must help. It must make a difference."

"Difference?" The moment she had asked the question, she knew it to have been a mistake.

"To us. To everything. You said – "

"Please, Victor. Not now. Let it all settle for a while. Let's sit tight, and see what happens by the end of the run." She didn't wish to hurt him, but she had to be firm, to establish she meant what she said. There was no point in continuing to hold out hope for tomorrow, or even next week. Whatever the outcome, it had to be well into the future.

"Does he – does he know you've invited me to the party?"

"Yes. I saw no reason for not telling him. There'll be lots of people there. He accepted it as a matter of fact."

The glow of her black velvet suit created a delicate aura around her pale skin, making her appear all woman, understanding, knowing, and above all compassionate. She was everything that the evil creature she had just portrayed was not.

"I'll see if he's ready. Come on, Victor. You go down to the stage door and I'll meet you there."

In Mitch's room Elizabeth leaned back against the door, taking in the mixture of perfumes trailed by recent visitors, and the thick cigarette smoke still clinging heavily in the air.

"Does the colour of your suit express your mood?" said Mitch.

"A medium shade of grey would have been nearer the truth. How do you feel now that it's all over?"

"A bit nonplussed. You know, uncertain." He ran a comb through his thick hair, recently plastered down under his wig, and now sticking up all spiky and startled. "Tony's called the company for ten thirty tomorrow morning."

"I didn't know that." She moved nervously, shrinking at the thought of yet another rehearsal.

"He's got sheaves of notes. He wants to tighten up certain scenes."

"Victor's waiting at the stage door. We'll walk over and pick up the car. I'll wait for you."

Mitch hesitated for a moment. "He's decided to opt in, has he?"

"I told you he'd be there, remember?"

"Look, I'm still feeling uptight. Suppose I stroll over on my own? I feel the need to be alone for a while."

Elizabeth tightened her lips. She could see that Mitch was edgy; he seemed restless and unpredictable. She was always scared that he would take off and not return – or worse, that something would happen to him as a result of his own stupidity.

He caught the mood of her sudden intensity and smiled his winning smile, a trick he had used to advantage on so many occasions. It was part of his theatrical equipment. On stage it never failed to warm an audience, off stage it had grown to be rather transparent; at least, as far as Elizabeth was concerned.

"You *will* turn up?" The question was blunt and to the point. She was tired of couching her words; tired of the constant fear that she might offend his sensibilities.

"Yes, of course I will. I just need to get some air. I need a little time to myself. I'll stroll along by the Embankment, and then cut up by Waterloo Bridge. I'll only be about half an hour or so. I'm still feeling rather tense."

The book Elizabeth had given Mitch was lying open on a chair, and she glanced at the page as he finished combing his hair.

> There was an Old Man of Peru,
> Who never knew what he should do;
> So he tore off his hair,
> And behaved like a bear,
> That intrinsic Old Man of Peru.

"Does this sum up the way you're feeling?"

"Just about. It was a sweet thought. Thank you." He wrapped himself into his coat, still damp from his earlier stroll, and smelling slightly of wet wool. "Come on, worryguts. I'll see you at Thomas de Quincey's. Have a quiet word with Kevin to make sure there's some food left for me."

They left the dressing room together and walked along the corridor, meeting a few members of the cast coming downstairs, still dissecting the evening's performance. There were the usual polite exchanges, but anyone unable to detect a guarded conversation would have had to have been totally insensitive to the human condition.

As they got to the bottom of the stairs Mitch hesitated for a moment, looking towards the door that led back on to the stage.

"Anything wrong?" said Elizabeth.

"No! No, nothing. I – I just want to go back in there for a moment. Do you mind?" He didn't wait for her answer but passed through the swing doors that gave on to the prompt side of the acting area.

The air was still heavy and thick and warm. There was very little light coming from anywhere within the building. He slowly walked on to the set, standing centre stage, listening to the dead silence, trying to recall the rush of sound that had greeted him so recently. The auditorium had a rich velvet blackness that vanished into oblivion in every direction. There was a single isolated reflection from the back of a seat in the second row. It seemed to flash like a mirrored signal, calling to him, begging him to stay. Somewhere in the void a door slammed unexpectedly, creating an echo that floated towards him and then beyond and away into the distance. The shapes of the false rocks on stage appeared to tower over him and push him into the floor. High above there was nothing but the same inky blackness that he had been unable to penetrate out front. It gathered on every side to envelop and crush him. He began to shake, to feel an alien in his own land of make-believe, a land where he had so recently been King, a wide dominion over which he had reigned supreme for so many years. He tried to breathe deeply, but his throat seemed to constrict. In his mind's eye he tried once again to gauge the success of the evening, but it was no use. There were no answers, only more confusion, more darkness, more conflicts.

It took a considerable effort of will for him to turn away and propel himself from the stage; to drag his aching body from the still echoing cheers, and into the sudden silence that seemed to cut across the noise.

"Mitch! Mitch! Are you feeling all right?" said Elizabeth, still waiting outside.

"Yes. Yes, I'm fine. It was stuffy in there. Difficult to breathe. I'm fine now. I'll just get some air and join you later."

"Stopped raining at last," said Joe, as they approached the stage door. "I bet you'll be glad to get 'ome to bye-byes tonight, Mr Dawlish."

"How right you are, Joe. Good night to you."

"Good night, sir. Good night, Mrs Dawlish. Congratulations to you both."

"Thank you, Joe," said Elizabeth absently, her thoughts still occupied with her apprehension for Mitch.

Outside, in the cold air, some fans were still waiting to greet them. It was amazing the extent to which strangers assumed a personal association with those they had only ever met across the footlights or, less formally, on the small screen.

Victor had moved away from the group, watching the eager faces of those patiently waiting, noting the actor's art of being polite even when under considerable personal pressure.

Elizabeth kissed Mitch's cheek and left him surrounded by the still excited knot of people, standing tall in their midst, smiling and nodding and exchanging greetings.

4

Once the last of the crowd had departed Mitch strolled to the front of the building. Experienced as he was, it still gave him a boyish thrill to read his own name spelled out in large letters above the title in front of a West End theatre. He stood there for a few seconds, drinking in the satisfaction of once again appearing in the heart of London. He had an urge to stop someone, anyone, and to point out that he and the name were the same person. He wanted to tell them about the play, to talk about the production and to boast about his family who were all appearing with him. He looked around, but no one was interested. They all had better things to do, better places to go.

He took himself along Northumberland Avenue, past the silently solid but dead office blocks, seething with activity during the day, deserted at night. Past the old Playhouse theatre, long abandoned as a live entertainment centre, even more recently cast aside by the BBC. Any misused theatre made him feel sad, one that showed no hope of ever reverting to its former glory caused him even greater pain.

The Embankment pavements were still very wet, evenly reflecting the wall-mounted streetlights balancing on their fish-tail pedestals. He stopped to lean against the grimy parapet, listening to the occasional lap of the water against the mossy flood-wall below. The lights from the Festival Hall opposite and the flickering neon sign above the Hayward Gallery demanded attention.

He moved on, then stopped again, his eyes fixed on the cold concrete edifice of the National Theatre clearly cut out against the dark sky, wondering when he would be invited to appear there. He mused on the type of role he would like to play; one of the Greeks, perhaps? Something with a bit of meat on its bones, a character that would allow him to explore subtle shades of meaning, and give full scope to his voice and its wide range of emotions. He looked away again, recalling that he'd just had such an opportunity that very evening.

He should have been exalted, but he wasn't; he was depressed and despondent. He couldn't help but conjecture what the national press would have to say in the morning, not that reviews meant all that much to him, but still – Most of them had seen more than one King Lear in recent years, and some would inevitably make comparisons. He recalled seeing Paul Scofield a few years back. More recently there had been Donald Sinden, Anthony Quayle and Michael Gambon. They'd all received their share of praises, and each had their minor shortcomings pounced upon. Too old, too young, too agile, too senile, too mad or not quite mad enough. Always a reservation, always *almost* but not quite. Perhaps he should have listened to his gut reaction when the role was first suggested to him, accepted that it was virtually impossible to play, and left it to others to prove the point. No, that would have been too easy, the coward's way out. Mitch knew there had been moments when his performance could not have been bettered. The adjectives "great" and "brilliant" and "inspired" had been shouted at him, and the chorus of bravos was still ringing in his ears. It couldn't all have been simply out of kindness.

He moved on again, his cold hands clenched against the warm lining of his pockets. There was an icy wind on his face, and he could hear the sound of his own footsteps steadily pacing out between the swish of cars as they sped towards wherever. Quite without warning he found himself in an isolation of shadows thrown by the bulk that was Cleopatra's Needle, meanly obliterating the distant lights. A monument of mystery, concealing its own ancient dramas.

Before he realised it he was at the steps of Waterloo Bridge, the time having been absorbed by his conflicting doubts and fears, his hopes and his despairs.

When Elizabeth and Victor arrived at Thomas de Quincey's they found most of the cast already there. Kevin, one of the youthful partners, was there to greet them. He led the way through the long bar and held open the door to the private room above.

"I heard it was quite a success," said Kevin.

"Sounds as though the jungle drums have been beating," said Elizabeth.

The restaurant was packed to bursting point with after-theatre diners, chatting against the background of clinking cutlery, and the occasional popping cork. The wicker-backed bentwood chairs cast tiny lace shadows thrown by the many flickering table candles. The waiters seemed magically to glide between the tables, there, but only just.

"Hullo, Liz, I hear it was a great night," a voice called to her from the far side. She stopped to squint into the shadows. It was an old friend from the Royal Shakespeare Company at the Barbican.

The noise issuing from the party indicated the continuing post-performance euphoria. Reservations about the outcome of the evening were being laid to one side for the time being.

"Liz, darling! I was beginning to wonder what had happened to you. Come and have a drink. You too, Victor." Maggie gushed towards them the moment they reached the top of the stairs.

The long buffet table was piled high with a selection of salads, some crayfish, others of Jersey Mids, and still others prepared with amazing concoctions of rice. There was a delicate soup made with cream and sherry and spices, and a dish of stuffed fish accompanied by an egg sauce. Fresh fruit salad heavily laced with a tangy liquor, and a strawberry flan supported by a layer of lightly whipped double cream were alongside addition- ally to tempt the palate. The silver servers sparkled in the light thrown from the candelabra which reflected shadows from the hanging baskets, thick with greenery, suspended below the glass roof, now screened by attractive rush blinds.

Most of the cast were there, some with friends, some with spouses, some with the usual complement of hangers-on. There would always be those too thick-skinned to question why they hadn't actually been given a personal invitation. It was all ebb and flow, all hustle and high-pitched laughter, below a ceiling of drifting thick smoke. Hands carried glasses high above heads, plates were lifted clear of faces.

Maggie led the way towards the buffet table. "There's some deliciously hot food over here. Come and help yourselves. Where's Mitch?" She had suddenly become aware of his absence.

"He'll be along shortly. He needed some time alone." Elizabeth began to fork out food on to the plates being dutifully held by Victor.

"He is all right, isn't he?"

"Don't worry, he won't run out on you." Elizabeth laughed at her own joke, knowing all too well the small element of truth behind it.

"What a fantastic ovation! It must have done his heart good. It shouldn't take long for the word to get around. There'll be queues all down the Haymarket tomorrow." Maggie sipped her champagne, eagerly looking over the top of her glass to see who was enjoying her hospitality.

Victor was uncomfortable. He would much rather have been downstairs enjoying an intimate meal with Elizabeth. He clung to his glass, trying to make the contents last.

"How are the advance bookings?" enquired Elizabeth.

"Almost sold out for the first month. They're the faithfuls. The rest wait for the reviews." She moved away, waving to someone on the far side of the room.

"I'm surprised. I would have imagined the season to be completely sold out in advance," said Victor.

"Just after Christmas is never the best of times to open. We might have managed an advance sell-out a few years ago, but Mitch hasn't got quite the box office pull he used to have."

"I would have thought all the advance publicity would have ensured success."

"Did I hear someone mention publicity?" A tousled haired girl in her mid-twenties had appeared alongside them.

"Well, yes," said Victor, not quite sure to whom he was talking.

"That's my department. I'm Sandra, PRO for the company. I'll be going through the reviews first thing in the morning.

Leave it to me. I'll soon have a few quotable quotes outside the theatre. Did you see the spread I pulled off in the weekend *Telegraph* last week? Then, of course, there was that bit in the *Daily Express*—"

"Oh! Were *you* responsible for that?" Elizabeth found it difficult to keep the sneer out of her voice.

"Beautiful double page, that was. All those pictures, too. Mind you, they took some finding." She gulped at her fast vanishing drink.

"It might have been better if some of them hadn't been found. We don't always like to be reminded of *all* the parts we've played." Elizabeth had now taken the stance of theatrical matriarch, her projection being brought to its full power.

Sandra laughed. "Well, you know what they say?"

"No. What *do* they say?"

"Get publicity. If you can't make it good, make it bad. But get publicity." Sandra grinned at them from behind her now empty glass.

"Yes, I believe Noël said it years ago." She turned away, leaving Sandra blinking at her back, trying to understand what she had said that could have caused offence. Sandra had only been with Maggie for the past six months; she still had a lot to learn about the delicate personalities of actors.

A little apart from the many tightly knotted groups, Bruce sat nursing his aching knee, annoyed at his disability, anxiously straining to catch what was being said about the production. Tracy hovered over him, feeding small titbits into his mouth. Whenever anyone came close enough to knock into him, he winced a warning glare.

"Come on, Bruce, you ought to be lying down." She tried to persuade him to his feet.

"I'm quite comfortable. Please, love, don't keep nagging at me." The pain was making him peevish.

Ernest Preston stood in front of them, manfully clutching a large glass of whisky, and slowly growing more and more rosy as the evening progressed. Many years ago he had played the Fool; now his advanced age dictated that he be content with Gloucester, a smaller role but nonetheless rewarding. His richly fruity voice was an instrument that had matured over the years and mellowed with age.

"You did very well, Bruce. Nice first entrance. Pity you managed to cock it up slightly. Still, not to worry, I'm sure the audience weren't aware of it. You could break a leg and most of them would think it was part of the action. Where's your father?"

"He ought to have been here by now. Who knows what he gets up to?" said Bruce.

"Who indeed?" But Bruce was in no mood for a prolonged encounter.

At the same moment, Mitch was entering the restaurant downstairs. Luigi, the more rotund and beaming of the two young partners, was there to greet him, extending a warm welcome as he ushered him towards the stairs. Before they had covered half the distance spontaneous applause broke out from the replete diners, many rising to their feet and extending their hands with filled glasses. Word had travelled across town, and these night people knew how much success meant to someone like Mitch.

The applause was picked up at the top of the stairs as guests turned to greet Mitch in his hour of success. Most seemed not to notice that he looked cold and tired, or that his face was drawn into abstraction. The cries continued as he progressed into the room. He endeavoured to give an all-embracing acknowledgment by waving and nodding his head in gratitude, but there were those who saw it all as part of the continuing performance.

"Please stay with me, Victor. I need your support this evening," said Elizabeth, under cover of the outburst.

His willing hand tightened over her arm. The fact that she and Mitch had arrived separately had not passed unnoted. Several of Fleet Street's more prominent gossip writers were busily asking pertinent questions with their usual tactless confidentiality. A blousy woman with coral rings on most fingers was croaking her less than casual enquiries towards anyone who thought they might get a personal half-line mention in exchange for a little dirt. She kept her glass constantly filled as an aid to oiling her nutcracker voice. In another corner a moon-faced man smiled his own brand of ingratiating charm, exuding a smooth flow of speech that matched his immaculate evening suit.

Andy had brought his guitar to the party and was standing with one foot on a chair, strumming an unmelodic series of notes and singing a tuneless song. He was there in isolation, simply adding to the general mêlée, a cigarette wedged in a corner of his mouth, the smoke floating into his eyes causing him to squint. He occasionally broke away to gulp at a glass of beer, only to return with renewed vigour to stamping one foot and swaying in time to his own broken rhythm.

Fiona stood in the middle of the room, surrounded by a small group of young actors. They were listening intently to all she was saying, mesmerised by the power with which she was making her points. One particularly tall young man was listening, although standing apart. He watched Fiona's expression, observing the way she carried herself, mentally making notes on aspects of her personality. Most of them were aware of the company she was trying to form and there may well have been more than a little enlightened self-interest in their undivided attention. They might not have agreed with her politics, but they still had to eat and there was no knowing when a contact such as this would be useful. To be able to say they had appeared with Fiona Dawlish, in her own company, would at least be indicative of their ability if not their judgment.

"I know it has box office appeal, but I really can't see any great advantage in having the six of us appearing in a production together. Anyway, that still doesn't answer the old question. What's being done to help the provincial theatre? They're still being starved of quality entertainment."

A wide-eyed young man edged his way forward. "I do see what you mean," he said eagerly.

"The Arts Council are still putting far too much money into a few grandiose national institutions, like that prison on the South Bank. It's the small reps who need the support. They do some bloody marvellous work, but they're left to struggle with inadequate budgets and crumbling theatres. No one really gives a bugger about them."

"Yes, but it's always been like that. There's not much any of us can do about it – "

"Tony, my love, do come and meet Lord Barrington. He's been saying some very complimentary things about you." Maggie was fraternising with one of the great powers of the British entertainment industry. Either he had a finger in every pie, or was about to insert a digit into those not yet set upon his table. He had been spotted during the interval and invited by Maggie to join them after the show. The fortuitous meeting had been one that she had long been trying to engineer without success. Now he was her guest, one among many, and there could be no question of ulterior motive.

"Always willing to listen to flattery," said Tony, extending his hand.

"Nice concept. Don't think it'll make money, but it's worth doing."

He shifted his double corona cigar from one corner of his mouth to the other. The phallic object, permanently wedged between his teeth, had long been accepted as his trademark. There were those, better informed no doubt, who saw this as a sign of his deprived childhood, but the suggestion had never been pursued.

"I do so agree with you. Money and high profits certainly aren't the sole criteria for mounting a production. I think we saw a little bit of theatrical history tonight." Maggie allowed this to drop into the conversation with a sense of personal pride. She knew she had been clever managing to get the entire Dawlish clan to appear on the same stage, even though her methods had verged on the devious.

"Maybe we can arrange for the production to be videod for TV. There should be enough interest around the world to make it worthwhile. I'm pretty sure the Public Broadcasting System in the States would jump at it. You could soon get back your production costs, and then some. Believe me, doll, there are more ways than one of getting around an unhealthy balance sheet. Difficult, I admit. But not impossible."

"I hear you've got problems with the new musical," said Tony, for the sake of something to say.

Lord Barrington seemed to be taken off his guard, but rapidly allowed his wide smile to cover the moment. "Everyone hears everything these days. When you hear it from me, then you start to believe it. OK! So we took it off the road for a couple of weeks. No problem. Now it's back." He rolled his fingers around the length of the cigar and then turned back to Maggie. "Tell you what, doll, give me a ring in the morning. We'll fix lunch and talk." His thick voice rasped out the instruction. Such ideas from him were never merely vague suggestions. His reputation had been built upon decisive thinking and quick action. He waved to someone else and moved away, the audience concluded.

Having come up the hard way had given him a keen sense of his own worth. Sam Bloomburgh, as he had been born, had started life in the back streets of Manchester, a child of immigrant parents with a raft of brothers and sisters. Having a reasonable voice, he had used his ability to get away from his poverty-stricken background and managed to get a job as a chorus boy in a long forgotten musical. Although he did get to playing second leads, progress was all too slow for his hungry ambition and he graduated to become an agent to a number of variety artists. Once the music halls began their metamorphosis he shifted his interests on to the production scene. Within five years he had emerged as a Midas of the theatre. His vast empire now stretched in all directions, embracing international connections with television companies and major cinema productions that ran into millions of pounds. Several West End theatres came under his banner together with a chain of provincial houses through which he toured his own productions. But he never relaxed; he still enjoyed working a twelve hour day, sometimes more. He was constantly hungry for new conquests and it was no secret that he wanted still more of the current theatrical scene for his ever-widening operations. There was no doubt about this man's power. Just a few of the right noises from him and success stood a great chance for whomsoever he smiled upon. Mind you, the pendulum had been known to swing the other way.

Not that Maggie needed him for her success. She had been clever and had clearly demonstrated that her own brand of cunning was not lacking. As far as she was concerned, she had managed to sew up as much of the West End as she wanted. She was ready to cast her net upon wider seas and now looked towards the crock of gold labelled video. She knew that Sam Barrington was pitching for a big video involvement, and rumour had it that it stood a good chance of getting off the ground. She was determined to find a way, any way at all, on to his board of directors.

Jake put his hand over Robin's glass. "Kid, you're getting soaked – "

"For God's sake, leave me alone. Why must you always treat me like you were my grandfather?" He pulled his glass from under Jake's hand, spilling most of the contents on to his trousers. "Aw, shit! Now look what you've done."

"If I treat you that way, maybe it's because you act that way."

"Oh, hell!" Another whinge escaped from him as he pulled a face and covered his cheek.

"Now what?"

"I've just reopened that cut inside my mouth."

"Try pouring some more alcohol into it. You never know, your mouth may seize up." He moved away, no longer bothering to disguise his impatience, leaving Robin to moan and nurse himself.

"You look quite knackered, dear boy," said Ernest, nudging up to Mitch. "Takes it out of you, that part. I remember doing the play with Wolfit. My God, now that was an experience and a half, I can tell you."

"Yes, I'm sure it must have been," said Mitch.

"Bruce has got a lot of you in him," went on Ernest, now well afloat with an abundant supply of whisky in his blood and insufficient food to soak it up.

"I doubt if he'll thank you for the comparison. He likes to think of himself as an individual with his own style of acting and his own brand of technique. Being the second somebody else is never that much of a compliment."

"Yes, but some of you must rub off. It happens to all of us."

"Who's that talking to him at the moment?"

"Can't remember his name. Worked for him once, a long time ago. Does successful tours of the classics. No royalties, you know. Puts on quite a good show – "

Bruce was showing more than a passing interest. "Three different productions, you say?"

"That's it. Haven't yet sorted out all the details, but they'd be good parts." Billy Caxton was working hard to persuade Bruce to sign with him for his next tour.

"Have you set any dates yet?"

"They're flexible at the moment. Here's my card. No need to rush into anything. Think about it – "

"Hullo, Mr Dawlish. I'd like to offer my laurels to those already piled upon your head." Jake had edged through the bustle.

Mitch looked up quizzically. He had met Jake on several previous occasions and was only too well aware of the liaison with his son.

"Thank you," said Mitch, polite, if a little curt.

"I found the production interesting. Perhaps a little too gimmicky for my taste – "

"It was intended to interest."

Jake insinuated his way on to the vacant seat alongside Mitch. "Oddly enough, I had plans to do something similar with Macbeth. I'd thought of making it more of an in-fight between tribes, possibly setting it in outer Mongolia." He grinned, his expansive oriental grin revealing his perfectly matched white teeth.

Mitchell turned his head, delighted to be able to put him down. "It's been done. Gielgud did a way-out Japanese-type production of Lear years ago. I seem to recall it was presented at the Palace theatre."

"Really? I didn't know that."

"Before your time, dear boy."

"Sounds like a lot of chi-chi nonsense to me," said Ernest. "The bloody thing's so obviously set fairly and squarely in Scotland. Dropping it in the middle of some outlandish place won't add anything to the action. Lot of balls, if you ask me."

"But he didn't ask you, Ernest. He was talking to me."

The obvious reprimand took the old man by surprise. His eyes darted from one to the other expressing his annoyance. He finally made the excuse of looking for something more to drink.

Someone had discovered that the light-switches doubled as dimmers, and turned them low. The harsh glare of the scattered spotlights grew kinder, although the volume of noise seemed to increase in perverse compensation with voices rising and falling in various parts of the room.

"Robin has spoken of you from time to time. Are you designing anything at the moment?" asked Mitch. He had now turned his complete attention towards Jake, speaking in a softly rich tone that seemed to come in under the general hubbub.

"Sure, there's a few projects I have in the pipeline. But I'm not for putting them about until I've got that piece of paper in my hand – signed. I'm sure you know what I mean." His light voice and the oddly uneven speech rhythms added another dimension to his engaging personality.

Mitchell sat back, looking at Jake through the dim light, observing the clothes he was wearing, taking in the well-developed chest and expensively tanned skin. He allowed his gaze to rest upon the tight trousers that disappeared inside the dark boots.

"Do you design your own clothes?"

"Some! I did this outfit. I've added some weight since this was made. Still, can't complain. It shows my gilt-edged security." He looked down at himself and laughed.

Mitchell joined in, patting Jake's thigh rather obviously. "I like your style. Tell me, how are you getting on with Robin these days?"

"Just great. He's an understanding lad. He knows how to please. Makes no demands – well, not many. You've brought him up well." Jake seemed to be playing cat and mouse with Mitch.

The older man was no fool. He'd had a lot of experience in the game. After all, he'd been at it longer. He knew exactly what was going on and enjoyed the volley.

Elizabeth had been anxiously watching them from across the room. She decided that she ought to join in the conversation, if only for the look of belonging. "Darling, it's been a very long day and I'm desperately tired. Don't you think we ought to be going?" Deliberately, she allowed her hand to rest on Mitch's shoulder, looking at Jake above his head.

"I'm just beginning to relax. After all, dear, I am supposed to be the guest of honour. Maybe I ought to stay just a little bit longer. You go on. I'll catch you up when I'm ready. I'm sure Victor will be happy to do the honours. I'll call a cab – or something."

She had tried, perhaps not very forcefully, but enough, and she knew when to admit defeat. It was a blueprint situation she had experienced many times in the past and she no longer felt inclined to put herself in a position of obvious humiliation by trying to persuade Mitch to leave with her. Her hand slid away from his shoulder, her cold gaze remaining in contact with Jake's eyes just long enough for him to understand what she was thinking. Neither of the men paid lasting attention to her. They simply smiled civilly, first at her, and then back to each other.

Elizabeth turned away, using all the control she had to hide her fury. Victor had witnessed the little episode and was at her side before she had taken more than half a dozen steps. They made their excuses for leaving ahead of the others, stopping to say goodbye to Maggie and Tony, and being as polite as possible towards anyone who happened to block their way to the top of the stairs leading down to the quietening restaurant below and out into the chill night air.

Victor said nothing, but simply held on to her arm as they walked to the parked car. The still simmering humiliation was evident from the set of her jaw, in the stony way she fixed her eyes on to the middle distance, in the iron grasp of her hands clipped on to the steering-wheel.

The atmosphere at the party had slowly degenerated from high jubilation through to careful avoidance of detailed discussion about the play. The family appeared to be at some pains not to talk with each other. There was an undeniable discomfort overlaying the laughter, an undercurrent of long established problems temporarily set to one side.

A great deal of food had been carelessly dropped and ground into the carpet. The air had grown stale with the acrid smell of perspiration, heavy liquor and smoke, all fighting for the same limited space. The candles were burning low. Some broken glasses were gathered in sad little heaps on the ravaged buffet table. The evening had taken its toll of sentiments and emotions and was slowly eddying towards its inevitable let-down. Such evenings always do finish that way.

There was still tomorrow to face, and the tomorrows that followed until the play had run its course.

5

"Would you like me to stay until he gets back?" said Victor.

"No, that's not necessary. Let me get you a drink before you go." Elizabeth switched on a table-lamp near the drinks table. The restricted low light cast eerie shadows into the furthest corners of the room.

"Make it a long one." He threw his coat over an armchair, watching Elizabeth prepare his drink, her hand shaking a little. "He's remarkably selfish, isn't he?"

"Not intentionally. I suppose it's partly my own fault. I ought to have given him an ultimatum years ago. But the time was never quite right. There were always too many reasons for not doing so."

"Such as?"

"Work, the children, simply choosing the right moment – "

"None of them very good reasons for putting up with that sort of boorish behaviour. He takes you for granted."

She held out his drink with a rigid arm, extended as a buffer. "No, please, Victor. Not now. Not tonight." She moved back to the drinks table and began to pour some gin for herself.

"You're entitled to your share of happiness. You've stood by him long enough, longer than most others would have done. It's your turn, Elizabeth." He tried to see her expression, to gauge her reaction to what he was saying, but the light was inadequate and he could only just discern the shape of her chin and see the outline of her open lips against the glass.

"Habits die hard," she said, relaxing a little as she took another sip. "It's been a long time." She threw herself into an armchair opposite Victor and reached out to switch on a second light.

"Some habits should never be allowed to start."

She was now seated within her own private circle of brightness, and he could see her face floating against the surrounding darkness. Her eyes seemed to be fixed in time somewhere in the middle distance, searching through the unhappiness of her married years.

Her head fell back on to the cushions as she moistened her mouth, chewing on her lower lip, breathing deeply and remembering. When the truth had first dawned upon her about Mitchell, she had been shocked, numbed into disbelief at her own lack of awareness. He had pleaded with her, claiming his inability to change, trying to explain to her as simply as he could that whatever he did, whatever she felt, it would make no difference to his love for her. They had talked and talked, endlessly discussing their true feelings, trying to dissect their emotions. Elizabeth's initial reaction was one of revulsion. She had wanted to run, and to keep running until she was as far away as possible. But her determination was slowly replaced by understanding, and then compassion, for Mitch's personal confusion and desperate needs. Their joint careers had taken a turn for the better, and the publicity of another divorce for Mitchell would have resulted adversely upon their growing popularity. They were appearing together in a romantic comedy at the time; it was doing well and they had been booked for a transfer to Broadway. The film version was under discussion, and they would have been foolish to jeopardise either their growing reputation as the ideal theatrical marriage, or the prospect of continuing popular acceptance. The paying public have always found a degree of cosiness in the knowledge that a couple playing husband and wife on stage were, in fact, married in real life. And so they had remained together, Mitchell trying to conceal the dark side of his personality, doing everything he could to keep it to himself, and Elizabeth presenting a bold face to the rest of the world.

There were also the children to consider. First Bruce, with his retiring nature and an insistent need for love and attention. Susanna, on the one hand assertive yet all too easily deflated. Finally, there was Robin, highly aggressive as a child, exhibitionist, and unashamedly gay as he developed into his teens.

Mitch had tried to ignore this trait in his son, having spoken to him with concern and understanding without actually having declared his own personal predilections. The children had absorbed a great deal of Elizabeth's time and devotion. She had never held that against them, never for a moment accused them of holding her back. There had been no expectation of thanks.

Victor had tried so many times to get Elizabeth to accept that her job within the family was over and that none of them actually needed her any longer. She was now a free agent, a person in her own right. He had said the same thing in so many different ways, but always with the same predictable outcome.

"He'd go to pieces if I left him now," she said softly, quite suddenly.

"And you'll go to pieces if you don't. You're being less than fair with yourself – "

"Please, Victor. It's been a long day. I love you very much, but I'm – I'm very tired. I'm very, very tired." Her hand came from the shadows to cover her eyes as she began to sob, her head thrown back into the pool of cruel harsh light. Her entire body shook as the tears flooded from her closed eyes. "Oh! Christ, I'm sorry. I – I didn't mean to do this to you. It's just that – I'm so tired."

He was on his knees at her feet, looking up at her, trying to prise her hand away from her face while offering her a soft white handkerchief with which to dry her cheeks. "Please, Elizabeth, don't do that. Please don't. Here, dry your eyes. You'll give yourself a headache."

"Joke! I've already got one." A brief laugh escaped from her throat as she choked on a breath and began to cough. "It must be the strain. I'm all right now. You'd better go, it's getting late."

He was about to protest but she placed her hand over his mouth, letting her fingers fall across his lips as they parted.

"Are you going to bed, or will you wait up for him?"

"I'll go to bed. Who knows what time he'll get back?" She pulled herself up from the armchair, moving away to pick up Victor's coat with an obvious finality, holding it out to help him into it.

"My, but you're a stubborn lady. I'll phone you in the morning."

They stood at arm's length, their faces concealed in the safety of the shadows. He drew her to him, kissing her with tenderness, fully aware that yet another attempt to win her over had failed.

"I'll call a mini cab for you."

After Victor had gone she stood at the window until the driving lights had disappeared into the darkness. She suddenly felt very dejected and desperately lonely, more alone than ever before.

The experience of loneliness was one not unknown to Robin. Loneliness was inherent in his world of casual liaisons and unexpected partings, incidents accepted by the twilight existence of his daily routine. That night followed an all too familiar pattern.

Robin, as usual, had managed to drink far more than he was able to contain. Seeing Jake in conspiracy with his father had sent him back to the bar far too many times. He knew that Jake was planning for the time when Mitchell would once again be in a position to demand his own designer. Jake was nothing if not an opportunist, delightful with it, if unashamed, and Robin had long since learnt to recognise the signs. He had begun to get boisterous with those around him, shouting across to Jake, trying to draw his attention, but Jake's ears had been blocked. The moment came when Robin had tried to stand, only to slurp his half-filled glass all over Sandra. She, silly lady, hadn't the wit to see what was happening and promptly created her own area of disquiet. Two members of the cast had intervened to gather Robin from his crumpled heap on the floor and managed to drag him back on to a chair. They forced him to stay put for a while until such time as he was able to get to his feet and remain reasonably steady. Bruce had hobbled over and quietly spoken to Robin, who then announced to Jake rather loudly that he was leaving. The only response from Jake had been to suggest that Robin didn't ride his motorbike. Being the perverse boy he was, Robin immediately informed everyone that he fully intended to use his motorbike and left.

The journey home had been one of near misses, both for Robin and the impatient buses and cars, all zooming around him in clusters only to open up in self-preservation. Pedestrians had fared no better, there having been at least three narrow escapes, with the motorbike swerving like a sidewinder to avoid a serious accident. Someone had tried to take down his number, but all they got was a stream of colourful abuse and two fingers towards the stars.

Having once managed to find his key and let himself in, he kicked off his overtrousers, slung his crash helmet into a corner, and proceeded to undress, letting his clothes fall where they may. Although the central heating was turned up quite high, he switched on the electric fire. Jake liked it hot everywhere. He shrivelled in the cold English winters. Having completely removed everything, Robin poured another drink for himself and then collapsed in front of the warmth of the dry heat. This was the only light in the room. Robin lay back, looking at the glow through half-closed eyes, allowing the steadily mounting heat to spread itself sensuously through his wiry body as he relaxed into the softness of the goatskin rug. The fire enveloped his nakedness, covering him in an orange tint that crept around his limbs, highlighting his features while throwing parts of his body into crimson shadows.

He drained the glass, but found himself unable to crawl across the room to refill it. He was now extremely drunk. The empty tumbler rolled from his hand, coming to rest against the front of the fire, reflecting a distortion of the glow and catching his drunken eye. He fell forward, pushing his face on to the glass, looking at the room beyond as though sighting it in the fisheye lens of a camera. A silly chuckle escaped from the back of his dry throat. He laughed a little louder as he finally fell into a drunken stupor and total exhaustion.

"Bastard! Miserable, arsehole crawling, bastard." The words slipped from him repeatedly as he rolled over again, now flat on his back, eyes closed against the fierce glow, hands outstretched.

He was in the same position a few hours later, snoring and breathing heavily, when Jake returned. By now the climate within the room was intolerable even for Jake. While Robin usually sank into mild aggression when drunk, drink relaxed

Jake into an easy-going affability that was never less than attractive and winning. He turned off the bars of white heat, still throwing their warmth on to Robin's motionless naked body.

"Come on, nakedness, you ought to get that skinny arse into bed. Get all your little bits and pieces toasted lying there." He tried to lift him but, slight as Robin was, the effort proved to be too much for Jake and he toppled over, landing across the body.

Robin let out an involuntary cry, startled and afraid. His head ached, his mouth was like the bottom of a gravel pit, and his muscles were stiff. He lifted his head with considerable effort, slowly becoming aware of what had happened, and then dragged himself away from Jake to leave him looking puzzled at the unexpected movement.

"Oh! It's you. Leave me 'lone. Wa' time is it?"

"Just after three."

"Rotten shit. Where you been?"

"There was another party being thrown by some of the stage crew. I – er, I decided to go on."

"On your own?"

"There were quite a lot of other guys there. Some I never met before."

"You know 'xactly wha' I mean." He pushed himself further away until he couldn't retreat any further, propped up across a heavy glass table, his head resting on one knee, and his hands supporting his weight.

"What the hell *do* you mean, Robby?"

The boy looked across at him, his eyes heavy-lidded, his head falling from side to side as though pulled by invisible wires and appearing terribly vulnerable. "Where do you think it's gonna ge' you, making up to my ol' man?"

"Let's not talk about it now. You're too pissed to know what the hell you're gassing about."

"I might be pissed, but I still know wha' I'm bloody well talkin' 'bout. I saw you, chattin' him up. You're nothin' but a rotten, crawlin' little shit. Tha's wha' you are. Crawlin' shit." He tried to pull himself up by holding on to the edge of the table, but it overturned and he fell across Jake.

Jake managed to extend his arms and so was able to break

Robin's fall. His cool hands slipped around the slim waist, clasping Robin to him firmly. "There, just like a baby."

Robin struggled for a moment. It was a gesture rather than a serious attempt to disentangle himself. "Le' me go. You're a miserable, crawlin' shit. Le' me go." The struggle subsided remarkably quickly, partly through genuine lack of energy, but more because Robin saw this as his chance to be close to Jake without any loss of face. The moment was more than opportune, and even through his inebriated mind he realised he would be silly to make too much of an effort to pull away.

"There's no need for you to be too upset, little Robin. I'm back. I'm here." He kissed Robin's chest, running his hand all over the boy's warm skin at the same time. "Come on, what you need is bed. I'll tuck you up."

Trancelike, Robin allowed himself to be guided into the bedroom. He allowed Jake to lay him on to the bed and to be stroked, and then to be enveloped in the soft luxury of the quilt. Jake took his time about undressing, carefully smoothing out every item of clothing before climbing in beside Robin. He was experienced in creating a mood of anticipation through a series of calculated moves, revealing himself without eager haste.

Jake fell on to the bed, lying on his back beside Robin and looking up at the reflection of the childlike figure next to him. He turned over, extending one arm as a comforting invitation. Robin shook his head sulkily, pulling away from the centre, annoyed because he had been denied his sweetmeats, wanting to be coaxed into submission. They each took their time, slowly giving way until they were curled together in the middle of the opulent bed. They clung together, warm and safe in each other's arms, the lovers' quarrel ended, the truce declared in the customary manner.

It was around eight o'clock when Elizabeth awoke having slept fitfully, worried about Mitch and concerned because he had failed to return home the previous night. She had lain awake for what seemed like an eternity. She remembered thinking, just before she finally closed her eyes, "I'll wake up when he gets back", but that was light years ago. She rolled out of bed and felt her way into her slippers while pulling on her dressing gown. The morning had burst upon her before she was ready for it. She sank back on to the edge of the bed, willing her thoughts to clear, to become more ordered, all the time trying to think about Mitch. It was at this moment that she became aware of the smell of freshly ground coffee. There were spasmodic sounds coming from the kitchen below. Someone was moving about as though trying not to be heard.

Once downstairs she stood in the doorway taking in the scene. Tousled and dressing gowned, Mitch was sitting at the end of the table, one newspaper in his hand, others spread around in disarray.

"Mitch?"

The newspaper rustled as he looked above it, his face bloated, his eyes heavy from lack of sleep, his jaw relaxed and flabby. There was no sign of the matinee idol, no indication of the greatness of less than a decade ago, no aura of the triumphant performer of less than twelve hours earlier. The mean early morning light was just managing to push its way into the kitchen, catching one side of his face. He remained motionless, allowing the paper to fold away slowly from him as he held it.

She moved further into the room, letting the door swing closed, creaking once again into the silence of their communication.

"What happened to you last night? I stayed awake as long as I could. I didn't mean to fall asleep – "

Her voice came to him as though being given a cue on stage. First the entrance, then the dialogue. His reaction was a rehearsed reflex born of a long run, but like most long runs it was carried on technique, facile and representational.

"Good morning, Liz. I – I got home much later than anticipated. I did look in and saw you sleeping. I didn't want to disturb you. I spent the night in Robby's old room."

Elizabeth's voice dropped to a whisper. "I see. That was very considerate of you. I wouldn't have minded, you know. It would have been – friendly." She paused for a fraction of a second, selecting the word with care. "Where did you go?"

"There was another small party. A sort of breakaway group. I was invited to go along. It would have been difficult to refuse."

"Yes, of course. Odd that I wasn't invited with you."

"It was something decided on the spur of the moment. You'd gone by then. Coffee?" He pushed the coffee pot towards her. Elizabeth reached down a large brown pottery cup and saucer. The aroma released a tight sensation in the pit of her stomach, making her feel an urgent need for something warm and comforting.

"What are they like?" Mitch pushed the scattered pages halfway across the table towards her.

"The general consensus would appear to be that I'm over the top. That indefinable something has left me. The muse has flown. So where do I go from here?"

Elizabeth began to read the reviews.

"Some brilliant moments of high tragedy", proclaimed one review. It then proceeded to qualify the word "moments", emphasising the unevenness of the production, and the lack of development of some of the performances.

"Pathetic and pitiable", declared another, slamming Mitch's interpretation as one that went for effect rather than truth.

"Raw and rugged". This one ran to very few lines, setting out to be clever at Mitch's expense.

"A noble attempt, but lacking greatness".

There was no doubt about it, they all felt that the production had been much too clever by half, and had not served the cast as well as it should have done. There were complaints of too many visual tricks that diverted attention from the emotional content. The general level of performance was considered to be too uneven to lift the evening to the heights it ought to have achieved. Mitch had been singled out as lacking both the lustre and the attack of his past performances in some of the great roles. His tiredness had seemed real rather than simulated as part of the characterisation. His grasp of the role lacked the grand scale, and therefore lacked conviction. It was generally agreed that there had certainly been some outstanding moments, and although these had served to carry the evening they had also served to highlight the shortcomings. The general consensus of opinion was that Mitch still had the potential for a great Lear, but this was not it.

Fiona, however, came in for her share of fulsome praise. She had reached a point in her career when merely to recite the telephone directory would have assured her of an award. Though her reviews were not entirely without reservations, some commenting upon her melodramatic heaviness towards the end. There was a feeling that Elizabeth had held back too much, allowing Fiona to overplay at her own expense, and so upsetting the balance between the sisters and their motivations. The reviews read as though there had been a conspiracy, a predetermined agreement to decide whose turn it was for accolades. In spite of the accident, it was Bruce who came off best, with unanimous acclaim for his highly original interpretation and his verbal agility with the convoluted structure of the lines. One or two likened him to Mitch at around the same age. Some actually forecast an even greater future than his father. On the other hand, Robin was universally dismissed as not giving sufficient serious attention to his small part. Susanna's Cordelia was brushed over with kind comment, and little adverse opinion.

"God, what a mess!" said Elizabeth, pushing aside the newspaper.

"As I've said many times before. A first night audience is no better than fond parents at the end of term play. They leave their critical faculties behind along with their expense account dinner."

"I'm sorry, Mitch. I still don't think it was anywhere near as disastrous as they would have us believe. The whole thing was given far too much of the wrong sort of publicity before we opened. Everyone anticipated more than it's humanly possible to give. Anyway, I gather we're booked solidly for the first month. I'm sure the rest will follow. I've read far worse notices that have resulted in long runs."

"Yes, so have I. *Charlie Girl*, for instance, but that was a musical, and we haven't got time to set *Lear* to music. Besides, that had its audience long before it opened. Anyway, I don't see myself as the coach-trade-type attraction, at least, not any more." The bitterness in his voice was difficult to ignore. Last night there had been storms of cheers. In the cold light of day they had turned to gales of jeers.

But it was Elizabeth who was crying, not for herself, but for Mitch. She still cared about his career, still knew what being on stage meant to him.

The intrusive ring of the telephone cut across their silence. "Here we go," said Mitch, sighing as he crossed to answer the wall-mounted receiver. "Hullo?"

It was Tony, sharp and to the point. "Have you read them?"

"Of course I have."

"Mitch, leave it to me. It just needs pulling together. They're all miserable bastards. I tell you, Mitch, the Butchers of Broadway haven't got a thing on this lot of crap hounds. These are the Slaughterers of Shaftesbury Avenue. We'll beat 'em, Mitch." His staccato delivery spat into the receiver now held about a foot from Mitch's ear so that Elizabeth could overhear what was being said.

"By the way, you might as well know it now as later. We're going to have to rehearse Bruce's understudy. His knee's come up like a balloon and he can hardly walk."

"Oh, Christ! That's all we need. He's the only one amongst us who's come out with consistently decent notices. Is that what we'll be doing this morning?"

"Among other things. The guy who's understudying assures me he's on top of the lines and knows most of the moves. He's keen – "

"So is a tiger with a dead carcase. Show me an understudy who isn't keen. See you later." He slammed down the receiver, turning to look at Elizabeth at the same time. Quite suddenly he was laughing. It was a broken sound, coming from the back of his throat, deep and rich and rising to an unexpectedly high pitch.

"Mitch! Mitch! Please don't." Elizabeth put her hands around one of his arms, pressing her fingers into him in desperation.

The laughter turned sour. He collapsed on to a chair, knocking over his half-empty coffee cup, covering his face with both hands and weeping until his entire body shook. "It's all too funny. You must admit – it's funny."

Before she could answer the telephone rang again.

"Don't answer it," he snapped at her, growling through his tears.

"It wasn't as bad as they claim. It needs tightening, that's all. Tony can do it – and so can you," said Elizabeth.

The telephone seemed to get louder, filling the room, blocking out the small comfort she was trying to offer.

Elizabeth picked up the receiver.

"Hullo, Liz, Maggie here. I've been trying to get through but you were engaged. Has Mitch read the morning editions?"

"Yes, we both have. Tony's already been on to us."

"How's Mitch taken it?"

"He's upset. Remembering last night's ovation and reading this morning's reviews, I think they must have been at another theatre."

Although Maggie sounded concerned, there was no telling to what her concern related. "Stay with him, Liz. Try not to let him get too demoralised. That's the very worst thing that can happen – "

"What do you mean, 'stay with him'? Do you imagine I'm going to walk out here and now – "

"You know exactly what I mean. We'll win through. I'll speak to Sandra, to see what sort of counterblast she can dream up. She's a clever girl, she'll come up with something. This is a brilliant production. I'm proud to have my name associated with it. It's prestige of the right kind for all of us. Can I speak to him?"

"I think not. He's really not in the mood to talk to anyone. Anyway, Maggie, it isn't prestige that's wanted right now. Mitch needs a hit, and he doesn't appear to have one with this bit of prestige."

"Leave it to me, Liz. Just leave everything to me." She was doing her best to be conciliatory.

"We haven't much choice, have we? Will you be at the theatre this morning?"

"Yes. We'll have something worked out by then. Goodbye." There was a sharp click at the other end, and the line went dead.

Elizabeth looked down at Mitch, his back hunched over the table, his head slumped forward, hands clasped in front of him.

"Did you have any sleep at all?"

"An hour or two."

"It's still only eight o'clock. Why not grab another couple of hours now? I'll take the phone off the hook."

"Only if you'll come back upstairs with me." There was a tone of childish pleading in his voice that would have been impossible to dismiss.

His moments of self-doubt, his indiscretions, all usually ended with reassurances from Elizabeth. Mothering in the time-honoured manner. She extended her hand to comfort him, and to help him upstairs. As they passed the telephone he took it down and left it twisting and knocking rhythmically against the wall.

6

In spite of the mixed notices there was a small queue at the box office by the time Mitch and Elizabeth arrived at the theatre for the special morning call. The numbers could hardly be described as a stampede, but there were sufficient people standing in line to raise hopes that the production might be nursed along until its reputation spread by word of mouth. It had happened before with lesser plays and a less auspicious cast. With the right sort of additional publicity they could just be in with a chance. They both agreed it was a welcome sight, and suggested that perhaps reviews weren't quite as important as the critics would like to think they were.

Even as they entered the theatre they could sense the doom-laden atmosphere permeating the shadowy auditorium, its mean working light coldly illuminating the stage. Sections of scenery were being shoved around in a listless fashion. Hushed voices could be heard issuing indistinct instructions. Members of the cast were clustered around in tight little groups, waiting to be called.

The diminutive figure of Tony was standing on stage with his back to the dark cavern, clearly outlined by the bright red dungarees that he always wore when directing. It had grown into something of an in-joke within the profession, that whenever Tony meant business it was "red for danger". He was deeply engrossed in the main objective for the day, that of hurriedly trying to coach Bruce's understudy for that evening's performance. Tony had managed to instil tremendous enthusiasm into the cast from the very first reading, and this had been maintained right up until the final preview performance. Now he was having to rekindle that early flame, and to cut away the rot that had set in overnight.

The understudy, Ralph Laughton, was a little older than Bruce but had enjoyed seasons with the National and the RSC playing a wide range of character parts with distinction and solidity, though never managing to blaze into glory. He was highly respected among the profession as an actor's actor, and had a fine reputation for simply getting on with the job. Ralph had been around long enough to be prepared for the unforeseen and by the opening night was almost word perfect. It was now a question of whether he could assimilate all the moves and the correct timing to ensure a creditable performance by that evening. Everyone accepted that perfect balance could only ever be achieved through a prolonged rehearsal period and early performances, and the best thing to do now was to pace out the essential details as economically as possible.

Mitch hung back under the low ceiling that formed the arch of the royal circle, and Elizabeth sensed his need to be alone. She walked on, waving to a few of the cast who turned as she approached. She smiled and nodded, exchanging a morning greeting as brightly as she could. They were all putting on a brave face, all acting for each other.

"No! No! Not like that, Ralph. It's got to be quicker, dear boy. Make the movements sharper. Try it again." Tony was waving his arms into the air and jumping about like a red india-rubber ball.

Maggie had established her own beachhead towards the front of the auditorium, seated at a small table with the light blocked off from one side so that it didn't distract attention from the stage. Sandra was hunched beside her, keenly marking up sections of the morning papers, scraping quotes for front of house.

Being new to the business, she was still a little starry-eyed about the theatrical scene so for the time being Maggie knew she could rely on the extra energy that was needed. Sandra was making a concerted effort to keep up with what was being demanded of her, but it wasn't easy.

"Perhaps I can lift a few lines from this one and let in some asterisks before going on to another section. I'll have a few words underlined. That ought to catch the eye."

Maggie glanced at the marked lines. She pencilled through a couple of words to tighten the praise even more. The word prestige kept dancing around in Maggie's head. She was animal enough to put up quite a fight to ensure that she came out of this venture with more than her fair share of it.

"I want you to prepare a small advertising campaign based on a series of six inch singles in several of the dailies. You can also include local newspapers around Hendon, Golders Green and Finchley. Our Jewish friends are keen theatre-goers. Mix in the right amount of culture and snob value and they might book a few charity performances. Do the same for the Sunday heavies as well. I'll work on alternative copylines to push the Dawlish name. I want a costing by three o'clock this afternoon. Where possible, try for right-hand pages on the centre spread."

"There's usually an additional premium for specified positions," said Sandra, trying to sound knowledgeable. She had previously worked for a publisher who couldn't afford such extravagances.

"I'm aware of that, dear. I also know how much it pays off to have the right announcement in the right place." Maggie looked up, turning her attention towards the stage. She remained alert, trying to assess Ralph's ability while taking in what Tony was telling him.

"I'm sorry, Tony, I'm simply not as athletic as Bruce. Not that it did him much good. Anyway, I'm at least a couple of stone heavier. I can't throw my bulk around with the same abandon as he does."

"All right! All right! Let's try it another way. But make it sharper. Give it angles. The character's got to be quick and edgy. Get more stylisation into the movement."

"I'm doing my bloody best. If I'd known this was going to happen I wouldn't have got quite so pissed at last night's party. My head feels like one of these rocks." Ralph kicked at the scenery, his patience beginning to run out, and his annoyance showing through his efforts.

"That's your problem, Ralph. My problem is to sort out a way to ensure that the paying customers get a performance tonight. This production has got to come together, and frankly I don't care how the fucking hell you're feeling right now. OK. Let's try again."

Mitch was taking it all in, remaining motionless at the back of the stalls making a conscious effort to relax before being called, before he had to repeat last night's performance. He enjoyed the anonymity of the darkened auditorium, the comfort of seclusion. The rest of the company had all too obviously left him alone. He felt they were embarrassed on his behalf.

"No use hiding at the back here." The voice came from just over his left shoulder, but he had no difficulty in recognising the crispness in the tone.

"Who's hiding?" He turned to Fiona, sitting with her arms folded along the top of a seat, her chin resting on her wrists.

She moved her position without looking at him. "We all set ourselves up just to be knocked down. Win a few, lose a few. That's what this whole rotten business is about."

"Maybe, but I don't seem to have won so many over the past few years."

"Don't take it to heart. Tony will soon iron out last night's little misdemeanours."

"Such as my entire interpretation?"

"That wasn't what I meant at all."

"What did you mean then?"

"Oh, Christ! Let's not go in for a self-knocking session. We're all in this together."

"Some not quite as much 'in' as others."

Fiona shrugged and pulled a face through the semi-darkness. "Think whatever you like. While I'm here I'll do my best. Apart from that, I've got my own plans to sort out."

"You mean you're definitely going ahead with your own company again?"

"Did you ever doubt I would?"

"I'm sorry, Fiona, but I've never seen the theatre as a place for the sort of blatant politicking that you go in for."

Fiona moved round, now sitting on the back of a seat to face Mitch, and almost obliterating the stage from his view. "I know. But it does provide me with more of a sense of purpose in what I'm doing. There's more to living than just money."

"I'd love to see you form your own company without it."

"Why the hell do you imagine I accept so many bloody awful movie parts? They subsidise my real work. I'm *your* daughter. I need to act. I need to be allowed to get up there and to pretend

I'm someone else. Well, that being the case, I'd rather do it for a purpose whenever I can."

"Can we have everyone on stage, please. Everyone on stage. Come along, hurry please, we've a lot to get through." The stage manager was standing on the edge of the stage, clipboard in one hand, shielding his eyes against the lights with the other. He was answered by a succession of thumps from various parts of the house as vacated seats tipped back and the cast resigned themselves to a job that had to be done.

Maggie had already removed herself through the pass door and was now on stage waiting for everyone to assemble, the inevitable cigarette fixed between her fingers. She pulled her cashmere cardigan around her shoulders, taking a deep breath as she stepped forward to face the cast. "Well, I'm sure you've all read the notices. They're not exactly fulsome, but they're not the worst I've read by a long way. There's still work to be done. It's going to take a lot of concentration and a lot of effort from all of us. By tonight I hope we'll have the right sort of publicity for front of house. There were enough good things said to ensure that we get more than a fistful of quotable quotes. I know we can pull this show together. Twelve weeks. That's all we're booked in for. Most of the first month is already sold out. We've got to fight for the other two. It's not a long season, but long enough. I hope that by the time this is over you'll all be proud to say you were a part of it. I wouldn't have attempted this production if I didn't have faith in it and feel it was something worth doing. But it's got to be right. You were all picked for this cast because of your reputations, because of your ability, and because it was felt that each and every one of you had something of value to contribute. There's always got to be strong teamwork in this type of play, and I know we have the right team. I can't say more."

"May I say something?" Mitch had hung back until this moment, but now he was trying to edge his way towards the front of the group.

"Sure, say whatever you like, but let's keep it short." Tony stepped aside for Mitch to take centre stage.

"Well, whatever any of you may say or think, I'm only too well aware that a great deal of the abuse has come to rest on my shoulders – "

There were several token mutterings of disagreement, but Mitch brushed past these waves, determined to have his say and get it over with.

"No! Please, hear me out. Perhaps my approach to the role has been a little too radical for the traditionalists, but I make no apology for that. Unless attempts are made at new interpretations such works as these will become moribund, they'll stagnate and die. I'm more than prepared to put in all the time God gives to get this right. If any of you have any scenes you feel you'd like to go through with me, just let me know and we'll arrange to get together."

Tony reached out and patted Mitch on the shoulder. It was an act of friendship, yet Mitch seemed to wince as though trying to avoid being touched, as if he wanted to have no physical contact with Tony. It was an odd moment, noticed but dismissed without further thought from the anxious red figure itching to return to action.

"Right, I think we all know what's to be done." Tony clapped his hands together and began to dart around. "Let's have some more bloody light for a start. Between being half-blind, and half-pissed, we'll all break our bloody necks."

"Lights. Sparks, more light. Come on, move it." The stage manager was swinging into action.

"We're going to run through for entrances and exits, taking in all the scenes in which Ralph appears." Tony had suddenly become bigger, his voice had assumed greater command. Those with whom he had worked before had experienced this metamorphosis and knew that it meant a gruelling time ahead. Others were taken by surprise at the unexpected outpouring of sheer energy. The Red Demon began to call instructions and dash to and fro with sharp little movements, demonstrating with actions and words exactly what he wanted. The illuminated area was charged with a magnetic quality impossible to ignore. Even hardened stagehands found themselves enmeshed in the proceedings as they witnessed the change that began to creep into the production. A tightening of pace here, a softening of emotion there. When added together the changes began to create a better balance of interplay between characters and situations. Perhaps they had all grown a little too blasé during the final rehearsals and throughout the previews. Perhaps they had believed too strongly in their own publicity. Whatever it was, the opening night had not been as compellingly consistent as were many of the scenes now being replotted.

They broke for lunch at around one o'clock, with strict instructions to return sharply at two. Mitch and Elizabeth left together, emerging through the stage door into the sort of winter's day that had a yellow tinge to it, holding the threat of snow but never quite realising the promise. They had booked a table at Giovanni's and sat in silence while waiting for their light meal to arrive, each trying to think of the right things to say, their emotions cocooned against the gentle hubbub of sound that filled in as a background to their silence. The restaurant had a steadying effect on what could have developed into a highly emotional exchange. The other clients effectively kept the steam at a lower level than otherwise might have been the case.

"That was very good of you this morning," said Elizabeth eventually.

"Good?"

"Offering to accept the blame for the notices. It wasn't really necessary, you know." She put down her fork and reached across the table to touch his hand. She sensed the barrier between them, and felt the need for more than just words as a means of communication.

"I thought it was. I had to say it." He smiled at her, pulling his lips together with determination.

"It will be all right, you know."

"No, I don't know. I'm no longer sure whether it will ever be all right again. I've gambled and lost."

"Mitch, that's a lot of nonsense, and well you know it. You saw them at the box office when we arrived. Don't you think they've read their morning papers as well? Nobody's paid them to queue up for tickets. Come on, love, where's your sense of humour? It's all part of the business."

"Fiona said much the same thing to me earlier this morning. Have you two been ganging up on me?"

"Is that likely?" She began to eat, but without much interest in the food, pushing it around her plate just to keep Mitchell company.

"Maggie seems to be as energetic as ever," said Mitch.

"She's one of this world's great survivors."

"You've never really liked her, have you?"

Her first reaction was to ignore the remark, but silence would have spoken more than words. "I've never had any real feelings towards her in any direction."

"That's exactly what I mean. You're usually far more positive about people."

"I'm no fool, Mitch. I know how much help you gave her in the beginning. She couldn't have made it without you. I also know why. You scratched each other's back a long time ago. Well, I hope you feel you've paid your debt by now."

He stopped eating for a moment, not exactly puzzled by her sharpness but a little surprised that she should have chosen this particular time and place to express her feelings. "She means no harm."

"And what worse can you say about anyone? The people who mean no harm are often the ones who cause the most."

"Oh, come on, Liz. What has she ever done to you?"

"Please, Mitch, let's not embark on a long list of reproaches. We've both had our lapses."

"Speaking of lapses, how's Victor?" It was a sharp riposte that would have been better left unsaid.

"You can be such a bastard when you don't try."

"I'm an interested party. When is he finally going to spirit you away?"

His lightness of approach was no true indication of how he was feeling. But Liz refused to allow herself to be drawn into a deeply domestic confrontation – at least, not there.

"I *need* Victor. He's one of the few totally undemanding people I know. There's never been any question of repayment for his friendship. Without him to lean on during the past couple of years I doubt whether you and I would be sitting here now."

"That really makes me feel great."

"I'm sorry, Mitch, but you know the truth of that as much as I do." She forced herself to concentrate on the food, but by now it was getting cold and tasteless.

"Yes." He watched her eyes begin to narrow in an effort to hold at bay her tears. "You're right. You always are."

"I'm not sure how much longer I can hold on, Mitch. Staying away from me last night didn't help. I've tried very hard over the past year or so, but you don't make it easy for me."

"Please, Liz, don't cry. Not here. I couldn't stand it. We're being looked at." He cast his eyes around the restaurant, catching sight of people nodding towards them, spotting half-inclined fingers pointing them out surreptitiously.

"Being looked at is part of our business. The time to worry is when nobody wants to look."

"There are times and places."

"You've chosen some very strange places in your time."

He leaned back in an attempt to hide, only to bounce forward again as though pushed from behind. His face creased slightly, as though in pain. The incident passed without comment from Elizabeth, but it registered at the back of her mind.

The afternoon progressed much as anticipated. Scenes were topped and tailed to ensure that Ralph knew the precise timing for his entrances and exits. Short sections that ought to have been easily rehearsed took longer than anticipated. Fractions of a second became vital to Tony who now seemed to be unhappy with everything and everybody. No one was spared his whiplash tongue.

By late afternoon they were all tired. They had endured more than enough of thunder-claps, of lighting cues, of pacing to and fro, and more than enough of each other.

Tony finally collapsed into a little red heap near the front of the stage. "That's it. We can't do any more today. Ralph, if you give me that much tonight I'll be more than happy. I'll want a bit more tomorrow, but we can talk about that later. Thanks, everyone. Now get some rest."

There was a concerted sigh as they allowed themselves to relax for the first time that day. As long as an actor kept going physical symptoms of exhaustion often remained unnoticed, but as soon as the moment of relaxation arrived, they were suddenly aware of the ache in their muscles and the stiffness across their shoulders.

They all knew that the second night of any run was a high danger spot. This happened time and time again after a successful opening. A universal feeling of euphoria would often create a state of contagious over-self-confidence that led to mistiming and to silly errors of judgment. On the other hand, if the notices were dismal there would sometimes be either an over-anxious straining to do better or an infectious sense of doom.

The house was full and all the standing room was taken up by the time the curtain rose. This was no longer the fashionable first night audience. These were people whose interest was in the play and, to a lesser extent, the players. Their reactions came in the right places and they gave, even through their silences, the right sense of participation, the oneness that every actor loves to feel coming back at him across the footlights.

By the time they arrived at the heath scene the audience were tuned to a fine pitch and ready for the ravages to be presented before them. Mitchell had dismissed Mrs Grace during the interval, telling her to return to wardrobe his act one costumes as his wife would be in to help him make up his back. Although she felt this to be unusual, Mrs Grace had worked with him often enough to know better than to argue. She simply gathered up the costumes and went out into the corridor, arms filled with trailing furs and heavy clothes.

Elizabeth was just coming from her own room as Mrs Grace closed the door. "Hullo! You're through early this evening."

"Not so much to do," she replied.

"You mean you've got the running of it already?"

"Well, if you're doing 'is back that leaves me free to sort out this lot." She waddled on her way, leaving Elizabeth looking puzzled by this remark.

Elizabeth remembered the long discussion she and Mitch had had about this particular scene, and how Mitch had decided to play it with his back made up to appear as though torn by brambles. Once Mitch had decided upon a course of action he seldom changed his mind, and to have suggested that she was going to make him up confused her. Her immediate impulse was to go in to Mitch, but as he had not said anything to her she decided against intruding. Instead she determined to watch the action from the wings.

Once the scene had started and Mitch's entrance established, she grew even more puzzled as there seemed to be nothing out of the ordinary in his playing. It wasn't until Mitch turned round, revealing his bare back, that she began to understand. Her eyes widened, first in shocked surprise, and then in sadness. His skin was a mass of bruises overlaid by numerous small weals that made her wince even to contemplate their application. It wasn't until this moment that she recalled the way he had started forward in the restaurant during lunch, and earlier that morning when Tony had patted his shoulder.

There was no doubt that from the front of house these marks must have appeared quite natural, with most of the audience hardly giving them a second's thought, and certainly not doubting they were anything other than stage make-up. But to have been alongside him, playing on the same stage and seeing this profusion of pain, could only have sent shivers of revulsion through the cast.

The final reception was not as wild as that of the previous night, but there seemed to be more sincerity behind it. When Mitch took his bow in front of the curtains there was a widening of the applause that soaked into him. It made him feel that perhaps all was not lost. Even Fiona, not known to be free with her compliments, felt bound to offer her congratulations to her father.

Neither Tony nor Maggie appeared backstage after the final curtain fell. This was accepted as *their* show of professionalism. They both knew when their presence would be just a little more than the cast could take and had decided to leave any remarks, good or ill, for the following day.

A call sheet had been placed near the stage door for the rest of the week, with understudy calls scheduled and general information about additional photo-calls.

From here on it was simply a case of doing a job of work to the best of their ability, and making sure the production remained on course for the period of the London run.

It had been a tough day for all of them, but it was generally agreed that the work had been more than profitable and the demands made were not all that unreasonable.

7

By the time the final curtain fell Fiona was tired and edgy. She had resented having to rehearse immediately after the opening night instead of going about her own, much more important, business. The day's divided attentions had involved her in running backwards and forwards to make furtive telephone calls whenever the time allowed her to break away.

This was not the first time she had undertaken to tour her own company. Although she was well aware of the countless problems involved before actually getting on the road, there was, inevitably, a mass of totally unexpected things that created a further demand on time and energy. There were actors who couldn't fit in with others for audition time. A director had suddenly decided that he ought to be given more of a free hand than Fiona was prepared to concede. One of the writers contacted her to explain that he had finally decided to accept a more lucrative offer, telling her that "Glory alone wouldn't feed his family".

She had driven herself home through Regent's Park, slowly allowing her mind and body to relax as she enjoyed the gentle background sound of Bach on her car radio, consciously encouraging the mounting heat within the car to creep into her bones. Her gaze took in the blackly silhouetted treetops as they swayed from side to side. There were very few cars using the park at that time of night, and it was far too early in the year for lovers to take advantage of the freedom afforded by the surrounding grassland. The lights from a solid terrace of houses on the left flickered into the corner of her eye as she accelerated to exceed the low speed limit. The night sky was clear and softly dark with thousands of stars, like specks of glittering dust reflecting from a fat moon. It was one of the better winter evenings.

By the time she drove into her garage she had managed to unwind a little, but this was to be short-lived. As she turned into her drive she couldn't help but notice the several cars lazily parked outside the front of her house. This usually meant that Andrew had decided to entertain a few of his friends. It was one of his methods of establishing his show of independence. If she wanted to use him, he insisted that it had to be on his terms. There were occasional arguments usually culminating in a threat from Fiona to throw him out, but when it finally came down to it – well, they were still together.

As she opened the front door her fears were confirmed. The amplifier was sending decibels of sound throughout the house to the accompaniment of pounding drumbeats and a battling of brass from somewhere in the background. A thin voice was wailing into the night, with other voices fighting to be heard above the din. This was one of those occasions when Fiona was glad to have exercised the foresight of fitting double glazing. It was an embellishment that had the side-effect of cutting down sound from within and without, but there were times when she was taken by surprise once the front door had been opened.

The few minutes of relaxation just enjoyed vanished as her anger rose and her muscles tightened in readiness for yet another confrontation. When she opened the door to the living room the sound seemed to throw her back. Through the half-light she could just make out Andrew leaning against the wall on the far side, apparently oblivious of all that was going on around him. He was fingering his guitar and shaking his head in time to the broken rhythm of the music. A small set of drums was ranged across another corner and a trumpeter was standing between them; no one seemed to be taking much notice of anyone else. Another couple were struggling together on the floor, copulating to the beat of the drums. Several others were either drinking from dented cans, or smoking from the ends of thin joints. The atmosphere was repulsive and quite the last thing that Fiona needed to return home to.

With swiftly practised skill she marched across the room to pull out the plug with the amplifier. She then proceeded to switch on every light in the room, and finally struggled with a window to let in a blast of cold air. It wasn't until this moment that there was any reaction to her appearance, or even awareness, from any of the others.

"What the bloody hell – " Andrew crossed towards her.

"I'll tell you what the bloody hell," said Fiona. "I don't expect to come home, to my own house, at the end of a hell of a day's work, and find it full of your layabout friends."

"What am I expected to do on the long winter nights? Sit and watch you perform all the time?"

The couple on the floor looked up, having completed their physical exercise before realising something was going on above them. "Turn the bloody lights off," shouted the dark-haired, grey-faced youth.

"Just who the hell are you?" Fiona was now standing dead centre, hands clenched against her waist, feet splayed out and almost digging into the carpet.

"I'm a friend of Andy's, that's who I am. Who are you?"

"Me? I'm the idiot who pays for this lot, that's who I am. I suggest that you all gather yourselves together into a single heap of crap and leave here, pronto."

There was a general rhubarb muttering of discontent as they chuntered at each other, and then looked towards Andrew for some sign of what they should do. He stood his ground, saying nothing, simply emitting waves of anger that Fiona should have done this to him in front of his friends. Perspiration clung to his brow and slowly trickled down his cheeks to disappear into his moustache. His hair was damp and hung around his shoulders as wet spikes of fern. His eyes narrowed and he gradually lowered his guitar, allowing it to come to rest on a chair.

He and Fiona locked each other in this glazed display of silent resentment for what seemed like an eternity. The only sounds were those of heavy breathing and the swish of an occasional car hurrying through the night.

"You'd better go," he said softly to the intent watchers.

They began to shuffle around, gathering up their belongings in a semi-stupor of pot and beer. After a few minutes they stumbled from the room in a sullen single file. The drummer was helped by the others as he struggled with his assorted bits of equipment. There was no question of taking time to pack things away neatly.

Even after they left, the room still stank from the airless atmosphere of stale bodies, alcohol, cigarettes and drugs. For a brief moment Fiona couldn't help but reflect that the smoking of pot in the eighties was a little quaint, but her continuing anger soon pushed this thought to one side.

"Don't you ever do that to me again," said Andrew.

"I could say the same to you."

"I mean it. You make me look like a little heap of shit in front of my friends again, and I swear I'll wipe the floor with you."

"I don't expect to come home, at this time of night, and find the place crawling with that sort of wildlife. If you want to entertain your so-called friends and provide somewhere for them to fuck, that's great. You go ahead. But I'm not that sort of landlady. Find your own pad. I've got more than enough on my plate right now."

"I'm not surprised. I read the notices. But there's no need to take it out on me. I've had to remind you before. I'm here at your specific invitation. You managed to crush the balls off two other guys who were idiots enough to marry you. Don't try it on me."

An unexpected blast of icy air from the open window made her shiver and realise just how tired she was feeling. She turned away to close the window, still shaking with anger. Her hair blew around her face as she reached out for the sill, gasping against the night air. She turned back to survey the room. There was ash on the carpet, cigarette butts had spilled over on to a couple of small tables, cushions lay where they had been flung, and beer cans ricocheted across the room as her foot connected with them. The general disarray made her feel physically sick. She crossed her arms around her middle as though to hold everything within herself, her anger, her breath, her tiredness. Her entire being needed to be protected against her own surroundings.

"Where's Kate?" In her haste to clear the room she had momentarily forgotten about her daughter sleeping upstairs.

"In bed. Where the hell do you think she is?"

"She might have been awake for half the night for all you care."

"She came down twice but I sent her packing."

"What the hell do you mean, you sent her packing?"

Before Andrew could say anything the door opened and Kate provided her own answer. The front of her nightdress was damp from her night of tears, and her eyes were red as a result of her fists being rubbed into them. She had short tousled hair and a rather flat nose that gave her face an elderly look yet at the same time adding a unique attractiveness.

"Mummy, I heard shouting. I couldn't sleep."

Fiona scooped the child up into her arms, pushing her head into the crook of her neck. "It's all over now, darling. It's all quiet. I'm sorry, my love. We were – we were having a discussion."

"Sounded very loud upstairs. Like the music. Very loud."

"Come along, darling. I'll tuck you up. I'm sorry we woke you."

"You didn't. I haven't been asleep. Andy was playing loud music. I couldn't get to sleep."

Fiona kept the child held tightly against her, looking across at Andrew above her head. There was no need for her to say anything. It was all there, plainly spoken in her eyes, in the set of her jaw and in the tightness of her mouth. At this precise moment she hated Andrew for having done this, but she hated herself even more for having allowed it to happen.

Being the au pair's night off, Andrew had agreed to stay at home, but he hadn't said anything about inviting his friends round to keep him company. Fiona had toyed with the idea of sending Kate away to boarding school. But having Kate at home with her, arranging for her to attend day school, ensuring there was always someone at home to meet her when she returned; all these were small problems that were there simply to be solved. When Kate had been younger it had been a lot easier in many respects, but more recently it seemed to be getting increasingly difficult. This was another of those incidents that pulled Fiona apart, that made her stop to question her own lifestyle. Yet, at the final reckoning, she felt she had the right to live the sort of life she wanted and to make whatever domestic arrangements she felt would best serve them both.

It wasn't difficult to settle Kate. She carried her upstairs, tucked her up in bed, and sat with her for a few brief minutes. Kate liked to hear about her mother's day; it was as close as she could get to being a part of it. Oddly enough, Fiona rather enjoyed recounting recent events as it often helped her to sort out problems in her own mind. She told Kate about the understudy call, and the rehearsals, and the evening performance. Perhaps she wasn't as totally honest as she might have been. There was nothing said about her countless telephone calls, or about the complicated arrangements she was making to get together her own company. This would simply have alerted Kate to the fact that her mother was preparing to be away yet again and that she would be left in charge of Trisha, the au pair, and with Andrew. There was no need to throw this at her just yet. Such departures were always well signalled by a few special outings to carefully selected theatres or films, or maybe a visit to the zoo. There would be meals with Mummy in restaurants and, of course, surprise *unbirthday* presents. There was no malice in Kate, no avarice, but she almost looked forward to these occasions. She accepted them as an inevitable part of her own particular lifestyle.

Once Kate was settled, Fiona returned downstairs. By this time Andrew had collected together most of the cushions and thrown them back on to the armchairs. His guitar had been carefully replaced in its case and there had been some small attempt generally to straighten the room.

"We can't go on like this. I think it would be better if you left."

"Aw! Come on! Surely I'm entitled to a little fun once in a while?"

"Not at the expense of my peace of mind," said Fiona. She threw herself into one corner of the settee, as far away from him as possible.

"Look, love, it's not as bad as you imagine. I'll have a good clear-up in the morning."

"Please, just leave me alone. I've got more than enough going on right now without you to contend with as well. I don't expect to come home after a performance and to find the place looking like a rubbish tip. Neither do I expect to find my own child having to cry herself to sleep in her own home because of your bloody selfishness. And I certainly don't expect you to take advantage of me after all I've done for you."

Andrew threw up his hands in mock horror. "Oh, bloody hell! We're not off on that tired old single again, are we? After all I've done for *you*. What the bloody hell am I expected to do? Shall I go on my knees? Would that make you feel any better? I've bloody well apologised. If you must know, I only invited two of them. The others tagged on."

"Then it was up to you to kick them out."

"They're friends of friends. They might be joining us as roadies when we start a new tour. I couldn't kick them out without upsetting the others."

"I've had enough, Andy. I've had more than enough. Now, for Christ's sake, just leave me alone."

Andrew leaned forward and kissed the back of her neck. He thought this would be a good move. It would help Fiona to relax. It would go some way towards showing her how sorry he was. "You're tired, love. I didn't mean to upset you."

"No, not this time." She pulled herself away yet again. This unexpected movement wasn't in Andrew's pre-plan. This resistance was something new. By now she ought to have been facing him, perhaps not totally forgiving, but at least facing him. "Look, I don't know what I've done that's so different this time. There's always got to be something you don't approve of – "

"I'll tell you what you've done. You've taken advantage of me for the last time. I can get someone like you any time I want. I don't need this sort of scene at regular intervals." She had now twisted towards him, her face composed, her voice still full of rage, her mind determined.

"Who do you think you're kidding? This is exactly the sort of scene you need at *very* regular intervals. That's precisely why I've lasted so long. I fill a very real need in your life. I apply the pressure when you want it. I act as your private brick wall so that you can throw yourself against me. It's part of the bloody thick streak of masochism that runs right through your family. You bloody well enjoy the hurt."

This wasn't part of the pre-plan either, but having now launched himself along this path there was no going back. "You love the pain and the fighting." He could hear the words bouncing around the room, and doubted they were his own. "You bloody well need what I give you. And believe me, there aren't all that many who would put up with your schoolgirl tantrums, or your moods, or your emotional uncertainties. That's why I'm here. I'm your private bloody hurt-machine. You engineer the whole thing to suit yourself. I took a small bet with myself that something like this would happen within the first week of opening night. I didn't have to wait too long, did I?" He pushed her away and pulled himself to his feet.

"That's not true, and you damn well know it. It's you. It's always you. You enjoy doing this to me. You get some sort of pleasure out of treating me like this."

"Balls to that. I do it for *your* pleasure. For your perverted satisfaction. Two husbands down, and third time lucky. Is that the name of the game? Well, don't count on me, doll. I'm not bloody well playing."

Fiona knew the truth of what Andrew had said. She knew only too well how much she needed someone whom she could allow to hurt her both mentally and physically. This was what had been wrong with her two previous marriages. Neither husband had been able to stand, or understand, the strange sort of biology that needed to inflict this treatment upon itself, and return for more. It was this truth that touched a raw edge within Fiona, and caused her to explode.

Without warning she suddenly rushed at him. "You rotten bastard. I hate your guts." Her hands shot out towards him as angry talons from a bird of prey.

Andrew let out a low moan as her nails clawed into his cheeks and warm blood ran into his beard. His hands shot up in self-defence, protecting his face from further mutilation. "You bitch! You stupid bitch." One hand reached out in an involuntary action and caught Fiona across the mouth. There was no resulting blood, just a fine sting as she felt his palm slide across her face.

It all seemed to happen within the fraction of a second as they found themselves rolling around on the floor, tipping over first a table and then a lamp. Arms and legs and hair flayed in all directions.

They rolled around until both were exhausted, lying back,

panting and crying through their respective private thoughts. They knew this would be the beginning of yet another attempt to meet each other on terms to be agreed. Another secret promise to have done with each other. Their heavy breathing slowly subsided. Fiona allowed herself the luxury of a few gentle sobs.

On other, perhaps less spirited occasions, Andrew had usually managed to persuade Fiona into bed, and to conclude the conflict by symbolically penetrating her, thus inflicting the final wound. Even he didn't feel he could manage that tonight. There had been considerably more violence than he could recall for a long time, and it had taken him by surprise and drained him of what little energy he had left. He felt he had served his purpose for that particular day.

This more direct approach at least had honesty as its redeeming quality. Mitch's needs were different, even though their origins were the same. For Elizabeth, the explosive confrontations had long been a thing of the past. Acceptance had become the name of their game. Agreement from her did not imply that she personally met his need, only that she had come to accept it was there and had to be filled in some way, by someone.

They drove home in silence, Elizabeth at the wheel and Mitch next to her sitting slightly forward in his seat, his back away from the support behind him. As soon as they stepped inside their own front door Mitch made for the kitchen. It was part of their routine after a show that he would make a hot drink and carry it upstairs to their bedroom.

"Not for me," said Elizabeth.

"Oh, really?" replied Mitch, his voice a little strained. "In that case I won't bother either."

"It's up to you." She threw her coat over a chair in the hallway and went upstairs.

Elizabeth had said nothing to him since the final curtain. Usually there was a certain amount of discussion on the journey home about the way a performance had gone, or a particular scene had been played. Tonight the silence had been like a great void between them.

"I'll just make sure that everything's locked up," he called up to her as she disappeared into their bedroom. There was no answer as he proceeded to go through the unnecessary motions of checking the already secure kitchen and side doors, before finally throwing the bolt on the front door. He walked up the stairs, switching off the hall light, allowing the pale moonglow to crease its way up the treads of the staircase. Elizabeth was already in bed. She hadn't bothered to switch on her own bedside light, only his, and one side of her face was clearly contoured across the darkness.

"I – I hope you're not in too much pain," she said with calm deliberation.

"Pain?" said Mitch, from the dressing room.

"Your back. It must have been quite painful to acquire." Her voice was flat. It was controlled with all the skill at her command.

"I'd had rather a lot to drink. Alcohol is a great anaesthetic." The words were only just audible, and they carried an apology in every syllable.

"One of the oldest," she said, lying quite motionless, continuing to stare into the darkness.

Mitch reappeared, now wearing pyjamas. He stood hovering above Elizabeth, trying to find the right words that would explain his reasons. But the words refused to come to his aid, and those that did were totally inadequate.

"You must be tired, you'd better come to bed."

"Yes, I am." He felt his way around the foot of the bed and sat on the edge for a moment. "I know what you're thinking, Liz."

"Do you? How clever."

"You're wondering *why*, after all this time."

"I *know* why. You were frightened after last night. The performance wasn't what you'd planned. You saw through the applause and you knew your performance hadn't quite measured up." She turned her head to look at his rounded back still perched on the edge of the bed.

He nodded agreement. "Yes, that's right. You know, I never really wanted to do this production. I was right. That's the trouble with King Lear. If you're the right age you haven't got the energy, and if you're the wrong age you're light on experience."

"We could have talked, Mitch. You didn't have to do this to me."

"To you?"

"You've never really thought about it like that before, have you? By the time the final curtain fell the entire cast must have known."

"I – I told Ernest that I'd had too much to drink the night before. I told him I'd fallen down some steps. He can be relied upon to make sure the right story gets around."

"I needn't tell you how well we've managed to scotch rumours over the years. You know how I've lied on your behalf. Can't you see how humiliating this is for me?"

"Yes, and I apologise. I'm deeply, deeply sorry, and ashamed. But it wasn't planned in that cut and dried way. It was the party that happened after you left. We went back to someone's flat. I think it was one of the stagehands. Jake, Robby's friend, invited me to join them. He seemed to understand. I agreed to go with them – with him. I – I had some more to drink. He was very kind. He was sympathetic towards my need for understanding." He banged his fist into the bed several times, emphasising his words. "I've done nothing but *think* about that bloody play for the past few months. Last night's cheers were partisan, they were misleading. But I wasn't misled. I – I needed to be punished in a different way. I'm sorry, Liz, there's nothing I can do about it now. I've tried over the years, you know that. God, but I've tried."

In some obscure way he actually resented the fact that Elizabeth had not tried to stop him from pursuing the practice.

"We agreed a long time ago that you would keep this *thing* away from us. That if you had to indulge yourself it would be a private matter. I love you, Mitch. I always have. I long ago accepted this trait in you. I couldn't bring myself to be a part of it, but I accepted that for you there could be no life without it. I've thought my way through all that. But to have finally exposed yourself publicly in that way, to have confirmed what had been strongly denied for all these years; I just don't understand your thinking. It's almost as though you've decided to throw away all our years of success. It's as though you want to destroy yourself, and me with you."

"Not you, Liz. Never that." He moved his head to look at her. There were no tears, these had all been shed many years ago.

There was anger, and deep pity, and above all a pervading sadness that seemed to envelop her. "I don't understand why myself. Perhaps you're right. Perhaps the exposure is all part of the self-inflicted pain I need to experience. I only know that – that I – I can't change, not after all this time." He slipped into bed, pulling the covers over himself lightly, and lay quite motionless on his side, as far away from Elizabeth as he could.

Elizabeth was recalling the very first time she had realised that Mitchell was a masochist. They had been walking on a beach covered in very sharp pebbles and he had insisted upon removing his sandals to walk barefoot over the razor-like stones. His feet had started to bleed quite badly, but he had continued to walk until he could no longer put one foot in front of the other. Elizabeth had expressed both surprise and distress at the incident, and he had merely laughed. It wasn't until he actually looked down at his feet that the nature of what he had done really dawned upon him. She was young, she had accepted this as part of his essential masculinity, if not virility. Although Mitch had shown concern, he had laughed it off. It wasn't until similar incidents occurred that she had begun to suspect. By that time their careers had grown so closely interlinked in the mind of the public that it would have been professional suicide for them to allow anything to have leaked to the press. There had been many occasions in the past when she had questioned the wisdom of her acceptance of his need to inflict pain upon himself. She questioned whether he actually wanted to damage their relationship and create a schism between them. Yet it was at times like these that her deep affection rose to the top and overcame all her other conflicting emotions.

"I – I think it would be better if I went away for the weekend," said Elizabeth. "I'll come back on Monday afternoon."

"You mean, down to the cottage?"

"No, not the cottage. I'm thinking of going to Victor. He's invited me often enough. I see no reason for refusing him any longer. As long as all this was contained I was willing to be a part of your conspiracy. Now I'm afraid I don't see that as being quite so important any more. I need time to think."

"I see." He sighed deeply, moving his position to ease the

ache in his back. "As you wish. I know you're right. I've had more than my share of your indulgence – "

"No, Mitch! *Not* indulgence. I've never done that. Call it understanding, or sympathy, or even compassion, but never indulgence." She fell silent again. "My only hope now is that Robin is happy."

"Robin?"

Mitch reached out and switched off his bedside light. The room was plunged into sudden darkness, until the cold moon-glow gradually reclaimed some of the light.

"That's something else I can take the blame for. Too many of *my* genes, and not enough of yours."

"That's the luck of the draw. I hope he manages to find a way to his own happiness. He's a lonely boy, Mitch. He needs a great deal of love and understanding. I'm not sure whether Jake is right for him. I hope so."

"We're all lonely in some way, Liz. He'll be all right. You'll see. He'll be fine." He reached out to pat her hand, but it wasn't there. He hadn't been aware of her turning away. This wasn't the way they usually slept, and it frightened him – it frightened him a lot.

8

Maggie's office was high above Shaftesbury Avenue, nesting in the rarefied atmosphere of London's theatrical skyline. It was an outmoded building, as indeed were most of its neighbours, but this added to its charm. Most of the other offices were occupied by assorted theatrical agents, film and TV production companies, and some obscure ancillary organisations who contributed little artistically to the end product, but always managed to ensure they were in at the box office kill.

Most of the names on the outer doors meant little or nothing to the casual passer-by. Production companies were always springing up, like weeds overnight, often to fade with equal rapidity. Many of them simply existed as a means of sorting out complex tax burdens, buying and selling properties several times removed until the money was out of the country, managing to keep the pages of the company ledgers turning by appearing to operate at base level.

When Maggie first started she had managed to squeeze in through the back door. She began as a lowly assistant stage manager. After that she moved on to stage manage a small repertory company for a summer season on the coast until she felt she had learned what went into the crafting of a production. Later she answered an advertisement in *The Stage*, and talked herself into an appointment as PA to a producer in one of the bigger companies. Once all this was behind her she turned to directing, aided by Mitch's insistence to his contacts that "here was a girl with something to offer". He, of course, having been the first to sample everything that was being offered.

Her office walls were covered with framed posters of past successes and current productions. There were several rows of framed photographs from international stars wishing Maggie "lots and lots of love", or whatever passed for affection. On the wall above Maggie's head was a complicated work-flow grid of current productions. Each week had a place name filled in to indicate the route of a touring company, and each production was identified by a separate colour. Perched at eye-level were scale models of sets for a new production and pinned behind these were a number of costume designs. A small table was piled high with unread playscripts and an assortment of theatrical reference books ranging from *Showcall* through to *Kemp's International Film and TV Directory* and various volumes of *Spotlight*. Maggie's heavy desk had two telephones: a white one which was always intercepted by her alert secretary, Brenda, and the other scarlet which she used as her own DDI and was a very hot line indeed. The furniture was overgrand, carved and padded, and gave the impression of being in store until required for a production. Nothing quite matched, neither was it terribly comfortable, but it scored triumphantly when it came to looks.

Maggie reached out for the white telephone, grasping it impatiently.

"Any news of that call, Brenda?"

"It seems they've got some sort of crisis on. He's been tied up in a meeting all morning."

"Try again."

"I've tried three times already. It's worse than trying to speak to God."

"Hell!" She slammed the receiver down, furious at having been kept waiting.

It was important to her that she spoke with Lord Barrington. She was never a person to let an opportunity slip. Having allowed a few days to elapse since the opening night party, she estimated that this ought to be just about the right time to try to take up his offer to present her production on TV.

There was a sharp knock on her door. Her minions knew better than to appear without first announcing themselves in the formal way.

"Yes?" She called out without looking up from the schedule spread on the desk before her.

Sandra popped her head around the door. "Hullo. Thought

I'd let you know that all the advertising spaces have now been confirmed. I've managed to arrange a series booking for some of the locals. It gives us wider coverage for just a little extra cost. I thought it was worth it. Might do some good."

"Have you made the weekend editions?"

"Some. A few lock up their pages earlier than others." She seemed to hover for a moment, as though wanting to say something else yet uncertain whether the timing would be right.

Maggie kept her head down until she sensed that Sandra was still there. "Anything else?"

"Well, I wondered whether you'd seen this?" She held out a copy of the *Daily Mail*, opened at the gossip page. There was a sub-heading, "The Long Farewell", and it dealt with the long-standing marriage of Mitch and Elizabeth. A recent unflattering photograph of them had been dug out.

Maggie stood up and grabbed at the newspaper; she spread it on top of the schedule and pressed down on the palms of her hands to keep it flat. "Trust him! Miserable sod! Well, there's not much we can do about it."

"I've already had several phone calls this morning," said Sandra. "They all want to know whether there's any truth in the rumours of a break-up."

"What did you tell them?"

"I – I told them I didn't know. I said they were a couple who kept their private lives very much to themselves, and would want to keep it that way."

"Next time deny it. Say anything as long as you kill the story. We've got enough problems without this adding to them."

"They'll never believe me. If I know the press they'll be hounding them in no time."

"Don't worry, I'll have a word with Mitch myself. He's due here at any minute. Have you managed to do anything about lining up a TV interview linked to the show?"

"It's very difficult at such short notice." Sandra hadn't counted on this one being thrown at her. She started to overstate the case. "They're – they're not too keen because the notices weren't so good – "

"I know about the bloody notices. That's exactly why I want Mitch to be seen." She threw herself back into the chair, her cheeks a flush of anger as she brushed aside the newspaper. Sandra bent to gather the scattered pages as the telephone rang.

"Hullo! At last! Put him through." She quickly cupped her hand over the receiver and whispered to Sandra, "Don't stop trying. I'll take this one on my own." Sandra was only too happy to be able to escape.

"Maggie speaking. Hullo, Lord Barrington. How nice of you to call back." The change in her voice was quite remarkable. "I was wondering whether we could get together some time? I thought we might be able to talk about the proposition you put to me."

"Proposition? Tell me, what proposition?" His voice was thick and powerful, with just enough of his original Mancunian accent to make his speech rhythms interesting.

Maggie knew of his reputation for saying things on the spur of the moment and then trying to wriggle out of them. His enthusiasms were legion, but it was also known that he never actually forgot anything unless he chose to. He liked to play the hard game. It fed his sense of power and he enjoyed manipulation. He had a generous nature but it needed to be massaged once in a while to ensure that everyone was aware that it was he who was pulling the strings.

"You suggested you might be interested in Mitchell Dawlish's *King Lear* for TV presentation. There were a lot of people about and a lot of noise. It could easily have slipped your memory."

There was a prolonged silence broken only by the sound of his heavy breathing. "Pity it didn't turn out so well. Maybe the public won't go for it on the small screen. You know what I mean? A bit too avant-garde for the great British viewer. Got to think commercial, you know, doll."

Maggie mentally called him a bastard, and dropped her voice half an octave. "I can think of at least a dozen other stage productions that have been transferred to television with great success. I think we ought to get together to discuss ways and means. For instance, well angled close-ups can cut away a lot of the more unusual visual effects. Anyway, you'll lose a lot of the detail when it's all reduced to the small screen."

"You got a point." He was beginning to soften.

Maggie could sense him reaching out for yet another cigar

and lighting it with his free hand. "Tell you what. Why not meet me for lunch, or maybe dinner if you'd rather?"

"Right!" he said. "I'll get my PA to call your secretary to fix a time." There was a minor bout of spluttering at the other end.

"Fine! I'll look forward to hearing from you. Bye for now."

She replaced the receiver and sat smiling to herself, her elbows on the desk and her hands intertwined to support her chin. Not for him a mere secretary, it had to be Personal Assistant. Well, she thought, if that's the sort of small status symbol that makes him tick, then good luck to him.

Before she could contemplate any further, the door opened and Mitch walked in without the customary politeness of being announced.

"Not too early, am I?"

"No, of course not. Glad you're early. It gives us lots of time to sort things out." She crossed to greet him, planting a moist kiss on his lips, and then called through the half-open door, "Brenda, some coffee, please." It was one continuous action, welcoming yet without involvement. She closed the door and turned back to Mitch who was now inspecting one of the models.

"Like it?"

"Nice shapes."

"You always did have an eye for a nice shape, Mitch." She smirked at him as she returned to her throne-like position behind the desks.

"Do you feel safer there?"

"It's my accepted seat for business."

"Well, you summoned, so here I am. What did you want to see me about?"

"I've just been speaking to Sam Barrington about the production. He's agreed to film it for the box." She sat back, watching his face, trying to read behind his eyes.

"Really?" The single word betrayed no feeling of any sort, his face was under complete control. "After the notices we got, I'd have thought he'd back out. He's a shrewd old sod is that one. Knowing the way he operates, I wouldn't be at all surprised if he read every notice as the papers rolled from the presses."

"He's keen on prestige. He's a bit of a snob that way."

"He's not the only one."

"You're very acerbic this morning."

"Put it down to bad digestion. I was speaking with someone from Sam's office only yesterday. Someone quite close to him. My informant was adamant that Sam had definitely gone cold on the whole idea."

"That was yesterday. I was speaking with him myself, just five minutes before you arrived. He's very excited about the project." She was a convincing liar into the bargain.

"Delighted – if it's true." Mitch sat down. He usually roamed around Maggie's office before settling, looking at whatever she had lying around, poking into the corners to find out about her future plans, but she had managed to tidy away before he arrived. She would much rather he hadn't even noticed the models, but these were too cumbersome to hide.

"When would you suggest we go on to the floor – "

"I'm going to try to persuade him to shoot the production on stage using lots of zoom camera work."

"Highly original," he said, throwing up his hands in mock surprise. "If there's anything I can't stand, it's cameras shooting straight up my left nostril for hours on end."

"Come on, Mitch, it won't be that bad."

There was a little tap on the door as Brenda rattled in with steaming coffee and some indifferent biscuits.

"Shall I pour it for you?" Her voice was thin and high, and she managed to end each sentence with a girlish squeak that added to her tiresome tone. She smiled at Mitch, her round face parting into a pair of narrow lips, and her small eyes vanishing behind a pair of fashionable owl-glasses. Her hands came together in a rather helpless way, a gesture more befitting someone fifty years her senior, and oddly quaint in one so young.

"I'll see to it. Thank you." Maggie began to fill the coffee cups, clanking the spoons alongside each one.

"This came a few minutes ago," said Brenda. "I knew you'd be wanting coffee, so I didn't disturb you." She carefully put down an envelope addressed to Maggie and left them together.

While Maggie finished pouring the coffee Mitch glanced across at the envelope which was long and narrow and an unusual shade of blue. He recognised both it and the handwriting.

"Help yourself to milk and sugar."

"Just dust and hot water for me. Aren't you going to open that?" he said casually.

"It can wait."

"I'd rather it didn't. It's from Elizabeth. Do open it. I'll pretend I'm not here, and then look over your shoulder."

Elizabeth's letter contained very few words, but they were sufficient to make a point. Maggie sat looking at the single sheet, not altogether surprised at the contents, but rather annoyed that its arrival should have coincided so precisely with Mitch's visit.

"Am I not right?" He sipped his coffee.

Maggie said nothing but threw the letter across to him. There had never been any secret that these two women had simply suffered each other for a long time. But as one was a bankable asset and the other held the key to the door, their sufferance was understandable. Daggers had always been well concealed behind backs, if not exactly in them.

Mitch read the few lines several times.

Dear Maggie,

I hope you now feel that Mitch has paid off his outstanding debt in full. This is the third and final production as demanded by that long outdated, though valid and legal, contract. I know that you had hoped for a greater success, but then we all did, especially Mitch. I needn't tell you how much store he put by the production. We're both grateful to you for what you have done, but let's call the account clear. Please Maggie, get off his back. Let him work out his career in his own way. And leave us to work out our lives in our own way. Mitch and I need to feel free to pick up the pieces and to forget the past. I needn't say more. I'm sure you'll understand.

Yours,
Elizabeth

"Obviously written before talk of the rift." Maggie couldn't resist dropping in that extra pebble to make even more ripples.

"What rift?" Mitch looked up sharply.

"Come on, Mitch. You must have seen this morning's *Mail*. Everyone else has seen it by now."

"If you really want up-to-date information, I suggest you come to me. You ought to know by now how much they like to exaggerate any situation into an interesting piece of muck."

"There have been some odd stories circulating backstage – "

He pushed his chair back with such force that it toppled over with a dull thud. The coffee spilled into his saucer as he rose to his feet. "I'm not interested in backstage snake rattles. They're like a lot of old women. I couldn't care a tuppenny shit about what's being said. I'm not interested. And if you've got any sense, you'll do your best to squash whatever is being said before anyone else starts to print more lies in the gossip columns. You've got a heavy investment to protect, and I've still got what's left of a career."

She hadn't seen him quite as angry as this for a long time. In fact, not since the time she had practically blackmailed him into signing the three-play contract. Maggie had secretly congratulated herself on that little incident. It had only cost her one full night alone with him but it could have made bad publicity had it got into the wrong hands. At that time other words were being hissed behind his back. Words that could so easily have undermined the enormous success that he and Elizabeth were enjoying. It was important that the marital edifice showed no cracks, and so they all did everything within their power to keep things to themselves. That had been the second time around for Mitch and Maggie. Earlier, he had used his position to get her her first directorial job, and subsequently persuaded the management to place her on the board of the production company. It was these involvments which had rankled with Elizabeth over the years and now precipitated her letter to Maggie.

The very fact that Mitch had allowed his anger to boil over in this way was all the proof that Maggie needed. She knew him only too well. It wasn't so much that outright lies made him angry, but facts that came closer to truth than the wild imagining of journalists really hurt him.

"I'm delighted they've got it so wrong. I'm even more delighted to learn that you and Liz are able to work out your little – differences." She really knew how to rub in the salt, but in the gentlest way.

"Look, Maggie, I've known you a hell of a long time. I know how your little twisted mind operates. Please leave us alone. We're getting on very well. We don't need any prodding from outside. You said there were several things you wanted to discuss. Let's concentrate on those?"

She didn't answer immediately; she simply sat and looked at him. She noticed the way he clenched his hands together, the fury in his eyes, the way he was breathing. And then she mentally turned the page.

"In view of what's happened to *Lear* I think you ought to plan for another production as soon as possible."

"What the hell's the rush? I'm still smarting from this one."

"I suppose it's the old saw about climbing back on to the horse as soon as you fall off."

Mitch gave a snort that spelt out his cynicism at Maggie's suggestion. He knew exactly what she meant.

"I'm not sure I want another stage production so soon. Perhaps a film, or TV or – or just nothing for a while."

"That would be a mistake. Believe me, Mitch. I know this business."

"I'm beginning to wonder if any of us ever really *knows* this business. It's like a greedy whore. It takes what it wants from you and then throws you aside for the next client." He pulled the chair into an upright position again and began to move about nervously. "And don't preach to me about not being compelled to take it up in the first place. I've heard it all before. Too many times before. Once you're in, believe me, you're right in up to the neck."

"Mitch, I'm offering you another production," she said quietly.

He stood still, unable to believe what he had just heard. How could she be willing to take another chance with him after what had happened only that week? What was she thinking about? There had to be more in the offer than simply giving him yet another chance.

"Don't make a fool of me, Maggie. I couldn't stand it again."

"I'm not making a fool of you. I'm dead serious, Mitch. I know exactly the right play. I'm not asking you to jump into anything at this precise moment. Take a few days to think about it."

"That's what I like about you. Plenty of warning."

"Why are you looking at me like that?"

"Because I know you well enough to be suspicious. Because I know you're not that generous. Because I realise there's got to be something more in it for you."

Maggie allowed a smile to grow into a small laugh. "I wouldn't want to leave it too long. I think the announcement of your next project would be good publicity. The general public still want to see you in *Lear*. It would be a way of nudging them back to you, of making them appreciate you. It would also help to recoup some of the production costs."

"How much do you stand to lose?"

"It could be as high as a hundred thousand. Depends whether the tour is taken up."

"What about the revenue from TV?"

"Sam will want most of that. I'll agree to almost anything he wants. I need to be on the right side of him."

Mitch could see the sense in what she was saying about himself but also felt he was being used for her own ends, and this hurt. "I'm sorry, Maggie, this production finished my debt to you. From here on I've got to take more time."

"I'm only asking for just one more production, Mitch. One, that's all."

"And then another one after that, and another one after that. I'd rather work with someone else. Someone whose only interest is the production. Not someone who wants to climb further up the crap-heap. I've honoured my debt – "

"Christ, but you can be bloody selfish." She blasted her words into his face, all guns firing. "I've stood by you, Mitch. I've stood by you and backed you. I've done a damn sight more than most of the other managements ever have. You made fortunes for some of them and where were they when you needed their support? I'm asking you to do this for me as a last gesture. To show me your appreciation for all I've done."

"I'll tell you what you've done, Maggie. You've mounted an expensive production simply to prove something to yourself and to certain other people. You think this is the way to buy yourself into the coffers of the Arts Council. You want their recognition and as much of their money as you can get. Well, ducky, there's a bloody long queue, and it's getting longer all the time. One production doesn't make an honest woman of you. Sam may be beguiled by your cunning, but I doubt it. I'll finish out this one with you and then it's goodbye. And don't you ever dare to have the audacity to throw in my face again that 'after all I've done for you' routine. When you blackmailed – "

"That's not fair," she cut in sharply.

"I chose the word with great care. You blackmailed me into that three-play contract because it suited you to have me in your debt. Well, it's taken a few years but the debt's clear. You're at the top, and I had more than a passing hand in putting you there. The score's now even." He was red with rage and trembling.

They stood looking at each other across the desk. The echoing silence was only broken by the faint tapping of typewriters in the outer office. It suddenly seemed as though a lifetime of working together, playing together, being hurt together, had all been encapsulated into the past few minutes and then allowed to explode and to disintegrate beyond redemption.

There was nothing more that either of them could say that would ever totally wipe out what had just been exchanged. *King Lear* would have to run its course, whatever length that might be, and then they would part, probably never to work together again.

After Mitch had gone, Maggie moved slowly towards the door. She wanted to silence the noise from the outer office. She wanted to keep out the prying eyes of the girls who must have overheard their raised voices. She felt she had made a complete mess of what she had intended to be an open-and-shut situation. It had never occurred to her for a moment that this could have happened. Even now she found it difficult to believe the brief scene had actually taken place. Yet, even though she was filled with regrets, another scheme was beginning to take shape in her mind.

9

It had been agreed that Bruce could return to the production towards the end of the third week as long as he was aware of his limitations. To begin with, certain of his more energetic moves had to be modified. This in turn meant adjusting aspects of characterisation so that the physical and emotional levels did not pull against each other. Everyone agreed that Ralph had acquitted himself admirably, with some actually suggesting that he had performed even better than Bruce. There were always the die-hards ready to line up to resist change, whatever form it took, and Bruce's interpretation was universally thought to be highly original.

Tony had worked hard to pull the production together, but the initial harm had been done and it was going to take time for word-of-mouth publicity to repair the damage. The critics had wrought their special brand of injury. In spite of good attendances at the early performances there had been no fantastic rush to book seats for the subsequent two months. This did not mean that the houses were thin; far from it. But only a decade earlier the mere announcement of a limited Dawlish season would have ensured a sell-out well in advance of opening night; now it needed something more.

To have been involved in lengthy rehearsals, and then to have played for a single performance, had had a dispiriting effect on Bruce. Of all the family he was the last person to think of himself as a potential star, although it had often been suggested that he had abundant talent. Forced to remain at home, resting his leg, there had been far too much time for him to think; far too much time to ponder his future career. To make it worse, Tracy had been away for a few days modelling swimwear in Corfu. The fashion industry was ever perverse with next season's bestsellers always being photographed at the wrong time of the year for weather.

Brooding in isolation, Bruce began to question whether he ought to continue in the theatre. If the public saw anyone more than twice a year on television they thought he was appearing too often. The viewers were ever greedy for new faces as well as new ideas. The younger generation demanded change, constantly, regularly. It was well known that they had few loyalties even to their most idolised pop stars. A few short years and it could all be over. What chance did someone like him stand of establishing an ongoing career and a lasting reputation that would carry him through for the rest of his life?

As soon as Tracy returned she sensed his mood. She was a clever girl, and was used to his constant self-questioning and his habit of self-knocking. Once she had unpacked, aided by Bruce who followed her around like a joyous puppydog, she presented him with a small parcel wrapped in flimsy paper.

"What's this?"

"Open it and see."

Bruce was never the person to save old wrapping-paper. He simply ripped the parcel down the centre, an indication of the way he was feeling. A neatly folded square of dark-blue cotton was revealed, and when shaken out to its heavily embroidered hem proved to be a kaftan. Tracy had often made lewd comments about Bruce's passion for passion, and buying the garment she had contemplated the laughs they would enjoy concerning the implications of him wearing it.

"Very nice. Thank you for thinking of me," was all he said.

"I never stop thinking of you. Don't you know that?"

"I suppose I ought to by now. You've told me often enough." He smoothed out the fabric, laying the garment across the end of the bed with an unaccustomed carelessness.

Tracy watched him. She was aware of his sluggish movements, aware of his efforts to make light conversation, but all his efforts showed.

"What's wrong?"

"Wrong?"

"It isn't just your leg, is it? I know you've missed me. I'm sorry I had to go away when you were stuck here. But you do the same to me whenever you go on tour. Work is work, and we're both in the sort of business that dictates where we have to be at any given time." She waited for a response. "Is it something you want to talk about?"

"No, not really. You've heard it all before." He moved away without looking at her, hanging on to the back of a small chair in the corner of the room, continuing to watch Tracy put away the last items of make-up from the bottom of her catch-all.

"Would it help if you spoke about it again? I think I'm a reasonably understanding person." She was trying to sound relaxed and offhand. It wasn't easy; she was tired and in need of a shower. She wanted to sit down and do nothing for the rest of the day.

"I'll make you a cup of tea," he said, and pulled himself across the room into the kitchen.

By the time Tracy had managed to put away her last few bits and pieces the tea was made and Bruce was sitting down waiting for her.

"Well, let's get it over with."

"I've had a lot of time to think during the past few days." He smiled at her. He was only too well aware that she guessed what was to follow and knew that she would simply sit back and let him talk it all out as she always did.

"And what did you decide as a result of all your thinking?"

"Is it worth the struggle, I ask myself? What the hell's it all about anyway? Who the hell am I to think that anyone really cares about me as an actor? Cares enough to wonder whether I'm making any sort of a living? And so on, and so on, and so on –"

"I get the picture," said Tracy. "Well, for a start, *I* care. Not whether you're making a living, but about *you*. I don't like to see you unhappy – "

"Part of my emotional make-up. I'm a natural pessimist. That way you get fewer disappointments."

"Anything else?" She felt it would be far better to encourage him to get it all out of his system at one fell swoop.

"My thinking's been a bit convoluted."

"So what's new?"

"It's an odd business, being an actor. Somewhere, at some level, there's got to be the right mixture of vanity, conceit, pride, self-confidence, self-awareness, humanity, humility, understanding of human nature, and a burning need to be heard."

Tracy smiled. "Well, that's not bad for openers."

He seemed not to hear her. "Given that I've got my share of most of those qualities, I then need to be *allowed* to step in front of an audience to confirm that the balance of the mixture is right. Not only that, I then expect to be paid for being allowed to do the one thing I feel I'm best fitted to do. I expect to be paid for the privilege of parading my vanity and my conceit before several hundred paying customers. People who have come along to watch me enjoying myself. Then, at the end of it all, having enjoyed myself, and been paid for it, I step forward to ask the customers to cheer me on and encourage me to start the process all over again. This, mark you, in spite of the fact that they've paid for the privilege in the first place. As I just said, it's a bloody odd business."

Tracy sat on the edge of her chair drinking her tea and meeting his gaze, listening patiently until she felt he had finished.

"How long have you been thinking like that?"

"Days – no, years really. I've always felt like that. It all seems so ephemeral. It's all so utterly pointless."

"Well, love, something that's been going on for thousands of years can't be all that pointless. It must fill a deep human need somewhere down the line. And if you're capable of helping to fill that need, I don't see you've any reason to doubt your considerable ability. Bruce, my love, you're just wallowing. Look, sweetheart, I'm the first to agree that it was a rotten bit of luck about your knee. That's over. It happens all the time – you know that. You also know, just as well as I do, that you'd live a slow death doing anything other than working in the theatre. It's deep inside your guts. It's part of you. You've really no choice. The hurts and the slaps, well, that's all just as much a part of performing as actually getting up there and doing it. It isn't called 'show business' for nothing."

"You sound like Donald O'Connor on an off day."

"Anyway, let's suppose you did give up. What else could you do?"

"Teach! You know the old saying, 'those who can, do, and those who can't, teach.'" He was being glib, and he knew it.

"Well, as you're one of those who *can*, there's no point in trying to teach others who can't." She crossed to him and knelt at his feet, forcing him to look at her. She deliberately took the cup from his hand and put it down beside her. For a brief moment she sat back on her haunches, smiling up at him, and then leaned forward to entwine her arms around his neck.

"Now, listen to me. You've got to stop being a stupid, silly old sod. We've been through this before. You'll be back on stage within a couple of days and then you'll forget this mood. You always do."

"It's the promises that get me down."

"Promises?"

"Remember the guy who was talking to me at the party? Billy Caxton, I think he said his name was. He said he'd phone me about a series of productions he was planning. Nothing! Getting on for three weeks and not a word."

"But, darling, they're all shits. You know that. Why don't *you* contact him?"

"God, I hate doing that. I'm the worst salesman that ever lived. And when I'm trying to sell myself, I'm absolutely hopeless."

"Then get your agent on to him. After all, Alan will be getting his ten per cent, so make him work for it."

"I sometimes think he's a waste of time as well. On balance, I've got more work for myself than he's ever got for me. The most he manages to do is up the salary, and that just about covers his own share. So I'm back to square one."

Tracy suddenly leaned closer to him and kissed him. At first it was merely a delicate contact, her lips only just brushing against his, but then it became more urgent, more devouring. She rained her kisses on to his face, on to his lips, pushing herself against him even harder, forcing him to respond. She had tried to remain aloof from his personal anguish. She had managed it successfully before, but even then it hadn't been easy. Now her tears were dammed between their cheeks, creating a salt taste in their mouths as they parted only to come together again.

The telephone rang as though calling the time. They allowed it to ring, hoping it would stop once it got tired, but it continued until they were forced to admit defeat.

It was Tracy who laughed and patted Bruce affectionately,

longingly, as she got to her feet and crossed to pick up the receiver.

"Hullo, Susanna here. I didn't know you were back."

"Half an hour ago. Everything all right?"

"Has Bruce seen today's *Guardian*?"

"I doubt it." She covered the mouthpiece and called across to him. "It's Susanna. She wants to know whether you've seen today's *Guardian*."

"Not my sort of paper, I'm afraid. I'll have a word with her." He crossed the room, wiping away from his cheeks the remaining streaks of Tracy's tears. "Hullo. What's all the excitement about?"

"I'll read it to you." She took a deep breath, changing her tone as though about to give a performance.

"The Editor.
Dear Sir,

I feel I must once again protest at the vast sums of money being poured into certain theatrical institutions at the expense of those outside London whose plight is seldom considered. The National Theatre, the Royal Shakespeare Company, and even the commercial production of *King Lear* in which I am currently appearing, are all heavily subsidised. The result of this assured box office protection is undue wastage on over-elaborate productions, unnecessarily drawn-out rehearsal periods, and an almost total disdain for trying to ensure independent financial solvency. It is high time that the large sums of public money being siphoned off went into areas where they are most needed. The provinces constitute the rest of Great Britain. Let them see the wealth of talent this country has to offer. They desperately need support in their efforts to keep the theatrical tradition of Great Britain alive, and they need it now. I, for one, am more than prepared to take my own company into the hills and valleys where I know there is a ready audience hungry for what I have to offer. I cannot do it by willpower alone. I, like others, urgently need support. Unfulfilled promises, and cuts in grants, can only ensure death to our living theatre. If more artists in my position were to speak out for the community as a whole, then

I am sure the situation would have to change. But until I am joined by others there cannot be any hope, and there certainly will never be any acknowledgment of the dire need for money.

Fiona Dawlish.

The 'subsidised' Her Majesty's Theatre."

Bruce was momentarily stunned into silence, his face growing red with mounting anger. "What the bloody hell does that stupid bitch think she's doing?"

"I don't know whether Mitch will have seen it yet. I haven't dared to phone him," said Susanna.

"This is the last thing he needs. How could she do this to him?"

"I wish I knew what to do."

"There's not much we can do. I thought she'd got off that particular hobby-horse."

"Not her! Bloody hell, and I have to share a dressing room with her."

"Whatever you do, don't start an argument tonight. It'll just about ruin the entire performance, and that's the last thing we want."

"I'm going to reply."

"How do you mean?"

"I shall write a letter to *The Guardian* myself. I'll put the other point of view."

Bruce thought for a moment. "You'd better clear it with Maggie first. My God, she'll be fit to be tied. There's nothing to be gained by upsetting her any more than she already is. Let me know what she says." He slammed down the receiver. "Stupid bitch!"

"Let me in on it. What's happened?" Tracy was bursting with curiosity. Anything big enough to distract Bruce from himself could only be a step in the right direction.

He gave her a rough outline of the letter, uttering oaths as a form of added punctuation. He loathed this sort of oblique political in-fighting for which Fiona had a reputation. It was totally beyond his comprehension how any management could be prepared to tolerate her. Several had vowed never to engage her again for fear of the trouble she brought in her wake. But for her being a Dawlish, Maggie would never have invited her to join the company.

Now it looked as though she was hell-bent on sabotaging the enterprise to gain her own small ends. Perhaps this was what she had planned from the moment she had signed the contract. It was impossible to judge.

At the moment when Susanna was reading the letter to Bruce, Fiona was taking a telephone call of her own. The nature of her call was not an altogether surprising request, although with Fiona's reputation the response was in doubt. Richard Gardner, the presenter of London Weekend Television's programme *Arts in Action* had ten minutes to fill in his hourly Sunday night slot, and had read the letter in *The Guardian*.

"Is that Fiona Dawlish?"

"Speaking."

"My name is Gwen Vickers. I'm a researcher on *Arts in Action*."

Fiona tried to sound surprised but Gwen was an old hand at the game and knew what to expect. "How nice of you to phone," Fiona said, to all intents and purposes unaware of what was to follow.

"We saw your letter in today's *Guardian*. We all agree that it's a subject that needs airing. Richard Gardner wondered whether you'd care to join him on Sunday week's programme."

"How long will I have?"

"About ten minutes."

"I hardly think that's quite long enough for a subject as far reaching as this. There's a hell of a lot that needs saying."

"Well, he might just be able to stretch it to twelve minutes. You see, we do have to consider the balance of the programme. It isn't often we can spare the time to devote to a single subject like this. However, if you feel you'd rather not, I'm sure Richard will understand. We shall have to tackle it another way."

Fiona had hoped for just a little more persuasion. "What time would you need me there?"

"We go on the air at ten fifteen. We wouldn't need you to run through, that would kill the spontaneity. If you could make it for eight o'clock, you could then discuss the item over a drink with Richard and sort out details from there."

"I'll be there. Remind me where your studios are again."

"Upper Ground, near Waterloo Station. On the South Bank."

"Oh, God! I always have trouble finding that terrible place." Fiona had the knack of making everyone feel she was doing them a special favour, regardless of the fee she was paid.

"I'll get one of the secretaries to send you a little map. We're quite used to people who have difficulty in finding us. If it's of any comfort to you, we haven't lost a single contributor yet. Oh, by the way. It's a standard fee of fifty pounds. I hope that's all right with you?" This wasn't so much a question as a statement.

Fiona knew enough about the scale of fees not to argue. She would willingly have given them fifty pounds to allow her ten minutes air time.

"Don't worry, I'm used to television rates. Standard fees usually mean the lowest you can honestly get away with." She laughed, and Gwen laughed with her, and they parted agreeing to see each other on Sunday week.

The cudgels were meanwhile taken up by several other newspapers and examined according to their own committed political beliefs. The *Evening Standard* jumped on to the bandwagon that same evening with almost a full column in its diary page. Fiona's already committed opinions were underlined and commented upon. Previous family friction was mentioned. Mitch had been invited to make some comment on his daughter's untimely outburst but he had declined to say anything. It was suggested, strictly off the cuff, that the animosity being expressed on stage at night was rapidly growing into reality off stage during the day.

The following morning saw an article by the *Daily Mail* theatre critic in which he expressed his personal opinions after having managed to interview Maggie. She, clever lady, had openly declared that there had been Arts Council money put into her production. Maggie made no secret of the truth, but she was quick to offer reassurances that the bulk of the money had been from other sources: mainly that of her own production company, and a few select backers whose prime consideration was their genuine love of the theatre, and not their percentage share. There were still enough angels around to make the venture work. However, the main point at issue was whether commercial managements *ought* to receive any subsidy at all, and whether the large fashionable London-based institutions got more than their fair share. The writer touched on the contention of tourist attractions, but it was generally felt that the British public ought not to be bled in order to attract foreigners to the capital. It was also mentioned that people in the provinces paid whatever taxes were demanded of them, but they had to make do culturally with whatever was left. These arguments were certainly not new, but they still had to be resolved. There were a great number of people within the profession who actively disliked Fiona's methods, but many of them had to agree with her in principle.

To say that Maggie exploded when all this broke around her would have been true British understatement. Sandra was called in to take down a press release that was to be circulated as widely as possible. The emphasis was to be placed upon the high quality of the production, the international standing of the director, and not least of all on the Dawlish name.

"Bring out the number of enormous successes Mitch has had. Mention some of the playwrights whose early work he has appeared in. List his credits as far as possible. Get his awards into some sort of order. Do the same for Liz. Dig out anything you can about the kids. Leave out Fiona. She doesn't need any help from us. Send photographs to all the nationals and the major provincials. I want as much coverage as we can get for this."

Sandra left Maggie gripping her red telephone very tightly. "Get me Lord Barrington right away." She might have hated the form the publicity was taking but, by God, she certainly knew how to use it. This may not have been exactly what she wanted, but in the final reckoning it was column inches that mattered, and she was determined to get her share. If Fiona wanted a public confrontation, then Maggie was just the person who could meet her.

Maggie was angry. She was furious. But she was also overjoyed to have been given this opportunity to let rip. Now she fully intended to keep the bubble of opinion as high in the air as she could, and for as long as possible. All she wanted were enough arses on seats at Her Majesty's Theatre to set the accounts straight.

10

Before the end of the week there were to be more column inches about Mitch and Elizabeth, and about the production, than even Maggie had dared to hope for. *The Guardian* ran a lengthy dissertation about the pros and cons of government money being used to support the arts in general, and about the comatose state of the British theatre in particular. The immediate effect was for bookings to improve for the two weeks succeeding the first month. The returns were scrutinised daily, and all the implications were that they were about to establish something in the region of seventy-five per cent capacity through advanced bookings. For the rest, it was reasonable to hope that passing trade would take up whatever remaining seats were available.

The greatest single threat to the entire venture now lay in the growing animosity that was developing backstage. Once the letter appeared, Fiona found herself all but ostracised by the majority of her colleagues.

It was inevitable that Susanna and Fiona would have a confrontation on the evening following publication of the letter.

Although she had decided not to say anything at all, not to give Fiona the pleasure of letting her know she had seen the letter, the moment she entered the dressing room Susanna's anger erupted.

"I suppose you thought that letter would make good publicity?"

"Of a sort," replied Fiona, applying herself single-mindedly to her make-up.

"The wrong sort. Christ, I knew you were bloody selfish but I honestly thought you'd draw the line at this sort of behaviour."

"You make it sound like gross indecency, darling."

"That's exactly what it is as far as I'm concerned. If you were so strongly against this production we'd all have been better off if you'd flatly refused."

"I did it for him."

"That's marvellous. I'm sure he must be feeling very grateful right now. Have you seen him this evening?"

"Not yet. There's no reason why I should. I'm sure he won't have much to say to me."

"For a while I thought he was getting over the reviews. I just passed him on the way in. He didn't say a word. He just nodded and dashed into his dressing room. Thanks to you, I wouldn't be at all surprised if he blows it this evening." She began to slam around on her dressing table, banging things down angrily, pushing her make-up to one side while trying to control her mounting fury. Her subconscious kept telling her to calm down but she wasn't listening. The damage had already been done. She knew that if she really let rip she would be in no state to give anything even remotely resembling a performance. She also realised that everyone else would be steamed up about this latest development and all be feeling much the same.

It was almost impossible to tell what Mitch was feeling. His make-up was so brilliant that the real self was totally obliterated. Yet the stoop of his shoulders and his slower pace were sufficient indication to the observant visitor of his mounting despair.

Elizabeth had made a point of getting to the theatre early that evening. She knew exactly how he would be feeling, and was still sufficiently involved to want to help him through the dilemma. They had said very little to each other during the past few days, their main contact being on stage.

She knocked on his door and went in, not quite sure what she was going to say once they faced each other.

He looked up, not exactly surprised by her visit, but choosing to remain distant. "How's Victor?" he asked, purposely not enquiring about her own well-being.

"Quite well." She knew exactly what he was doing, his knack of picking on sensitive subjects and treating them casually. She knew him well enough to accept this as an old ploy.

"Good. Then you must be feeling better."

"Mitch, I'd rather not go in for small talk. I saw Fiona's letter. Is there anything we can do about it?"

"Yes, nice piece of concise writing, wasn't it? If there wasn't more than an element of truth in it, I'd have said she ought to take up fiction."

"I'm not so concerned with the truth as with the effect it's going to have on the box office. It's no secret that I've always disliked her. The fact that she's the daughter of your first marriage has nothing to do with my feelings. I know you've always said it has, but that's not true. I tried very hard in the beginning, but she seemed to go out of her way to set up barriers. She's got a wide streak of selfishness. I've been aware of it for years. But I didn't think she'd stab you in the back like this."

"I appreciate your concern." He turned to her, puzzled and smiling weakly. "As a matter of interest, why are you so concerned?"

The simplicity of the question sounded strange to her, almost as though from a casual acquaintance. "Whatever else has happened, I'm still your wife. Believe it or not, I do still care – "

"Only care?"

"Caring isn't to be brushed aside. It means I'm still involved. It means that I still think about you. I still want you to be happy and still want you to be successful."

He turned back to the mirror. "That's nice of you. Is that so that you can finally go to Victor with a clear conscience?"

"Please, Mitch, I'd rather we didn't get into the deep waters of conscience. I came to see if you were all right. I know how this sort of thing gets to you. Try to forget it while you're on stage. Don't let it eat into your performance." She made a half move towards him, but then changed her mind. He was being too remote, too self-assured. She saw no reason to put herself in a situation that invited rejection.

"I'll allow technique to dictate emotion tonight. I'll keep the rest in reserve."

There was a single curt rap on the door breaking the controlled tension that was beginning to arise between them.

Elizabeth opened the door to find Ernest looking glum through his pallid make-up.

"This a good time?"

Mitch recognised his voice and called out to him. "Always a good time, my dear chap. Come in! Come in!"

Ernest rolled himself into the small make-up room and stood behind Mitch who was now applying the finishing touches to the edges of his wispy beard. "Had to see you, dear boy. Don't think much of Fiona's idea of a joke."

Mitch laughed. "It's hardly a joke. In fact, that was quite a restrained outburst for her."

Elizabeth could tell that Mitch was exercising enormous restraint in order to hold at bay the anger bubbling just below the surface. "Wouldn't you do better to tackle her about it? It's hardly fair of you to expect Mitch to be able to do much."

"Not really concerned one way or the other. Simply don't want it interfering with the performance, that's all. Got to keep politics off the stage. Can't stand it when things are dragged out and flaunted in front of the public."

"A little flaunting might be good for the cause," said Mitch, having now decided to bait Ernest.

"Yes, her own goddam cause, not ours, old boy. Not yours or mine. In my young day, we managed to keep all this sort of thing to ourselves. Our private lives were our own affair. The only thing the general public ever wanted from us was glamour. Good old-fashioned glamour. They got it too. My God they got it, and lapped it up, and that was enough for them. When I think of those lovely ladies like Gladys Cooper, Constance Collier and the Vanbrughs. Not to mention Ivor Novello and Boo Laye and that lot. Bring it back, I say. The general public know far too much about how every bloody thing works these days. Too many artistes let their arses hang out in public these days." He turned to Elizabeth who had decided to allow him to talk himself to a standstill. "So sorry, my dear. I'm sure you know what I mean." He smiled courteously.

"I think so. Perhaps it would be better if we let Mitch have a few minutes to himself before they call beginners."

"Don't worry about me – "

Ernest threw up his arms, and waved his hands in the air. "She's right. Elizabeth's always right. Don't worry, old boy. We're all still behind you. We'll beat this lot of miserable buggers yet, you'll see. Good luck." He blew an extravagant kiss to both of them and then flurried from the room.

Had the situation not been quite so unfortunate they would have allowed themselves the luxury of laughter, but the humorous side of the incident took second place to their real problems.

"If you want me to, I'll come back with you this evening," said Elizabeth.

Mitch was deeply touched by this. He knew just how much the offer meant to Elizabeth. "Only if you really want to," he said, his voice now reduced to a whisper.

This was as much of an acceptance as she knew Mitch could give her, but it was enough. "I'll wait for you." She awarded herself a gentle pat on his shoulder, and then left him alone.

Once on his own he seemed to shrink in stature. His shoulders sloped, his stomach sagged and his neck appeared to stop supporting his majestic head as he allowed his chin to fall low on to his chest. If he could have retreated within himself he would have done so. But there was still a performance to give. There was the paying audience of some twelve hundred people who had the right to expect the very best he was capable of giving. These people weren't interested in family feuds, at least not the real, only the unreal. And yet, he mused, at this point the edges can sometimes become blurred. Clothes and time alone cannot alter a basic human situation of desperation, of mutual dislike and distrust. He told himself he had to rise above it all. He had managed to submerge his personal feelings before, whatever the reasons. This was all part of the actor's make-up, all part of being on top. And he was at the top. The theatre in which he was playing and the role he was performing were proof enough of that. He was at the top, and by God he bloody well intended to stay there.

"Act one. Beginners, please. On stage, beginners, please." The call brought him back to the job on hand. It *was* simply a job of work. He checked his appearance in the vast mirror and walked out into the corridor.

He stood back, watching the near-naked extras making their way down the stairs, their bare bodies gleaming through their total make-up. Their thick thighs and buttocks tensing as they walked. The sheer ostentation of it all and the thick smell of grease paint as he went on to the darkened stage, intermixed with the warmth of the enclosed atmosphere, brought the unique intoxication that is summed up in a single word, theatre. It made him pause for a fraction of a second, and he breathed deeply, absorbing it all like a medication.

"I'll give these sods a performance they'll remember for the rest of their lives," he murmured to himself in the semi-darkness.

He pulled back his shoulders and proceeded to put himself through a few elementary breathing exercises. He shook his hands from the wrists, then rotated his neck and flexed his muscles, as he cleared his thoughts of everything but what lay ahead of him for the next three hours.

There was the call of "house lights". This was the one place where he knew himself to be in total command. He felt safe, completely exposed, yet oddly safe. From the first moment when he stepped on to that stage, until the final curtain, he allowed his emotions to show without shame. The anger, the passion, the raw humanity that played one feeling against the other, were all part of the whole, and the whole came together in a way such as it had never done before. The cast sensed the drive emanating from Mitch.

The audience almost felt as though they were eavesdropping on a private family feud, but one in which they had never seen such a display of hatred and loathing, of cunning and desperation, but above all of human suffering. The final ovation was not that of a first night audience doing what was expected. The cheers were still ringing through the theatre long after the house lights went up.

Mrs Grace was waiting for him in the dressing room. She handed him the small glass of whisky standing ready. It was a tradition with Mitch that had long become established as part of the performance. It warmed his belly and aided instant relaxation. He accepted the glass from her as though in a daze. He was both elevated and exhausted, tired yet burning with vitality. He knew he had done well and no one could deny that to him, no one at all.

There followed the usual procession of camp followers paying the usual lip service and filling the room with gushing banalities.

Mitch accepted their homage with his usual charm, but without encouraging any of them to linger, although he didn't actively hurry them either.

As Mrs Grace collected together his costumes she simply said, "Nice one, that. I think they really enjoyed theirselves tonight. Lots of tears. I could 'ear 'em sobbing their 'earts out at times. Like a good cry meself. Does you good now and again. Just take these things back." She toddled out, arms full, breasts bouncing above the pile of rags that passed for Mitch's costumes.

True to her word, Elizabeth waited for Mitch and they left the theatre together. Outside there was an unexpected biting wind. The night had assumed a sudden cold aspect with low clouds obliterating the earlier clear sky and creating heavy threatening shadows. There was a fine screen of sleet falling to settle in the gutters and produce tiny ridges between the uneven paving stones. The weather had deteriorated so rapidly that only a few stoics were still hanging about outside the stage door. Autographs were signed and greetings exchanged until the small gathering had dispersed into the thin blanket of fine white haze.

As they drove home the sleet turned slowly into snow and began to settle more rapidly, drifting against garden walls and around the unprotected sides of chimney stacks. Once home they went through their routine of locking up and Mitch making the hot drink.

"I bumped into Alan Scott today," said Elizabeth.

"Oh, really! I saw him yesterday. He phoned me."

"So I gather. He's a good friend as agents go. A very good friend," emphasised Elizabeth.

"Yes, I suppose so."

The room fell into silence. Elizabeth had hoped that Mitch might show a little more interest.

"Did he – did he say much to you?" asked Mitch eventually.

"Not a great deal. He's a very honourable man. He much prefers his clients to do the talking. He simply sits on Olympus, sifting the offers on their behalf."

There was another long silence as they seemed to be mentally sussing each other out. Finally, Mitch said, "He told you, didn't he?"

"Told me?"

"Liz, this is no time to be playing cat and mouse. Out with it. What did Alan say to you?" He was beginning to unwind, beginning to loosen the tight knot in the small of his back, to allow the sensation of tiredness to overtake him and dictate his reactions. His guard was slowly being lowered, and the obvious defiance of early evening was now showing the cracks.

"He – he told me about the new offer."

"Oh, that! Well, I haven't yet made up my mind. After tonight, who knows! This one could bounce back into the success we'd all hoped for. I've been doing a lot of thinking. Even if Maggie decides not to proceed with the provincial tour, I might have a go myself. I've still got quite a following out there in the sticks."

"Whatever else I may think of Maggie, I know her well enough to respect her judgment. If *she* isn't prepared to back the show for the tour, then I'm inclined to think it won't stand much of a chance. It could cost us a fortune."

"Us?" He looked across to her, genuinely surprised.

"Yes, of course. I'd be as much a part of the venture as you."

"I'd find backing somewhere. Don't you worry yourself on that score, my love. My name still means something out there in the great wild yonder."

"Don't do it, Mitch. Please, don't do it. If you're so sure the audience will follow you, why not go into the new production?"

"Because I don't fancy carrying an entire play again. At least, not so soon after *Lear*."

"Alan didn't say which play. He only mentioned there had been an offer."

"*The Apple Cart*." Even as he said the title his voice became crisp and clipped, an echo of the speech rhythms he had used when playing Shaw in the past.

Elizabeth looked surprised. Mitch had appeared in this play about twelve years before to considerable critical acclaim, and she couldn't understand his reasons for rejecting the revival.

"But, Mitch, you adored the part when you played it before."

"Which is precisely why I don't want to play it again. King Magnus is hardly ever off the stage. Then there's that bloody enormous speech in act one that goes on for an eternity. Even Noël called it 'a bit of a pill'."

"I think you look very handsome in uniform." It was almost as though she were flirting with him.

"Flattery will get you everywhere. Anyway, what I was able to manage more than a decade ago is quite different from what I feel I can cope with today."

"It must be easier than *Lear*."

"I was thinking of the rough and tumble towards the end. Not only did I strain my back last time, but I also finished up with a sprained ankle. Anyway, you know as well as I do that comedy always takes a hell of a lot more energy than tragedy. Any fool can play heavy drama, but you've got to be far more serious about comedy."

"Stop talking like a drama school student. We both know you're a past master when it comes to Shaw. You've certainly done enough in your time."

"How would you feel about playing Orinthia?" This one was a shot across the bows, and Elizabeth wasn't prepared for it.

She had not even vaguely considered joining with him in a new production. Her prime consideration was to make sure that Mitch had something lined up immediately after the end of the present production – whenever that might be. There had been several offers for her to appear on both stage and screen, but she was feeling the strain of the past few months and her intention was to take some time away from the theatre. She wanted to think things out. She had had enough of being in the public eye, of shuffling after work, of being the subject of newspaper stories and of the constant awareness of being looked at. Always having to look her best. Always having to say the right things to people. She was beginning to feel ready to put it all behind her and merge into the background – or perhaps into Victor's background.

"Alan didn't say anything to me about that."

"I just thought of it. You haven't played it before. I think you'd enjoy it."

She looked at him across the room, trying to read his thoughts through the half-light. "Are you saying you'll do it *only* if I agree to join you?"

"No, not exactly – "

"Sounds like emotional blackmail."

"The part gives you a wonderful wardrobe."

"Anything would be an improvement on simulated fur and sackcloth."

Mitch put down his cup with a clatter and stood up, unable to conceal his excitement. "It could be a lot of fun."

"You mean you'll do it?"

"On certain conditions. I want to direct this one myself. I've managed both before. And as I've already appeared in this play once it shouldn't be too difficult to stand back and take an objective look at myself."

"I thought you wanted something less demanding."

He laughed, almost boyishly, full of easy charm, his tiredness dropping away from him as he contemplated the prospect of having total control. "It's bound to have its problems to begin with, but once we were on the road – "

"On the road? Alan didn't mention anything about touring."

"Provinces first, and then overseas for a few months. If it takes we then go into the West End with a ready-made reputation. Take up to about a year."

Elizabeth frowned. This was more than she'd bargained for. Four months at the most, maybe five, but to be forced to live out of suitcases again for so long, that needed time for consideration. She put her cup down carefully and got up.

"Victor could tag along if he wanted to," said Mitch, with just a little more of a sneer than he'd intended.

"That was unworthy of you, Mitch. It's just that, well, a year's a long time. I've been seriously thinking about calling it a day..."

"You're right. Let's forget the whole thing. A year is a long time. I won't do it."

She turned on him quite fiercely, taking him by surprise. "That's not fair. I refuse to carry the responsibility for making up your mind. You know that's unfair."

"I told you earlier, I don't really want to do it."

"You soon changed your mind when you thought I might opt in."

"Pity! I know a great designer who could bring an unusual quality to the sets. Three of them, remember?"

"Yes, I do remember. I remember very well. What makes you think you'd have that much say about a designer?"

"Because when Alan put the idea to me, that was one of the points I raised. He was sure it could be arranged."

"The management must be very keen to get you if they're prepared to go that far." Now it was Elizabeth's turn to sharpen the cutting edge of her tongue.

"It's a management that hasn't done anything for some time. Alan mentioned the name but it didn't mean much to me. They're going to concentrate on 'high-quality revivals for the masses' I think he said."

"You must make up your mind, Mitch. I'm not going to argue with you. I'm not going to argue with you ever again. I'm tired of it. We seem to have wasted so much time arguing. It really isn't worth it. Life's too short to waste any more. The choice has got to be your own. I'm going up to bed."

He watched her go, went around the room switching off the pools of light, and then followed her upstairs. His mood had once more swung back into a black sombreness. For a few moments he had been able to live off the adulation of the evening and so regain a little of his lost confidence. For a few moments he had managed to engender some personal excitement from the prospect of another production and all that was involved in its preparation. But it was only a few brief moments, and now those moments were over.

The tiredness crept back into him as he mounted the stairs. They undressed without exchanging any further conversation. He glanced from the bedroom window at the white sheet now covering everything in a phosphorous glow as far as the eye could see. It seemed as though they were high above the earth. As though they were looking down on mile after mile of clean white linen, lumped up to conceal secrets. Hidden mounds smoothed over by the continuous white plateau that now stretched into infinity.

He was feeling hot and decided to sleep without his pyjamas. He wanted to enjoy the sudden rush of cold sheets against his skin when he first climbed into bed. There was something deeply sensuous about this, something he enjoyed and needed to enjoy at that particular moment. His warm body gave a minor protest as he snuggled down into his pillows, pulling the covers up around his neck.

"Thank you for coming back tonight," he said to Elizabeth.

"You don't have to thank me. You knew I would sooner or later."

"I was beginning to doubt it this time. There wouldn't have been any point in my complaining if you'd said you'd had enough."

"I could have said that many times over the past few years."

They fell into silence once again. The snow was still falling, creating a finely changing pattern across the room as though a rather tarnished witch ball was slowly revolving and just missing the light. The sounds outside had become flat and dead.

"Please, Liz, stay with me. You'll never know how much I need you. Now more than ever before." He was pleading with her, yet exercising all his skill to keep the note of pleading from his voice.

The first flush of innocent adolescent love had never been quite their scene, but they had certainly enjoyed a richly romantic beginning with more of the exotic trappings than any young couple could ever wish for. Shared happiness and shared success. Money, adulation, lots of friends, and above all else they had enjoyed each other. Only they knew exactly what the past years had meant, and only they could understand the need each filled for the other.

Mitchell stretched out his hand towards Elizabeth and felt her fingers close around his. They gripped tightly, almost too tightly. He pulled her towards him and rolled over to kiss her face only to discover it was wet. She had lain there, silently crying, keeping her sorrow to herself, too proud to admit her anguish, and too concerned openly to deny it. He tried to wipe away her tears as he then reached down to kiss her breasts, causing her to gasp in little delighted breaths of surprise. They clung to each other. They were full of despair, knowing their situation to be one of utter interdependence, and unable to shake free from it. Buried deeply within each of them was the need for the other, and within each of them was the weakness of being needed.

11

The following morning saw the culmination of a night of constant snow. True to form, London was almost brought to a standstill. Most of the trains serving the Southern Region were either cancelled or running late. The heights of Highgate and Hampstead were virtually inaccessible. The early morning news announced that blizzards had hit all parts of the country and snowstorms could be expected to continue for at least the next week.

Inclement weather of this severity was one of the few factors that Maggie had not considered. There were a wide range of hard and tried methods that could be employed to combat inferior notices, mishaps during a performance and failing box office returns, but weather was quite outside the normal duties of administration.

Predictably, the box office telephone started to ring the moment the theatre was open for business, on the dot of 10.00 a.m. The ringing continued non-stop throughout the day, with people from the suburbs trying in vain to gain a refund, or to transfer their tickets for a future performance.

Redcliffe Square, like so many other green patches in the middle of London, looked like an enormous white sheet with trees sticking up through it. This was the scene that greeted Robin when he woke that morning. The brightness outside drew his attention, causing him to shiver as he made his way to collect the morning papers and then return to the warmth of his bed and snuggle up to Jake.

It was Jake's turn to stir and to blink into the dazzling brightness that now flooded into the room. He scratched at his hair and rolled across to meet Robin. "So what's exciting in this morning's world?"

"Looks like the poor man's St Moritz out there. The snow must be acres thick. I bet this'll keep the audiences away by the hundreds."

Jake pushed himself even closer to Robin, throwing one leg across his loins. "Read me the funnies."

Robin had been pulling open the pages with a considerable amount of rustling and general activity; he was mainly interested in the assorted arts information. He suddenly jerked his arms into a rigid position as he caught sight of the letters page. "Bloody hell! Susanna's in print. Bloody, bloody hell! She's lambasting Fiona like there's no tomorrow. Good for her."

Giving in to her anger, Susanna had written her own letter to *The Guardian*. The reply suggested that Fiona ought to make up her mind about whether she really wanted to be an actress, or to meddle in politics. If the former, then she ought to concentrate upon entertaining the public. She ought to be helping them to understand human emotions through the expression of the art of the theatre. If the latter, then, Susanna said, Fiona should get out of the theatre as soon as possible. She went on to point out the number of times Fiona had castigated some of the larger subsidised companies and then subsequently appeared with them. It was also pointed out that on numerous occasions Fiona had openly declared that she had had enough of the theatre. The theatre no longer held any challenge for her and she was considering the possibility of going into something quite different. Social work had been mentioned at one time, and then again, perhaps some politically motivated organisation. The letter concluded by pointing out that Fiona still enjoyed the luxuries brought by her huge film earnings. It finally mentioned the extent to which some of her income was kept out of the country in order to avoid high taxation.

Jake pulled away to lie on his back. "Man, you know, your lot amazes me. They really do. Your whole goddam family's worse than the Borgias. You're all at each other's throats."

"Someone had to answer back."

"Not you, I notice. Not liddle ol' Robby. I gather Fiona's gonna be on the liddle ol' box on Sunday night. Got to hand it to her. She sure does know how to wave her dirty knickers in public."

Robin wasn't really listening. He allowed the newspaper to float away beside him on to the floor. He found he was thinking about his father. Jake's hand ran along Robin's belly, nestling between his legs, and they wriggled even closer. But for Robin it was more of a well-practised reflex than a desire for action.

Jake caught his mood. "Say, what's wrong, Robby?"

"Thinking."

"At this hour of the morning?"

"My brain, such as it is, manages to function right around the clock."

"Come on, man, out with it. What's on your mind? When you get like this, there's got to be a reason."

Robin sat up, pulling his skinny white arms towards his head, and cradled his hands to support his neck. His narrow chest heaved with the intake of breath. "I – I heard you on the phone yesterday."

"When in particular? There's a lot of phone calls I make during the course of a day."

"Yesterday afternoon, around three o'clock. Is that precise enough?"

Jake frowned for a moment, trying to recall the time, and then his face showed a moment of recollection. "What is it you think you heard?"

"You were talking about a new production."

"I'm always talking about new productions."

"You mentioned the designing of three sets."

"That could be because I'm a designer."

"I know who you were talking to."

"So?"

"It was my father, wasn't it?"

There was no immediate answer. Now Jake lay back, looking up at his own reflection in the overhead mirror. Robin continued to stare straight ahead, almost afraid to turn and read Jake's expression. He knew that his deductions were right, yet he still hoped he had been mistaken. The silence seemed endless. Even the usual noises that penetrated from the street were now deadened by the thick snow.

"You haven't answered. That can only mean I'm right."

"Sure, you're right."

"How far advanced are the arrangements?"

"No more than a single phone call. *That* phone call." Jake turned towards him, propping himself on one elbow.

"Are you going to accept?" Robin's voice was flat and controlled.

"I haven't been offered anything yet. It was simply to find out whether I'd be interested. It was also to find out what other commitments I might have on my distant horizon."

"Jake, you're hedging. Are you going to accept the offer if it comes off?" Robin was nothing if not persistent. It was a trait that had its annoying side.

"I need the work."

"I happen to know you were offered something in New York only last week. Why don't you take that?"

"Say, listen, kiddo, are you trying to hustle me out of the country?" He was now sitting upright, exuding indignation and hurt, his light olive skin with its satin texture cleanly contrasted against the dark blue of the decor.

Robin turned to meet Jake's questioning eyes. "I know just how ambitious you are, Jake. If you designed a production in which my father starred, that could be a big step forward for you. I also know what happened on opening night. One of the backstage queens told me."

Jake threw himself from the bed and stood in the full light of the large window, his muscular legs set astride and his arms folded tightly against his chest. "I thought we'd sorted that one out. I thought it was agreed that we forget all about it. I'd had too much to drink that night. Don't forget you were pissed out of your tiny mind as well. It's a small wonder you didn't manage to finish up under a bloody bus."

"Might have been better if I had."

Jake swung round to him. "Now listen to me, man. Don't let's have that bullshit all over again. You're too fond of life to leave it behind without one hell of a fight."

"Please, Jake. We – we've got a good thing going between us. Please, don't spoil it."

"*You've* got a good thing going." He lowered his voice,

speaking with a finely controlled tone that was far more effective than shouting. "I'm getting just a little bit tired of jealousies whenever I happen to speak with anyone else. I'm getting more than a little tired of you spying on me – "

"I don't spy. I can't help but know what goes on. You make no attempt to hide it. Christ, man, I love you. Doesn't that give me a right to care?"

This declaration was totally unexpected, and Jake found it difficult to reply. He reached out and wrapped himself into a vermilion silk kimono heavily embroidered with peacocks. The effect was quite stunning. He appeared to have stepped from a mediaeval tapestry; a demi-god of infinite beauty and superb proportions.

"We don't own each other," he said, softly.

"Is that your way of saying you want me to leave?" Robin now sounded remarkably cowed, very beholden, vulnerable and very, very young. There was a quiver in his voice, as though the threat of severance would be more than he could cope with.

Jake knew Robin well enough to recognise the tone. They had lived together long enough for him to have heard it many times in the past. It was not unusual for Robin to sound off, and then try to backtrack. Whether this was a clever device or natural self-preservation it was almost impossible to tell, but it was certainly effective.

"Robby, you know that's nonsense. If I decide to go to New York, it's because I want to. If I decide to stay, it's because I want to. It's as uncomplicated as that. I follow my feet wherever the work's most interesting. Now, please, kiddo, do me a favour and stop being a schmuck." He moved around and sat on the edge of the bed near Robin.

Robbie stretched out his hand and smoothed it across Jake's chest. It was a small gesture, but one that he needed to make if only to reassure himself that all was well between them.

"Christ, Jake, but you're beautiful." Robin was suddenly up on his knees, kissing Jake, holding him firmly across his shoulders and forcing him back. This open display of his love was the nearest that Robin could come to an apology for his outburst. He loathed these minor disagreements and was frightened whenever they happened. It was the fear of being unwanted and left to seek another bed. He had his own way of inflicting a hurt upon himself, his own perverted desire to self-destruct, but for the most part he managed to keep it under control.

Robin pushed himself on to Jake, enveloping him, almost afraid to let go. Jake was happy to lie back and allow it to happen. He finally embraced the boy in a bear hug that set the seal on their reconciliation.

"Come on, sonny. Tell you what, let's get dressed and go for a walk in the snow," said Jake, as he playfully pushed Robin aside and rolled away. "I'll see if I can find my fur lined jock strap."

"Great idea. I haven't seen snow like this for years. Better keep something across my mouth though. The last thing I need right now is a sore throat."

"Don't worry. Christ, man, if you're that concerned, wear your crash lid with the visor down. You'll look like something from outer space."

"Great idea!" He ran from the bedroom to return stark naked except for his crash helmet as he stomped around the room with stiff legs and jerking arms, enacting the movements of a robot getting dressed. Harmony was restored.

For Fiona, the word harmony was rapidly becoming a long forgotten state; it always seemed to belong to yesterday. It was now her turn to express anger when she read Susanna's letter. She was furious to find that more personal issues were creeping into the discussion. It came as a surprise to her that Susanna should have burst into print at all. As far as she was concerned, Susanna was the sort of person renowned for spending a lot of time moaning in corners, a considerable amount of energy brooding, but never actually going out of her way to correct an unpleasant situation. For Susanna to have blazed out with such a hysterical letter infuriated her more than she could put into words.

"Can't blame her, love," said Andrew, once he had read the letter.

"She's no bloody right to jump on the bandwagon. I've got a valid point to make. Her letter is nothing more than a personal attack. Anyway, what I choose to do with my money is entirely my own affair."

"Not when you're complaining about the way other people spend theirs."

"I can hardly wait until Sunday week. My God, I'll really say what I think about the whole lousy rotten business of grants and subsidies."

The kitchen clock began to chime ten, making Fiona forget the newspaper and gulp at her coffee. "Oh, God! I had no idea it was as late as that. I've got someone coming in half an hour."

"Oh, yes! What about?"

"He might be joining my company for the tour. He wasn't able to fit in an audition at any other time so I agreed that he could come here this morning."

"Ta for telling me," said Andrew, banging down his cup.

Fiona looked across to him, startled by his inexplicable annoyance. "What difference does it make to you?"

"I bloody well live here as well."

"Are you suggesting that I ought to confer with you before I arrange for anyone to call?"

"It's been like Heathrow airport for the past week. I'd have thought we could at least have breakfast in peace and quiet before the bloody hordes start to descend again."

Her voice was slow and deliberate. "Listen, Andy, I'm beginning to get just a little bit fed up with your calm assumptions about what you think should, or shouldn't, happen in *my* home."

"Oh, for Christ's sake! Don't tell me we're in for another one of your 'if you don't like it do the other thing' moods."

"I'm not telling you anything of the sort. But I am warning you. The time is rapidly approaching when I'll simply open the door and show you the pavement."

"That's what I like about you, doll. You've got such a delicate way of putting things."

"You're here at my invitation, and to suit my needs."

"You mean, I'm a bloody good stud."

"Balls and brawn are no substitute for brains. I'd much rather have someone with an equal share of all three, but until I can find the right person, I've settled for you."

"Bloody hell! Here we fucking-well go again." He threw his breakfast cup across the room smashing it into fragments.

Fiona stood her ground, almost laughing. "I hope you feel

better for that. But if you really feel the need to start breaking things, perhaps the time *has* come for you to look for a pad of your own."

"Perhaps I'll do just that. Then let's see who you'll take up with, and for how long."

"With what I've got to offer, that shouldn't be difficult."

"I *know* exactly what you've got to offer. A bloody great outsized ball-crushing ego. That's what you've got to offer. And it's *all* you've got to offer, believe me."

"It's suited your purpose for the past six months."

"Right! That's precisely what it has done. Suited my purpose. With the row of gigs I've got lined up they might just about set me free."

He had spoken like this before, but in the past it had always been speculation. There was something about the way he said it this time that was different.

"What do you mean?"

"I mean the Apollo in Glasgow, the City Hall in Newcastle, two nights in Southampton, a couple in Hammersmith. Twenty-four dates in all. What the hell do you think all the rehearsing's been for? Just to keep my hand in? This could be the big one, and then I'm on my own, with my own group."

"You mean a tour?"

"That's right, love. A tour! *T-o-u-r*. Tour! What's the matter, didn't you think it would ever really happen?" He was goading her, shouting into her ear and making her wince at the noise.

"Don't bawl at me like that," she snapped back at him, moving away. "I don't give a damn what the hell you do. You've taken advantage of me from the moment you moved in here. I thought you had more depth, more character. You're just the same as any other man. You want to take all the time. You give back nothing. Nothing at all!"

"I give you what you asked for. No more, but certainly no less. It was an exchange, remember?"

"I remember only too well. What I offered you was a roof and food in exchange for emotional support."

Andrew began to laugh, sarcastically. "Emotional support! That's a bloody new name for it. What you get from me is a hell of a lot more than just emotional support. I'm the best poke you ever had, and you bloody well know it. Take it from me, I've certainly had better ladies than you. The groupies aren't all scatterbrained little misses who wet their knickers every time they hear a guitar twang. My sort of music brings 'em all running. I can take my pick. And while we're at it, let me put the records straight. It wasn't *you* who picked *me*. *I* picked *you*. I knew you were going to be at that rally, that's why I made sure I played there. I knew the type of person you were, and *are*."

"There's a word for bastards like you," she shouted at him. "You're nothing but a ponce. A layabout, sucking me dry."

There was a sharp sting on her cheek as Andrew's clenched fist connected with her, throwing her on to the floor and making her knock over a chair.

"Don't you ever call me that again. I've paid you in kind. I've danced around you, and followed you wherever you've wanted me to be. You've enjoyed showing me off to your snotty-nosed friends. You've enjoyed proving that you can pull someone like me. Don't you ever call me names again." He stood towering over her, his legs astride her sobbing body, his eyes showing the extent of his fury.

"My face! What have you done to my face?" A fine trickle of blood was running down her cheek. Her hair had fallen about her eyes. She staggered over to splash cold water on to her still-smarting face and examine her reflection in the small mirror next to the sink. There was a cut just below her cheekbone. It wasn't more than half an inch, but enough to make her wonder whether it would leave a scar.

He had never actually injured her before, not to make her bleed that is. This was a new departure. This was something that could affect her stock-in-trade, her looks. A scarred actress was not often sought after. His momentary anger was spent, and he stood watching Fiona move about the room, listening to her little whimpers as she inspected her face. He wanted to go and help, but this would confirm he was in the wrong, and neither of them would ever readily admit to that. He did love her in his own way; strange, hurtful, thoughtless though it might be, a physical merry-go-round off which either could jump at any time, but they both remained aboard because they enjoyed the rough ride.

There was a ring at the front door. Fiona dabbed at her face and brushed past Andrew. He reached out to touch her as she passed but, still frightened, she sidestepped to avoid his grasp. Andrew followed her, trying to think of something to say, as she opened the front door to admit a tall, extremely good-looking and obviously virile young man. Andrew was not slow to recognise a threat when he saw one.

"Hullo, Miss Dawlish. Neil Hamilton."

"Do come in. You must be frozen." She continued to hold her hand against her face.

"Not really. Once it stops snowing it seems to get warmer straight away. Oh! Have you hurt yourself?"

"It's nothing. Silly accident. I – I just walked into the edge of the door." She turned and led the way into the living room.

"We have met before," said Neil. "It was at your first night party. But I'm sure you won't remember me. We didn't actually speak."

Andrew remembered him. He remembered noticing him standing slightly apart from the others when Fiona had been holding court. He remembered watching Neil's eyes follow Fiona around the room. He remembered thinking at the time that here was someone who could become very much to Fiona's liking. He watched them disappear into the living room at the front of the house, but then lost their words as they continued to talk behind the closed door. He was about to follow them, but changed his mind and went upstairs, hating himself for his own stupidity. There was no way of telling whether he had gone too far this time, whether he hadn't supplied just that little bit more than the bargain had called for.

12

Maggie's publicity machine had done all it could. Sandra was bright and learned fast, but she lacked the right contacts. Most of the "old pal" network had been milked before the play opened. The usual round of expense account lunches, dinners and drinks had been plied to all and sundry. There was now a great reluctance to give additional space to what was essentially a dead story. The further flurry of gossip that appeared related more to Fiona's letter and her anticipated Sunday night appearance rather than direct comment on the production.

Now that the weather had joined forces with the other furies, it seemed that the enterprise was doomed to early failure. It was with this in mind that Maggie had once again tried to contact Lord Barrington. He was as difficult as ever to speak with and she was forced to leave messages in the hope that he would return her call. The anxiously awaited response from him failed to materialise and this made Maggie more determined than ever to get to see him. Although his highly trained watchdog of a PA had given firm assurances that the call would be returned, for any one of a dozen good reasons the telephone on Maggie's desk remained silent.

As luck would have it, the two of them came face to face at an opening night, and she took the opportunity to pin him down. Sam gushed his apology with all the charm he could muster. He even removed the cigar from between his teeth in order to give greater sincerity to the occasion.

"Sorry not to have phoned you back, doll. You know how it is. Busy! Busy! Busy! Not enough hours in the day."

The crush in the bar had been unbearable and every time they began to speak yet another face would thrust itself forward with a smile of recognition and a few words of false goodwill. For the most part the faces belonged to actors or singers who felt they ought to be seen talking with Sam and, to a lesser extent, with Maggie.

"Don't worry," Maggie had said. "I do know how difficult it is to fit in everything. Why not let's make a date here and now?" She had broken away to wave at someone across the bar and to call a lack-lustre "Hullo" as a way of playing down the urgency from the suggested meeting. She had smiled, and she had laughed aloud, but she had insisted. It had all been conjured in the nicest way possible, but having finally wedged her small toe in Sam's door she was hardly likely to allow the door to close.

"Let me see," she said. "Today's Wednesday. How about this Friday afternoon?"

"Impossible. I got meetings like other people got fleas. We have a few little problems to sort out."

"I've been reading about them," said Maggie knowingly.

"Believe me, the record business ain't what it was. We'll sort it out, but it takes time. We got to have meetings. All day it's meetings."

"There's no real hurry," she said, smoothly. "Let's leave it until next week."

"Sure, next week'll be better. I can manage next week." He turned to go.

"Let's say Friday afternoon around three-thirty. That should give you time to sort out the week's left-over business. I always find Fridays are perfect for considering new ventures and for talking about ways and means."

Sam's face broke into one of his lemon squash smiles. "OK! OK! My, but you're a persistent little lady."

"I'll get my secretary to phone your – PA." She paused before the letters in order to give them the right emphasis. "That way we'll make sure it gets put into your diary."

And so she gushed on. By the time the final bell had announced the end of the interval, the situation had been taken out of his hands. For once, the occasion, and the noise, and the press of humanity on all sides, together with Maggie's powers of persuasion, had been too much even for Sam.

The words "International Entertainment Management" were spelled out in enormous letters across the front of the imposing office block that was Sam's West End headquarters. The organisation enjoyed a superb view of Hyde Park from the highly expensive Park Lane control tower that formed the hub of the complex entertainment industry over which Lord Barrington presided. An entire floor was devoted to the promotion and distribution of tapes and records, discs that had sold around the world in their millions. IEM Records Ltd was a holding company with several labels and a list of contract players that was still the envy of the entire industry. Until recently they had always managed to find new and exciting personalities, performers who could satisfy the insatiable appetite of the young disco demons. However, over the past eighteen months the new talent had been lacking and, with the price of LPs rocketing, sales had dropped off dramatically. The company was also into catering at the quick turnover teen-end of the market with lots of chrome and glass and bright colours in the darker corners and changing patterns of light. International touring productions, plays, musicals and concerts of all types were heavily promoted. Television productions had recently grown into an important area of operations. Not least because Sam enjoyed the wheeling and dealing that was part of every major contract and to which he gave a great deal of his time. It was a standing joke that if he wasn't in his office he was up in the air flying around the world to sell his company's wares. Alongside all this were movies for the big screen that cost many millions of pounds to produce and featured the world's stars. Sam was known to be interested in anything remotely interesting. The profession had long expected him to keel over as the result of a coronary, but he continued to astound everyone by rushing around the globe at a pace that left younger men gasping. Recently he had announced the formation of yet another subsidiary company, this one to meet the fast-expanding video market.

It was this new scene that Maggie had set her sights upon.

Sam's office was surprisingly elegant. It was big, very big, with a twelve-foot-high ceiling, its ornate cornice picked out in pale-green and lemon. The walls had panels of olive-green raw silk set into plaster mouldings. There was a central chandelier that reflected the fading sunlight edging its way across the park. Matching wall-brackets protruded from the silk panels. At one end of the office was a long rosewood conference table with twelve matching chairs around it and a large bowl of fresh fruit in the centre of its highly reflective surface. Sam's desk was gently curved and matched the table. It had a large coloured photograph of himself seated between his children and his many grandchildren. Immediately behind his own high-backed chair was a portrait of himself executed by Bratby in purples, reds and pinks, the ever-present cigar painted slightly larger than life. The carpet was in a toning olive-green, and it was this that had given rise to the office being known as "The Bowling Green". The finished effect was of tastefully expensive style.

"Come in! Come in! Nice to see you. Glad you could make it." He greeted her expansively, as though genuinely pleased he had been able to persuade her to visit him. Maggie returned his greeting with a typically feminine kiss on the side of his cheek.

"You're looking good, doll. What are you drinking?" He rolled across the open field of carpet towards a long rosewood cabinet.

"A little dry sherry might be nice."

Sam delicately poured just the right amount of sherry for Maggie and a large glass of whisky for himself, clinking in some ice to fill the glass. He seemed to take a childish delight in the preparation of the drinks, as though showing off his toys. Beneath his outwardly ostentatious display and screened behind the smoke of his very expensive cigars, there still lurked the small-time dancer from Manchester who was constantly surprised by his own remarkable success. There was an enormous amount of pride in his achievement, but there was also an odd mixture of embarrassment as well.

Great play was made of serving the drinks, of putting Maggie's on to a small coaster and of placing his own on the open blotting pad. He lit a cigar, drew deeply and with well-practised skill, blew the smoke high into the air. He leaned back and smiled another broad smile at Maggie. The opening ritual had now been completed.

"Well, so what do you want to see me about?"

"I thought we ought to try and sort out the details concerning the suggestion you made."

"Which particular suggestion was that, doll?" he said vaguely.

"About filming the Dawlish production of *King Lear*."

"How's it doing?"

"How is anything doing in this weather?"

"The crazy weather, yech! Believe me, I have it on very good authority that it won't last." Sam pulled a face, wrinkling his cheeks into layers.

"I've spoken to Mitch about the project. He feels we could just about manage it in two shooting days. Leave the production intact on stage and arrange several cameras around the auditorium."

"You make it sound so easy. Believe me, when it comes to filming, nothing ain't that easy. I know!"

"It could be. I realise it would need very careful planning. But it could be done. Two full Sundays could see the job in the can. The boys could then take their time in putting it together."

"How does Mitch feel about doing the show for TV?"

"Can't wait. He feels it ought to be presented as soon as possible. There's a lot of interest in the production right now."

Sam nodded, rolling his cigar between his fingers. "Yeah, I've been reading about the interest. His daughter must be some kind of a nut."

"Well, the publicity's been useful."

"I'll have to work out a budget and then see what we can come up with. No promises mind."

They were interrupted by a buzz on the intercom. Sam switched through, nodding his apology to Maggie. "Yeah?"

A clipped voice answered from the desk. "Martin here. I'm afraid I've drawn a blank. It doesn't look as though any theatre of the right size is going to be available until well into May. Either we try to extend the tour or we put the production into cold storage for a few weeks. It needs a big stage. We might be able to keep the cast on rehearsal pay. I'll have to have a word with Equity."

"My muzel! OK! OK! See what you can do and report back." He flicked off the instrument and turned back to Maggie. "Wouldn't you know? I got a smash-hit musical waiting to come in and there ain't no bloody theatre to take it. It'll cost a fortune to keep it cold until May. I tell you, a fortune it'll cost." He banged his plump fist on to the desk, causing the drinks to dance obediently.

This came as no surprise to Maggie. She had known about the show for several weeks and now it was as though she had arranged the timing of this call herself. She knew of the costly teething troubles there had been while the show was on the road. But for the past few weeks the production had broken box office records around the provinces and was now poised to arrive in London. The scenery was complicated and needed space, and the cast was quite large by present-day standards. If anyone was aware of costs, it was Maggie.

"I heard that the Criterion may be dark the week after next." She knew this was a pointless suggestion, but felt she had to appear to be helpful in order to create the right atmosphere for her own lead-in.

"That underground lavatory! It wouldn't even take half of the smallest inset. It's a great little theatre for one man shows, providing the one man happens to be a midget. I need space, and I need it fast."

"I do sympathise. However many theatres you've got, it's never quite enough, and certainly never the right ones." She sat back, sipping her sherry while trying to be conciliatory. A breathing catalyst waiting for awareness to set in.

"I tell you, Maggie, the past few weeks have been a sell-out wherever we've played. We even had an extra two weeks in Manchester."

"I know. I did read something about it in *The Stage*. I gather you've already had nibbles from Broadway."

"Sure we have. It'll take every Tony award that's going. The Shubert Organisation went berserk when they heard we got in first."

"That's understandable. After all, it is an American play."

"So what? I tell you, doll. It was a smash-hit when it played straight at the Savoy way back, and it'll be a smash again. But for God's sake, I need a lousy theatre that can take it."

"You ought to try to get your hands on more of your own properties. That way you don't have to rely on anyone else."

"Don't you think I know that? I got seven already. How many more do I need?"

"Obviously more than you've got." She shifted in her chair, pretending to be unaware of the magnitude of the problem while selecting a cigarette and then taking her time about lighting it.

Sam had lifted his bulk and was now slowly circling the middle of the floor, blowing gales of smoke through the thin shafts of sunlight, stopping to think, only to perambulate again through his own smoke.

"How much longer have *you* got to run, Maggie?"

"Until the end of March. At least, that's how long I'm booked in for." Now it was her turn to ooze smoke and smile through the shifting atmosphere to meet his thoughts.

The game was interrupted once more by a polite knock on the door to announce that Mitch was waiting outside.

"What's Mitch doing here?" said Maggie, eyes widely questioning as her fingers flattened the end of her darkly lip-sticked cigarette.

"Didn't I tell you, doll? He wanted to pop in to see me. Thought you wouldn't mind if he joined us. Send him in! Send him in!"

"Does he know I'm here?" said Maggie.

"Don't think I mentioned it." He shrugged, and returned to the throne-like security of his desk, cigar growing from the centre of his face and sending out irregular smoke signals.

There was another sharp rap on the door as Mitch entered. It wasn't until he was completely inside the office that he realised Maggie was sitting to one side of the desk. He allowed his face to show the surprise he felt.

"Maggie! I had no idea."

"Come in, Mitch. Pour yourself a drink, you know where it is."

"Thanks." He crossed to the drinks cabinet, glancing sideways towards Maggie as he passed her still figure.

"Is this a special meeting? I mean, is there a reason for us both being here together?"

"You wanted to see me. Maggie wanted to see me. So why not together? We got no secrets from each other."

"I'm just as surprised as you, Mitch."

"Really?" He raised his glass in her direction and savoured the clean taste of vodka.

"Sam's thinking of presenting the show for TV. I'm sure it's a good idea. I told him how keen you were to do it."

"It had crossed my mind, right at the beginning. I'm not so sure now."

"Maggie said you were keen."

She leaned forward, looking into his face with great intensity. "It would give you an audience of millions, Mitch. You haven't appeared on the box for about nine months or more."

"There have been offers, but I wasn't taken with the subjects."

Mitch continued to drink, trying to hear the silent anger that was bubbling around inside Maggie's head. He was also doing his best to keep at bay his own sense of irritation at being tricked into this confrontation.

The whole rotten business was crammed tight with people at the top playing off each other. Each trying to score top marks for presentation and content and entertainment value. It was all just like one great big bloody talent show. Mitch knew he was a star, he knew his own worth. Yet in spite of all this, he also knew that without the backing of people such as Maggie and Sam he could so easily find himself locked out. He had sat in on this type of scene before, and he had learned. He had learned to play the game their way. So he waited.

"We're not doing very well, Mitch. With this weather set to last for at least another week or so, I doubt if the box office advance will cover production costs."

Mitch's face flickered concern, but nothing more. "I see. And what about the provincial tour?"

"They were never more than provisional bookings. The first three dates have already cancelled."

"I would have thought that Brighton and Norwich would be all right."

"But they're not enough."

Sam leaned forward. "Mitch, I think Maggie's trying to tell you that you might not even manage to run the full three months."

"But surely there's enough of an advance to carry us over the next four weeks? Once we're over that period, the weather must improve and the audiences will come back. I've seen it before. Given a few bad weeks in the winter, the public are only too eager to get out of their homes and be entertained."

"It's a big cast, Mitch. My organisation can't afford to subsidise the show beyond the overcall, and we're almost into that now."

Maggie's information was news to Mitch. The overcall meant that the reserve of cash allowed for after initial production costs had been met would be dipped into, and once that happened it usually spelled death to an ailing production. The larger the project, the more certain was the end once they reached this situation.

"Suppose I took it on the road myself? I'm not asking for any financial help. I'll raise it somehow."

"Don't be a pots, Mitch. It would cost you a golden fortune, and it still wouldn't work. You know it. I know it. The lousy public knows it. What you really need is a new production so that you can put all this behind you."

Mitch laughed wryly, but with an undertow of feeling. "If I didn't know, I'd say you've been plotting with my agent."

"Common sense, my boy."

"Which isn't all that common," said Mitch.

Maggie had sat back, holding herself apart from this little exchange. She was trying to gauge the feeling of the occasion, watching Mitch's face, listening to what he was saying, and also to what he wasn't saying.

Sam had been doing some remarkably quick thinking. He knew as well as anyone else exactly what it meant to an actor to be out of work, no matter how high up the ladder of success the actor might be. There was never such a thing as a successful actor *without* an audience. To be unemployed was tantamount to cleaning off a canvas after an exhibition; there was nothing to look at, nothing to applaud. He pushed back his chair, pulling himself up with another puff on his cigar as though getting up a head of steam.

"I got an idea. Maggie, you want me to put the show on film, video, or whatever, right?"

"It was your own suggestion, remember?"

"If you say so." He waved the point aside. "OK! OK! Suppose I agree and manage to get access to screen time. I'll give you a percentage of the take. That way you get back some, if not all, of your investment."

"I'm listening."

"If you put up the notices tomorrow, you close in two weeks' time. I can get a director to sit in on performances all next week. He can make notes, decide where he wants to position his cameras and how to organise his crew. We can start to shoot by the end of the week, finish the following week, and then think about our edits."

"What happens if we run over?" said Mitch.

"With my boys, we finish on time. That's why I book 'em. Then with you closing in two weeks, I can move my production in and we can open without a break."

"That doesn't really give me very much, does it, Sam?" said Maggie. "I mean, short of getting back a few pounds, which in this case I'm not over-worried about. I think I'd like a little more than just money."

Mitch was beginning to feel uneasy. He disliked being in on the scheming side of the business, but he disliked even more the feeling that he was being bandied about in an exchange system simply to satisfy the needs of two of the moguls of the entertainment industry. "While we're on the subject, what do I get out of it? I'd like to feel there was a bit more than a few hours of screen time at the end of a lot of hard work."

"You could finish up with a few more awards," said Sam, laughing so that his heavy frame bounced up and down.

"Awards are cash in the bank at the box office, Mitch. You know you could do with a little collateral at the moment." Maggie knew she was being a bitch, but she was past worrying on that score. She was beginning to edge her way towards her main objective with Sam.

"Listen, Mitch," said Sam. "Be sensible. I'm prepared to arrange another shop window for you. You can even suggest your own property. I'm reasonably open-minded."

"You must really need that theatre pretty badly."

"I've spent a little over two million on getting that little lot together. It'll have to run for at least nine months to a year before we're into profit. The company's in a bit of trouble, and I don't feel inclined to spend any more than we need right now. I can't afford to sit back and let it all drain away. What do you say?"

"I'll tell you what I say. I don't need a production from you, but I do need your money. I've been offered another shop, but I haven't yet made up my mind about it."

"You didn't tell me, Mitch," said Maggie, showing the first real sign of interest in the conversation since Mitch had joined them.

"It doesn't concern you, Maggie."

"Sorry I spoke."

"What do you want with my money?" said Sam. "Let me do the job and I'll present whatever it is."

"*No!* I want to direct this one myself, and I also want to have total artistic control. I've had enough of people pushing me into productions I don't want to do. I'm fed up with all the airy-fairy nonsense that passes for direction and costumes and scenery. Those who want the experimental theatre can take themselves to the grubby fringe warehouses. I want to present something I can be proud of. Something I can enjoy and that I know the public will enjoy."

Maggie clapped her hands together. "Bravo! If I hadn't heard you say it, I would never have believed it possible. Such a pity you didn't let me know your feelings six months ago when we first discussed *Lear*. I'd have taken Wembley Stadium and produced it on ice for you."

"What's the play, Mitch?" said Sam, with growing impatience.

"*The Apple Cart*. I've done it before. I was good then, and I'll be even better now. If you agree to put up half the capital in my name, I'll buy into the management on my own terms. We'll work out a percentage of the returns for you."

Maggie was unaccountably laughing. "You make it sound like a game of Monopoly."

"That's exactly what it is. Isn't that why we're in Park Lane right now?"

Sam thought for a moment, but it was only a moment. "If I agree in principle, will you then agree to the other arrangements?"

"Why not? I've always been a great believer in the operation of mutual back-scratching."

"OK! OK! You're on, Mitch. Let's have another drink." He began to cross towards the cabinet.

"Just a minute, Sam," said Maggie. "I'm still standing on the corner with the wind blowing up my knickers. When I came here to see you, I had no idea that Mitch would be here as well. There are a few other details I'd like to discuss before we go any further."

Sam turned back to her, surprise on his face. "I thought you agreed. You'll get your share. What more do you want? Blood?"

"I've got more than one theatre, Sam. I'm only prepared to release that particular one in exchange for another kind of deal."

Sam continued to pour the drinks, his back to the others. He didn't ask for much from this life, just an easy row to hoe, and the right theatre whenever he needed it.

Mitch was watching Maggie's expression as it spread into a feline grin of self-congratulation. She hadn't got quite what she wanted yet, but she sensed that with the right manoeuvering it shouldn't be too difficult to obtain.

"What would you say to a merger, Sam?"

The rounded shoulders of the old man stiffened in amazement. He was the one who always made this type of suggestion. He, Sam Barrington from Manchester, the little dancing boy who made good, was the one who led the others through their paces. He slowly turned round to them, a filled glass in each hand. He seemed to glide across the Bowling Green without taking his eyes from Maggie's face. They both knew she was nursing her trump card very close to her small chest, not letting it see the light of day until she was sure she knew what hand the opposition was holding.

"A little ambition is admirable. Too much can be a dangerous thing, my dear."

"It didn't do you any harm," replied Maggie.

"Times were different then," he said, extending his hand with the drink without taking his eyes from her face.

"Times are always different. Well, what do you say?"

"Suppose I refuse?"

"Then she won't close the show. Right, Maggie?" said Mitch.

"Right!"

"You must be bloody raving mad. To keep that one running to half-empty houses would cost you a fortune," said Sam. "A fortune!"

"It'll cost you a fortune as well, Sam. My show is still capitalised, how's yours?"

"What do you want?"

"I'll exchange forty-nine per cent of my little dominion for a seat on the board of your empire."

Mitch almost choked on his drink. He felt he had been given complimentary tickets for a special show being performed for an audience of one. "You can't be serious, Maggie?" he said.

"Why not? I know as much about this business as anyone else. I've got a successful track record second to none. I can do anything most of the others can do, and better. My theatres are in prime sites. They all get a lot of passing trade and it's a growing market. I'm not joking, Sam. Forty-nine per cent of my company for a seat on your board and a long-term contract."

"You've got a head on your shoulders, darling. You've got to have some yiddisher blood lurking there somewhere."

"You still haven't given me an answer. What do you say?"

"I'll have to go into it. I'll have to speak to my board. This one I can't decide for myself. You know what I mean? Share-holders' interests, future plans, and so on and so on."

"Let me know by five o'clock tomorrow at the latest. After all, I've got plans to make."

"But, doll, tomorrow's Saturday."

"That's right." She carefully placed her sherry glass on the coaster, stood up and pulled on her coat with the casual charm of a tame cobra. "Goodbye, Sam. Thanks for the drink. I'll expect to hear from you one way or the other."

Mitch and Sam were left together, speechless at the speed with which the little exchange had been played, and marvelling at the technique that had supported it.

Sam moved to his intercom, clicking the tiny levers impatiently.

"Yes, sir?"

"I want you to arrange a full board meeting for nine thirty tomorrow morning."

"But it's Saturday!"

"I know that. OK! OK! So lay on lunch as well. But I want everyone there. *Everyone*, do you understand?"

"Yes, sir." The machine clicked silent.

Mitch had sat stunned, watching Sam's reactions throughout the proceedings. "Are you going to agree?"

"Keep your eyes on the city pages next week." He lit another cigar and began to surround himself in a great cloud of smoke, sitting behind his desk as though Mount Etna was about to erupt.

13

There was still no improvement in the weather and Friday night had seen yet another heavy fall of snow. Generally speaking, unless anyone really had to go out they chose to stay at home for fear of being stranded.

Elizabeth had had a restless night, feeling at first very hot, and then shivering in the small hours of the morning. By the time the alarm went off at eight she knew she was cooking a heavy cold. Worse than that was the realisation that she was almost voiceless. It is one thing for an actor to feel listless and low yet still able to present an acceptable performance through sheer technique, but all the technique in the world would never summon up a voice where there was little available.

This had long been a problem with which Elizabeth had had to battle throughout her career. If she was feeling tired, anxious, depressed or anything other than in top health, her voice was always the first part of her to succumb to the strain. Being Saturday meant there was a matinee, and her immediate reaction was to insist upon going to the theatre as usual, struggling against her voice as best she could.

"We're in enough trouble," she croaked. It was obvious to Mitch that every word she spoke was causing her considerable pain.

"Listen to yourself. You'll never get through the first act. You'll finish up without any voice at all and then have to be off for the whole of next week." Mitch was patience personified, and even this was part of an irregularly repeated scene.

Elizabeth allowed her head to loll back on to the plumped up pillows. The cotton wool in her head seemed to swell up into her eyes and made them run. There was a dull ache behind her cheekbones that indicated her sinuses were mildly infected.

"I've – I've got to go on this afternoon. I'll be all right. This sounds worse than it is." She smiled feebly, swallowing her saliva with great difficulty and breathing with some effort through her half-open mouth.

"I'm not arguing, Liz. I'll phone Maggie and warn her. Your understudy's been hanging around like a vulture ever since we opened. Let's see if she can spread her wings."

"That's unkind of you, Mitch."

He picked up the telephone and was about to dial when Elizabeth put her hand over his, waving him to a standstill with her free hand. "Wait a minute. Suppose I agree to stay put for this afternoon and come along for this evening's performance? If I don't speak too much, my vocal chords should be able to relax during the day. I've still got my laryngeal spray to help me through. I can use that."

"Darling, you've got a roaring temperature," said Mitch.

"I've appeared with worse than this."

They might have been playing a tape-recording, so often had the same dialogue been exchanged before. Elizabeth had always refused to admit defeat, regardless of how badly she was feeling, and sheer willpower had often carried her through. It was always Mitch who flapped around her and panicked for fear of her becoming seriously ill. It was on occasions such as this that he realised the extent to which he depended upon her for support in every respect. His concern revealed itself as fear, not only for Elizabeth, but for himself as well.

He went downstairs and prepared breakfast for himself. He poured some grapefruit juice for Elizabeth and made two thin slices of toast for her as he knew this would help her throat. It was all neatly placed upon a tray together with a pot of china tea and some slices of lemon. He took his own breakfast up to the bedroom simply to keep her company, and sat at a small table in the window. It was an oddly suburban scene. He took his time, first showering, then shaving and getting dressed. Once this was over he made Elizabeth comfortable with the morning papers, and then went back downstairs hoping she would manage to sleep for a while.

At nine o'clock he called Maggie. The cast bumbled into the depths of despair as soon as it was announced that Elizabeth was off. The house was very thin, with the upper circle closed completely. Those who had booked seats there were moved down to the next tier in order to bulk up the audience. The performance proved to be no more than adequate.

During the course of the afternoon Elizabeth had rung Victor to tell him of her cold. Before she realised it, he had come over to the house, letting himself in by the back door. Victor had been keeping a low profile for several days. Now he spent the afternoon sitting next to the bed, holding her hand and making her hot drinks.

"It was very sweet of you to come," she said, between gasping for breath and trying to carry on a reasonable conversation.

"It was the least I could do. Listen, my love. You've asked me to be patient, and I have. But the time has come for me to say what's been on my mind for several weeks."

Elizabeth began to tug at the handkerchief now gripped between her teeth. She knew what was coming, wanted it to be said, yet did not wish to be forced into making a decision.

"You've often told me that you've had enough of the theatre. That you had thought of giving it all up before very long. I want you to give it up, Elizabeth. The longer you postpone making the final break, the longer you'll go on. And the longer you'll continue to be unhappy."

She reached out and put her hand over his mouth, trying to stop him. He merely pursed his lips and kissed her palm very tenderly, taking hold of her hand and stroking it with weightless fingers.

"Not now, Victor. Please, not now," she whispered.

"Not ever." He rose to look vacantly from the window, beyond the dirty furrows in the road, out over the glacial rooftops and the undulating purity of the snow-covered heath, where little grey blobs of humanity bounced their way cautiously as Lowry-like figures in a landscape. It was a scene of great beauty, yet it managed to fill him with a sadness that seemed to numb his senses, not because of the cold but because he felt so helpless. He slowly turned back to Elizabeth.

"You've tried, Elizabeth. You've done your best, more than

your best, but what's the sense in going on? You're not being fair to yourself, or to me either for that matter. Forgive me if I sound selfish. Perhaps this isn't the best of times to talk like this, but there seem to be so few opportunities lately. I've waited for nearly two years. How much longer am I to be kept in the wings?"

"You make it sound as though I've been using you."

"Haven't you?" The answer arose spontaneously. "Let's be honest. Whenever you've needed a shoulder to cry on, I've been there. Whenever you felt the need for someone to talk to, it's been me. Not that I've minded, or objected. I've always felt very close to you. But I've reached a point when feeling close is no longer enough. I don't really believe it's enough for you either. I want us to *be* close. I want to love you as part of me. I – I need you as much as he does, Elizabeth. And I'm sure I have a lot more to offer you than Mitch has, or ever will."

She suddenly reached up and pulled his face towards her own, kissing him with great passion through her tears.

"You need to get away, Elizabeth. Somewhere in the sun. As soon as this production is over, let me take you away."

"I – I know you're right, Victor. I know that what you're saying is the truth. I still don't feel I – I can do it to him." She turned her head away from him, burying her tears in the pillow.

"As soon as the show closes, I'm going to take some time off and arrange for us to go away together. We owe that much to each other. *He* owes us that much," said Victor.

"Let me think about it. My mind's not clear enough right now. Let me have time to think about it, Victor."

"Have you got another play in view after this one?"

She shook her head. "Not exactly. Mitch has asked me to partner him in something. I've – I've already told him I'm not sure that I want to do it."

"You don't sound very convincing. You've got to say it, and mean it." He held on to her arms, forcing her to look straight at him. He seemed to be exercising a physical strength she had not noticed before.

She lifted her head to look into his eyes, aware of the set of his jaw, the firmness of his chin. Then she caught sight of his slightly balding head reflecting the rapidly fading light from the window. Victor was no matinee idol; he was too short, too plain, too portly, but he did exude a love for her that she had never felt before in her entire life. He wanted her for herself alone, and not because of the support she would provide for him, or the lies she would tell on his behalf, but simply because he wanted to be with her and to look after her. The odd sensation lasted no more than a few brief seconds, and then her head filled with the rolling cotton wool once more and her eyes began to water again. She sensed that her nose was red and her cheeks flushed. She suddenly felt unaccountably shy. She wanted to sink below the bedcovers, to hide her blotched face and angry complexion.

"If you can fancy me like this, you really must love me," she said with some difficulty.

"I do, very, very much. I only wish you'd believe me. You've got to be strong willed, Elizabeth, and make up your mind."

Before he could say any more there was an unexpected telephone ring. Victor reached out to pick up the receiver but Elizabeth managed to get there first. As she anticipated, it was Mitch telephoning during the interval to ask how she was feeling.

"I'm a lot better," she said, manipulating her voice to a low register.

"Who are you kidding?"

"What's the house like?"

"It matches the weather, frigid."

"I'm coming in this evening," said Elizabeth.

"There's really no need. Your understudy's doing quite well. The house isn't all that big this evening, either. You'd be well advised to stay put. You'll be a lot better by Monday." There was a strained note in Mitch's voice and Elizabeth couldn't help but catch it from him.

"Is everything all right, Mitch?"

"Why do you ask?"

"Just something in your tone."

"I'll tell you this evening. Don't worry."

"I will worry unless you tell me now."

There was a silence until Mitch spoke again.

"I wasn't going to mention it until tomorrow. I suppose you might as well know now. The notices have just been posted."

Elizabeth stopped breathing for a moment. This was something she had been afraid of. They had hoped to have been able to last for at least two months, if not the full run. This would be just halfway; a mere six weeks and then out.

"I'm sorry, Mitch." This was all that she could say. It was all that she wanted to say. She knew how hurt he must be feeling, how great an injury this would be to his personal pride. She also realised that whatever else happened he was going to need a lot of moral support to get him over the next two weeks.

"Don't bother about this evening's performance, Liz. Save it all for next week. Got to go." He hung up without waiting for her to reply.

Victor took the receiver from Elizabeth's motionless hand and replaced it on the cradle.

"What's happened?"

"We're out! The notices have gone up. We close in two weeks' time. It means that Maggie can't hold on any longer. Things were beginning to pick up but the weather turned against us. You can't fight the elements. Sounds as though it ought to be a line from the play."

She laughed a little, more with a sense of relief than despair. "Oh well, it looks as though I'm about to be unemployed again."

"Two weeks, Elizabeth. You'll be free to come with me in two weeks."

She shook her head violently. "Not unless Mitch has got something else lined up. He'll be out of a shop. This will – this will be a blow to his pride. This was intended to be his big return to the top. It's been a – a disaster right from the opening night."

Victor got up, pulled his jacket straight and adjusted his tie.

"Don't be angry with me, Victor."

"I'm not angry, just a little sad. I'm going now. Try to get some sleep." He moved over to the door and held it open.

There was no longer any trace of daylight. The shadows had crept across the room while they had been talking. It was difficult to see features, but they each knew what the other was feeling. They each knew the hopelessness of the situation.

"When will I see you again, Victor?"

"That's rather up to you, Elizabeth. I'll be ready in two weeks' time, if you want to come away with me. If you decide not to, then I shall have to admit defeat."

"Please, Victor – " Her voice was more childlike, crying through the advancing darkness, holding out her arms to be protected from an unseen enemy.

"There's no longer any point, my love. It's for you to decide. Two weeks." He slipped from the room but remained outside for a few seconds, listening to Elizabeth's tiny sobs coming towards him.

14

Elizabeth was sleeping deeply when Mitch let himself in and went up to see how she was. Trying not to disturb her, he fingered his way around the room without switching on any lights, but he walked into the dressing table stool and sent it over with a clatter. Elizabeth woke with a start, momentarily confused as to where she was, and even which day it was.

"Sorry, darling, I didn't mean to wake you." He leaned over and kissed her head. "You feel cooler."

"What time is it?"

"Nearly midnight."

"Damn! I really had intended to play the second performance."

"Just proves how much you needed the rest. Don't worry, the few people who did turn up got what they paid for." He switched on his own bedside light.

As he passed the dressing table he couldn't help but notice the ashtray with several blackened butts screwed into the grey mess of ash. He stood looking down on to the evidence of a visitor and then cast a glance towards Elizabeth. She was lying back with her head resting on the pillow, her eyes closed against the bedside light. Mitch knew instinctively that Victor had been with his wife that afternoon, and the knowledge festered. It was his turn to be hurt.

The next day being Sunday, they slept later, until the winter sunshine icily spread into their bedroom. Elizabeth was aware of feeling much better and realised that her temperature had dropped. She was now left with a simple cold and this she was well able to cope with. But Mitch persuaded her to accept breakfast on a tray, and sat with her while she nibbled at the toast and gently swallowed the steaming coffee.

They ate in silence for a while. The tell-tale ashtray was still within Mitch's line of vision. The several parts of *The Observer* were shared between them as a means of concentrating on other things.

"Oh, Christ! Here we go again," said Mitch. "There's another piece here about the production. We're all mentioned. It starts off by stating that *family disunity* is not enough. This is linked to Fiona's appearance tonight. God alone knows what nonsense she's going to come out with."

Elizabeth put down her colour supplement. "Richard Gardner's nobody's fool. Don't forget I was on his programme last year. The last thing he'll do is allow her to turn the evening into a three ring circus in which to present her own political viewpoint."

"I hope you're right." Mitch's anger was evident by the way he began to bang around on his breakfast tray; first the teapot, then his cup and saucer, and finally the sugar bowl. It was an uneven tattoo in a rising crescendo of clatter.

Elizabeth watched him from above the rim of her own cup, observing the way he tossed his head to clear the still tousled hair that had fallen across his brow. For a brief moment she saw the schoolboy she had never known. She saw the stubborn petulance that must have been quite amusing at the beginning, but which now had dissolved into a furious figure of impotence.

"We'll just have to be patient, won't we?"

Nothing more had been mentioned about the closing of the production. She felt it would be better to allow any comment to come from Mitch. But if he continued to say nothing, she decided, it would be up to her to broach the subject.

Before anything else could be said the telephone rang and Elizabeth picked up the receiver.

"Hullo? Oh! Robby, how nice of you. Yes, I'm fine. Feel a bit of a fraud actually."

Robin's light voice expressed concern, greater concern than the situation demanded, but then this was part of his nature. Either he concealed the way he was feeling with an endless stream of rather bad jokes, or he allowed himself to swing in the opposite direction and treat everything with great earnestness.

At the moment, he was quite certain that his mother must be at death's door. He knew how professional she was in her attitude to her work, and for her to have missed two performances could only imply that she was at the point of extinction.

"Are you sure you're really all right?"

"Stop panicking, darling. It's nothing more than a rotten head cold. I'll be back tomorrow night."

"Is there anything I can get for you?"

"I've got all I need. It's very nice of you to ask," said Elizabeth, trying valiantly not to laugh aloud at his exaggerated concern.

"I'll pop in to see you later," he suggested.

"I'm sure you must have a great many better things to do," said Elizabeth.

"Not in this weather. I'll be round later."

Elizabeth held her hand over the receiver while she hissed at Mitch, "He wants to come over this afternoon."

Mitch beckoned the receiver from her. "Nice of you to be so concerned, Robby. There's really no need to come rushing over. We've folded up the oxygen tent and packed her in ice. She's doing very nicely, thank you."

"Are you trying to put me off?" He sounded hurt, like a small child sulking as only he could.

"Not exactly. Mother feels she'd like to rest a little more, that's all."

"I'm not suggesting we all go to a disco. Bloody hell, surely I can come over when she's not well?"

Mitch realised Robin was determined to visit the sick bay and there would be no stopping him. His eyes rested on the ashtray once again and an idea occurred to him that he thought would restore a little of the current imbalance to which he took exception.

"Very well, Robby. Why not make it for tea?" said Mitch, smiling wryly.

Elizabeth turned sharply.

"If that's OK with you? Love to," said Robin, fully buoyant again.

"Oh! Why not bring Jake with you? He's never been before," he said as a well-timed afterthought.

There was an obvious silence from the other end, a pause that spoke through its emptiness.

"I'm – I'm sure he's got something else to do."

"Why not ask him? I'll hold on."

Elizabeth took this opportunity to cut in. "Is this meant to be some kind of sick joke, Mitch?"

"Of course not. I thought it might help to have someone else around. They can sit here and talk to each other and lighten the load on us."

He blew her an extravagant kiss. It was a finely turned gesture, one he sometimes used when he felt particularly good and knew that he had managed to score off someone.

Robin returned to the telephone, his voice now a little more subdued. "We'll be over around three thirty if that's OK with you?"

"Fine! Fine! See you both then." The receiver was replaced with due ceremony and the instrument purposefully pushed back from the edge of the bedside cabinet. "That ought to be quite pleasant. Sunday afternoon tea for the family."

"I hope so, Mitch. I sincerely hope so."

"Why do you say it like that?" said Mitch, still looking at the ashtray.

"Because I think you're up to something."

He picked up the ashtray between his thumb and forefinger and lifting it very high, walked across to the wastepaper basket and proceeded to make a great play of emptying the contents. "Can't stand the smell of dirty ashtrays. Filthy habit." He strode into the bathroom and turned on the cold tap, allowing the jet to splash around until all traces of ash had vanished.

He returned to the bedroom, making as much play with the clean ashtray as he had made with the dirty one, setting it down on one corner, and then moving it slightly to one side, standing back to admire the symmetry of the arrangement with the hairbrushes and combs already there.

"I'd better get up. I can't stay in bed all day – not if we're to have a tea party." Now it was Elizabeth's turn for a small volley.

By lunchtime Elizabeth had made a small sponge cake. In all this time there was still nothing said about the closing of the play. It was almost as though Mitch had decided to pretend the notices hadn't been posted.

During the early part of the afternoon the telephone seemed to ring in an endless series of broken melodies. First Maggie called to enquire after Elizabeth's health and to check whether she could be expected to perform the following evening. It was during this brief conversation that Elizabeth first discovered the possibility of the play being presented on television.

No sooner had the receiver been replaced than Elizabeth cornered Mitch with more questions. "You said nothing to me about a TV film of the play?"

"It's – it's still not certain. I didn't want to bother you about it yet."

"Is it likely that I'd feel bothered? After all, I imagine I am to be involved?"

"The final details have got to be sorted out."

"What details, Mitch?" Elizabeth was beginning to be suspicious of the venture.

"I've – I've agreed to do it only on condition that Sam puts up fifty per cent of the backing for my next shop. It has to be in my name."

Elizabeth's incredulity was growing by the second. "I wasn't aware that he was interested in the game of blackmail."

"Don't be so melodramatic, darling. It's nothing like that. It's a simple deal – an agreement – "

"Nice for you." She fell to musing for a moment. "What's the play?"

"Probably *The Apple Cart*."

"The one you weren't too sure about. Interesting. What happened to make you change your mind?"

"I'm rather taken with the idea of having total control. Casting, direction and so on. You know, darling, I have mentioned all this to you before. You must have forgotten."

"You also said that you would only consider it if I played opposite you. Or have *you* forgotten?"

"Well, there are some things one just has to accept. If you're dead set against appearing with me, then there's no point in trying to force you to tag along." He sounded very matter of fact, very offhand about the project.

"I see. I've never seen myself in the light of a camp follower before."

"Obviously, it's early days yet. I haven't even begun to cast the play, so you can still have first refusal. Let me know. Anyway, I hardly think this is the right time to discuss something that may not even get off the ground."

Had he been able to get hold of Maggie at that precise moment, he would willingly have throttled her. He knew that she very seldom said or did anything important by accident and he felt this to be no exception to the rule.

Further discussion was diverted by yet another telephone call, this time from Susanna, a dutiful daughter enquiring about an ageing parent. Bruce also made contact during the afternoon, much in the same way as Susanna, if perhaps in even greater haste. Several other members of the cast telephoned as well, as did Tony who was recently returned from New York.

It was around a quarter to four that the doorbell announced the arrival of the visitors. Mitch jumped to his feet immediately he heard their voices outside, slapping his son on the back as he entered and shaking hands with Jake.

"Come in! Come in! Nice to see you both. Hullo, Jake! Good of you to come."

True to form, Jake was wearing something exotic, though highly appropriate for the weather. A thick cossack hat of pale fox fur was slanted across his head, teamed with a tan leather coat that had a wide collar trimmed in the same fur. High knee-boots completed the ensemble, making him look as though he had just arrived from the Steppes, leaving his wild horse to roam until recalled by some magic chant. His face was bright from the cold and his eyes gleamed through the fine snowdust still resting on his dark lashes. His white teeth flashed the warmth of his smile as he handed Mitch his hat and coat. Robin was dressed in a black leather jacket and had a red silk scarf wrapped around his neck several times.

As soon as they entered the living room Robin dashed across to his mother, planting a dutiful kiss on her cheek. Jake had arrived armed with a splendid bouquet of assorted spring flowers and now placed them on Elizabeth's lap as though presenting a peace offering.

"Where did you manage to get these lovely flowers?" asked Elizabeth.

"Leave it to him," said Robin. "He could find ice-cream in a desert if he wanted to."

"How terribly talented of you, Jake. It's very sweet of both of you to come, but it really wasn't necessary."

"Something to do. Got to pander to the aged p's," said Robin.

"Is that intended to make us both feel wanted?" said Mitch.

"You know what I mean." He turned back to Elizabeth. "Anyway, how are you feeling?"

"Apart from a shiny nose with a dew-drop on the end, fine. I've had colds before, and worse." She was determined to make light of the occasion and to keep the conversation at a meaningless surface level until they had finished their tea and were ready to depart.

"I'll go and make the tea."

Mitch handed round small plates and encouraged them to pile high the sandwiches. They all fell to munching in silence until Elizabeth returned with the covered teapot.

"How do you like your tea, Jake? Milk? Sugar?" She allowed the pot to hover above his empty cup.

"Neither, thanks. A little lemon would be fine if you have it."

"I'll get it." Robin jumped up and scurried into the kitchen like a faithful puppy.

"He seems to know your likes and dislikes."

"Habit." Jake smiled broadly, a little embarrassed.

Mitch had settled himself into the corner of a high-backed armchair, absently nibbling on a sandwich and watching Jake's every move. Jake's shirt pulled across his muscular chest to fit snugly into the top of his well-cut trousers. The boots with their stacked heels shone, reflecting the curve of his calves. Nothing escaped Mitch's gaze. Jake was aware of the interest. Elizabeth was aware of both of them.

"You have a very charming home," said Jake, feeling the moment had arrived to offer his brand of flattery.

"Nice of you to say so," said Elizabeth. "More tea?"

"Thanks. It's got a nice smoky flavour. I take to it."

"It's Souchong. I get it from Fortnum's."

"Great store. Whenever I feel hungry, I dash in for a quick sniff and emerge replete. It's the nearest I ever get to buying anything in there."

"You'll have us all in tears in a minute," said Robin.

They all joined in the laughter, and then fell into one of those strained silences during which everyone tries to think of something bright to say.

"Robby told me about the play closing. Pity! It deserved better treatment," said Jake, unaware of the minefield he had just exploded.

It was as though Elizabeth and Mitch had been programmed to look at each other. Their eyes flickered across the room.

"These things happen," she said. "London is becoming more like New York than New York. Unless a show is a sensation overnight, then it's doomed to failure."

"Well, I guess there's been plenty of shows that folded long before six weeks," said Jake. He was vaguely aware of the undercurrent that had suddenly spread across the room.

"Nevertheless, I must admit to being disappointed," said Mitch. "Anyway, off with the old and on with the new."

"Oh! Does that mean you've definitely got something else lined up?" said Jake.

"Hey! I didn't know anything about that," said Robin. He wasn't exactly hurt but did have a feeling of being left out.

"Your father's going into *The Apple Cart* again. He's planning to have full control over this production. Isn't that so, dear?"

"Is that the one you mentioned to me a few days ago?" asked Jake.

"It seems as though you've been taken into Mitch's confidence ahead of us, Jake. I hope you feel honoured," said Elizabeth, pouring a second cup of tea for herself.

Now it was Jake's turn to be embarrassed. "Sorry. I had no idea it was top secret."

"Not to worry," said Mitch. "It's just that I never like to broadcast my plans until I'm sure they're going to happen. I've grown superstitious over the years."

Jake looked at Mitch, trying to read what wasn't being said. He put down his cup and stood up. "This really has been very pleasant. I'm so glad you're feeling better, Mrs Dawlish." He glanced around the room again, standing awkwardly admiring the memorabilia and taking the opportunity to read something in a frame from an early production.

Mitch took his cue and rose as well. "I'll show you around, that's if you can spare the time. I've got a small study upstairs. Terribly cramped for space. You might be able to advise me as to how I can get more use out of it."

Robin tried to say something, anything to avoid prolonging the visit. "I really think – "

Jake had already made the obligatory gesture of consulting his watch. "Perhaps another few minutes won't matter."

"Good!" said Mitch. "As a matter of fact, I've already got one or two ideas roughed out for sets. You might like to see them. Give you a little something to think about."

"You mean, if you decide to go ahead, you really want I should design the show?"

"Let's talk about it while we're looking round upstairs." Mitch held open the door and allowed Jake to pass in front of him. He turned back into the room. "Won't be long." The door closed behind them and their fading footsteps could be heard ascending the stairs. Their conversation was punctuated by the sound of Jake's high-pitched laughter.

Robin made a few half-hearted steps, as though intending to follow them, but changed his mind.

Elizabeth watched as her son was transformed from the bright easy-speaking youth of a few minutes earlier into a tense young man, holding back his fury and his growing distress. She was aware of the sudden rigidity across his shoulders and the reddening of his neck.

"More tea, Robby?"

There was no answer. He simply shook his head and walked aimlessly over to a window, making sure he kept his back to her.

"Have you – have you ever thought about coming home?"

"No," he said, almost inaudibly.

"Your room's here whenever you want it."

"That's not really the answer, is it?" He turned to face her, now pale and trembling, his tears being forced back by a tremendous effort of will. A small boy looking for his lost toys.

"I really did do my best to dissuade him from coming with

me. I only wanted to see you. Just to make sure you were OK. That's all I wanted."

"I appreciate the kind thought."

Robin kept glancing at his watch with a nervous twist of his head, counting the seconds into minutes and listening to the muffled voices coming from directly above them. He looked up at the ceiling as though trying to penetrate the solid mass, and then jerked his head back to his watch.

"Have you got anything else in view, Robby?" said Elizabeth.

"Not yet. There doesn't seem to be much going on right now. Being in a flop isn't any great recommendation, is it?"

"It takes more than a single individual to make a flop. It takes more than one to make a success as well. Something will turn up."

"It's getting quite dark. I'd better give Jake a shout."

"They'll be down in a minute."

"All the same – " Robin pulled open the door and bounded up the stairs, two at a time.

The landing at the top was now quite shadowy and he could just hear the two voices issuing from Mitch's study; softly spoken exchanges delivered through the fading daylight. He stood outside the study door for a moment, undecided whether to enter boldly, or simply to stamp around as a way of announcing himself. There was a sudden unexpected burst of laughter from Jake, causing Robin to react as though released from a coiled spring.

The study door was flung aside to reveal the two of them standing close together in the shadows. Mitch, bigger and taller, standing with his hands on either side of Jake's shoulders. Jake was perched on the edge of the desk looking up into Mitch's face; his own hair was tousled as though there had been something stomping through his dark locks.

The three of them stood looking from one to the other. Jake stood up, running his hand over his head and tucking his shirt back tightly into his waistband to make it pull across his chest. The movements had no meaning in themselves, but there was a degree of furtiveness that was impossible to ignore.

"It's getting late. We ought to be going." Robin turned and made his way downstairs without looking back. He collected his jacket and wound his scarf around his neck without any show of emotion.

"Thank you, Mrs Dawlish," said Jake. "It's been a very pleasant afternoon. I'm delighted you're feeling better." He turned to Mitch. "Mr Dawlish! I'll sure look forward to hearing more about the project. Goodbye."

After they had gone, Elizabeth went to the window to watch them disappear into the twilight, aware of the distance between them as they walked down the road. She shivered a little.

"He's quite a nice boy, is Jake. Seems quite bright, too," said Mitch.

"Yes, I expect he is."

"Probably make a good job of the play."

"Yes, probably."

"I think I'm going to enjoy working with him. He's biddable," said Mitch.

"I'm sure that will add to the enjoyment." She moved away from the window, passing around the room to switch on the low lamps to create their usual small island of light. Mitch's face was illuminated in isolation. He was smiling contentedly, knowingly. He was smiling as Elizabeth had not seen him smile for several weeks. She looked away again, her eyes being caught by the bright yellow flowers waiting to be arranged in a vase. Jake certainly appeared to have all the virtues.

15

It had been quite some time since Fiona had last worked in the studios of London Weekend Television and she had forgotten the exact location. She knew they were somewhere near the National Theatre complex on the South Bank, but there were a number of small twists and turns to be navigated before a visitor actually arrived at the right place. The company had offered to send a car to collect her or, alternatively, to pay for a taxi, but Fiona always preferred to drive herself and so not have to rely upon the uncertain promptness of others.

When she finally arrived she was a few minutes late because she had missed her turning in the darkness. She had found herself revolving around the Waterloo Bridge roundabout at least three times before making up her mind that she ought to have gone sharp left after crossing the bridge. By the time she arrived at the studio reception area she was well and truly pent up.

A short bespectacled young girl made towards her. "Hullo, Miss Dawlish. We were beginning to get a little worried about you."

"That's hardly necessary. It isn't as though we require a lot of rehearsal time, is it?"

"No, I suppose not. I've already taken care of your visitor's pass. I'll show you where you can park your car." It was only a matter of seconds before Fiona was being taken back into the main building.

"My name's Angela, by the way. I'm the production secretary on this particular programme. If there's anything you need, just give me a shout."

"Thanks. I will."

"We'll go straight up to hospitality, if that's all right with you?"

"Anything you say."

They took the lift up to the fourth floor and made their way into an L-shaped room that had been set up with a small bar and a table arranged with plates of curling sandwiches. There were several small knots of people gathered together in exclusive groups, each emitting their private buzz of conversation. In a corner Fiona vaguely recognised a pop singer whose photograph she had seen in one of Andrew's magazines. There was also an American movie writer who was to be interviewed about his latest screenplay, the finished production having already been tipped for an Oscar.

"Can I get you something to drink?" said Angela.

"Whisky and dry ginger, please," replied Fiona, resenting her isolation and trying to spot at least one familiar face.

"Hullo, Fiona. Glad to have you with us." A tall greying man, clasping a clipboard under one arm, held out a long slim hand in greeting. "Richard Gardner."

"Oh! Hullo! Nice to meet you." Fiona softened slightly.

"I'm delighted you were able to make it. I'm sure you appreciate that we try to be as up to the minute as possible in this segment of the programme. It gives the whole show a special lift."

"Yes, I know exactly what you mean. I have managed to watch from time to time."

He relaxed on to the edge of the table, bringing his hands around the clipboard in front of him. "What did you think?"

"Quite honestly, the show I watched seemed rather static. I thought it needed to get out and about a little more."

"Really?" There was an undisguised note of condescension in his voice; a verbal looking down his nose at yet another critic. "Let's sit over here, shall we?" He sidestepped between the outstretched legs of seated technicians and finally managed to clear a way so that Fiona could follow him.

"Is it like this every week?" asked Fiona, waving her hand towards the middle of the room.

"Sometimes it's worse. If we have a large company in to perform something special, then it's like Paddy's market. Ballet dancers are the most tiresome. You know, delicate feet in all directions, and gestures like fading butterflies. I'm sure they each have more limbs than anyone else. And last time Ken Russell was here he brought his dog and insisted it appeared on camera with him." He glanced at his clipboard. "Now, how would you like me to introduce you?"

"I really don't mind."

"I mean, I do feel I ought to make some reference to the production you're appearing in and, of course, the fact that the entire family are together."

"Why not? Everyone else has used that platform."

"Now, I know all about your own company and how you feel towards the powers that be. What we've got to remember is that we are trying to present a balanced programme. You know, entertainment for the masses."

"Are you trying to tell me to soft-pedal?"

"Not exactly. However, there has got to be a sort of – well, an easy compromise, if you follow me."

"I think I do. Let's face it, Richard. It's hardly likely that I'm going to be able to say a great deal in twelve minutes."

"I'm afraid we've had to cut back on the time slightly. One of the musical items is a little longer than anticipated. It's impossible to snip a few bars from the middle."

Fiona put down her glass. "Oh, bloody hell! How long am I left with?"

"If we're tight on captions and introductions, I'd say eight, perhaps eight and a half minutes."

Her voice was beginning to rise. "Do you mean to say that I've been dragged all this way for a lousy eight minutes of screen time?"

"Well, it's not to be sneezed at. We had thought of bringing someone else in with you, just to put the other point of view. In the end we decided that it would only fragment what you may have to say."

"What makes you think that cutting it to eight minutes isn't going to bloody-well fragment what I have to say?"

"I can think of at least a dozen people who would be delighted to have the opportunity to present their case in eight minutes of free screen time."

"Wouldn't it make sense to have fewer items but more depth of coverage?" She grabbed angrily at her glass.

"That really isn't my decision. I don't structure the programme. I'm merely the presenter. I do assure you, Fiona, I would dearly love to spend more time on certain subjects, but there, what can I do?" Richard was not a presenter because of his good looks alone, but because he knew how to handle people. If someone got really het up, he would allow them their full head, and then use the anger to draw from them their reasons for the fury.

But the last thing he wanted was for Fiona to get so incensed *before* she appeared that there would be nothing left by the time she went in front of the cameras. He turned to her engagingly. "I ask you, what *can* I do?"

"What a lot of balls you talk. You know as well as I do there's always room for discussion." She leaned back, holding her glass tightly into her lap, looking around the room while speaking. It was impossible for her not to be aware of the glances she was getting. She began to relax and to become curious about what they might be saying of her. Perhaps it was the general ambience, or the number of people, or even the drink, but she was beginning to feel a little nervous. It was just sufficient to get her tingling and to make her alert to her own senses. It was enough to engender the right feeling within herself to be able to give a performance, and she was almost teed-up for her entrance.

"Like another drink?" said Angela, appearing from the midst of the crowd.

"Same again, please."

"I do hope it won't affect the interview," said Richard.

"Hardly likely. I assure you, it takes more than LT's hospitality to affect what I've got to say."

Soon the clock above the drinks table indicated just past ten o'clock. The technicians began to drift away into the studio and Angela took Fiona down to make-up. The make-up girl smiled her welcome and held out a cloth to cover Fiona's blouse. She stood behind Fiona, squinting at her face in the brightly illuminated mirror, covering her ears with her hands in order to see the shape of her face more clearly. It was all a little laborious for this type of programme.

"I've got a small sore spot on my cheek, see if you can cover it." said Fiona imperiously.

The girl looked at the spot indicated and proceeded to apply a little more colour. Finally, she powdered and whipped away the cloth with a well-practised flourish, as though revealing a rabbit at the end of a conjuring trick. "There we are. All finished." She stood to one side, admiring her handiwork. "Just a moment. You've got a little shine just here." She stepped forward once again to add another spot of cover to Fiona's injured cheek. Unfortunately she was a little more heavy-handed than she realised, and in pressing on to the cheek she had applied pressure on the cut area.

"Bloody hell, you're not kneading dough." Fiona jumped back, clutching her face and disturbing the make-up. "Oh, Christ! What a mess."

The poor girl had no idea what she had done wrong and was full of apologies, as Fiona herself rummaged among the make-up sticks until she located the right colour to patch the marks. Angela exchanged a knowing look with the still quivering make-up girl and began to move around impatiently while waiting for Fiona to finish. "As soon as you're ready, Miss Dawlish. We'd better make our way to the studio."

By the time they arrived at studio three, rows of lights had been switched on high above the performance area. They flooded their blurred patterns across the floor. Richard had settled himself into a chrome and leather chair and began to adjust his tie. He then made a minor performance out of shaking the unseen creases from his trousers. He called over the stand-by girl from make-up to ensure that the passage of time hadn't allowed his applied glamour to wear thin, suggesting that additional powder be patted on to his slightly balding forehead. Once this was completed he then turned his attention to the notes on his clipboard, flicking through the sheets and adding a few pencilled instructions to himself as he paused over certain sections. The small red lights on top of the cameras began to wink on and off as they were lined up for the opening shots. Whatever the programme, there was always this moment immediately before transmission when a sudden surge of adrenalin created a sinking feeling in the pit of the stomach. The red light over the door was flashing to indicate silence. Several people were standing by the scattered monitors to watch the final details of the week's news.

The image of the newsreader faded to be superseded by that of a smiling announcer.

"Next on London Weekend we have *The Arts in Action*."

Harpsichord music faded in together with a montage of arts images, eventually giving way to Richard Gardner's face.

"Good evening, ladies and gentlemen. Nice of you to join us. This evening, as always, we hope to bring to you a little of everything interesting to present *The Arts in Action*." More music, more bright lights flashing over theatre canopies showing the titles of current plays in the West End. It all finally settled into the first item which was a filmed insert from the new musical touring the provinces, *The Man Who Came To Dinner*.

Two more items followed, and then there was the commercial break, during which brief respite Fiona was beckoned on to the set. The lights began to flash to indicate the end of the break as camera one winked its red light and faced Richard to present him in close-up.

"I'm sure that most of you will have read something about the unusual production of *King Lear* currently playing at Her Majesty's Theatre in London. I'm equally sure that most of you will have heard, and seen, the name of Fiona Dawlish on your TV screens at home and on the larger cinema screens up and down the country, to say nothing of her many inspired appearances on radio and in the theatre. Tonight, we are delighted that she has been able to join us for this programme. She is known to millions for her many movie roles, for her brilliant playing of the world's classical drama, and more recently for her outspoken opinions on the current state of the British theatre. It is my very great pleasure to introduce to you, Fiona Dawlish."

Fiona smiled her acknowledgment. It was just in time to catch the wide angle of camera two now exclusively directed on to her. Aware of the mark on her face, she was doing her best to keep in profile.

"Thank you, Richard, for that very flattering introduction. You make it sound like a lot of hard work."

"You make it appear so easy. But then, I suppose that's the

art behind the art. A cliché, but also a truism. But we're not here to discuss any of that this evening. There has recently been a vast amount written about the entire Dawlish family, but particularly in relation to yourself and the letter you wrote to a recent edition of *The Guardian*."

A copy of the letter was inserted on to the screen, picking out certain words and phrases as the camera followed the lines from side to side. There was a final dissolve back to both of them in a mid-double shot, before the camera focused on Fiona.

"Perhaps I ought to explain. I know it's all been said before, but it really can't be said too often. In my own humble opinion, far too high a percentage of the Arts Council subsidy is allocated to the great institutions such as the National Theatre, the Royal Shakespeare Company, the Royal Opera House, and so on."

"But they are our showcases. They do present the finest theatre to be found anywhere in the world."

"Have you seen who it is that makes up the bulk of the audiences in these theatres? Vast numbers of tourists. Why the hell should the British taxpayer be saddled with a bill of such enormous proportions simply to subsidise the entertainment of those people?"

Richard glanced at his clipboard. "Actually I do happen to have some figures here. For instance, tourists recently spent over three thousand million pounds in this country. The business of tourism alone employs over one million people. Surely that's justification enough for continuing to encourage them to our shores. We would be very much poorer without them. We need their millions of dollars and yen and francs, and whatever else they care to spend."

"Not if it means that the theatre in the provinces is going to die because it's unable to keep itself solvent."

"Forgive me, Fiona, but you do have a vested interest in airing this particular subject just now. I mean, you're not simply shouting in the wilderness on behalf of the faceless starving theatres up north, are you?"

Fiona had not intended to admit her own interest. "If you're referring to my own company, well, I've presented one before. I'm not afraid to tour and to play to small audiences. The people out there have as much right as anyone else to see the best the British theatre can present. There's no chance of that at the moment because they're being denied the right by the tight fists in Whitehall."

"But your company does have a strong political bias towards the left, doesn't it?"

"You make it sound quite Marxist. It isn't anything of the sort. It's called CHASE, which stands for Community Harmony And Social Education. It's a form of socio-drama or community theatre. I aim to present work specially commissioned and designed to broaden a community point of view. As I see it, there's far too much bureaucratic direction as to what should or shouldn't be done. I think the people of this country ought to be given the opportunity to control more of their own destiny, more of the wealth in this country. The works I intend to present are designed to clarify certain incidents in the past and, hopefully, to give them a relevance for today."

"Is all this part of the reason why you attacked the production in which you're currently appearing?"

"I merely pointed out that it was a commercial venture undertaken with a great deal of the taxpayer's money."

"How have the rest of your family reacted to the onslaught?"

"With dull predictability, of course. I'm out in the cold."

Richard glanced down at his notes. "It has been said that you only engage indifferent performers for your own company. You use them as cyphers merely to get across your own message. Is this a fair accusation?"

"Certainly not. I always engage the very best people I can afford. With more government finance for companies such as mine, there could be infinitely better touring productions playing to wider audiences. For instance, why should the Arts Council invest in revivals of expensive musicals when that can be undertaken by commercial managements?"

"Perhaps because the audience wants them."

"With more down to earth companies like mine, perhaps the general public would be more aware of how they are being bled dry to pay for overseas investments that are only designed to assist the country of origin and bring nothing back. They could be made to realise just how many millions upon millions of pounds are going to support the defence machine of this country.

They would also get to know about the vast sums of money advanced to countries as a way of keeping them quiet about trading activities and the exchange of information for defence and war." Her voice was getting its hard edge back and she began to speak faster, only too well aware that time was not on her side.

"We do seem to be getting off the point. You have said, from time to time, that you were seriously considering giving up the theatre and going into some sort of social service. Have you given any more thought to this recently?"

"Yes, I have. But I still feel I have something worth saying to as many people as I can reach. In my position, that is from any stage that will allow me the honour of filling its time. I have something worth presenting to the general public, something they ought to know. I've done it before, and I'll do it again. But I need money to support my company. I think it is iniquitous that that great tomb on the South Bank should be allowed to vacuum millions of pounds and then spend it on inferior productions, inept new works, and wasteful administration. The building alone costs over one million pounds each year simply to maintain. Let the Arts Council think again. Let it divide its largesse more equally between those more deserving."

The floor manager appeared just to their left out of shot, circling his arms to indicate the wind-up of the interview. He looked rather anxious as he began to make mock throat-cutting gestures and pointed to his watch.

"Thank you, Fiona. I'm afraid that really is all we have time for this evening. May I take this opportunity to wish your little venture every success. I'm sure that if there have been any philanthropists watching out there, your coffers will be filled by tomorrow morning."

Fiona realised that she hadn't covered anywhere near as much ground as she had intended to. It had all happened so quickly. She felt she had been tricked into a fireworks display that hadn't quite materialised into the right patterns.

The red light on camera two was no longer winking at her. The floor manager had now moved over to camera one, continuing to wave his arms even more frantically at Richard. Richard smiled a broad smile straight into millions of living rooms, nodding to Fiona now out of shot. The monitor faded and it was all over.

Fiona remained seated for a second as the blinding lights were slowly shut down. The studio became hushed with just the swish of the camera wheels and the slap of cables being pulled back like the entrails of some huge rotting prehistoric monster. The remainder of the programme consisted of filmed sequences that were controlled from the production box and were already being transmitted.

"That was fine," said Richard.

"Glad you enjoyed it," said Fiona, still smarting from the experience.

"Let's hope you get something in your begging bowl soon. Thank you so much for joining us." He moved away, dodging between the cameras, ducking below a cable that swung out towards him.

Fiona got to her feet, no longer sure whether she had said the right things or whether she had managed to say enough. She saw no point in her hobnobbing with the rest of the team. She knew how they all felt towards her. The light make-up could easily be removed once she got home, and she decided to leave immediately.

Once outside she breathed deeply: for a brief moment her mind went to Mitch, who she was sure must have been watching – but it was only a very brief moment.

16

Once the boys departed an odd surface lightness had enveloped Mitch, creating in Elizabeth a sensation of anxiety. Mitch could so easily undermine the delicate and caring relationship that existed between Robin and Jake. She was of the opinion that the ability to love was a considerable achievement. If it had to be someone of the same sex, so be it; at least it appeared to offer understanding and companionship.

Although Mitch had decided not to watch Fiona that evening, he now felt that her appearance offered a focal point away from the atmosphere that had unexpectedly developed between himself and Elizabeth. She had used her cold, and a fading voice, to collude in the uneasy silence. During the transmission Elizabeth had glanced at Mitch in an effort to penetrate his thoughts, but his looks betrayed nothing.

The daily papers carried their inevitable coverage. The critics and gossip writers appeared to conspire to keep the family before the public. Even this renewed upsurge of media interest failed to dampen Mitch's spirits the following morning. He remained unperturbed by Elizabeth's sustained withdrawal and rose early to prepare breakfast for both of them.

Elizabeth's cold was short-lived, having awoken with the discomfort of the after-effects but a firm determination to return to the theatre that evening.

The weather finally appeared to be brightening. The persistent night's drizzle had left temperatures above freezing point, with most of the slush washed away and a dripping landscape.

"Do you want to meet me for lunch?" said Elizabeth, unexpectedly.

"Might be difficult, my love. I'm seeing Alan at around eleven and I've no idea how long the meeting might last."

"I see." She diligently applied her make-up as though protecting herself from the outside world. Elizabeth knew the psychological value of looking good.

"I phoned him at home from the theatre on Saturday. Once the notices went up I thought I ought to sort out my plans for the future."

"You mean *The Apple Cart*?"

"That's right. It seems he's already spoken with the management and wants to report back to me. You know how it is. Unless I actually go there then things can drift on for ages."

"Yes, I know how it is. Well, I'll see you this evening on stage, if not before." She swung away from the dressing table, her hair pulled well back from her face, her eyes enhanced to bring out the colour, her lips perfectly shaped and her cheekbones accentuated to lift them higher. The crisply cut Chanel suit of knubbly tweed picked up the delicate shades of blue from her silk blouse.

Mitch would have been blind not to be aware of the painstaking effort she had put into getting ready to meet the world. Her cool resolution radiated towards him. This had always been her special way of behaving whenever she was hurt. In spite of the still lingering effects of her weekend cold, Elizabeth had surpassed herself on this particular morning.

"You look good," he said, not quite grudgingly, yet not with total enthusiasm either.

"Yes, I know. I can when I try." She swaggered past him into the dressing room to select a pair of hand-made boots in leather and suede, and finally wrapped herself into a superbly tailored travel-coat. Having flashed a cursory look at herself in the cheval mirror, she brushed past Mitch, throwing him a knowing kiss. "See you when I see you. Bye."

He heard the front door slam, and watched her from the bedroom window as she sauntered down the road. It was not unusual for either of them to leave alone, though usually turning to wave as they went. Today Elizabeth simply pulled back her shoulders and flicked up her coat collar in defiance of his gaze. He watched her for another few seconds as she diminished into the distance, returning to his own preparations, and left the house about half an hour later.

Alan Scott's office was above Regent Street, within easy reach of the other agents and managements. The outer office was dispiriting with its clutch of hopefuls, sitting there waiting to be seen, all eagerly chatting to each other about what they had done and what was on the horizon of "if" and "perhaps" and "maybe", even if most of the work spoken about always seemed to finish up elsewhere. These were the steady stream of agentless performers who went from one office to another like gypsies, ever hopeful of picking up whatever was left after the contract artists had been placed. Though some of them were fortunate enough to be accepted on to the books and placed under personal management contracts, this alone did not signify that they would always be working. It simply meant that an agent would endeavour to place them before anyone else. Nothing was ever certain, least of all work, in the theatre.

There was the obligatory assortment of photographs around the walls, plus the GLC licence that allowed Alan to act as an agent. Long out of date theatrical magazines littered the chairs and rickety table. Two doors led from the reception office: one into Alan's own suite, and the other into that of the junior partner who was responsible for the general run of interviews and good wishes.

As soon as Mitch arrived he was shown into Alan's office – not exactly a splendid example of modern decor, but comfortable. Alan looked upon the theatrical scene entirely as a job of work. He was short and thickset, and his face behind the small moustache and heavily framed glasses was lined with the years of heartburn and worry encouraged by the business he was in. He had a reputation for never making a false promise to anyone, and for refusing to raise hopes above a possible "maybe". Alan's technique was to wait until he could come up trumps, and then to make the artiste feel agreeably surprised whenever a contract was presented for signature. This way ensured fewer disappointments, and there were many who found themselves delighted with the unexpected news of a job.

"Hullo, Mitch. How's Liz? I gather she was off on Saturday."

He shook hands warmly, pulling Mitch towards a comfortable chair.

They spent the next five minutes exchanging pleasantries while coffee and a plate of remarkably plain biscuits were brought in by an office junior, clearly delighted to have been entrusted with providing succour to such a distinguished client.

Eventually Mitch put down his coffee on the edge of the desk. "Well, how far have you got?"

"I'm going to be honest with you, Mitch. They're not so keen for you to have quite so much control."

"Then that's that. I won't do it."

"Shut up and listen. It isn't easy to interest managements in your sort of projects."

"Come on, Alan. I'm not quite that much over the hill."

Alan was feeling uneasy, and he wasn't very clever at covering it up. He was the last person to want to hurt anyone, least of all a client with whom he'd enjoyed a long association, yet there were things that simply had to be said.

"I've spent a great deal of time on the phone, Mitch. A couple of lunch meetings and so on. First of all, you know as well as I do that a big-cast play like *The Apple Cart*, with more than one set, is getting difficult to fund."

"That isn't altogether true. There are still enough people around with a little money who want to dabble." Mitch swilled down some more of the coffee, absently aware of the bitter aftertaste of the chicory in the blend.

"That may be, but the managements still feel they have a moral obligation to protect the investment as much as possible."

"Is that why they look to Broadway for second-hand successes?"

"I don't know why it is, Mitch. I suppose it's all just part of the fashion in things."

Mitch got to his feet, roamed around the office to end staring down on the bustle of Regent Street below. His eyes followed the bright red oblong tops of the London Transport buses and the smaller black shapes of taxis. There were cars weaving between them, and tiny antlike dots of humanity. Everyone seemed to be going somewhere, doing something, being busy, earning a living. He couldn't help but wonder how many of them woke up every few months, or weeks, and had to ask themselves where their next job was coming from? He turned back to Alan who was still sitting patiently waiting for him to make some other comment.

"What *will* they agree to?"

"They're still keen for you to star, and to share artistic control. You can invest if you want to . . ."

"Yes, I bet I can." He could sense there was more to follow. "Anything else?"

"They – they want to appoint another director."

"But that's absolutely bloody ridiculous. I've directed plays before . . ."

"You haven't starred *and* directed before. Had you suggested this ten years ago – it might have been different. If this one is a success, well, maybe it will be different again in a couple of years' time. Right now they'd rather hedge their bets."

"Who have they in mind to direct?"

"Several names have been mentioned."

"Such as?"

"Patrick Garland, Peter Coe, Anthony Page – it depends upon availability."

"Anyone else? I get a feeling you're holding something back."

Alan nervously smoothed his moustache. "There is one other name that's been suggested."

Mitch said nothing.

"They think that Matthew would do a good job."

"Matthew! He might be my son-in-law, but he couldn't direct traffic up a one-way street."

"You're not being fair to him. His work's good. I saw one of his productions at the Kings Head, and another at the Gate. That boy knows what he's doing, Mitch. Lots of bright ideas. He'll bring something fresh to the play. That's what is needed, a different approach. He'll rethink it . . ."

"Since when does Shaw need rethinking? It plays itself."

Alan threw up his hands, making a small gesture of despair as much to comfort Mitch as to indicate the way he was feeling himself. "I know you've set your heart on directing this one. Perhaps it's not such a bad idea to give it a miss. Think about it. You've had a hell of a lot on your mind lately."

Mitch began to drum his fingertips on the back of a chair, sifting his way through a maze of questions. "Listen, I've had a thought. I'm not happy with the arrangement, but I'm prepared to work with any of the other three if it comes to it. But if the final choice is Matthew, what are the chances of me going in as associate director?"

"I don't know how Matthew would feel about that."

"If he's got any sense he'll accept. I can still teach him a thing or two, and he'll finish up with a major credit behind his name."

Alan was a highly experienced agent and knew how to reach a compromise so that no one was left with egg on their face. "All right! All right! Leave it with me. I'll see what I can sort out. It's not going to be easy."

"For Christ's sake, Alan, my name must still mean something above the title. Call it give and take. I don't care what they say. I'm entitled to some consideration. It's not as though I've been in the business five minutes."

"Calm down, Mitch. I'll do my best. Have I ever let you down before? Have I?"

Mitch shook his head slowly. "But don't start now. I couldn't take it. While we're at it, what about casting?"

"No problem. You can be in on that."

"Bruce? Did you contact Bruce?"

"He should be here at any minute. I thought it better for us to get all this out of the way first."

"That's very thoughtful of you, Alan. I appreciate it."

"Listen, Mitch, there's no need to take it quite so personally . . ."

"How else can I take it? It *is* personal. Acting is a bloody personal business."

"Most of you go through a patch like this at some time or other. For the most part it all goes right, then, before you know it, it's suddenly going wrong. That's not to say your ability's in question, or that you've lost the know-how. It's just one of those things. Maybe it would be better if you took some time off first. You know, recharged your batteries, stood back, and assessed what you really want to do."

"All I want to do is get back on top with a thumping great hit."

"You will! You will! Don't worry." He removed his glasses with a circular gesture and began to wipe the lenses.

The junior appeared at the door to announce that Bruce was outside. It was eleven thirty and he had arrived with his usual stopwatch precision. He was somewhat thrown to find his father present.

"I had no idea... Seems a bit silly, all this cloak and dagger nonsense."

"Mitch is contemplating a new production. I thought it would be better to sort out a few of the details before speaking with you."

"Why the secret? Is this the Shaw play?"

"Yes."

"The jungle drums have been on to that one for the past week. You've done it before, very successfully. You ought to be on to a good thing." There was an undisguised note of disdain in his voice. It was almost as though he felt his father ought to have more pride than to attempt to resurrect a past success.

"That's the general idea," said Alan.

"Why call me in?"

"I – I thought you might like to join me."

"Playing what, exactly?"

"There are several interesting roles. You could have your pick."

Bruce shuffled, embarrassed at the position he had been placed in. "Don't you think it's time we all stopped trying to live in each other's pockets? I mean, we've just had mud thrown in our faces. Why leave ourselves open for a second helping?"

"Is that what you honestly think it will be?" said Mitch.

"For Christ's sake, father. You know as well as I do, once those bastards get their knives into you, they take a sadistic delight in twisting them until it hurts."

"And you'd rather not give them the opportunity to twist. Is that it?"

"It isn't that at all. I simply feel that I've reached a point when I've got to find out what I can do. We've appeared together in the past. I've enjoyed being with you. Please, don't feel hurt. Try to see it from my point of view."

"It's going to be a very fine production, Bruce," said Alan.

"How the hell do you know?"

"I know the extent to which the project will be capitalised. It may be projected for a tour, but there's every intention to bring it into town eventually."

"If it doesn't bloody well die on the road first," said Bruce. "Come on, Alan, we both know that most tours are *intended* to come into town. Hope springs eternal, and all that crap. How many actually make it?"

"This one will. Believe me, Bruce, *this one will*." Mitch leaned forward and spoke directly into his son's face, and for the first time Bruce saw there was pleading in his eyes. This wasn't the matinee idol of twenty years ago. This wasn't the great international star. This was his own father, and he was fighting to climb out of the shit.

For a moment he found himself wavering, but it was only a moment. He hated himself as he said, "I hope you're right, Father. I really do, but it will have to happen without me, I'm afraid."

Mitch sat back again, tapping the top of Alan's desk thoughtfully. "First your mother, and now you."

"What do you mean?"

"She's not interested either. It seems as though my evil reputation is really getting about. If my own family are no longer prepared to back me up, maybe I ought to take the hint."

Alan got up from his chair and came around behind Mitch, patting him on the shoulder. "There's no need to take it like that, Mitch. You know there's no malice in your family."

"Caution, perhaps. Self-preservation." He seemed to withdraw into his chair, to be not quite with them. His mind raced back over his countless past successes, recalling the applause and the cheers and the adoration. It all flashed before him as, it is said, does the life of a drowning man going under for the third time. But he wasn't drowning, and he had no intention of going under – now or ever. He pulled himself from the chair, as though shot through with an electric current.

"I'll do it, Alan. I'll do it and prove everyone wrong. It'll be a great tour. We'll pack them in. And we'll bring it into town for a long run. It'll be the longest run that any Shaw play has ever had. I'll bloody well make sure of that. I don't care who the hell doesn't want to join me. I'll get my cast together. My name alone will bring them in. Just you watch me. Just you bloody well watch me."

Alan looked towards the younger man. He could see the expression of puzzlement, of concern at the unexpected outburst.

"I'm sure you're right," said Bruce. "I'm sorry, but I hope you see my point of view."

"Yes, of course. Forgive me, Bruce. I shouldn't have asked you."

"Think nothing more about it," said Bruce.

"Have you got anything else in view?" asked Mitch, now fully composed once more.

"I'm not really sure. The Billy Caxton management have approached me. It sounds interesting."

"I bet it does," said Alan. "He's one of those play-it-for-the-experience merchants. You know, great parts, but always pays the Equity minimum."

"What has he offered you?" asked Mitch.

"*The Caretaker*, *Private Lives*, and *Otherwise Engaged*. The idea is that we play two weeks at each date and split the plays so that all three can be seen in any one week."

"You must be raving mad," said Mitch.

"Perhaps, but I've got to find out what I can do. I know it'll be bloody hard work, but I happen to think it's worth doing."

"When will you know for sure?" asked Alan.

"Within the next week or so. I did tell him to contact you about the contract."

"That must have put him off." They all enjoyed the joke.

Alan was known to be a hard bargainer and to stick out for the very best terms he could possibly obtain for his clients. He was both loved and hated within the profession for exactly the same qualities, depending upon whether you were a buyer or a seller.

"How long will you be on the road?" asked Alan.

"Six to eight months, with an option of another four months tacked on to the end. It rather depends on how the tour works out."

"Sounds like hard work. I wish you every success." Mitch extended his hand to Bruce who accepted it willingly, placing his own spare hand over that of his father's to sandwich it in a firmer grip.

"I hope everything works out, Father. I'm truly sorry not to be able to join you, but I'm sure this will be better for both of us."

"You're right! You're right! Think no more about it." He laughed loudly. It was way over the top, but he had to do it. "There's no shortage of actors. I could go into Alan's outer office right now and cast the play before I leave."

The others joined in the joke, aware that the truth behind the statement wasn't all that funny.

After Bruce had departed Alan turned to Mitch. "Don't take it too seriously. You know he's right. He's got to be allowed to spread his wings on his own. He's got a lot of talent. He'll make it big one day."

"Bigger than me, probably. And he'll stay there. He's a lot more level-headed than I ever was." He turned back to Alan. "But how can we tell? How the hell do any of us ever know what the future's going to bring in this fucking rotten business?"

Alan shrugged his shoulders. The simple questions were always the most difficult to answer. He brought the conversation back to *The Apple Cart*. "Are you going to accept all their terms, Mitch? Not that I want to persuade you one way or the other, but I think you should."

"Yes! Yes! I'll accept. Let's be honest. Do I have any real choice? Either I say yes, or I don't bloody well work. It's as simple as that. Yes, I'll accept. I'll accept. See you around."

No sooner had the door closed than Alan picked up his telephone and dialled a number. "Hullo. Alan here – How are you? – Good. Good. Mitch has just this second left. He wasn't too happy, but he's agreed to accept – We had some words about who's to direct, but I expected that. Anyway, we agreed on a sort of compromise – You can tell him yourself when you feel the time is right. I don't enjoy doing things in this underhand manner, especially with Mitch – If you prepare the contract, I'll see that it's signed before the end of the week – Many thanks. We must meet for lunch some time. Sure. I'll phone you – bye."

He put down the receiver and allowed an escape of breath as though relieved the morning was over.

17

Upon reflection, Fiona decided that she wasn't quite as upset about the interview as she had first imagined. At least she had managed to air her grievance on a national network, and a few of the morning newspapers had carried brief reports about what had been discussed.

"Did I tell you we're closing in two weeks' time?" she said to Andrew over lunch.

"No, but I'm not all that surprised. Anyway, you ought to be pleased."

"Not entirely. I'd rather we saw the run through to the end. At least with that much behind us we could have claimed a success. I don't much care for being associated with flops."

"Who does?"

She was very preoccupied with thoughts about her own preparations but, in spite of this, there was still a small corner of her mind available for other things. "Any more news about your own tour?"

"Oh? You interested?" He was flicking through the *Sun*, devouring the triple nudes on page three, and leaning back with his feet up on a chair. He didn't bother to look up.

"It would be nice to know. More coffee?"

"Yes, ta!" He pushed his beaker towards her, putting a lot of effort into not disturbing himself too much.

"Perhaps it will work out just right for both of us."

"How do you mean?"

"The company are going to be rehearsing here for a while. There will be all sorts of people in and out, coming and going. You don't care much for that, do you?"

"Not much. It's a bit like living on Paddington Station. You going to take on that guy who called here the other day?"

"Do you mean Neil? Neil Hamilton?"

"That's him. You taking him on?"

"I haven't quite made up my mind, not yet. He's certainly very presentable."

"Depends what for. Seemed a bit of a pretty boy, for my taste."

Fiona shifted in her chair and turned over the page of her newspaper. "This really has nothing to do with *your* taste, does it, Andy dear?"

He allowed his feet to drop to the floor with a loud thud and lowered his own newspaper on to his lap. "Tell me, are you auditioning for the boards, or for bed?"

"You've got a nasty mind. It goes with the music you make. A lot of noise but lacking in depth."

"Ha! Bloody, Ha! Don't knock it, doll. There's a bloody big audience out there, just waiting to lap it all up. If your little circus manages to get the attendances I do, you'll be doing bloody well, believe me. While we're on the subject, what the hell makes you so sure that the great British public are sitting on their collective arses waiting for you to bring them messages? Who the hell do you imagine you are? What right do you have to go knocking everything in sight simply because you haven't got a share?"

"I'll get my share. Don't you worry your little empty head about me. I've done it all before, and I'll do it again." For a moment she sounded very like Mitch.

She folded the newspapers into a small pile, and began to clear away the remains of their meal. Andrew stayed seated, watching her, observing the defiant tilt of her head, aware of her dressing gown falling open just enough to reveal her breasts swaying beneath the satin lapels, and then opening even further as she twisted her body. He sat smiling to himself as he recalled some of their past romps, and began to feel randy at the recollection of a few of their more bizarre moments. He knew that he had only to approach her in the right way, to allow his hands to caress her back and smooth their way around to her front and inside her dressing gown, and they would be upstairs before he could say, "poke". He allowed one hand to drop between his legs as he continued to think himself into a state of minor excitement, and he began to feel stirrings at the memories. It had all happened before, so often, and he had enough faith in his own prowess to know he could make it happen again whenever he wanted to. He rose to his feet and moved towards her straight back.

There was a sudden ring at the front doorbell. Fiona dodged neatly below Andrew's outstretched arms and went into the hall, amused at the interruption to his all too clear intentions. On the doorstep was Mitch, looking pale and a little damp from the drizzle that had been falling intermittently for the past hour. Father and daughter remained looking at each other for a moment, seeming to be total strangers. There was an embarrassed silence. Fiona reached up instinctively to pull her dressing gown across her front, tugging on the sash with both hands. She felt trapped within her own home.

"May I come in?" said Mitch.

"Yes, of course. Sorry – it was just that – well – you were the last person I expected to see." She allowed the door to open wider, standing back so that he could pass into the hallway.

"Let me take your wet things." She extended her hands, almost as a gesture of supplication.

The kitchen door banged open as Andrew came thumping out. "Who is it – ?" His voice died away as he caught sight of Mitch.

Mitch looked from one to the other, concerned in case he should have descended at the wrong time. "I – I can always come back later. I'm sorry. I should have phoned first. Thoughtless of me."

"You're not interrupting anything. I slept late this morning and we had a sort of scrap brunch. Andrew's clearing up for me. Aren't you, Andy dear?"

"Yes, sure thing. You carry on. You're not interrupting a thing." He was far from convincing, and he allowed the teacloth to fall across his front in an effort to conceal the evidence of his forward planning.

Fiona showed her father into the living room, clearing away some of Kate's toys from an armchair.

"Messy child. I keep on talking to her about it. You know what kids are like."

"She must be getting quite grown up."

"She likes to think so. She stays at school for lunch."

"I see." He looked around, trying to find something that would make a point of conversation. He was trying desperately to be relaxed and to sound casual, but the simple fact of him being there gave the lie to all that. It had been several years since he last visited Fiona, and he felt oddly isolated within her own home. They had remained on cordial terms, meeting at theatrical functions and following each other's career. They had occasionally appeared together, but the relationship could never be described as warm and loving. It was never one in which confidences could be shared or successes mutually enjoyed.

There was an unexpected sadness about his eyes that Fiona had not noticed before. His cheeks looked cold and pale, and his usually neat hair had been blown about in the wind. She felt a moment of pity, not the warm familial pity one feels for a father, but more that for any living creature who seems to have lost the spark of vitality to keep going.

"Have you – have you had any lunch?"

"All I want, thanks."

"Can I get you a drink, or something hot?"

"Some whisky might be nice."

She knew he only drank at this time of the day when he was feeling really low. She poured out slightly less than she would normally have done and added an additional piece of ice. He held on to the whisky inside his mouth, allowing it to burn into his cold breath.

"That's better."

Fiona lit a cigarette and propped herself in front of the dead fireplace. "What brings you here?"

"I felt I had to come. We seem to get so little time to speak in the theatre." He sipped some more of the whisky.

"I wasn't aware we had all that much to talk about."

"How – how are the plans going for your own company?"

"They're shaping up nicely, thanks."

"Good! Good! I'm glad to hear it."

"Are you?"

"Yes, of course I am. Why do you say it like that?"

"I suppose I'm surprised that you're interested. After all, it's not exactly your type of theatre, is it?"

"No, not exactly. But there's room for all types. The public is a wide audience. They're entitled to have a choice."

"That's exactly what I think." She drew on her cigarette uncomfortably and wished Mitch would say whatever it was he had come to say.

"I – I saw you on the box last night."

"I'm surprised you bothered to watch."

"I was interested."

"And?"

"Quite honestly, I thought you overstated your case. But then, I'm sure you must know exactly what you're doing."

She laughed. "Yes, I think I do. I'm sure you didn't come here to make small talk, father."

"No, you're quite right. I didn't. I – I – " He emptied his glass. "May I have another drink, please?"

Fiona wanted to refuse for his own sake, but she took the glass and refilled it.

"Thank you."

"You still haven't told me why you're here."

He began to rotate the glass between his hands. "I was with my agent this morning. We had a meeting about a new production that I'm – I'm probably going to do."

"Oh, good! I'm delighted for you." Her reaction was genuine, and she was thankful for something about which she could sound enthusiastic.

"Things are not quite settled yet. I wanted to direct as well, but the management have refused. Can't blame them, really, I suppose. It would have been nice, but there, I'm in no position to argue." His concentration was on the bottom of his glass, watching the ice change shape and observing the tiny eddies of water as it mixed with the whisky.

"Why are you telling all this to me?"

"Fiona, I'm asking you not to stir up any more trouble."

"Trouble? A letter in *The Guardian* can hardly be called trouble."

"You know what I mean. I'm not saying that letter alone had

anything to do with the fortunes of *King Lear*, but it was yet another factor. The notices, the weather, you, it's all part of the same thing. I know nothing but acting. It's all I've ever done in my entire life. I need to be allowed to go on."

"You're being just a shade melodramatic. I can understand a management insisting on a separate director. It's never all that easy to do both. I can't understand why you're attaching so much importance to their refusal."

"Because I see it as a beginning. A running downhill until I reach total rejection. I couldn't stand that. I've seen it happen to so many others. I don't want it to happen to me."

She looked down upon his slouched shoulders, and another great wave of pity swept over her.

"It isn't *you* I'm against," she said. "You must know that. I've nothing against you personally. I agreed to do the production to help you. I'm sorry I wasn't able to agree to the tour as well. Anyway, that's not on now."

"Both Liz and Bruce have decided not to join me. They haven't said so, but it's quite obvious they don't wish to be associated with another flop."

"I hardly think that's fair. I know that Liz has been feeling tired. Rumour has it that she's seriously considering calling it a day. Surely you must be aware of that better than anyone else? As for Bruce, he's entitled to make up his own mind. He can't act as a prop to you for ever. He's got to be allowed to get out and do his own thing. After all, he is twenty-eight."

"Don't you understand? With you campaigning as you are, and both of them refusing to join me, it doesn't look all that good from the outside. Please, Fiona, don't push your politics any more. You've had your say. You've made a lot of people sit up and take notice. Now, let it rest for a while. At least – at least until I'm off the ground again."

"I'm sorry, but I've got to do what I feel is right. If it looks as though something may rebound on you personally, then I shall try to avoid doing it. On the other hand, I've got to seize my opportunities when and where I can."

"Yes, I do see that. I do understand." He looked up at her, staring squarely into her face for the first time. "Perhaps I shouldn't have come. I'm sorry. I couldn't see any other way round it. You know, Fiona, when you've been at the top for as long as I have, it isn't easy to accept that the climbing has stopped. To realise suddenly that the only way left is down makes you desperate. I'm not ready for that yet. I happen to think that I've still got something worth offering. I just need one big smash and I'll be back. Just one hit. That's all it will take. It seems so little to want. I know I can do it. I'm not asking for your help. At least, not help in a way that requires any sort of effort from you. I think that what I'm really asking you for comes under the heading of 'masterly inactivity'."

She laughed; it was the same wry laughter that she had developed as a filler for so many pauses in so many plays. It was all beginning to take on such theatrical proportions that she was suddenly finding it difficult to take the parental confrontation seriously. "You make it sound so easy. I suppose it should be simple to stand back and do nothing. I'll try. That's all I can say. It'll be a novel experience for me."

He got to his feet clumsily, draining the glass. "Thank you. That's all I ask. I'd better be going. I knew if I spoke with you, face to face, you'd understand." He leaned forward and kissed her cheek, letting his lips close on to the still scarred section of her face.

It was the single moment of unnerving for Fiona. Mitch's unexpected movement had taken her by surprise. She stifled a gasp and had to fight to hold back her tears. He had demeaned himself by coming to her. He had begged for her aid, and she had sensed what this must have cost him in pride. The realisation was more than she could take, and her own tears began to run down her cheeks. She hated herself for having given way. She tried to push away the tears with the back of her wrist.

"Hell! Bloody, bloody hell! I wish you hadn't come here. No! I'm sorry, I don't mean that. I mean – shit! I don't know what I do mean any more." She pulled on her sash and turned away trying not to let him witness her tears. She still retained sufficient respect for him to want him to leave with some remnants of his dignity intact.

"Thank you for listening. I'll be going now. See you this evening at the theatre."

"Yes, see you this evening." She kept her back towards him while still dabbing at her eyes.

Mitch would dearly liked to have made some physical contact with her again, even to have patted her on the shoulder, but her back was too much like a closed door. The satin of her dressing gown caught the dull light as her small movements made it ripple. There was the sound of a gentle click that signified his departure.

"He's gone then?" Andrew appeared behind her.

She nodded, still watching him disappear into the continuing drizzle, her tears caught in the reflection from the window.

"What's happened? What are you crying for?"

"You couldn't even begin to understand."

"Try me."

"He's an old man, Andy. He's suddenly started to fall apart. I think I've contributed to that."

Andrew crossed towards her with two long strides. "Come off it, doll. He's been going downhill steadily for the past few years. Nothing you or anyone else can do could save him."

"You don't know him. He'll save himself. Just you watch. He'll bounce back simply because he's got to. There's nothing else he can do."

He placed his arms around her and reached up to smooth her tears. His head dropped against her cheek to kiss her face gently. He could feel her arms encircling him and her fingernails digging into his back. She needed him.

"Don't go, Andy. Don't leave me, will you?"

"Would I do a thing like that?" H's hands began to explore her body. "You got anyone coming here this afternoon?"

"No. Not a soul."

"Let's go upstairs. I know just what you need right now."

"You think that's the answer to everything, don't you?"

His hand was inside her dressing gown, fondling, tickling, playing. "Not quite everything, but a hell of a lot of things."

He led her out into the hall and upstairs towards the bed and sat her down in front of him to take off her slippers, first one and then the other. Each time he kissed her toes, allowed his lips to encircle the tips of her toes and felt them wiggle inside his mouth. He reached up and undid the slippery sash, watching the dressing gown fall open to reveal Fiona's smooth body and well-rounded breasts. It pleased him to keep her waiting, as he slowly removed his shirt and unzipped his trousers to stand all but naked in his tightly fitting briefs.

She looked up at him. "You mean bastard. You know what you're doing to me, don't you?"

"Patience, my love. We all have our price. The really good things in life are worth waiting for."

"Bighead!" She reached up and pulled him down beside her. "Tell me I'm being silly. Tell me everything's all right."

"You're being silly. Everything's all right."

"The very last thing I want to do is to hurt him."

"Who?"

"Mitch. I've no grudge against him."

For a moment Andrew's spirits faltered. "Bloody hell! I don't bring you to bed to talk about your fucking father."

"I'm sorry. I – I can't forget the way he looked. So old. So very, very old."

Andrew was no longer listening to her. He kissed her face, and allowed his lips to caress her breasts and then find their way on to her belly and kiss her neat navel. He felt her squirm beneath him. He had succeeded in locking Mitch out of the bedroom – at least for a few minutes.

"Love me, Andy. Love me." She reached up and drew him on to her. It was Andrew she was holding. It was he who was providing the love she so desperately needed to compensate for the hundreds of years she had been alone. It was Andrew who was there caressing her body. But it was still Mitch's face she saw through her closed eyelids.

18

With the slight improvement in the weather came the promise of a return to fuller houses. Once the closure was announced to the general public, long queues began to form at the box office for the remaining performances. A full house inevitably acts as an elixir to any cast, but it had arrived too late to dispel totally the atmosphere of creeping despondency that pervaded backstage.

There was no doubt in anyone's mind that the performance had been smoothed out and modulated to highlight all the finer points in the action that had been so narrowly missed on the opening night. There was a unified sense of achievement on that score, but knowing they were good was a hollow compliment alongside the knowledge that it was too late to save the show. It was a large cast and, for the most part, they would find themselves on the breadline yet again on Saturday week. A few of them would get together to hold a wake and the following Monday would see them back to square one. They would put on their brightest smiles and their neatest clothes and once more begin the dreary rounds of agents' and managers' offices. They would visit the accepted theatrical coffee bars and pubs to pick up whatever gossip they could about pending productions, about imminent auditions, anything at all that vaguely sounded like a hope of work. It was always the same heartbreaking routine and always required the same determined effort.

Maggie had decided to see Mitch before the rise of the curtain that evening. She knew his habits and guessed he would be early. Having obtained his dressing room key she let herself in and turned on a small table-lamp. She decided to sit in the semi-darkness to await his arrival. The glow of illumination from the street outside cast long shadows that picked out details within the room and caught the smoke as it drifted from Maggie's cigarette. Within five minutes of her settling into a wicker chair Mitch pushed open the door and stood looking at her shadowy figure. It was impossible for Maggie not to notice a greyness about his face that she had never seen before. She poured some whisky for him without waiting for the request.

"What's wrong? Can't we even afford the light?" he said.

"I was resting my eyes. It's been a long day and I'm tired."

"I know the feeling," he said, hanging up his damp coat.

"Mitch, are you feeling all right? You look terrible." She handed the half-filled glass to him.

"Fine! Fine! What brings you here?"

"I wanted you to know how sorry I am about the show having to close."

He stood back from her and gave one of his toneless laughs. "I'd have thought you'd be delighted. Cheers!" He raised the glass towards her and downed some of the drink.

"Hardly. I had quite a lot hanging on the success of this production."

Mitch looked across his glass and smiled. "I'd have thought you'd got what you wanted from this production. Obviously Sam's agreed to your terms."

"Not entirely. I'm only on his board for four years. There's an option of another three after that. I'll have to prove that I'm worth keeping on. I can't imagine that he'll willingly agree to take up the option."

"So you sold out. Congratulations." He raised his glass again. His hand was shaking slightly. "It won't be as easy as you think, my love. Sam's nobody's fool. He's charming and outgoing and full of bonhomie. But I warn you he has a reputation for never forgetting anything. He isn't likely to forget that you trapped him into this deal."

"I'm a big girl, Mitch. I can cope. I know this will take away some of my independence, but I'll gain in other areas."

"Good for you." By now the sharp taste of the whisky no longer stung his throat.

"What are *you* going to do?" she asked.

"Does it make any difference to you?"

"I suppose not. I'd like to feel this isn't going to be the end of the road. I'd hoped we could still be – good friends."

"Sure, if that's what you want." He drained the glass and then flicked it into his wastepaper basket. "You know if that were big enough I'd probably jump in beside it."

Maggie was perched on the edge of a small table, looking at him as he slouched deep into an armchair with his legs outstretched and his hands pushed into his trouser pockets. "I've got such ideas, Mitch. There's not enough real *human* drama on TV. I've got several ideas that could well become a winning series. Nostalgia, that's what the public's into. But I'll make damn sure I get a percentage of the action before I part. I'm not going to be put down that easily. Just you watch me. At the end of the four years Sam will be begging me to stay with him." She was burbling on as though Mitch were there solely as a sounding board to reflect her enthusiasm for herself. Maggie had never been any different.

"Got to hand it to you, Maggie. You certainly know how to get what you want."

"I could get some of it for you as well, if you'd let me." For a brief moment she had stopped talking about herself. A new note of seriousness had crept into her voice.

He pulled himself from the depths of his armchair and moved away like a caged animal trying to hide. Maggie followed him, taking hold of his arm and making him turn back towards her.

"I mean it, Mitch. I still care enough about you to want to make it right. Why the hell do you insist on being so bloody stubborn?"

"Because whatever is right for me has got to be bought in my own way from here on in. I'm not in the 'favour' market any more."

"There was a time when you weren't quite so proud. What's happened?"

"I'll tell you what's happened. I've grown up. It's taken a hell of a long time, but I really do think I've finally grown up."

It wasn't easy for Maggie to accept rejection quite as simply as this. It was something she wasn't used to. She had been on her own for a long time. Manipulating, twisting, cudgelling if need be, but always scheming to ensure she got exactly what she wanted, and invariably finishing up successfully. It had cost her a lot throughout the years, not least as a woman. She had never been anyone's fool, and knew exactly what men wanted her for, why they agreed to go to bed with her. She had always managed to play the deck from the bottom up, pulling out the trump cards as they were required. There had been a time when Mitch had thought nothing of spending nights away from home with her to take illicit weekends in Paris or Rome. It wasn't the sort of affair that could easily be forgotten, or one either could pretend had never happened. She knew every part of him intimately, every part that is except what went on inside the very private part of his mind. She had always known there was one section of himself that he clung to and refused to share, but she had never been able to discover what it was. This was the single aspect of Mitch's marriage that she had resented, because she had always been aware of the fact that between him and Elizabeth there was this something extra, something in which she played no part. It was a special dimension that had kept them together throughout all the storms encountered in the professional theatre, and her resentment at being on the outside was monumental. In the end she had reluctantly settled for whatever Mitch would part with of himself and pretended the rest didn't exist.

She went up to Mitch and put her arms around his neck in an effort to draw him towards her. "I think you're being rather silly about this."

He reached up with great purpose and unhooked himself from her grasp. "Silliness is my middle name at the moment. Don't worry about me, Maggie. I've all but got my next shop lined up."

"I've – I've heard something to that effect. I'm delighted for you."

"I hope to sign by the end of this week. I'll let you know when it's all sorted out."

"Nice of you. I hope that whatever it is, it goes well for you. At least let me thank you for helping me to get what I wanted out of Sam. Strange are the uses of adversity. Or whatever the saying is."

"Like the phoenix rising from the ashes – or whatever the saying is."

"You're a great actor, Mitch. A very great actor. I mean that most sincerely." There was an unexpected tenderness in her voice that made him look up at her face. She wasn't expressing pity or sympathy, or any of those trite emotions. Maggie was making a simple statement of fact. She was trying to instil some of Mitch's former self-confidence back into him. He felt all this coming from her and he was touched by the concern. He moved towards her involuntarily and then placed his hands on either side of her face to kiss her. It wasn't a full-blooded kiss, but something much more knowing, something that can only ever pass between two people who had enjoyed a long standing relationship in which most of the words spoken no longer have adequate meaning. Maggie brought up her arms to encircle his neck, clasping her hands behind his head to pull his face closer towards her own.

"I still love you very much. In my own way I still care enough to want to see you back right on top." She kissed him again, but with more desire this time, with greater urgency.

The only thoughts that crossed Mitch's mind were those of the moment, those that related to what was happening to him then and there. After a day of rejections and disappointments, he clung to her, returning the kisses she gave him. He was unable to hear the door as it opened behind him. The dressing room was flooded with light as Elizabeth stood facing them, her hand on the switch.

"Sorry if I'm disturbing anything."

"I was just saying goodbye to Mitch," said Maggie. She sounded like a naughty schoolgirl caught in the act.

"I always prefer to say my goodbyes with the light on. It's so much easier to look the other person straight in the eye," said Elizabeth.

"I've got a dozen things to sort out. I'd better be going." She slipped past Elizabeth, offering her a weak smile.

"What have you been up to today?" said Elizabeth as she ventured further into the room.

"Not much. I saw Alan and agreed to the terms being offered. I'm – I'm not going to direct."

"Does that mean you'll not have artistic control either?" said Elizabeth.

"No, it doesn't. They've agreed to that much. Sorry to disappoint you on that one. It looks as though I'm going to be able to bring in whoever I want."

"I see. Well, I hope it works out for you, Mitch. Does Maggie know about the production?"

"I get a feeling that Maggie knows a hell of a lot more than she's letting on. There's a certain air of unlikely disinterest. I can't put my finger on what it is."

"Maybe she's been secretly signed to play Orinthia."

"Very funny. I'd still like you to play the part."

"No, Mitch. I've had enough. I've already told you. Once we close I shall probably go away for a few days."

"Down to the cottage?"

"No, I feel the need for some sunshine. I want to lie out on hot sand somewhere and let the heat soak into my bones. I'll be going abroad for ten days, maybe a fortnight."

This was something Mitch had not thought about. "I see. Thanks for letting me know."

"I shall be going with Victor."

Had she reached out and hit him, she couldn't have hurt him more than at that precise moment. His expression changed to one of total injury. Elizabeth read all this in his face, but she felt justified in her decision.

"Victor's been asking me to go away with him for some time. I've constantly refused. I would have continued to refuse but for yesterday."

"Yesterday?" He looked puzzled, and cocked his head to one side as though to underline the question.

"You purposely encouraged Jake to visit us. You had no regard for the way I was feeling. But that was the least of it, Mitch. There was very little regard for Robby's feelings either."

"I thought they enjoyed themselves."

"*You* enjoyed yourself, and I imagine Jake did as well. Robin was deeply hurt that you saw fit to spirit Jake away into the privacy of your study. I don't know what went on – "

Mitch extended his hand as though about to offer some protestation but Elizabeth didn't pause long enough. She knew there would only be involved excuses, lies and half-truths, and she had had enough. There was no longer any room in her life for the sort of double standard that had existed between them for so long.

"Please, Mitch, don't. Whatever you have to say isn't important. I've tried to reason with you. I've tried to conceal and to lie and to stand by you. But you seem determined to throw discretion to the four winds. If that's what you really want, fine. Then the time has come for me to follow suit. I'll take my cue from you. I was going to wait until we got home this evening. But seeing you in here with Maggie made me realise that there would be no point in waiting. Let's get everything out in the open, once and for all."

Mitch had that frightened feeling again. This didn't sound like Elizabeth speaking. This wasn't the woman to whom he had been married for all these years. The woman who professed to love him and to protect him, not only from the outside world, but from himself. None of it sounded real to his ears.

"What are you saying, Liz?" He asked the question, almost afraid to hear the answer.

"I'm saying I have to start to live for myself. Not for you. Not for the children. Not even for *us* any longer, but for *myself*. I can't be stifled any more. I've got to be allowed to breathe and to enjoy whatever there is left."

It was all sounding like a well-rehearsed speech in a rather bad play. Stiff upper lip and terribly thirties except that her lips were quivering with every word she spoke.

"If you've really made up your mind, then there's nothing for me to say. I know how justified your remarks are. I suppose I'm lucky to have had you standing by me for so long."

It was the sort of situation where the leading actor ought to make a final gesture and leave the stage, but life isn't ever quite like that. The final gesture is never quite final enough, and the advent of a subsidiary character in the form of Mrs Grace was all that was required to introduce the anticlimax.

"Nice and early tonight you are! 'Ullo, Mrs Dawlish, didn't see you 'iding behind the door there. 'Ow's your cold?"

"Almost gone, thank you, Mrs Grace. Nothing serious."

"Good! Glad to 'ear it. Must say you don't look too bright, Mr Dawlish. Mind you don't go catching your wife's cold." She began to potter about, spreading out the small bits of costumes, checking hems and inspecting fastenings all over again.

"I'd better leave you to get ready," said Elizabeth quite softly as she left the room.

Mitch switched on the lights around his mirror. He sat down and leaned back in his chair to look at himself. He tried to recollect what he would have seen there ten years ago, or even five. The clean-cut features and the square jaw were heavier. His eyes were puffed and his hair, previously never out of place, was now over his ears and criss-crossed on to his forehead. His ability was in doubt, his personal relationships were wavering, and now his physical appearance seemed to be echoing the last lie about his entire existence.

"Here we are. This ought to warm your cockles." Mrs Grace was holding out a small glass of whisky. It was part of her regular routine. It gave Mitch the additional fortification he needed to get through the first part of the evening. A second glass usually backed up the second act and added to his willpower. He had always needed something to support him until he actually arrived on stage and delivered his first lines. There was a time when he and Elizabeth had laughed about this little prop of his, but the laughter had ceased a long time ago.

It was a different performance that evening. The tiredness was not simulated, and the age projected reflected the way he was feeling. The bitterness with which he confronted Fiona and Elizabeth was more fact than fiction. The differences did not escape the rest of the cast, and they simply tried to meet the changes of nuance as they arose. At the final curtain the applause, intermingled with some cheers and bravos, tended to tighten the family group as they swayed down towards the front of the stage to take their collective bow.

Behind the closed curtains the usual hasty replacement of props and mobile scenery took place before lights faded into the deadness of a lifeless stage, leaving behind the smell of heat and glue and stale air and make-up.

As they made their way upstairs Mitch called to Robin, "I'd like a word with you. See me before you leave."

Robin waved his acknowledgment from the top of the stairs as he turned right into his dressing room. He was still smarting from yesterday's experience. He hated the way he had all but fallen on his mother's neck and pleaded for help. He was so certain that he had learnt how to deal with his own problems and shortcomings. Yet without warning there had been this rush of helplessness. The summons to see his father after the show now filled him with unease as he returned to his dressing room.

"Father wants to see me. Did I go wrong during the performance?"

"Not nearly as much as he did," said Bruce. "I don't know what he was thinking about, but for a great deal of the time it certainly wasn't the play."

"I thought he was a bit off," said Robin, scraping his grease paint on to a soft tissue.

"I don't think he's feeling too well. I saw him this morning, he looked terrible then."

"Oh, why did you see him? Is he giving us all the once over in turn?"

"He asked me to go into his next production. I refused."

Robin stopped cleaning off and looked at Bruce in surprise. "Bloody hell, that must have rocked him back a bit. I say, you don't suppose he's going to invite me to join him, do you?"

"I wouldn't know. It's none of my business. Unless he asks you to play Orinthia. You've certainly got the height."

"Very funny," said Robin, throwing a piece of thick sticky cotton wool at Bruce.

By the time he had finished his ablutions and knocked on Mitch's dressing room door, Mrs Grace had completed her duties and departed for the evening.

"Hullo, Robby. Come in and shut the door." Mitch was acting a part again. It was somewhere between that of fading actor-manager and paterfamilias. Unfortunately he lacked the weight to carry off either with total conviction and found himself performing against type. It had always been a bone of contention between him and Elizabeth that, when the children were smaller, the main part of their upbringing had been left to her. For Mitch suddenly to assume a long forsaken role placed him at a considerable disadvantage through lack of familiarity with the script.

It had been a long time since Robin last found himself in quite this situation, sitting opposite his father, waiting to be advised or told something he wasn't sure he wished to hear. He sat on the edge of a bentwood chair, his feet spread wide, leaning forward with his hands lightly clenched across his knees. His face was openly expectant without being quite sure what he ought to expect.

"Has Jake told you anything about my plans?"

"Not in any great detail. He simply said he might be doing a play with you."

"Well, I hope to sign the contract some time this week. I'm – er – I'm not going to direct after all. I decided that it would put too much of a strain on my attentions. Better to concentrate on one aspect only, and do it well. That's worth remembering."

"Yes, I'm sure you're right," said Robin.

"However, I will have some say in the choice of a designer and I'm going to recommend Jake."

Robin said nothing for a moment. It was what he had expected, but secretly hoped wouldn't materialise. If Jake got involved with his father's production it would mean him joining the tour for a while, certainly until everything was run in. They could well be apart for a month or more, and he didn't take kindly to that idea.

"I wanted to tell you this myself. I thought you might like to know the capacity in which he'll be employed. I know how much you – how much you care for him. And he for you. What are your own immediate plans, Robby?"

"Haven't got any, really. There's been some talk of a company going to New York with a production of *Valmouth*, but I believe there's an objection from American Equity about taking over a completely British cast. Anyway, I'm not too sure I really want to go. You know what I mean? All that camping about."

"Sounds as though it could be a lot of fun. I'm sure you'd enjoy it." Mitch was trying not to sound over-enthusiastic in case Robin might feel he was trying to get rid of him.

"I think I'd miss Jake too much. There was an offer for him to work over there as well, but he's tended to let it hang fire. He had a feeling there would be something over here. I suppose this is what he was thinking of."

"Could be. Would you be happier working together with him?"

"Yes, I certainly would."

"Well, I'm going to have some say in casting. I can't promise anything, mind, because I'm not actually directing. But I'll see what I can do. How's that?"

Robin leapt to his feet, animated for the first time since he stepped into the room. He slapped his father across the shoulders. "That's fantastic. I'd be so grateful if you could manage that for me. Thanks, Father. That really is great. Fantastic!" He kept repeating the word over and over again.

Mitchell couldn't help but wonder whether he had oversold the case. He hadn't been through the cast requirements in any detail. He had merely thought of this as a way of keeping the boy happy. Now he began to wonder whether the idea was such a good one after all.

"Jake will be tickled when I tell him," said Robin.

"I'm sure he will. I'd like you both to be happy together. Do give him my very warmest regards, won't you Robby?" He turned and smiled at his son, a wide smile of beneficence. He looked better than he had looked all day.

19

The first public indication of the merger came through the gossip columns of the *Daily Express* and the *Daily Mail*. Both headlined the success behind the success, and each conjectured reasons for the link-up. The financial pages of *The Guardian* picked up something about the nuts and bolts of the deal, indicating hard bargaining with Sam while setting out their own theories about motivation. Declining record sales were mentioned, together with the state of the British theatre and the general lack of investment money on all fronts. Even the *Financial Times* had its share of column inches spread across its puce pages. With its usual air of authority on all matters industrial it gave the main reason for falling record sales as complacency about talent.

There were also all sorts of prophecies as to what difference the enlarged conglomerate would make to the British entertainment industry. Fiona lost no time in letting it be known that she was totally against this sort of monopoly within the industry. For her, it spelled an even larger circle from which she would be excluded. But there was no doubt about it, most of the shows produced were concerned with pure entertainment value and box office returns, often catering to the lowest common denominator. It was all pap, mush, and revivals, not what Fiona wanted the theatre to be, and it certainly wasn't what her own company was about. Fiona had finally managed to assemble her small company and there had been a couple of meetings to sort out a rehearsal schedule. Their contracts were as much in default of alternative offers as because they desperately wanted to work with her.

Mitch's contract was ready by the middle of the penultimate

week of the *Lear* production. Alan Scott's technique was to request everything he wanted and then settle for whatever he could get. In this case the settlement wasn't all that bad. Mitch was to be given top billing, together with a handsome weekly basic salary, plus a percentage of the box office over a certain sum. Once full production costs had been recouped and the break-even point passed, the percentage was to be increased.

Matthew was confirmed as the director. At first, although flattered by the offer, he had demurred at the play, seeing it as the waste of a good theatre. He would have preferred something with a bit more bite to it for his West End debut. When told that Mitch would be associate director he had been ready to turn the offer down flat. Compromise was not his way. It was Susanna who had prevailed upon Matthew to accept, and to realise that he and Mitch could play to each other's strengths. Jake had been settled upon as designer and it was already agreed that Mitch would be allowed a say in casting. In some respects the terms had been agreed with remarkably little opposition.

During those final two weeks everyone was busy making whatever plans they could towards shoring up their own future. It was always like this in any West End production regardless of the length of the run. In the initial stages everyone lived in everyone else's pocket. The long hours of rehearsal threw unlikely personalities into close proximity. Whenever they weren't actually on stage, being put through their paces, they would be huddled in corners finding out about each other. The conversations would be guarded at first, but then slowly more revealing as they approached costume fitting time and stripping off in front of each other. It was this sort of creeping intimacy that helped to mould a company together almost as much as the business of appearing on stage. There is no period of settling in. In the theatre everyone finds themselves in the deep end together, and it is sink or swim en masse.

By the time the end of a run is in sight, the tension lessens and everyone looks beyond the last performance to whatever may lie ahead – if anything. Some would hype-up every whisper of work to make those about them think all would be well. Others tended not to count on anything until they had a contract in their hands. Having been in a West End production tended to spoil actors. They felt they ought to remain in London and only accept similar work, but the cold fact was that similar work was not always available.

It was with this in mind that Bruce had decided to accept the three-play contract. Although there had been nothing firmer than a suggestion of him being engaged, he had assumed this would be followed through, so as he had still heard nothing, he called his agent.

"Hullo, Alan. Bruce Dawlish here. Thought I'd check about the Caxton offer. What news?"

"He's been bloody nigh on impossible to track down. I've been trying to contact him every day for the past week. He's one of those characters who enjoys keeping people on the end of a piece of string. Builds up his own sense of importance."

"Have you managed to speak with him at all?"

"I made contact last night. In fact, I was just about to call you."

In Bruce's experience this was usually the line that preceded something you didn't wish to hear. "Well, tell me the worst."

"I'm afraid he's cast someone else. Nothing I could do. He made all sorts of feeble excuses for not letting me know sooner."

It was difficult for Bruce to conceal his disappointment. "What reason did he give? He must have given a reason?"

"He told me they finally decided that they needed someone better known. He's got someone who's recently done a successful TV series. You know what it's like, Bruce. The TV personality means a bloody sight more to the provincial box office than real ability."

"Then why the hell don't you get me a TV series? You're always saying how good I am. You've told me a dozen times that I'm right for the bloody square-eyed monster. Well, for Christ's sake, Alan! I'm on the breadline again in a few days' time. I need some money."

"Leave it to me. There are several things going on at the moment. There's a new production of *The School for Scandal* about to be cast. I've already got out some feelers for you. I was thinking of Charles Surface."

"More bloody costume. I'm sick and tired of boots and breeches. Isn't there anything modern on the horizon?" Bruce knew he was being unreasonable, but to have been approached direct and had his hopes built up, only to be dropped out of hand, left a nasty taste of rejection.

"Sorry, Bruce. The number of interesting new plays are few and far between. You know what they're all after these days. A cast of two and a single tatty set. If they could manage it with one and in drapes, they'd settle for that. Leave it to me. I'll do whatever I can."

"Yes, I'm sure you will. Sorry." He lowered the receiver and sat looking into the middle distance.

Tracy came out from the bedroom. "I'm sorry, love. I couldn't help but overhear. Had you really set your heart on that one?"

"Not exactly. It was all that was being offered. It's when I get to this sort of situation that I ask myself what it's all about. It's all so – so ephemeral, so bloody pointless."

"You're not to get depressed. I won't have it. And don't start the self-knocking bit either. It's got nothing to do with your ability."

"I've been thinking a lot lately. You know I was offered a teaching job some time ago."

"We discussed that and decided against it, remember?"

"I wouldn't have to take it up until the beginning of the next academic year. Suppose I said yes, just as a long stop?"

"No! You're far too good to waste your talent that way. Anyway, you'd be bored out of your tiny mind. Most of the girls use the place as a finishing school, and most of the fellas tend to drop out after the first few years. It's such a waste. Don't do it, Bruce. Please, don't do it." She leaned over and kissed the top of his head, allowing her cheek to rest there for a few seconds.

"It's not fair on you. We'll never be able to get married and have a place of our own."

"I'm not complaining, am I?"

"I wish you would. It might help me to make up my mind. If I thought I could manage to make a decent living out of this rotten business, I'd have no second thoughts at all. You must know that." He turned to her. They had been through this so many times in the past. Whenever an engagement had come to an end, or whenever there had been an unsuccessful audition, or whenever a promise had not been fulfilled. The entire profession was full to busting with these moments, and an individual had to be totally insensitive not to stop and question, not to wonder if he had what it took to remain a part of the rat race. Every time the question came up it was getting increasingly difficult to make the right choice.

"Have you got a cigarette?"

"Help yourself." She threw her handbag across the room and it landed at his feet, falling open and spilling the contents. "Oh, hell! Just a minute, I'll – " But it was too late to stop him collecting together the assortment of things that had fallen out.

Bruce picked up her lipstick, her comb, and a small container of artificial sweeteners, some coins, a few safety-pins, a bashed packet of cigarettes and a crumpled letter. He turned it over and then back again to reread the few words.

"How long have you had this?"

"Two days. I was going to tell you, but you've been so distracted lately."

"When is it due?"

"About the end of October. I'm sorry, Bruce. I don't know how it happened. I've always tried to be so careful." Tracy turned away, her hand covering her mouth to stifle her small sobs. "I did a test myself and thought I might have got it wrong. You know how stupid I am about that sort of thing. So I thought I'd better have it done properly before saying anything to you." She took the letter from him and looked at it herself. The heading "Pregnancy Advisory Service" would have been impossible to miss.

"I wasn't aware that I've become all that impossible to talk to. After all, it's as much my baby as yours."

"I can arrange for an abortion if you want me to." She pulled the words from herself, but the manner of their delivery conveyed the opposite meaning.

"Do you want to have the baby?"

"I don't know, Bruce. I – I honestly don't know."

He stood up and went to her side, making her sit down and then kneeling in front of her to raise her face, streaked and tear-stained. He kissed her and held back his head to look at her again, still trying to search out what she really wanted to say.

"Maybe the teaching job isn't such a bad idea after all," he said.

Tracy burst into tears all over again. "I'm not going to let you throw away your career because of this. It would be too much for any child to have to carry around. You'd resent it, Bruce. I know you would. You've got to make your decision in isolation. We'll have the baby, and we'll manage. People always do. Somehow they manage." She was calmer now, blowing her nose and pushing back her hair. There was a beautiful expression on her face. It was a warm loving compatibility that spoke all she was feeling, all that Bruce wished to know.

Elizabeth had confirmed with Victor that they would leave on the Monday after the final performance. She knew her own weaknesses and was only too aware that if she delayed it would take very little pleading from Mitch for her to change her mind. She knew how much he needed her when he was about to embark upon a new production. His need would be even greater on this occasion because of the failure of *King Lear*. Yet if it hadn't been this production, it would have been something else. There was always something else, there always had been. This was the pattern of their lives, and the lives of all who set themselves in the public eye, asking for praise and often receiving nothing but abuse.

Victor had lost no time in reserving two tickets on a plane to North Africa. He had promised Elizabeth sunshine far away from the cold and the grey skies of London. She had protested that it was just a little too far away, that it was too abroad, but he had insisted.

No decision had been made beyond the two weeks planned as an escape. Elizabeth had no other theatrical commitments. She had refused parts that had been offered as soon as it was realised that she would be available. The theatre had taken a great deal from her over the past few decades and she felt the time had come to pull a little back. She was going to do and be what she wanted, just as she had tried to explain to Mitch, but she doubted whether he really understood what she meant. For Mitch there was only one way of life, his own, and she felt it was getting to be impossible for her to share this with him any longer.

Robin had little choice but to accept his father's offer. Although he was part of the Dawlish legend, he had no illusions about his relative position. His talent was small, and his range limited. His notices had seldom been more than polite. Nothing had been said about what he would play. His contract simply stated "to play as cast". This usually meant doubling in all sorts of tiny ways and perhaps understudying if the opportunity arose, but he had sunk his pride and accepted.

The only member of the family who was really doing what she wanted was Susanna. She had been offered a secondary role in a film to be shot in Italy in the spring. It was a love story about a holiday romance between a young crippled girl and a married man with three children. Somebody had called it a good clean cry. Susanna would not be required until the end of May and so this gave her enough time to sit back and accept an odd television engagement if such should come in, or even do nothing for a while.

She was glad she had managed to talk Matthew round into working with Mitch. It wasn't exactly emotional blackmail, but she did want another success for her father, and with Matthew's involvement she believed this could be achieved. She knew him to possess sufficient strength to refuse to be pushed into a wrong artistic decision by her father. At the same time she had enough faith in Mitch's sensibilities not to try to force his ideas to the detriment of the production.

"A few more performances and *Lear* will be behind you. I should think you'll be glad to see the back of it." It was Thursday morning and Mitch had arrived at Alan's office to sign the new contract.

"It's taught me one or two lessons, Alan. Not least of which is what I can't do."

"I'll take a bet with you now, Mitch. You'll have another stab at it within a few years. After all, Sir John's played it three times, or is it four? It's a great part and worth taking a second bite at."

"I'm not Sir John. For that matter, I'm not even Sir Mitchell, either." They both laughed, but there was the perennial question-mark behind Mitch's quip. He had toured and appeared on Broadway. He had encouraged new performers and new writers. He promoted the finest in British theatre throughout the world, and yet he remained out in the cold as far as official recognition was concerned. There had been rumours that his time would come. It had been pointed out to him that quite a number of eminent people had been kept waiting a hell of a long time before honours had been piled upon their stooped shoulders. Ben Travers had been mentioned as a case in point, and Charles Chaplin another. For Mitch these comparisons meant very little. He had always been impatient, not only with those who were less efficient than himself, but with his own shortcomings as well. He hated to take too long about getting things right, or about getting his priorities in the correct order. It was because of this that he had wanted to get the contract signed and the formalities out of the way as soon as possible. He would liked to have had more information about the management before signing, but as Alan had assured him that everything was in order he had decided to go ahead.

He leaned over the contract, muttering the clauses through to himself. The words "Shaftesbury Productions" were typed near the top. Thereinafter "The Management".

"You know, Alan, Shaftesbury Productions is ringing bells at the back of my mind."

"Just another company. The West End's full of them. You probably talk about Shaftesbury Avenue a dozen times a day."

"You really think that's it? I've got a feeling it's something else." He put down his pen, trying to think his way through the haze of words that kept eluding his memory. Brightly lit canopies flashed across his mind. Play titles with which he had been associated jostled for space. The more he tried to clear his mind, the more jumbled everything became.

"No good, I can't work it out. It'll probably come to me later. There's not much I forget, Alan, you know that." He returned to the finely printed sheet of paper and scribbled his impressive signature. A very bold M accompanied by several looped uprights that took care of the christian name, and an exaggerated

D with most of the surname cutting across the half-circle. The formalities were concluded. Mitch had committed himself to the production.

The intercom sounded. Alan answered the call. "Yes?" There was an indistinct burble from the instrument. "Yes, by all means." He smiled towards Mitch, almost self-congratulatory, but warm and friendly and happy that the contract had been signed.

The door opened to admit the junior who announced, "Miss Roxborough."

Mitch lifted himself from his chair and swung round to meet Maggie as she sauntered into the office looking for all the world as though she had just swallowed the cream.

"Shaftesbury Productions! Maggie, you bitch!"

Alan was on his feet within seconds and holding on to him. "Let me explain, Mitch."

"You knew all along. You were in on this. You bastard. You stinking shit!"

"Come on, Mitch. Surely it's not quite as bad as that?" Maggie said.

"I'd rather busk in Leicester Square than tie myself to you again."

"I'm afraid that will have to wait for a while. You've signed, Mitch."

"Maggie did it for *you*. She made me promise not to tell anyone it was her company. She knew you would never agree. You need this production, Mitch. Get this one right and you're out there in front again. Believe me, I did try to get you an alternative shop."

The situation was one with which Alan would much rather not have been associated, but he had acted in good faith. He, above all others, had come to accept the impossibility of obtaining the right shop for Mitch's next venture, and the last thing he wanted was for this giant of the theatre to find himself cast upon the rocks of failure after all this time.

Mitch felt completely trapped. Had he been able to reach out and rip up the contract, he'd have done so, but the paper was in Alan's hand and clasped very securely.

"Anyway, the company isn't mine any longer. Sam's taken over everything so you're really in his stable now. I'll have very little to do with the planning of the operation. I – I do care, Mitch. I always have."

"This is really going to be some party. You've both excelled yourselves this time."

The smugness had left her and she was no longer smiling with her unique brand of self-satisfaction. She was trying to make him see reason and to accept that she had acted in his best interests. There had always been a hardness in her approach, but now it was being held at bay. For once in her life, certainly for the first time in years, she was giving as much of herself as was possible. Once the rot was allowed to set in it could take many years before the process was reversed, and this production was designed as a checking operation.

Mitch removed himself from them, crossing to pour a large glass of whisky. Nothing was said, although Maggie would have liked to stop him. She would like to have been able to take the glass from his hand and throw it on to the floor. Alan motioned her to leave well alone and allow Mitch to take the drink. The only sounds were the clickety-click of typewriters in the outer office and the gurgle of liquid being poured from the bottle. The click of glass upon glass was followed by several quick gulps as Mitchell downed his drink, still holding his back to them.

"God! But I hope you're right. I sincerely hope you're fucking right." He hurled the glass across the room. There was a resounding crash as it smashed through a glass-fronted cupboard. Fine splinters shattered in all directions to compose a sound of discordant temple bells.

Maggie covered her face instinctively and backed away, at the same time colliding with Alan who put his arms around her shoulders. She was frightened. She hated violence of any sort, and however verbally violent she could be in her dealings with people it never went further than that.

"You make me want to vomit – both of you!" He banged out of the office, leaving the two of them looking after him as he wiped a torrent of papers from the desk in the outer office while storming into the corridor beyond.

20

For the remainder of that week Mitch kept himself very much apart. He had a sense of having been whipped in public. Exposed as requiring assistance to get up off his knees and rejoin the human race again.

Maggie had made several, albeit half-hearted, attempts to dispel his sense of being used by her, but he refused to meet her, or even to speak with her at remove. His reaction hurt her but there had never been any suggestion of offering to cancel the contract – that was not her way. In any case, the moment it was signed it had passed into the domain of IEM as part of the assets she was selling off. As far as she was concerned, the subterfuge and the secrecy had been insisted upon out of her genuine concern for Mitch's career. She saw it as her way of saying a simple thank you for their years together. It was her final gesture of gratitude.

Throughout the whole of that penultimate week Jeremy Woods had sat in the audience, making copious notes about the production in readiness for the filming. He had decided to use three cameras and to run them simultaneously in order to cover every angle so that he could select whichever shots he wanted. There would be far more film than could be used, but it would allow complete freedom to edit and splice as required. Jeremy was a skilled director and now enjoying the challenge of the smaller screen. He achieved his results by careful planning which resulted in economical budgeting. He never forced his interpretative ideas upon a cast, but always allowed them to arrive at their own conclusions by whatever personal devices they decided upon. In the present situation, he saw little purpose in attempting to change things within a production that had already worked its way through difficulties and settled into a smoothly flowing presentation.

The company had a very early call first thing on Sunday morning, arriving to discover that the cameras had been set up overnight and the additional lighting already hoisted on to platforms spread across the front rows of the stalls. A mobile intercom system linked the camera crews with Jeremy and the entire operation was ready to roll from the moment they appeared on stage.

It was an odd sensation to perform in a theatre on a Sunday morning. The cast went about their business in unusually hushed tones, aware of the echoes that bounced back from the darkened auditorium, aware that once their performance was on film there was no going back. One or two of the opening sequences had to be reshot due to poor sound levels or unexpected noises that crept in from the street. On another occasion there was trouble with the film catching as it went through the gate of camera two.

It was a day in which everyone appeared to play more on technique than emotion. The camera would expose anything too exaggerated. Everything had to be played in a low key: small and controlled, as though placed under the wrong end of a telescope to appear in miniature. Whatever alchemy was operating between them during that day, it had worked to perfection.

They finally finished at around eight thirty that evening, having gone into overtime. But they had managed to get the entire first act into the can, plus a small section of the opening sequence of the second act.

"That's about it," called Jeremy. "Wrap it up. Thank you everyone. You've all been absolutely marvellous. Get a good night's sleep and save your guns for next Sunday. I'll try and make it as easy as possible for you all. God bless."

The auxiliary lighting was systematically doused. Technicians wasted no time in dismantling the platforms, pulling out the cameras, and trailing miles of cable back into the vans in Charles II Street.

The final week seemed to gather together the best of all the performances that had taken place throughout the previous five weeks. They played to packed houses. The "House Full" signs were displayed in prominent positions on the pavement outside the theatre, with standing room being willingly accepted by those devotees not wishing to be disappointed.

Mitch's performance had undergone a subtle metamorphosis from his original conception of the role as played on opening night. The underlying pathos had been submerged and replaced by the anger of abused age. Being able to borrow from his innermost emotions had afforded his playing considerably greater strength. His volume of unqualified rage, his sense of betrayal and his degeneration into madness were all expressed with a terrifying degree of truth that outdid anything the backstage pyrotechnics could manufacture. Those who were fortunate enough to witness these few wondrous performances knew they had been present at a remarkable theatrical achievement.

The London theatrical scene was soon abuzz with the minor miracle that was taking place at Her Majesty's Theatre and those amongst Mitch's peers who were able to take in a performance did so. Throughout that last week there was an endless procession of the famous and the would-be famous backstage to offer their congratulations. In some small way this helped to re-establish his confidence in his own ability. He knew he had managed to master the unmasterable, yet he remained saddened at the way it had come about.

When the curtain fell on the final performance on the last Saturday night, there followed a scene of fantastic enthusiasm. The audience went wild, recalling Mitch for countless solo calls. The entire house rose to its feet, cheering and shouting and begging him to make a speech. This was something he hadn't done for years and for which he was totally unprepared. Even after the house lights were raised, the audience refused to move. It was an ovation one occasionally hears reserved for a Diva in an opera house.

Behind the closed curtains the cast caught the still mounting excitement.

"Mitch, you'd better do something," said Elizabeth, above the clamouring that came at them through the heavy curtains.

"I can't. I don't want to. There's nothing to say."

"Why not just thank you?" Elizabeth pressed his arm.

Mitch looked around at the cast. He knew there would be nothing left for most of them by Monday. All the faces were turned towards him, asking him to step forward, asking him to acknowledge and accept what they all agreed was rightly his. It wasn't until Ernest started to applaud alongside him that the rest of the cast joined in. They were then followed by the stage staff who slowly edged on from the wings. It was a precious moment.

Mitch had to agree. The house lights were reduced to half as the curtain swished through the wave of sound still drumming towards the proscenium arch. Mitch took a few short steps forward, raising both hands for silence. There was a tattoo of seats thumping back into place. The immediate silence was as stunning as the recent sound.

"Ladies and gentlemen, you have made this into a very special evening for me. An evening I have always dreamed about, yet never dared hope would ever be my privilege to experience. There are a great number of people I have to thank for this. Not least of whom are those you see sharing this stage with me. Their participation is no less than mine. Perhaps it wasn't quite right at the beginning, but we have since tried to rectify that."

"And succeeded," cried a voice from the back of the stalls. This was joined by shouts of "Hear, hear!" from various parts of the house and another round of applause.

"There comes a time in every actor's life when he feels there is nothing more he has to give, nothing more worth striving for. I have sometimes thought, during the recent past, that I had reached that point. I know there are some critics who would endorse that opinion. Your kindness and your generosity and your understanding have all gone to prove to me that it is you, the paying customers, who will always be the final arbiters. Without you out front there would be little point in us being up here. A theatre without an audience is like a bed without lovers. The two are indivisible. As long as you are there, I shall remain here, as ever your obedient servant. And now,

'As you from crimes would pardon'd be,
Let your indulgence set me free.'

God bless you all. Thank you and good night."

He bowed very low to the audience and turned to repeat the bow to the massed cast behind him. The audience had been tamed. They remained quite still. Then there was renewed cheering as the curtain slowly fell for the last time.

"Well done, Mitch. A bloody marvellous speech. Wolfit would have been proud of you, and believe me, *there* was someone who really knew how to milk an audience," said Ernest, ever one to put his foot in it.

Susanna was at her father's side, kissing him, tears of joy running down her face. Elizabeth followed with her own special brand of congratulations. Whatever else stood between them, or whatever developed in the future, they had shared this evening of Mitch's greatest triumph.

By the time the last well-wisher had finally left his dressing room all Mitch could do was to turn off most of the lights and slump back into his chair. He let his head fall forward into his hands and began to weep. The past few weeks had taken far more from him than even he realised. The sheer strain of trial and error to get the part right: the newspaper attacks, the abuse, and his own efforts to force himself to go on. He had a sense of being drained mentally and physically, and suddenly he felt he was falling apart. His head ached and his body felt unable to support him. He had pains across his shoulders and in the small of his back, and he was weary right through to his middle, but he knew, positively knew, that he had triumphed, and no bastard critic could ever take that away from him.

Elizabeth had come in unnoticed and remained standing behind him without saying a word. She wanted to reach out and comfort him. She wanted to say something, anything at all that would let him know she was there, but the right words eluded her. There had been so many words, so many moments of compassion, but this felt different. It felt more important. It required the sort of unspoken comfort that can only exist within a certain type of close relationship, and she no longer felt this applied to them. She made a small movement towards him, still wanting to offer him whatever comfort she could, but it just wasn't possible. Elizabeth turned as silently as she had entered, and left without making contact, full of guilt, full of silent sorrow.

The following day came as an anticlimax. Last night had been a mixture of sadness and high jubilation. All that was now required of them was a routine performance of half a play, but this involved diving cold into the high point of emotion, continuing in a rising crescendo, and remaining at that pitch for the entire day. They were tired and listless.

The eye-gouging scene had to be reshot because something went wrong with the lighting and because when viewed through the monitor it came across as being a little farcical. When viewed a second time it was almost too realistic. There were also problems with the final scene due to the loud scraping of the dead bodies as they were pulled up over the rocks. Jeremy seemed to spend more time soothing the army of technicians than directing the actors. Technicians were a notoriously temperamental breed who would walk out at the drop of a hat, and there was no time for that sort of behaviour. The stage was being struck first thing the following morning, and Sam's expensive sets were scheduled to take over. Where there had been gore and mayhem there would now be bright lights and high kicks. There was no longer any time for expensive mistakes. A bad soundtrack could be redubbed, but a faulty visual image had to be lived with.

It was another late night, this time running until just after nine o'clock. Eventually the cry went out, "Save the lights", and they knew it was all over. The final leave-taking is always the hardest part of any show. There were the usual clutch of promises to keep in touch.

"Phone me."

"We must meet for lunch."

"See you at the labour exchange."

"Codron's auditioning tomorrow at the Savoy."

"I'm going to spend a week in bed."

"Who with?"

"I'm going up to the Crucible next week. I'll let you know what's happening."

"If I see another bloody spear, I'll shove it right up someone's arse."

"I should be so lucky."

"Here's to the next time."

"Christ alone knows when the ghost'll walk again."

It had all been said before and would be repeated many times in the future. They were a unique group, actors, joining together to create a single unit of entertainment and then brushing it away when it was all over. When they were working there was no profession quite like it, but when they were unemployed the good times were swallowed by the pangs of hunger that occurred all too regularly for far too many of them.

Now as they walked up the Haymarket or fell tired and dulled into small cars parked outside, all scattering to their various corners of London, no one in the wide world gave a damn whether any of them ever surfaced again.

21

Victor had booked a mid-afternoon flight from Heathrow which left Mitch and Elizabeth with a morning together while she attended busily to her last-minute preparations for departure and he looked round the house for things to do. Elizabeth asked him to sort out the two suitcases she needed and the matching hand-luggage. He did this for her and helpfully dusted the cases before handing them over. They were both being very considerate, very polite.

"Anything else I can do to help?"

"Not really, thanks. I'm better left to my own devices. I always was a better packer than you."

"Yes, I know."

In that moment Elizabeth could tell he was remembering their days on tour, when they had been "that lovely couple", as their friends reported, to a succession of provincial landladies. For a second it gave her pause, a blouse half-folded in her hands.

At twelve thirty Victor's car hooted twice discreetly from the drive. Mitch was upstairs at the time.

"I'll let you know when to expect me," Elizabeth called.

"Yes, do that," he replied, without descending. He waited until he heard the car drive away before going to a window to watch it out of sight. The house suddenly seemed very empty.

He wandered into their bedroom and stood in front of the dressing table, aimlessly straightening Elizabeth's remaining combs and brushes, pushing her make-up into rows, and then changing the pattern of the jars and bottles. There was a discarded handbag lying on the bed where she had left it. He picked it up, aware of the smell of her perfume clinging to it. He took himself into Robin's room, empty and cold, unused for so long, apart from the single occasion when he had slept in the bed himself a few weeks ago. There were odd cups and saucers on the draining board in the kitchen; he made a point of returning these to their rightful place in the cupboard. The living room looked comfortable, yet uninviting. He gazed out into the garden, at the barren trees fingering their way towards the grey clouds and at the stunted rosebushes ready for a spring that still seemed light years away.

For the first time he began to appreciate what it could mean to be on his own.

He needed someone near him. It wasn't until he returned to his study and began leafing through his script for the new production that he thought of someone to contact. He reached out for the telephone, showing all the outward signs of an anxious lover taking his first faltering steps towards making a date.

"Hullo, Jake? Oh! Sorry, I didn't recognise your voice. How are you, Robby? It's Father." He didn't use the word very often. It sounded like someone else saying it for him. Hearing Robin's voice had thrown him.

"I'm OK. How's Mother?"

"She's just left."

"Yes, of course, I was forgetting." There was a brief silence. "Sorry."

"Don't lose any sleep over it."

"Was there anything in particular that made you call?" said Robin.

"Not really. I simply wanted a word with Jake, if he's around, that is."

"Oh! I'll give him a shout."

There seemed to be a minor altercation, not raised voices exactly, but certainly a dialogue.

"Hi there! Nice to hear from you."

"Are you terribly busy?"

"Not terribly. Why, what do you have in mind?"

"Well, Elizabeth's just left. There's no one here to disturb us. I thought you might care to pop over for a chat about the designs for the play. Only if you've got nothing better to do, that is. We ought to get down to it soon anyway."

"Great! Love to! I've already made a few preliminary sketches. Very rough ideas. We can kick them around. See you soon." He put down the telephone. "Mitch has just invited me over to start work on the play."

"Oh! Really? I'd have thought that would be the director's job."

"I'd like to hear what your old man has to say. Don't forget he's done the show before. It could be a valuable meeting." He began to rush around collecting together an A2 drawing pad in which he had already made a few rough pencil sketches, and some pencils and a rubber which he threw into a battered portfolio. The roughs were really no more than a few doodles, but they served as an excuse to obey the command and present himself.

"Shall I come with you?" said Robin.

"You'd be bored out of your tree. I won't be long."

By the time Jake arrived at the house Mitch had busied himself tidying the corners and preparing a tray with some tea things. He was at the front door the moment he heard the car drive to a halt and remained on the top step waiting to welcome Jake. He took the portfolio with an eager hand and clamped his other arm around Jake's broad shoulders, giving him an extra hug as they entered the living room.

They began to discuss the play in some detail, Mitch explaining his own ideas, the other taking copious notes and listening intently, sitting at his feet on the floor with sheets of paper spread in widening circles all around them.

There were three sets in all and Mitch felt they ought to be designed with as much style and sumptuousness as possible. He envisaged the first set as being rather baroque to the point of being oppressive, using deep shades of crimson and maroon with lots of gilt. This was to be in direct contrast with Orinthia's boudoir which he wanted in sugared almond shades using miles of satin and with a chaise-longue placed high on a dais. Mitch wanted this setting to be as feminine as possible and to serve as a background to the froth of the comedy with Orinthia that culminated in the important fight scene. The final set was to convey a certain melancholy with the terrace being shrouded in deep greens against shaded and stained brick walls.

Jake waited until Mitch had finished before saying anything at all.

"Say, your ideas are great. All of a piece. I just feel they're a little old hat. Know what I mean?"

"Not exactly. I have appeared in the play before. I do know what I'm talking about."

"Sure you do. But let me tell you my ideas. The whole thing ain't quite real as I see it. It's all a sort of no-man's land. Suppose the sets didn't go quite up to the flies? You know, we left them with jagged edges set against a changing sky. That way, there would be a sort of – well, you know, not-quite-of-this-world quality about the whole thing. I can give it the treatment you want but, by doing it my way, we get the best of both worlds." Jake sat back on his haunches, pulling out the sheets of paper on which he'd dashed off a few sketches.

Within half an hour Mitch began to feel tired. He hadn't anticipated the meeting being quite so concentrated at this early stage. He had simply felt the need for company and now he wanted to relax.

"I've made a tray ready. Let's have some tea."

"Sure thing. I'll fix it."

They moved into the kitchen and Mitch left Jake to find his way around. He sat at the table watching him move, observing the way Jake's shirt almost pulled away from its fastening every time he twisted his body. He was aware of the tightness of Jake's trousers, of the slim waist and the fullness around the crotch. He remembered their last encounter, but said nothing. Neither of them had ever spoken about what took place although they had passed each other in the corridor at the theatre. There had been an exchange of smiles, but nothing more, no words, not even a casual touch.

"Some of your ideas sound interesting," said Mitch once the tea had been prepared. "I think we need a little more time to sort them out. Have you got much going on at the moment?"

"Not really. I left myself pretty clear for this show. I want it to have my undivided attention."

"I'm glad to hear you say that. Very wise of you. It could well open up other doors – "

They munched biscuits and sipped tea, neither saying

anything more about the play. They were both equally alive to the other's awareness of what was happening. Mitch suddenly brightened, giving the impression of just having had an inspired idea.

"Surely it's going to be rather silly for you to keep coming backwards and forwards. I've got this entire house to myself for a while. Why don't you move in for a few days? Until we get the basics sorted out. That's only if you want to, of course." He concentrated on his teacup.

Jake sat thoughtfully, trying to make up his mind.

"OK! You're on. I'll be back late tomorrow evening, if that's all right with you."

"Suit yourself. I don't want you to feel obligated. It was merely an idea. A way of saving time for both of us."

"That's great. No need to elaborate. I know what you mean. I get the idea."

Once this had been settled Jake had many things to do, materials to sort out, some clothes to throw together, and Robin to pacify.

"It'll only be for a few days. Only while we're getting the broad ideas on paper. You won't even notice I've gone."

"I don't see why you have to move in with him."

"To save travelling time. We've a hell of a lot to get through."

"I can imagine." Robin knew he had no hold over Jake. It was more a case of letting him go willingly than making a scene.

During the following few days Robin made several telephone calls to Jake, using the excuse of postal deliveries and odd messages that had been left for him. He knew precisely where the telephone extensions were sited in the house and couldn't help but notice the length of time it took for anyone to answer the calls. It was always Mitch's guarded voice at the other end. There was usually a delay before Jake came to the telephone, and then he sounded annoyed at having been bothered with silly messages that both knew were unimportant.

The play was discussed in all its details. The props, the type of furniture, the costumes, the general balance of colour required to enhance a particular scene. For part of the day Mitch often had to be out. He had to attend final auditions and give his yea or nay to the actors eager to join the company. He loathed having to say no to any performer for not looking or sounding right, regardless of the abundance of talent an individual may have paraded. This was something that he personally hadn't had to endure all that much. But he had been remarkably lucky and he knew it.

Matthew sat out front, calling a few words across the rows of empty seats as the actors appeared under a mean working light. Some had prepared a small piece of their own choosing, and then went on to read a few lines from the play with the ASM filling in for all the other characters. Some seemed lost the moment they stepped on to the stage. Auditioning was an impossible business. There were actors who were brilliant sight-readers but who seldom progressed to produce a fully rounded character. There were others who stumbled over every word on the printed page, but who found their way to the finer points of characterisation through knowing direction and lengthy rehearsals. This was one reason for so many productions being cast on the old boy network.

It was on days like this that Mitch returned home tired and a little sad for the unsuccessful ones and determined not to discuss any aspect of the play. He simply needed to be with someone, and Jake was there waiting for him. Jake was ready with meals, willing to be an obedient servant as long as it suited both of them.

By the end of the first week Robin felt that Jake ought to be ready to return, but he was wrong. Jake made the lame excuse that changes were being made and he felt he ought to stay put. They had spoken by telephone, but as the days passed, Jake's conversation had become more and more terse.

Although Fiona was only a half-sister, there had been times when Robin felt he had far more in common with her than with Susanna. She did appear to understand what he felt and how much he seemed to want from a relationship. In Robin she saw a weaker version of herself, a reflection of some of her own past mistakes. There was a driving force within Fiona that seemed hell-bent on self-destruction. That same force lay restlessly within Robin. In him it revealed itself as a weakness. In Fiona it showed as her strength. Yet where one started and the other finished would have been impossible to decide.

On a Saturday afternoon he decided to call upon Fiona. He got on to his motorbike and zoomed away to St John's Wood. He didn't bother to telephone first and give her the chance to refuse to see him. He hesitated on the front steps, sensing something going on within, almost changing his mind but being prevented from turning back by the unexpected opening of the front door. Fiona was showing someone out.

"Robby, what are you doing here?" There was no mistaking the surprise in her voice.

"Can you spare me a few moments? I need to speak with you." He took off his helmet and shook out his hair awkwardly, shifting from one foot to another.

"Better come in." She held open the door for him to pass her.

There was a jumble of voices coming from the living room and others from somewhere upstairs. A bold bass drum thumped and echoed through the house.

"Perhaps I should have phoned?"

"No need. I can't spare you long. We're in the middle of rehearsals. We're due to start in ten days' time in Wolverhampton. We'll finish knocking it into shape on the road."

"Where can we go to talk?" he asked.

She ushered him into the kitchen, closing the door behind them to blot out most of the sounds, although it was impossible to prevent the thumping from throbbing through the ceiling above them.

"Sorry about the noise. Well, what is it?"

Robin clutched at his helmet, rolling the edge around between his fingers, looking at the pattern as a means of concentrating his thoughts. "Do you think you could talk to Father for me?"

"Me? What about?" There was no denying Fiona's amazement at the suggestion.

"Jake's been there all week. Father called him to go over and talk about designs for *Apple Cart*. He then suggested that Jake stayed. We both know what that means."

"And what do you think I can do about that?"

"Father will listen to you. You and he – well, you're alike in so many ways. You don't have to spell it out exactly, but you can talk to him in a way that I can't. He still looks upon me as a small boy."

"We've hardly spoken for weeks. Not since my letter in the *Guardian* and the TV programme. How long has this been going on?"

"It first started after the opening night party." He began to splutter and to fall over his words. He wanted to find the right phrases without making the situation appear too melodramatic, but he found it difficult to make sense. "I know how he must be feeling now that Mother's gone away. But that's not my fault. Why – why does he have to take it out on me? It's unfair. Why doesn't he leave Jake alone? Please, Fiona, isn't there anything you can do?"

A disembodied voice called from somewhere upstairs, "Fiona, darling, we're ready."

She opened the door and called back, "You carry on. I'll be with you as soon as I can." She returned to the room, unable to conceal her growing impatience, and with more than half her mind on the group waiting for her upstairs. "I'm sorry, my love, but this is something you'll have to sort out for yourself as best you can. Mitch is a big boy, and so are you. You've got to stand up for yourself some day. You might as well start as soon as possible."

"Then you refuse?"

"I *can't*. I've got more than enough to contend with right now. The last thing I want to do is to get involved in any affair of yours." She knew she was being unkind but she was determined to leave no doubt in his mind that she meant what she said.

"I see," he said, almost whispering. "Sorry I troubled you. I promise I won't bother you any more – ever." He pulled open the door to find Kate dancing up and down the stairs outside, trying to keep in time with the drumbeats.

"Hullo, Uncle Robby. I didn't know it was you in there with Mummy."

"Hullo, Kate. You've grown since I last saw you."

"Then you should come to see me more often." She was a self-assured little madam, but that was hardly surprising.

"I've got to go now. Perhaps I'll see you some other time." He bent down and kissed her cheek.

She threw her arms around his neck and hung on until he picked her up and swung her round. It was a game they used to play when she was much smaller. It was one of the few games anyone ever bothered to play with her or seemed to have time for.

"You must let him go now, Kate, there's a good girl. Go on, back upstairs, and see if you can help with the tambourine." Fiona made a conscious effort to produce a different voice for Kate, firm yet kinder, but it came out as cold and incisive as the way in which she had spoken to Robin.

Kate allowed herself to be put on the second step before throwing another kiss to Robin. She then went upstairs making a booming sound in time with the drum.

"She doesn't seem to mind having lots of people around," said Robin, watching her go as he pulled on his helmet and fastened it below his chin.

"I've always encouraged her to behave as a person. We're all grown up a hell of a lot longer than we're children."

"Don't you think she's missing out somewhere along the line?"

Fiona shook her head. "No, of course not." There was a practised tone of defence in her reply. "I've always conducted my life so that *she* lives with *me*. I've never felt the need to have to pretend that *I* live with *her*. It seems to be working out."

He climbed on to his motorbike and revved as loudly as he could, pushing his foot down hard several times before finally moving off. He knew they could hear him inside the house and it pleased him to think that they would have to wait until he moved off before they could continue with their miserable rehearsal.

He then made his way across Maida Vale, pushing towards the Harrow Road and on to Gloucester Road to see Susanna.

In the past she had often sorted out the minor battles he used to have with Bruce. She understood him and she accepted him without asking too many questions. There was always a meal for him whenever he felt the need and even a bed in the living room on occasions, but Matthew had never really encouraged this. He was never less than polite, but it went little beyond that.

By the time Robin arrived outside Susanna's flat he was very upset and angry now both with Fiona and Jake. Susanna welcomed him, explaining that Matthew was out watching Fulham. She was being a housewife, ironing, and preparing an evening meal. Its very ordinariness made it seem so extraordinary to Robin.

"I've just come from Fiona. I went to her first as I thought she might be willing to do something."

He began to tell Susanna about what had happened during the past week. He felt he had to be more circumspect when telling Susanna about the affair. There was an inner quality about her that made her so much nicer than Fiona. There was no malice in her, no envy, no deviousness, not a great deal of ambition either. She listened to Robin without once interrupting him, allowing him to order his thoughts as he gabbled on.

"I'm fed up with being accepted simply because my name happens to be Dawlish."

"We all have that cross to bear, darling. Mind you, there are times when it comes in handy," said Susanna, trying to lighten the conversation.

"It's almost as though my only worth lies in being part of the family. For Christ's sake, I'm still a person in my own right!"

"I'm sorry, I didn't mean to make it sound unimportant, Robby." She reached out to comfort him, but he shrank away from her.

"There's not a bloody soul in this world who really cares. Really cares for me. I've always got to be in someone else's shadow. I'm sick of it."

"Surely that's not altogether true. There must be other friends you can turn to? People who share your problems – "

"If you mean other gays, forget it. It's a tight, mean little world. There's no one who cares a jot apart from Jake. Now it looks as though *he's* about to drift away." It was the desolation in his voice that made Susanna feel so ineffectual and unable to offer him the support he so painfully wanted.

"Are you sure that your affair with Jake hasn't blown itself out? Are you sure you want to go chasing after him? Because there's no one else at the moment, that isn't really a good enough reason for not letting him go."

"You don't seem to understand. I really *need* him. I do care, and I'm sure he still cares for me. He's dazzled by Father at the moment. He feels flattered. Once that lousy play is on Father will drop him. You know that as well as I do."

"If I'm to approach Father at all, then I've got to take my time. Go at him bald-headed and you get nowhere fast. You know that, Robby."

"Yes, I suppose you're right."

"Suppose I funded you for a while? Gave you some money to help get yourself to LA? There's a lot going on there. You've got a few friends who have often invited you over. Why don't you go for a short stay in the States? See how you like it. You could get work there. You might even decide to stay." She sounded older than twenty-five, older than a hundred and five. Her entire manner was motherly. This wasn't what he wanted.

Robin shook his head slowly. "It won't help, Susanna. I know it just won't be any good. It's got to be sorted out. I'd really appreciate it if you could find a way to speak with him for me."

"All right," she sighed. "Leave it to me. I'll see what I can do. But it will have to be in my own time."

"Thanks. I should have come to you in the first place. Don't leave it too long, will you?"

"I'll do the best I can. You'd better go before it gets too dark. I hate it whenever you're on that terrible machine of yours."

Back at the flat Robin dropped his helmet into a corner and flung himself on to the settee, unable to control himself any longer. It had taken a considerable amount of courage for him to go to his sisters, and now he simply had to let go. There was nothing left for him to hold on to. There was no dignity, no pride, nothing, only the overriding knowledge that he desperately wanted Jake back with him, whatever it cost personally. He curled up into a corner and began to sob.

22

With so many people in and out of the house, Andrew had been made to feel redundant. He had played no part in helping Fiona to get her company on the road; if anything he went out of his way to make life difficult. He would spend ages on the telephone blocking the line against incoming calls, and any messages he took were scribbled on odd scraps of paper and usually allowed to get buried.

Andrew would dearly like to have told Fiona about his own plans, about the gigs he would be playing and the size of audiences anticipated. There had been an isolated occasion when he managed to get across to her that his audiences would be measured in thousands rather than hundreds, but even this brought no response, so completely absorbed had she become in her own preparations. This was an important break for Andrew, important enough to launch him into the international scene, and he was taking no chances on any of his own arrangements being fouled up through lack of attention. An experienced road manager had been appointed and the twelve man team of roadies all but selected. Smoke effects, lighting and amplification equipment had all been decided upon. He had as much reason to feel a sense of tightness in his guts as Fiona.

She had told him of her need to rehearse at home as a way of saving on her restricted budget. She had also informed him that if he wanted to bring in his group he must let her know well in advance. Andrew was nobody's fool and apart from being made to feel more like a transient lodger rather than the ardent lover, he was quite sure that Neil Hamilton was playing more of a domestic role in her life than she was prepared to admit. But he needed to stay put for another few days before being able to risk a confrontation.

By mid-week their differences were being allowed more air. Their hours at home no longer coincided. They occasionally met in bed, at which time life was lived for the moment, but by morning, they had slept away their togetherness, and mutual disdain once more took over as they went their separate ways.

Fiona's company had reached a point in rehearsals when they were running through for timing. A drum and tambourine had been introduced to create a rough fairground atmosphere, and to break up the evening's programme. She had finally decided to dispense with the skills of a writer, yet another economy, and allow the cast to find their own way to the truth of what she wanted to put across by the simple method of improvisation. There were points Fiona wished to make about Trade Unions and workers in relation to employers, about government controls and the general economy. All these details were slowly absorbed into the action by means of preliminary discussion groups. The company had to work out little scenes to make their points. Characterisation was to develop from the demands of these vignettes. It had proved to be an interesting method of presentation, but it was hard work and they were all feeling tired. What they now needed was a live audience.

By about seven o'clock they had been through the piece twice and were taking an evening break before returning to discuss the day's work. The company went their separate ways, sorting out little restaurants around Swiss Cottage or further over along Haverstock Hill. It was an area that had long since mislaid its Victorian grandeur, with most of the enormous houses being converted into flats or bedsitters. As was customary in such areas, they were well served for eating houses.

Fiona had been invited to join Neil at one of his favourite haunts in Finchley Road. It pleased her to feel that she could still appeal to a virile young man at least ten years her junior and she was delighted that her sexual prowess could satisfy him enough to make him return for more.

It amused Fiona when Neil fussed about the temperature of the Niersteiner, sending it back to be chilled a little more, and she accepted his attentions with as much charm as was possible for her. They chatted about the project and about what it was that Fiona was trying to get across.

"I admire the way you take so much in your stride," said Neil.

"I long ago made a conscious decision to do what's right for me. At this moment in time you're the rightest thing there's been for ages." She pursed her lips and blew him a silent kiss across the table, causing the flame on the stub of candle to dance drunkenly.

"Good! I'd like to think it will go on being like that. Coffee?"

Fiona glanced at her watch, forcing herself to be aware that time was pressing. "We really ought to be getting back. Another hour or so should see us through."

Neil paid the bill, but not before checking every item and the total, Fiona noticed, and they drove back up Fitzjohn's Avenue, past the large houses rising high above them on either side, catching the spasmodic street lighting as it streaked into the car and observing the silhouettes of people moving about in their always dimly lit rooms. They were both relaxed, well fed, and ready to resume work.

When they arrived outside the house, several other members of the company had already returned and were standing about outside looking worried. Lights flooded on to the front steps and out across the pavement through the semi-darkness, producing an oasis of brightness that could be seen right across the road. The all too familiar throb of pop music smashed its way through the brickwork. A synthesiser was creating ear-piercing vibrations backed up by staccato drumbeats. In the background were the faint cries of a nasal vocalist of indeterminate gender. Although the double-glazing held back some of the harsher notes, the musicians appeared to be oblivious of the volume of sound that still managed to issue forth. It was surprising that there were no neighbours beating on the front door.

Fiona went cold at the thought of the confrontation that lay ahead. As she opened the front door the sound increased, blasting its way into her ears, throwing her back and rousing her fury.

The scene was much as it had been several weeks ago, except that now there were more people, more instruments, more equipment filling the corners and spilling out into the hall. It looked as though the entire episode had been prepared as a bad joke, but Fiona was not in a humorous mood.

Her wide eyes told everything as she flung herself into the middle of the room, seeking out Andrew pounding on his electric keyboard. His eyes were tight shut against the cigarette smoke curling on to his face and sweat streamed down his cheeks. The other musicians were no less absorbed, their minds were encapsulated in sound.

"Andy, for Christ's sake turn that bloody thing off!" she screamed.

He appeared not to hear her. The vocalist was the only person to have ceased making his particular contribution to the noise.

She raised her voice even louder. "If you don't stop this within two seconds, I won't be responsible for my actions. Will you shut up, all of you?"

The others had become aware of her standing in their midst, and one at a time they allowed their music to die until the only person left playing was Andrew. Fiona was now in full flood. Her rage was monumental, and words alone were no longer enough. With a couple of quick strides she was beside Andrew, pulling and tugging on every wire lying around his feet. Sparks flew in all directions. This finally had the desired effect of forcing him to acknowledge her presence.

"Stupid bitch! Stupid bitch! You'll ruin the gear." He reached out and grabbed her wrists, twisting her arms to force her to stop.

"Let go of me, you miserable bastard. You knew I had work to do here. Get this lot of shit out of my house. If they're not out of here within five minutes I'll call the police."

"You wouldn't dare," he snarled at her, looking at her minions standing around not quite knowing what to do or say. "I'll make life so bloody difficult for you, you wouldn't know what day it was."

"Get out! Get out and leave me alone. I've stood about as much as I can take from you. I've been reasonable. I've given way. I've supported you. And if this is your idea of repayment, then let's call it a day."

"That's great by me. I don't know who the hell you think you are, but you're not *that* great a lady. In fact, you're no lady at all. You're a raving fucking nymphomaniac. Believe me, the man who can satisfy you hasn't been born yet." He shot a glance across to Neil who had now pushed his way to the front of the small circle of actors.

Fiona had a banging in her head and a fierce blinding ache behind her eyes that made her want to scream out in pain. There were no longer enough words to express what she felt, no longer enough emotions to encompass what flashed through her mind and seared into the pit of her stomach. Her hands shot out. It was all over before Andrew realised what she was doing. There were great red trenches down both sides of his face, blood oozing on to his neck and running down to stain the front of his shirt.

Andrew let out a scream of pain as he drove his fist into her jaw, spinning her across the room against the actors who were standing around in stunned silence.

Neil leapt forward and punched Andrew in the stomach causing him to double with pain. "You bastard. You miserable, rotten bastard!"

The two of them were rolling around, upturning furniture, tangled in the wires caught between their legs and all the time hitting each other as hard as they could. Actors and musicians rushed forward to try to separate the two men before either was severely injured.

The noise carried through the house, all the way up into Kate's room where she had been trying to get to sleep by pulling the pillows over her head and diving below the bedcovers. She had grown accustomed to the music at all hours and had learned to accept the general noise as part of her strange lullaby. The sounds that travelled up to her now were quite new. The raised voices, the excitement of angry words and the crashing below, made her wake up and run downstairs. The others were too preoccupied to notice a small child peering into the room from halfway up the stairs. No one saw the terror in her eyes or the way she stood transfixed, biting her fingernails. It was all more than she could take. She ran back upstairs in a blind panic and flung on her clothes, grabbing at whatever she could find in her money-box and then dashed down the stairs again and out into the street. At that precise moment she had no idea where she was going or what she was doing. She only knew that it was all too much for her, too terrifying, too horrific. She had never witnessed this sort of adult scene before. There had been arguments, disagreements, but nothing quite as violent as this and she wanted no part of it.

By the time Neil and Andrew were parted the room was a complete wreck. Broken furniture, damaged upholstery, several ornaments in pieces and some of the equipment in ruins. Fiona was taken out into the kitchen, sobbing and insisting that Andrew be kept away from her and that everything belonging to him be thrown out and him with it. Andrew left, physically supported by several of the group. The company did their best to straighten the room and then departed, leaving Neil to comfort Fiona.

It was some time before he managed to get her to stop sobbing, plying her with a strong drink through her tears. An angry mark was appearing on her chin and she could feel the ache settling into her jaw.

"Leave all this and go to bed," said Neil. "I'll come round and help you to get straight in the morning."

She looked at him as though she hadn't quite heard what he'd said or understood his meaning. There was a look of puzzlement on her face, now pale and tear-stained, streaked and smudged with her mascara. She looked like a badly painted doll waiting to be repaired.

"Yes. All right. Stay with me, Neil. Please stay with me."

Although he had slept with her before, he had never been invited to stay the night.

"Are you really sure you want that?"

"I don't think I could stay here alone tonight. Please, don't leave me alone. Stay with me. Please stay with me." She began to sob again, muttering her request over and over again as though pleading with whoever happened to be available. From being a woman who was proud of her ability to cope and to rely on no one but herself, she had suddenly collapsed into a helpless shaking jelly.

"If that's what you really want, yes, I'll stay. Let me help you upstairs." He held out his hand to steady her as she got to her feet but she swayed and had to hang on to the table to stop herself falling on to the floor.

"My head. Everything's going round and round. Help me, Neil. Please help me."

He put his arms around her and picked her up. Her head flopped close to his chest as he carried her upstairs and into her bedroom.

Robin managed to sit it out for another few days before contacting Susanna again. She was now his only hope.

"Hullo, Susanna. It's Robin." His voice was hesitant and subdued, and there was a quiver in his throat. "Have you – have you managed to contact Father yet? You did promise."

"Not yet. I told you, I would have to do it in my own time. Have *you* thought any more about my suggestion of you going to the States?"

"It's not on. I couldn't face that. It would be like running away. Anyway, I wouldn't know what I was running *to*."

"I see." She sounded oddly abstracted, as though she wasn't really listening to him.

Hurt by this unexpected tone, he persisted. "When do you plan to phone Father, then?"

"I'm sorry, Robby. Something – something else has come up. Something that's taking up rather a lot of my time at the moment. Leave it for a day or two. Just until I can sort myself out. I'll phone him and try to arrange to meet him for lunch, or something."

"OK. If that's the way it's got to be. I'll – I'll wait until I hear from you. Bye." He banged down the receiver very hard, holding on to it and shaking in his distress and utter loneliness.

"Robby! Robby! Are you there? Robby?" But he had gone and there was nothing more Susanna could do to explain why she hadn't yet got round to calling Mitch. Then, she thought, even if she explained, there was little likelihood that her brother would accept the reason as being greater than his own need.

Robin slowly lifted his hand from the telephone and glanced at his watch. It was just half past eight. He knew that his father seldom got up early when he wasn't rehearsing and so made a snap decision to ride over to Highgate for a confrontation. He decided that it was unfair to expect others to act as his mediator and that it was too easy for him to stand back bemoaning his own fate.

It didn't take him more than three quarters of an hour to get across London on his motorbike. When he arrived at the house he noticed that the bedroom curtains were still drawn and congratulated himself for managing to get there so early. This small confirmation of his reasoning supplied him with additional courage for the anticipated meeting. He saw himself confronting his father and talking with him in a calm, rational manner. Robin was quite sure he could make him see reason and get him to agree to release Jake. He rang the front doorbell very lightly and stood still while he allowed enough time for someone to come down from upstairs. He rang again. And again. He pressed the bell just long enough for the sound to mean something in the upper regions of the house, but there was still no response. He gave up and made his way round to the kitchen door, hoping it would be unlocked. This was a small failing in Mitch's memory that had often led to slight words between him and Elizabeth in the past. Robin let himself into the house, stealthily walking across the polished floor, aware of the smell of freshly made toast and ground coffee. It felt odd to be back in his own home, creeping about as though he had no right to be there. The living room still had several sheets of paper spread on the floor showing set designs and a number of half-drawn costume sketches with small cuttings of fabric pinned to one corner. Signs of work, but not of the workers.

He put his foot on the bottom step and then took the others two at a time, halting as one of the middle steps creaked below his slight weight. His sensibilities told him that he ought to be walking about without caring whether there was any noise, yet he found this impossible. There was a definite sense of being an intruder, of being uninvited into his own home. He did still feel this was home, more so than the flat.

The study door was slightly ajar and he looked in. There were three small uncoloured balsawood models of sets constructed on their own bases and resting on the floor against a wall. The sharp winter light was beginning to slide in at the window to produce a series of tiny shadows through the smaller windows of the sets and giving them a ghostly appearance. As he passed the door to his own room he had an urge to look inside, to see if many of his things had been moved. The bed was rumpled and Jake's possessions were lying around in little heaps. There was a pair of socks on the floor, his high boots in need of some polish, his trousers and a pair of briefs caught over the corner of a chair. There was no sign of Jake. Robin moved slowly along the landing until he was outside his father's bedroom door. He noticed a sliver of light shining from below. There seemed to be sounds, nothing obvious. It could have been a sensation rather than an actual noise, but it made him feel uncomfortable. He began to shake through his discomfort as his hand reached for the doorknob.

A flash of images raced across his vision as he threw open the door. Mitch was sitting up in bed, obviously naked, and being served breakfast by Jake who was standing alongside, equally naked, with one foot on the bed. They were looking at each other, smiling and murmuring. The daylight continued to push its way below the curtain line, creating little bright streaks of whiteness against the dull yellow of the bedside light. It wasn't easy to make out the details, but there was enough to send Robin into a fit of hysteria.

"Christ! No! No! No! You miserable, rotten bastard! I trusted you. My own father. I trusted you. Why did you have to do this to me?"

Jake turned, totally unprepared for the sight of Robin, his obvious excitement leaving him almost immediately. There was nothing Mitchell could say. The scene said it all. There was no denying and no sense in attempting to lie.

Robin fell into the room, hanging on to the half-open door. "Couldn't you even allow me this much? All my life I've had to trail after you. I've known what you are. I've known why I'm like this. All my life I've tried to respect you and understand you. I've looked up to you for what you've achieved. I've always known I could never be as good an actor as you. But I've tried. Christ! I've tried in every way I know to make you feel as proud of me as I am of you. I hate you! I fucking well hate you for all you've done to me. Now this! Why? Why did you have to take this from me as well? There's nothing now. Everything's gone.

You'll get no more respect from me. You should have stuck a knife into me. It would have been a bloody sight kinder. You're just a rotten father. A miserable bastard. If I'm gay, it's because of you. That's all you've handed on to me. Fucking hell, I've been a damn sight more honest than you've ever been. Than you'll ever be."

Jake moved towards him, holding out one hand as though to comfort him, but Robin pulled back as though hit by a bullet.

"Don't touch me. You're no better. You're just using him and he's too stupid, too bloody senile, to see through you. You'd bed a bloody ape if you felt it would do you any good. I wish you were dead, both of you. I wish I was dead! I wish I was dead."

Mitch made as though he was about to get out of bed, instinctively reaching out for a silk robe thrown across the foot. "Robby! Robby! Listen to me – "

"Don't bother. I've listened to you all my life. Not any more. Not to you, nor to anyone, ever again. I wish I was dead! I wish I was dead!"

He ran from the room, stumbling down the stairs as he continued to repeat his own death wish. He could hardly see what he was doing through his blinding monumental rage. His hand reached out to pull at the front door, forgetting that it was still bolted and he had to search for the bolt before he could get out. He flung himself on to his motorbike and sped into the distance, swerving from side to side, almost blinded by his own tears. The wind lashed at his face, causing his hair to fly in front of his eyes.

23

Throughout the first few days away from Mitch it was impossible for Elizabeth to escape a feeling of guilt. She could not forget the atmosphere of strained politeness in the house the morning she had left and this had at first thrown a constraint on her relationship with Victor. There had been an odd coyness between them at Heathrow as they waited to board their plane.

It had been obvious to Victor that her mind had not yet adjusted to the break or the determination to think only of herself for the first time in many years. There still existed the emotional barrier that could only be broken down by time, and Victor told himself that, at last, this is what they now had in abundance, and there was no need to rush into things. Although the weather was heavy, with the damp, cold winter being pushed on to London by the deeply etched clouds, they suddenly found themselves high above the layer of gloom. They were unexpectedly dazzled by a burst of brilliant sunshine that blazed in through the portholes and exposed an explosion of azure blue sky.

Victor's fingers tightened around her hand as an unspoken comfort. She turned back to him and smiled. He ordered small bottles of champagne to accompany the plastic meal. Eating was another something to do; something else to fill in the time and concentrate her mind away from more pressing thoughts.

As they circled over Gibraltar they were able to pick out the single flat surface set into the rock, and then it disappeared as they seemed to land almost on the very edge of the coast, floating in past the assorted boats moored alongside the runway.

"My wife used to hate this moment," said Victor. "Laura was always sure we would hit the rock or plough into some boats."

"I know the feeling." This was one of the very few occasions

Victor had ever mentioned his first wife, and it made her feel odd. She remembered the single word "understudy" crossing her mind. There had been a minuscule glance in his direction during which she felt she had caught him in an unguarded moment. She thought she detected a glimmer of regret. Perhaps a fleeting moment from the past, or a less than fleeting conjecture about the future, but it was a mood, a sensation carried through the air. The result was a small wave of discomfort at the back of Elizabeth's mind.

Their stop-over lasted no more than twenty minutes and they were on their way again, climbing towards the African coastline. The Hotel El Saadi in Marrakesh was all polished brown marble elegance. Their room was large and airy and overlooked the sharply geometric pool with its island palm tree that arose, startled, from the centre, like an Esther Williams film set.

Elizabeth strolled out on to the balcony, shook out her hair and breathed deeply for the first time. It was as though she had signalled her moment of acceptance. The fading sunlight caught the outline of her head as she turned back to Victor. It was a fragmentary moment of beauty that vanished as she moved back into the room.

"Thank you for bringing me here. You were right to insist. It's all very beautiful!"

"Glad you like it. We'll spend tomorrow round the pool, just doing nothing. We've lots of time. Later, I'll enjoy showing you around."

"How long is it since you were last here?" They had begun to unpack and she arranged her cosmetics on the dressing table. A few books were spread around together with the magazines purchased at the airport.

Victor had taken charge of the suitcases, delicately unfolding Elizabeth's clothes and arranging them in the wardrobe, leaving the small items for her to put in drawers.

"About four years. But I doubt if anything's changed all that much. Progress takes time out here. Lots of time." A suitcase was clipped closed and deposited out of the way.

This was another of those odd moments. She had wondered whether he had selected this place because he knew that nothing would be changed. Was Victor looking to lay some personal ghosts of the past? He had certainly assumed a more relaxed and carefree personality.

The following days were spent lazing by the side of the swimming pool, listening to the splatter of the fountain at the foot of the palm tree island. They had swum and then lain out in the sunshine again on the white slatted lounging chairs to allow the warmth to insinuate itself into their bones, while dark-skinned waiters walked with an easy swing to their hips, fully attentive. The bright orange umbrellas splashed colour against the dark green of the cypress and palms and figs.

Neither of them spoke directly about their situation, but each was aware of it. Each wondered what would be the outcome of their time in such close proximity, and only vaguely thought about the future.

"Let me show you the souks tomorrow," said Victor, one night over dinner. "I feel the need to get away from here for a few hours."

"Very well," said Elizabeth. "What's so special about them?"

"It's like all the markets you've ever seen put together – and then some." He laughed. It was a lighter more boyish laugh than he usually allowed himself. "And as a basic principle, you never agree to pay the asking price for anything."

"I couldn't possibly argue about prices."

"You've got to. They respect you for it. Leave it to me. I always had to do it for Laura as well. I'm sure I haven't lost my touch."

"You mean your wife wasn't very good at it either?" She seemed to push the words at him. Her own forcefulness had taken her by surprise.

"That's right. She was always too willing to pay up, whatever the cost. Got to beat them down a bit, you know."

"If you say so." They continued their meal, commenting lightly on the other guests, but still not discussing their own future. Things were referred to obliquely, as though removed from themselves.

When they went up to bed it was to lie side by side reading. Elizabeth allowed the words to ride past her eyes without taking in their meaning. The book fell back as she remained looking into space.

"Why not switch out your light?" suggested Victor.

"I'm not really tired enough just yet."

"What are you thinking about?"

"It doesn't matter."

"What is it?" He put down his own book and raised himself up on to one elbow to look down at her face. They had both managed to encourage a little suntan during those early days and were beginning to unwind.

"I – I was wondering what the weather's like in London."

"Bloody awful. I caught sight of someone's paper as they were booking in today," he said. And then added, "Is that really all?"

"I was also wondering how Mitch was coping. I'm sorry. That's not very polite of me, is it? Being here with you and thinking about him."

"At least you're honest. Are you having regrets?"

Elizabeth didn't answer immediately, as though she needed time to consider the question and balance her answer against its implications. "I think I'm still rather more tired than I realised." She knew she was cheating, but she also knew that to have given an immediate answer in the affirmative wouldn't have been totally true.

Victor leaned over and smoothed back her hair. He looked down on to her, his bare chest just touching her breasts, making her more aware of him as a sexual partner. She reached out and curled her arms around his neck smiling up into his face and pouting a kiss at him. He slowly lowered his body against hers. His skin was still tingling from the day's warmth. He knew how tense she had been since the day they arrived. He had forced himself to exercise great patience and consideration at all times, but his own physical need had been mounting during the past few days in a desire to enfold Elizabeth in his arms and love her totally. He moved his body closer to hers. It was a signal without words. He wanted her to know how ready he was and how urgent was his desire, and she responded fully, ashamed of her own preoccupation with things more distant. She slowly pulled his face closer to hers and allowed him to possess her as never quite before. It was over within a matter of seconds. Not exactly a complete success as they were both over-anxious, but it was an unspoken acknowledgment of their relationship.

Victor cradled her in his arms, kissing her cheek several times before he finally fell asleep, breathing heavily into her ear as she continued to lie awake. She was tired, but not enough to fall into the deep sleep she would have enjoyed to block off her mind from the thoughts that were still nagging at her. It was some time before she was able to drift into a broken sleep, finally interrupted by the intoning of the muezzin calling the faithful to prayer at dawn. It was an odd sound, strange in its antiquity, yet warm and reassuring about things past. The unknown words floated through the growing dawn as she slipped from the bed and padded out on to the balcony to look at the minarets being stroked by the rising sun. The faint morning breeze caught fine wisps of her hair as she listened to the eerie silences between the sequence of devotional cries. She tried to ask herself what she was doing there, and be objective about her relationship with Mitch, about her feelings towards continuing in the theatre, and above all about her feelings towards Victor. There was a rustle of movement from within the bedroom as Victor turned over, unaware that she was no longer by his side. She could just make out his shape sprawled across the bed, half uncovered and suspended in sleep. There was no way in which he could possibly share in all of her most private thoughts and feelings.

After breakfast Victor superintended his promised tour of the souks. The silverware stalls were dazzling in the sunlight, a granite-faced storyteller was surrounded by eager listeners, mostly men in dark robes and with covered heads, a row of scribes sat on their haunches. Stalls were piled high with richly coloured rugs and carpets, basketwork and western denims alongside eastern djellabas. An aged water-carrier jangled his metal jugs past them, his clothes embroidered and hung with fringing and tassels. There were crowds everywhere, jostling, pushing, elbowing; voices were raised to mingle with the thump thump of the snake-charmer's drumbeat. Camels and cars nudged each other for space.

It was all a little frightening to Elizabeth. A small boy appeared from nowhere with his hand outstretched begging for money. No sooner had Elizabeth handed him a few coins than they were surrounded by a dozen others who materialised as though on a magic carpet.

"I'd rather you didn't do that," said Victor. "It only encourages them. They're cunning little bastards. Memories like demons. I guarantee if you come back here in a week's time they'll follow you for miles. Come on, let's go into the souks."

Victor took hold of Elizabeth's hand, as though about to lead a child who might wander off and get lost. He elbowed his way between the covered lanes of tiny shops. Gap-toothed smiles were set into darkly lined faces, and hands outstretched in servile invitation. It was a world apart that carried its own mystique, intriguing and fascinating and vaguely frightening.

Victor was enjoying every moment of the excursion, remembering little lanes and odd shops as they progressed further into the centre of souks. He insisted upon buying a neat little leather handbag for Elizabeth, colourful if not very well made. She stood back, embarrassed by the discussion that ensued relating to the price to be paid. The negotiation was resolved at just under half the asking price, and the seller was more than happy.

"Wasn't that fun?" said Victor, handing over the small parcel.

He stopped outside another leather shop to pick up a small box and inspect its workmanship. Elizabeth took herself further along the narrow road to look at some lace. A thick London accent cut across the bustle and the smell of leather and wool and oil.

"Well, I never. Ain't you Elizabeth Dawlish, the actress?" The woman was wearing a much too tight crimplene floral dress with a square neckline and buttons down the front. Her face was bright red and her hair a mess of dark curls that charged out below a wide-brimmed straw hat.

Elizabeth was caught quite unawares, turning towards the unexpected greeting with eyes that spoke her incredulity. "I beg your pardon?"

"Ain't I seen you on the telly?" The woman nudged her look-alike companion, dressed differently but the same.

"Yes! I do appear from time to time."

"There! What did I tell you, Doris? Soon as I saw you, I said to my friend, 'She's on the telly,' I said. Knew I was right." There was triumph in her voice.

Victor had heard the exchange and now joined them. "Everything all right?" There was an edge to his voice.

"Oh! This is your hubby?"

The question was one that Elizabeth had not looked for. "No! No, we're here on business." It was a stupid thing to have said and she had no idea why she had lied so instinctively. She turned towards Victor, sensing his annoyance.

"Oh! I see." There was a sneer behind the comment that verged on the impertinent. "Anyway, can I 'ave your autograph? Fancy coming all this way and seeing you. Small world, really. That's what I always says. Very small world." She turned to her nodding companion. "Got a pencil, luv?"

"Here, use this." Victor held out his own ball-point pen, anxious to have done with the incident.

"Ta!" She rummaged amongst the untold mysteries of her bulging handbag and pulled out a small sheet of what appeared to be lavatory paper, and held it out with a trembling hand, over-jewelled with cheap rings and dangling bracelets obviously just purchased. "This should be all right. It's all I got anyway."

Elizabeth signed the paper and handed it back with a polite smile reserved for such occasions. It was all over within a matter of minutes, but it had broken through the mood of the morning. They engaged the services of a horse-drawn carriage and returned to the hotel.

"I'm sorry about that," said Elizabeth, as they entered their room.

"I don't know why you bothered," he replied.

"I could hardly do otherwise. Short of being downright rude, what alternative did I have?"

"It's a damned liberty. Why can't they leave you alone?"

"I'm afraid it's one of the penalties for appearing in their living rooms. Once you enter their homes, they own you body and soul."

"Only if you allow them to. You could have ignored them. Stupid bitches." He walked out on to the balcony, gripping the handrail firmly and allowing his anger to produce a rigid tension throughout his body.

"It's part of the business, Victor. The time to start worrying is when I'm not recognised and when no one cares a damn."

He turned back to her, still tight around his jaw, and still holding back his anger. "Does it really matter all that much?"

"It depends."

"On what?"

"On whether I intend to continue in the theatre or give it up."

"You've been talking about giving it up for ages."

"I know I have. That's when I've been particularly tired or worried. But it's easier said than done. I doubt now I could really ever settle for anything else. It's been an awfully long time."

"I think you actually enjoyed that moment this morning," he said, accusingly.

"I was flattered. They might have recognised me, but they needn't have let me know. After all, I'm not one of the great luminaries, am I?"

"Stop knocking yourself. You're bloody good, and you know it." He moved about impatiently, hunched and trapped within his own confusion of thoughts and feelings. He had enjoyed being on the perimeter of her very separate world, but in truth it was as foreign to him as the souks, and the incident of the morning remained with them and between them. They chose to remain close to the hotel for the next few days, soaking up more sun and swimming. The following week Victor suggested a trip to the Atlas Mountains and Elizabeth was happy to fall in with the plan as she was beginning to have a desperate sense of sitting it out until their two weeks came to an end.

This was to be their single memorable day. It was a day during which they both felt equally at ease in the other's company, and shared a sense of fun. It was fun that had been missing; it was the laughter in small things, the sharing of amusing thoughts and incidents.

They were required to be up very early in order to catch the coach. As they began to climb there were scattered rocks that announced the foothills of the mountain ranges edged against the brilliant blue sky. Their snowcaps and murky red tones caught the crystal quality of the light. A fortress rose up in front of them like a cheap setting for a touring production of *The Desert Song*, complete with cardboard oasis a short distance away. Women with mountains of sticks piled high on their backs waved at the passing coach, their deeply etched faces wizened from the sun and the sand and the wind that blew in from the Sahara Desert. They were allowed within the fortress, and climbed high into an upper story where a tiled room overlooked a sunny yard filled with school-children laughing and playing games. The world was being put to rights as school-children are wont to do anywhere.

There was an unexpected cry as two boys began to thump each other while the others stood around shouting and taking sides. For a fleeting moment Elizabeth was reminded of Bruce and Robin. Particularly Robin, who always managed to get the worst of a fight, and who used to do anything rather than protest or make his voice heard.

"I think we ought to be going." Victor's voice came at her loudly, as though he was repeating something already said.

"Sorry, my mind was miles away. I was looking at the children." She couldn't resist casting a glance back over her shoulder between the lace ironwork that crossed the narrow window.

High into the mountains there was snow on either side, icy in the shade. They had travelled as far as they could in a single day, to the beginning of the endless desert. It was strangely eerie.

It was quite late when they arrived back at the hotel. They were both agreeably tired, certainly happier than either of them had been since their arrival and perhaps a little closer to each other because of it. They had finally jumped the hurdle of defensiveness without being aware of it, and yet each knew the moment had arrived. This represented their own oasis, their own moment in time when what was happening around them seemed less important than being together on that particular day.

As they went through the main lounge, Elizabeth's eye happened to catch sight of an English newspaper left on a low table. She stooped to look at the front page held down at one corner by a coffee cup. It took her a moment or so before what she read sank in, and then she allowed a startled gasp to escape from her constricted throat.

"Oh, God!"

"What is it?" said Victor, holding on to her as she seemed to sway.

"It's – it's Robby. He's been killed in a road accident." She pointed to a section in the newspaper and sank in an armchair, not crying, but muttering to herself and staring blankly.

Victor read the item two or three times. There was very little information other than the fact that Robin had been killed while riding his motorbike. The names of Mitch and Elizabeth were mentioned, but very little else.

"I must get back, Victor. I've got to get back." She looked up at him, her eyes finally filling with tears and her lips tightening. The colour in her face was fast draining away, leaving her looking as tired and drawn and lined as the day they arrived.

"I'll see what arrangements I can make." He turned away, and then turned back to her, kneeling at her side and lightly touching her face. "I'm sorry, Elizabeth. Deeply, deeply sorry."

Uncontrolled tears were now streaming down her cheeks. Her lace handkerchief was too small to be of any practical use, although it did provide her with something to tug against. She wanted to scream, to protest and to ask *why*? But she managed to control these several aspects of the single emotion that was utter despair. She managed to hang on to her memories, and the mixed thoughts of happy family occasions that were already beginning to stir. There was confusion and chaos and questions, countless questions all pushing and jostling for space within her mind. She had to return to England, to be with Mitch and the rest of the family. She had to take her share in their grief and in their misery and in their guilt.

There was always the guilt. Whatever happened to other people there was always an abundant share of guilt waiting to be soaked up as a means of saying "sorry". It was never enough, but it helped.

It was at times such as this that Victor was able to rise to the occasion. Elizabeth needed no further proof that he was reliable, unflappable, and well able to get things organised, despite an uncaring hotel staff who complained of having to get hold of people out of hours. They moved slowly. Time was not of the essence to them.

In their room Elizabeth tried to contact Mitch. The phone rang on and on until she heard the operator confirm that there was no reply, and would she care to try again? Instead she called Susanna.

"Speak up, Susanna, it's a bad line. I read about Robin in the *Telegraph*. What's happened?"

"His motorbike skidded. He was going very fast and he skidded into a lorry coming in the opposite direction."

"I've been trying to get through to Mitch but there's no answer. What's going on?"

Susanna's voice was tearful and full of distress. "When – when will you be returning?"

"As soon as possible. Victor's trying to organise it now. Where's Mitch? Why doesn't he answer the phone?"

"I – I don't know. Ring me as soon as you know your flight number."

"Yes. Yes, I'll phone you. Tell Mitch I called, won't you? You will tell him?"

For all Victor's efforts it was the following afternoon before they were aboard a plane. Once settled into her seat Elizabeth reached out for Victor's comforting hand and pressed it very tightly. "Thank you."

"What for?"

"For being you. For simply being there. Whatever happens, Victor, I shall always be grateful for everything you've done. For everything you've wanted to do."

"You sound as though you're saying goodbye."

"I don't mean it to sound that way. I just want you to know how much I appreciate your kindness. Not just during this holiday, but all the time." She was once again fighting with her own emotions. She was saying one thing, but thinking something quite different.

"I understand." He patted her hand in his customary fashion and leaned over to kiss her as the aeroplane slowly taxied to take off.

24

The return flight seemed interminable, beginning with half an hour's delay before take-off, then an extended stop-over in Gibraltar, to be followed by an unexpectedly strong head wind that further prolonged the journey.

Elizabeth was unable to conceal her tears. Past years ebbed and flowed through her mind's eye as she tried to knit together the fabric of Robin's short life. The single burning question that kept repeating itself was simply, "Why?"

She and Victor said little. He offered her whatever comfort he could, but at the back of his mind was the growing conviction that he was fighting a losing battle. The past days had proved to him that the family ties were too strong to allow him to cut the cords and carry her away into the comparative comfort he knew he could offer.

After some time Elizabeth fell into a fitful sleep that served to stimulate wild dreams and imaginings. At one point she awoke with a start, accompanied by a loud cry of "*Why?*"

"It's all right, darling," said Victor, leaning over her shivering body and trying to kiss her.

She looked up at him, still half-asleep. It was as though she were a million miles away, seeing him as a stranger, unable to focus her eyes on his features while trying valiantly to remember where she was and who this strange person was leaning so close to her. Then it all came back to her as she sensed the gentle motion of the aeroplane and felt the seat holding her in its grip and looked out at the fast fading daylight.

"I'm sorry. I – I must have been dreaming. How long before we land?"

"About another half an hour or so. Would you like a drink?"

She shook her head. There was no point in fuzzing up her mind. She was relieved when the seat-belt light indicated they were about to land.

"I'm so confused," said Elizabeth as Susanna drove them back into London. "I don't understand. How did it happen?"

Susanna forced herself to concentrate on the road ahead. She made a conscious effort not to sound too angry or too distressed, and gave only the barest of facts.

"He – he wasn't wearing his helmet."

"The idiot. The stupid idiot." Elizabeth's grief was now being expressed as white anger. She had never liked the idea of Robin using the motorbike, and it was this mixed sense of pain and needless waste that now expressed itself as fury.

"I know how you're feeling," said Susanna. "But there's no point in recriminations."

"Where was the helmet?" said Victor, almost as much to join in rather than simply to occupy space as a cypher.

"At home," said Susanna.

"How *could* he leave it at the flat?" asked Elizabeth.

There was a pause as Susanna changed gears at the traffic lights, grabbing at the tiny incident not to answer directly.

The question was repeated.

"It wasn't at the flat. It was on the floor of your kitchen."

There was another silence as Elizabeth exchanged a puzzled look with Victor. "I – I don't understand. How did it come to be there?"

"I really think it's better if we wait until you're home before we go into too many details. The light's bad and I ought to concentrate on the driving."

"You're hiding something, aren't you, Susanna? You're not telling me everything?"

"It's all very complicated. I'd rather wait until you're home. In some respects I feel I'm as much to blame as anyone else."

"You? But – I'm sorry, Susanna, I don't understand. I don't seem to understand anything at all. Robin's dead, and you're not telling me the things I want to know. What happened? I want to know. *I want to know.*" She began to cry deeply, bitterly, in great waves of sound that filled the car.

Victor leaned across the seat so that he could put his arm

around her shoulders. He gently patted her head on to his chest, and then sat silently stroking her wet cheeks. From the moment Elizabeth had first read about the death she had managed to hold her emotions partly in check, but now she had finally given way completely. There were no passing strangers who might ask for her autograph. She was away from the public gaze, and suddenly consumed with all the raw emotion that had been pent up since she first realised what had happened. Now it was all exploding in great waves of utter despair.

By the time Susanna had driven them back to Highgate it had grown dark. The house stood like a blind person, solidly there but waiting to be linked with life. Inside there was a sense of desolation, as though the house had been empty for several days. There was no indication of Mitch being around, and a pile of letters had gathered on the front door mat.

While Victor busied himself unobtrusively bringing in the suitcases, Elizabeth roamed about the living room, idly touching objects. Then, quite unexpectedly, she seemed to find an inner strength as she clasped her hands together and turned back to Susanna.

"Now, I'm quite calm. I've got a lot of tears out of my system. I want to know what happened. Everything!"

"Let's go into the kitchen. I'll make a hot drink."

"*Now! I want to know now!*"

Susanna edged away, trying to decide how best to give her the facts she now demanded. She took a deep breath and sat down on a low stool.

"Robin came to see me last week. He asked me to speak to Father on his behalf."

"What about?"

"Jake."

Elizabeth showed only an inkling of what she felt at the mention of his name, but it was enough to let Susanna know of her mother's awareness.

"Once you left, Jake moved in here to sort out designs for the production. It went on longer than Robin wanted. He asked Jake to go back to the flat, but Jake made excuses for staying. That was when I was asked to intervene."

"I see. And did you?"

"Something stopped me."

"Stopped you?"

"It was Kate."

"Kate? What has she got to do with this?"

"It seems there was some sort of – upset, at Fiona's. Kate saw it all and ran away. She came to me."

"Oh, God! What a mess," said Elizabeth.

"I didn't know what to do. Kate was in a very emotional state, very disturbed. She begged me not to contact Fiona. You know the sort of messy life Fiona leads. Well, it obviously upset Kate."

"Did Kate actually tell you what she'd seen?"

"It was some sort of fight with Andrew. I didn't press for details. I tried to phone Father to arrange to see him but he didn't seem to be in. Anyway, I didn't feel I could just leave Kate on her own."

"In the circumstances I really don't see that you need to blame yourself for anything that's happened."

"Well, that's what I keep trying to tell myself, but I find it difficult to believe. If I hadn't waited quite so long, maybe I could have persuaded Jake to go back sooner."

"I doubt it. Where are they now?"

"I don't know."

"Have you spoken with the police or – or anyone?"

"Yes. I was asked to – to identify the body." Her face paled at the memory and her hands went up to hide her own tears. "He'd been taken to St Mary's hospital for various tests. At first they thought he might have been drunk, but there was nothing."

"It must have been a terrible experience for you."

"They'd – they'd cleaned him up quite a lot by the time I saw him. It was an odd experience. Not what I'd anticipated." She began to talk, almost trancelike. "They'd removed him to the – the public mortuary. There was a small plate-glass window, with little curtains either side and some flowers in the background. He didn't look as though he'd been in pain, or even distressed. He looked more as though he was in a deep sleep. Quite composed and relaxed and sleeping. I almost felt happy for him. It was all over very quickly. I didn't have time to get emotionally involved – not then. Not at that precise moment."

"I should have been here," said Elizabeth.

"It wouldn't have made any difference. Something was bound to happen sooner or later. They're due to do the post-mortem tomorrow."

"I hadn't thought about that," said Elizabeth.

"Apparently it's a formality for all road accidents of this type. I was told they'd managed to take a few statements from passers-by. There was one report that seemed to imply that he – " She stopped short shaking her head as though trying to deny what she was about to say.

"That he what?" urged Elizabeth.

"It was an eye-witness report. Someone said they thought Robin drove straight into the thick of the traffic."

"You mean – suicide?"

Susanna nodded slowly, her eyes heavy with the image of the horror that must have taken place.

"The poor boy. My Robby! My poor boy. There never was a lot of fun for him. Always behind Bruce. Always the different one. Looking for something special, seeking attention, seeking an impossible relationship. Always out on his own. Now completely alone."

"I – I still don't know what to do about Kate. I haven't been able to locate Father, either."

"I'll look around upstairs. Maybe there's a message. Perhaps he's gone away for a few days. He used to do that years ago. Whenever things got too complicated he used to just up and away for a few days. He needed to be alone. Have you tried to contact Jake?"

"No, I haven't phoned the flat. Frankly, I didn't want to speak to him."

Elizabeth went upstairs in a daze. She stood outside Robin's room for a moment, and then went in to try to recall a few of the happier moments of her son's short life. The bed remained unmade, crumpled as it had been left by Jake. The rug was slightly kicked up at one corner and a couple of gay magazines lay open on the dressing table. She smoothed her hand across the glossy pages, almost as though she were trying to stroke the bare chest of the model, imagining it to be Robin smiling up at her, blatantly admitting his gayness by posing in the nude and boasting of his exhibitionism. Yet she knew he would never have done that. He was always too concerned for her feelings to leave this sort of magazine lying about even in the privacy of his own bedroom. Her hand reached out to claw at the pages, tearing them into shreds as they made uneven patterns of chests and thighs and genitals floating to the floor. Although Jake had used the room and his particularly sweet-smelling aftershave still clung stalely in the air, she was aware of there being nothing of his around. Everything belonged to Robin. The hairbrushes and the comb, the half-used bottle of cologne left for the odd occasions when he slept over.

The sound of Victor finishing the unpacking in her bedroom brought her back to the present, reminding her of her lack of answers and making her close the door on those particular memories.

"There's no sign of Mitch having been around recently," said Victor.

"I know. Jake obviously used Robin's room, but that's just as empty."

"I'm deeply sorry, my love. If there's anything you want me to do, you've only to ask, you know that."

"Yes, I know. I'm very grateful to you, Victor. I don't know what I'd have done without you. Not just recently, but over the past year or so." She wasn't looking at him, but seemed to be expressing one thing while thinking something quite different. She went past him and into the dressing room to open one of the wardrobes.

"What are you looking for?" said Victor.

"Something has just occurred to me. There might be a suitcase missing." She ran her eye over the little row of luggage until she came to a gap on the shelf. She then opened Mitch's wardrobe and ran her hand through his suits and odd trousers, noting a few empty hangers. "He's gone away somewhere."

"Surely he couldn't just walk out and leave everything?" said Victor.

"That's exactly what he can do. You don't know him as well as I do. No one knows him as well as I do." There was far more substance to that statement than Victor appreciated. Far more than most people could ever understand, or even begin to accept.

The telephone began to ring in Mitch's study, a sharp sound that dissolved the silence of the house and intruded into the corners. It seemed to nag for an eternity until Elizabeth picked up the receiver just ahead of Susanna downstairs.

"Yes?" she said softly.

"Hullo, Matthew here. I wasn't sure whether you'd got back yet."

"A short time ago."

"How are you?"

"I'll do. Did you want to speak to Susanna?"

"I really wanted to find out about you. I'm – I'm sorry. If there's anything you want me to do, any way I can help, you know I'm here."

"That's very kind of you, Matthew. Everyone's being very kind."

"How's Mitch taking it?"

"I really don't know." There was a silence at the other end. It was the sort of silence that spoke its own meaning through its very lack of communication. "Why did you ask?"

"We've started rehearsal. He – he hasn't been for the past two days. I haven't contacted him for obvious reasons. We've managed with a stand-in. I thought he needed time to get over the shock. Isn't he there?"

"Some of his things are missing. He's probably gone away. He does that now and again. When things get too much for him he likes to be on his own."

"I see. But he can't hide away for ever, can he?" said Matthew.

"No, I suppose not. If I find out anything I'll let you know. Do you want to speak to Susanna?"

"Yes, please. Just keep your chin up."

Elizabeth went out on to the landing and called down to Susanna in the kitchen where she could hear her rattling cups and saucers. The extension was picked up downstairs and Elizabeth replaced the receiver in the study. It wasn't until she turned to go back into the bedroom that she noticed a coloured envelope propped up against a book on a small table near the door. It was addressed to Mitch in an unfamiliar handwriting. She picked it up, tapping it against her palm as she went downstairs followed by Victor.

"What's that?" he asked.

"I just found it in Mitch's study. It's addressed to him. I – I don't seem to recognise the handwriting."

"Are you going to open it?"

Susanna was just finishing her conversation as they walked in.

"There's something odd," said Susanna. "When I went to put the kettle on just now, there was some warm water in it."

"Then someone must have been here quite recently," said Victor.

"Maybe the person who left this," said Elizabeth.

"You'd better open it," suggested Victor.

Elizabeth turned the envelope over in her hand. "Let's hope it doesn't constitute police evidence of any sort."

"You've seen too many bad TV shows," said Susanna, trying to brighten the moment.

Elizabeth inserted her forefinger under the flap and ripped it open. Inside there was a single sheet of notepaper written in neat small handwriting. The loops were carefully completed, the t's crossed with an exaggerated curl, and the i's dotted with complete circles. She let her eye run down to the foot of the notepaper to see who had signed the letter; it was Jake. She read through the contents very rapidly, her heart seeming to race faster as the entire situation became clearer to her. The letter was more in sorrow than in anger.

Dear Mitch,

Although I did what you asked me to do, I'm sorry man, but that just ain't my scene. I can't take any more. Make no mistake, I'm not ungrateful for the help you've offered, but the price is much too high, even for me.

Robby meant more to me than anyone I've ever known. Now we've both got to live with that load of guilt for the rest of our lives. If you decide to have me put off the production you've only got to say the word. I'm not the sort to carry a grudge. Here's the front door key of your house. Give Elizabeth my love, she needs it from someone. We could have managed some great work down at the cottage, but not with the demands you made. I hope it hasn't taken you too long to [here there was something finely crossed out and other words written alongside] sort yourself out. I hope it wasn't too painful.

    Yours ever,
    Jake.

It was a florid signature, with large curves and an enormous letter K rising above and below the other letters. It was flamboyant, artistic in the extreme, yet delicate and caring, reflecting the various facets of the writer's personality.

Elizabeth handed it over to Susanna who glanced at the words and then passed on the sheet to Victor. There was an exchange of glances between the two women that spoke all there was to say. Perhaps Susanna was only able to half guess at the truth as she had done for most of her adult life. But she sensed the renewed pain that had been caused to her mother. It was Elizabeth who spoke first.

"Mitch must still be at the cottage. I must go to him. He might need me."

"Why not telephone first? He could have decided to move on," suggested Victor.

"I doubt it." She crossed to the telephone and dialled a number. As the flat ringing-tone burred in her ear she pictured Mitch crossing the living room of their Cotswold cottage, bought for a song many years ago. They had used it as regularly as commitments allowed when the children were small and it had grown into a comfortable cluttered bolthole away from the demands of London. But over the years they had used it less and less, a status symbol now overgrown with moss and mildew. She hoped Mitch had remembered to air the bed. The phone rang on; she willed him to answer – but there was no response. She shook her head and replaced the receiver.

She immediately dialled another number. This time it was only a matter of seconds before the American voice of Jake answered.

"Yeah?"

"Jake, this is Elizabeth. Please don't hang up on me. I've got to talk with you."

"What do you want? I'm surprised you're talking to me," said Jake. His speech sounded slightly slurred, as though he had been drinking.

"Tell me, is Mitch still at the cottage?" There was a pause at the other end of the telephone, and a gulp as though something had been swallowed. "Is he still there, Jake?"

"Yeah, he's there. He asked me to go with him. I didn't wanna go, but he asked me to. He was in one hell of a state about – about Robby. Christ! Why the hell did you have to phone me? Leave me alone. It's all over – finished. I'm sorry. Goddammit! I'm sorry, but it wasn't my fault. It – it just happened. It happened."

He seemed to be talking wildly, running together his words and saying anything that came into his head. It was as though he were trying to apologise as best he could, but not terribly successful in the attempt.

"Please, don't hate yourself, Jake. You and Robby had some good times together. I'm sorry if I sometimes seemed less than friendly towards you. I hope you now understand a little better. It was nothing to do with you as a person. Do you understand what I'm getting at?"

"Sure, I understand. We all need to live according to our lights. I – I gotta go now. By the way, Robby's things. What do you want I should do about them?"

"I'll let you know. Try not to feel too guilty, Jake. We've all got a share in that. Goodbye." She spoke quite softly, almost in a whisper. She saw his olive skin behind her eyes, recalled the finely chiselled features and the set of his mouth that always struck her as being so carefully constructed to reveal the whitest teeth she had ever seen. This was the first thing she remembered noticing about Jake, the even teeth set against his dark lips as though designed for a glossy toothpaste commercial.

"I've got to go to the cottage," she said calmly.

"Not tonight," said Susanna. "It's gone eight o'clock. It'll take you over an hour to get there."

"Mitch needs me. He needs me more than ever before. I know he does. I've got to go now." She began to pull on her trench-coat before either of them realised what was happening.

Victor reached out and clung on to her arm as she made

towards the door. "Elizabeth, you're overtired. You must be worn out. You've hardly eaten a thing all day. Why not wait until the morning? I'll drive you down then."

"I'll go by myself, tonight." She pulled free from his grasp and made towards the front door.

Susanna tried to stand in her mother's way, but it was no use.

"I'll come with you," said Victor, confident that he was making the right decision.

"*No!* I don't need anyone to watch over me. I don't want anyone to come with me."

"But you're overtired. You might even fall asleep at the wheel," said Victor.

"I doubt it. If you'll feel better, I'll telephone you when I arrive there. But I've got to go alone. There are reasons, strong reasons. Believe me, I know exactly what I'm doing."

25

Elizabeth drove carefully, but fast, very fast indeed. It would be the longest single journey she had ever made. She had to navigate her way across London on to the Western Avenue and the motorway. The cold amber sodium lights along the first stretch of road formed murky shadows just beyond her range of vision, shadows that clustered and disappeared as headlights penetrated them and were carried away behind her. There seemed to be considerably more traffic lights than she remembered; a greater number of delaying roundabouts than she recalled from past journeys.

Once she reached the M40 near Denham she knew she could open up the throttle even more. The sight of the name "Denham" brought back unexpected memories of the time when she and Mitch had made a film there, way back in the dim past when they were very young and riding high. It was almost the last film made at those particular studios. Their problems had seemed so infinitesimal then, almost non-existent. They were happy times. The times of fulfilment and growing reputations and public adulation. It was all so many light years away.

The road wound through the countryside in great sweeping curves, through the High Wycombe escarpment with its myriads of lights signalling their personal brand of comfort in the ticky-tacky houses below. The road narrowed and widened around unexpected roadworks, constantly challenging. The trees and bushes swished past the windows of the car like a nightmare tunnel in a funfair, darkly sinister, reaching out to clutch and claw at the vehicle. Occasional light was admitted only to be blacked out with even more menacing darkness and ever more confusing shadows. Oncoming headlights flashed and dipped and flashed again in rapid succession as Elizabeth's control of the car began to waver. It had been a long day after a restless night, and she had taken very little food. Fatigue was beginning to take its toll. Her head ached and her eyes were sore. Her hands clenched around the steering-wheel, pulling and twisting it through the English countryside, almost as though she were trying physically to turn the wheels faster through her mounting anxiety.

At the Headington roundabout, just outside Oxford, she turned right and began the final stage of the journey. There were still more roundabouts that had to be navigated, more unremembered bends in the road to slow her down. Always having to slow down when she wanted to accelerate, always having to hold back, hold back, *hold back*. That's what she had been forced to do throughout most of their married life. Visions of the years continued to float before her. When the children were young and needed her personal attention. The time when Robin had appeared in the middle of a dinner party dressed in her clothes, and created a moment of enjoyment linked with gentle admonition. Was that the beginning? Was that the moment when she first began to suspect where his emotions would lead him? It was all so long ago. It was all so dim and distant, like the velvet darkness that had crept up and wrapped itself around the speeding car. The occasion when Bruce had had the lead in the school play and revealed his undoubted family talent for the first time. Mitch's first faltering attempt to explain himself. His driving compulsion for self-indulgence and his need for pain. His desperate cry for human understanding, and his plea for charity.

Elizabeth found her attention wandering as she realised the extent to which the car was swerving across the middle of the road. An oncoming lorry flashed its headlights several times, pressing down hard on the horn as it passed. The sound and the brightness brought her back to the present and to a concentration that had begun to slide away. She took the old road through Witney, passing through it as though under remote control.

Her headlights picked out the metallic glow of the road sign indicating the village of Minster Lovell off to the right. There were more advancing cars with headlights blazing to instruct her to wait until they passed. She hated being so near to the end of her journey, yet still so far away, and being forced to conjecture what she would find when she finally arrived. After an eternity of moments, she was able to drive down the sharply sloping lane and over the narrow stone bridge that led to the single road of the old Cotswold village. There were no streetlights, just a few glimmers from the latticed windows of the Old Swan.

Elizabeth pulled to a halt outside a large cottage at the far end of the village on the left. The stone building was crouched below a large chestnut tree with bare spiky branches and was surrounded by low bushes and a walled garden that formed a corner with the road running across the top of the village.

She turned off the headlights and almost fell from the car, standing against the warm engine while she surveyed the windows for signs of life. The sky had now cleared, and a sudden movement of cloud had created an opening to allow the full moon to cover the countryside in a steel blue light that gave everything a strangely ethereal appearance. The parish church shaped itself against the cyclorama of stars and distant horizon. The hedges and isolated farmhouses looked as though they had all been cut out of cardboard and strutted for the occasion. The ancient ruins of Minster Lovell rose hugely, shrouded with mystery and menace. The sound of the River Windrush completed the background to the monochrome landscape.

There was no sign of activity from within the cottage, no drawn curtains with fine chinks of light, no sounds of radio or television, no indication of any form of habitation, yet she knew that Mitch must be there. Elizabeth let herself into the cramped front hall and switched on the light. Mitch's raincoat was clumsily hanging from the hallstand. She noticed some recently dried mud on the front mat. For a brief moment her instincts told her to return to the car and drive home again, but she knew this would be silly.

"Mitch," she called softly, fearfully. There was no reply, but she hadn't really expected one. The sound of her own voice acted as a comfort to her. It established an awareness of things solidly around her.

She passed into the living room and noticed a script of *The Apple Cart* open on the settee. Sections of dialogue had been underlined and stage directions pencilled in. In the kitchen were a few pots and pans upended on the draining board, and the table had some scattered crumbs. The emptiness worried her, making her feel cold so that she pulled her coat about herself, puzzled and trying to fathom what had happened and where Mitch could be. He certainly wouldn't be down at the Old Swan as that never had been his scene. In fact, the villagers thought them to be stand-offish because they so seldom mixed with the local inhabitants and seemed to take away more than they brought to the neighbourhood. She called his name a second time as she mounted the very narrow twisting stairs that led up to the small bedrooms. All was stillness and silence. The only sound was the creaking of dried-out floorboards as she passed from one room to another.

The bed was smooth, as though it had not been slept in for some time, and a suitcase was lying open in one corner. A few of Mitch's clothes were spread about. A crumpled shirt was hanging over the back of a chair, some socks on the floor, discarded underpants and trousers nearby. The disarray seemed to be superimposed upon the basic order of the room, as though something had happened in a hurry. It was unlike Mitch to be untidy and to leave his things strewn around. In the next room the bed was unmade with the sheets and blankets dragged down one side and the mattress showing below as though the occupant had spent a restless night. Elizabeth was about to go when a vaguely remembered smell drifted into her nostrils. It was the same sweet smell she had noticed in Robin's room a few hours earlier.

It wasn't until she looked into the bathroom that her fears began to mount. A small stained white towel had been thrown across the side of the bath to hang as a blood-spattered flag. The dried crimson had now congealed to a dark maroon. A few drops of blood were domed across the floor in an uneven line from the handbasin to the towel.

"Mitch! Mitch!" His name escaped from her throat before she realised it. The final words of Jake's note washed back into her mind. There was the crossed out section and then something about sorting himself out. "*I hope it wasn't too painful.*"

She began to feel sick with fear. She opened the bathroom window to let in some fresh air. The slight wind stroked her face, causing her to gasp, drinking in the clean night air. She allowed her head to drop forward as she began to relax and to regain a little of her composure.

It was at this moment that she saw a glimmer of light coming from the barn at the end of the garden. It was an outhouse that led on to the side road, and had been used for general storage, stables and workshop. There had been a time when the children had colonised it for their clubhouse. The building had its fair share of memories. Once again she allowed the name "Mitch" to escape from her lips. This time there was a resignation about the way she whispered the single syllable. It was no longer a question, but rather a moment of anticipation. The nausea began to rise again, and images took hold of her imagination as she looked back towards the bloodstained towel.

She ran from the bathroom, stumbling down the dangerous staircase and out through the kitchen into the garden at the rear of the house. The flagstone path was overgrown with clumps of grass and moss, and was slippery from the late night dew. She was able to see where she was going as the moonlight spread its sinister glow across the bedraggled lawn, seeming to beckon her towards the barn. The light became a little brighter as she brushed past the barren bushes and emerged from below the overhanging branches of the chestnut tree. The faintly yellow glow announced the end of her journey. It seemed to confirm that this was where she would find her husband.

The entrance to the barn was set well back from the road at the end of a cobbled driveway. This forced her to feel her way through a patch of darker shadows around to the other side. By now she was thinking only of Mitch, and how she would find him. The inset door was slightly ajar and allowed a minutely faint line of dull light to escape across the cobblestones as though indicating the way. She pushed open the door, listening to the scraping of rusty hinges as the moonlight took over and filled the entrance.

"Mitch? Mitch? Are you there?" She called softly, full of the fear of her own wild anticipation, consumed with foreboding.

There was still no reply, yet she knew in her heart that he must be in there somewhere.

Her feet seemed to lead her into the barn, pulling her forward slowly, cautiously, stopping to listen and then advancing another few steps before she stopped yet again. She passed a shelf full of long-discarded cobwebbed toys, things they had planned to pass on but never got around to. A pile of broken garden tools was lying unevenly stacked, yet another sign of long-abandoned activity. It wasn't until she reached about halfway, and her eyes had become accustomed to the dim light, that she was aware of a slight groan coming from the far end, behind a slatted partition.

"Mitch, is that you?" She remained quite still, petrified in case it was someone else. There was always the remote chance that she had made a mistake and come across an intruder. The silence was unnatural. The groan was repeated, and now mouthed into a single word, "Help", rasped through a choked throat, effortful and pained. Elizabeth went quickly towards the direction of the sound, bracing herself to face what awaited her.

The sight was more devastating than her wildest imaginings could have led her to believe. She reeled back in horrified incredulity, her hand covering her mouth to prevent her crying into the night.

Mitch was spread-eagled, face forward, on to an enormous cartwheel, his wrists and ankles lashed with rough rope that had become bloodstained through his unsuccessful efforts to release himself. He was totally naked and his back was covered in fine lash marks that had opened his flesh and allowed blood to trickle down the length of his bruised torso and over his legs. His buttocks were discoloured with dark patches of swollen flesh that showed the yellow and red areas where he had been beaten. Perspiration had dried on his face. His eyes were sunken from pain and lack of sleep, and his beard had begun to establish itself as a dark stubble around his sallow cheeks. His hair had become matted. He resembled something from a mediaeval torture chamber, now left to rot until such time as retribution had been satisfied.

"Oh, my God! Mitch! How – Why – " Elizabeth was unable to find the right words, the right questions. There had been times in the past, but nothing to compare with this.

"Liz, help me. Please, help me." His voice was nothing more than the merest rasp, yet there was still a plea for understanding and compassion mingled with his cry for help. "Untie me, Liz. Please, untie me."

Her fingers tried to grapple with the rope, but the knots were corroded with the dried blood and she wasn't able to see clearly through her own tears and the renewed throb in her temples. The light was on the wrong side and she felt weak. She looked around for something with which to cut the rope, and remembered the pile of tools. Her hands flung aside useless items until she finally found an old pair of rusty secateurs that had long since been discarded as useless. One blade was broken, and she had to use the thick part of the cutting edge in order to get any leverage that would allow her to gnaw into the rope. However fast she tried to work she had to be careful not to cut further into Mitch's still bleeding wrists. He continued to gasp and to sob until the first rope was cut free. Once this much was achieved he managed to take the secateurs from her and painfully release his other wrist. He was then able to work on his ankles until he was totally free.

Mitch raised himself, using the spokes of the wheel to pull up his weight. He managed to hang on to the upper spokes with his head resting against the backs of his hands, too ashamed to turn and face Elizabeth, too ashamed to say anything at all.

She leaned back against the wall opposite him, looking at his back, watching his own tears mingling with the newly flowing blood that oozed from his wrists, shaking her head in total disbelief.

"I'm sorry, Liz. I'm sorry! I'm sorry! I'm sorry!" Over and over again, first quite loudly, and then softly until it was just a murmur being burbled into the wheel.

Elizabeth took off her coat and covered his shoulders with great tenderness. "Let's go back into the house. We'll – we'll talk inside."

He allowed her fingers to unclip his grasp from the wooden spokes, and then lead him back through the cold air into the kitchen. He stood apart from her, leaning against the door, still in considerable pain. "I'm sorry, Liz," was all that he could find to say.

"You've apologised so many times, Mitch. So many times, over so many years. Why now? You've made so many promises. Until recently I really did think it was all over. All behind us. I thought we were finally through it all, until the opening night of the play."

"Me too. It was the play, Liz. They hurt me. I had to get back somehow. I hate myself. I loathe myself for what I do to both of us, but I can't help it. I try not to, then something happens, and I'm on the treadmill all over again."

"Why this time?" She now forced herself to look across the room towards his hunched figure, still clutching her inadequate coat across his naked loins, dirty and bloodstained and looking ill.

"It was – Robby. He's – he's dead."

"I know. That's why I came back. I read about it in someone's newspaper."

"How long has it been? What day is it?"

"Does that matter?"

"I killed him, Liz. It was my fault. I – I took Jake away from him. It was only for a few days, but he saw it as being permanent. You were away, and I needed someone. We – we were working on the play together. There was nothing . . ."

"Please, Mitch, don't say any more. I'd rather not know."

"I had to punish myself. I had to pay for what I'd done. This was the only way I knew in which I could suffer with him."

"You're talking like an idiot. Do you honestly believe that he knows about your suffering? Do you think this will bring him back? He's dead, Mitch. *He's dead!*" Her voice was high and hysterical, her eyes wildly out of focus, and her own lack of sleep and anguish now taking control of her emotions.

"Jake? Where's Jake?" he asked.

"He's gone. How else do you imagine I could have known where to find you? He left a note for you at the house. I opened it. Christ, but I hate you. I hate you for all the years you've taken from me. For all the suffering I've had to share with you. I hate you for the lies and the deceits. I hate you for robbing me of what I might have been. I hate you! I hate you!" She collapsed on to a chair, sobbing and heaving and banging her tightly clenched fists on to the kitchen table.

Mitch wanted to go to her, to put his arms around her and express how he was really feeling, but his shame held him back. He looked down at his bruised and bleeding ankles and held out his shaking hands, inspecting them as though they were no longer a part of himself, as though they belonged to a stranger in supplication. He crossed behind her and stood over her for a moment. And then dragged himself upstairs into the bathroom to begin to wash himself clean.

It was some moments before Elizabeth realised that he had gone. It wasn't until she looked up towards the ceiling to listen to the sounds coming from the bathroom above that she knew where he was. It took a considerable effort for her to follow him, and to begin to help him. She bathed his wounds with remarkable tenderness, cleaning away the congealed blood from his feet, and then drying the semi-open wounds on a soft towel, gently dabbing at the raw flesh while trying not to inflict any more pain than he had already suffered. Elizabeth cleaned his legs and his arms, sponged his back, and all the time he simply sat on a low stool and allowed her hands to touch him, to administer aid to his battered body. They were more like mother and child than husband and wife, and it was oddly comforting for Elizabeth to be able to help Mitch in this way. After washing his hair and drying it with large towels, she guided him into the bedroom and helped him to lie down, avoiding touching the injured parts of his body, and ensuring the bedclothes covered him lightly.

"I'll sleep in another room tonight. You'll be more comfortable," she said.

"Liz," he said, holding out his hand.

"What?"

He raised his head and looked at her. "Thank you. It might not sound much, but there doesn't seem to be any other way of putting it. I shall always be grateful to you."

Elizabeth almost laughed as she recalled having said much the same words to Victor. It seemed as though everyone was always in someone's debt. She sighed and looked away. Mitch's face seemed to have aged ten years since she last saw him. The lustre in his eyes had gone and his cheeks were drawn. Even the strong line of his jaw seemed to have disappeared. He was suddenly an old man, old before his time. Old and helplessly crying out for more understanding, more help, greater charity.

"You ought to eat. I'll make something for you."

"No, it doesn't matter. Please don't – "

His words followed her downstairs as she returned to the kitchen to sort out whatever she could find. There was only some bread suitable for toasting and an old piece of cake that was dried out but still edible. She made a pot of tea and took it all upstairs.

"You're being very kind. Thank you." He was straining after saying the right things, trying to keep from the brink of another explosion.

"Not kind at all. You've got to eat something. Not that there's much downstairs." She poured the tea for both of them and put his on the bedside table together with the toast and the cake.

There was a noisy silence between them, filled with the crunching of the toast and the stirring of the tea.

"Is this the end, Liz?" he said quietly.

"I don't know, Mitch. I really don't know. I'm too tired to think about it tonight."

"How's – how's Victor?"

"Oh, he's fine." The sound of his name reminded her of the heat of Marrakesh, and the single day when they had laughed a lot. It also served to remind her how different was Victor's way of life and his expectation from marriage. She recalled the way he had sometimes spoken about his first wife, and the minor intimations of comparison with Elizabeth. Above all there was Victor's genuine regard for her own welfare, his attention to her creature comforts, and the other side of his personality that had only been revealed once they were away from London and in a completely different environment. It had been an odd experience being alone with him for so long. Alone and together, yet still apart.

"Yes, Victor's fine. He arranged for us to return the moment I read about Robin's accident. He was very understanding, very concerned."

"I see." Mitch sipped at his tea, allowing the hot liquid to slide down his dry throat and warm his belly. He felt it penetrate into the cold ache of his entire body and relax his stiff muscles.

The telephone rang loudly, making both of them suddenly aware of the outside world. "Hullo?" said Elizabeth.

"Susanna here. I couldn't wait until morning. Is he there?"

"Yes. Yes, he's here."

"Why didn't he answer when you telephoned?"

"He – he was out in the barn. He – he couldn't hear the phone ringing from there. You know what it's like."

"What about the note? Jake's note? What did all that mean?"

"I shouldn't worry too much about that. He's a highly emotional young man. He had a slight argument with Father about – about something to do with the sets for the new production. He suggested they get someone else to work on the designs. That's what he meant about 'sort yourself out'. Tell Matthew not to worry about the production. I think we'll stay down here for another day or so. We need time to be together, and to talk about things. Time to talk about – about Robby. I'm sure everything will be fine. Now, you get some sleep, and remember to kiss Kate for me." She didn't wait for a response but replaced the receiver immediately.

Mitch remained motionless throughout this brief conversation, listening but not registering. "Thank you," he said. "Oh, God! Why are we like this?" The words demanded a reply and an explanation, but there was no one who could answer such a simple question. He reached out for a piece of cake, but it crumbled in his hand; he shrugged his shoulders in a half-laugh. "Let them eat cake." He took a small mouthful, allowing it to linger on his lips as he looked down on to the remaining fragment held between his fingers.

> "There was an Old Person of Rheims,
> Who was troubled with horrible dreams;
> So to keep him awake,
> They fed him on cake,
> Which amused that Old Person of Rheims."

He spoke the lines slowly, with a self-mocking inflection. Puzzled and amused at his own situation, yet confused as to why he should find himself where he was.

"I think you ought to try to sleep now, Mitch." As she took the remainder of the cake from his hand, she saw renewed tears welling into his eyes. She opened the bedroom door to leave, the landing light casting a shadow down one side of her face.

"Liz?"

"Yes?"

"Try to remember I *do* love you. Whatever you're thinking, or whatever you're feeling right now. Try to remember I've never stopped loving you."

She said nothing, pausing only for the smallest fraction of a second. There was nothing more she could say, not now, not after the past few hours. The door closed slowly, cutting down the shaft of light until the room was consumed by darkness. The moonlight dissolved into the room, spreading its gentle glimmer across the bed and picking out Mitch who was still awake, glassy-eyed, and now crying more bitterly than at any time in his entire life.

26

Being alone, and in a bed she hadn't slept in for a long time, encouraged another restless night for Elizabeth, weighing up yet again the needs of Mitch against those of Victor, always putting herself at the end of the line. The dark hours of waking and sleeping knitted together and were interwoven with memories of Robin. He had never been a really happy child, never outgoing and sociable like the others. Over and over again she awoke to blame herself, crying bitterly and asking questions to which there could never be any conclusive answers.

Mitch's own tears had lasted no more than a few seconds. He had succumbed to sleep almost as soon as he heard Elizabeth's door closing, too utterly exhausted to pursue his own train of thought. He too spent a restless night, occasionally waking as he thrashed around. The sheets pulled at his raw flesh, causing some of his wounds to gape and weep their small tears of blood on to the white linen.

Elizabeth got up at about eight thirty and prepared whatever passed for breakfast. She took the tray up to Mitch, still sleeping fitfully and showing all the signs of his own uneven night's rest. He opened his eyes as she entered the room, smiling weakly, unable to find any words that were appropriate. She set down the tray beside the bed and began to pour the coffee. It filled the small room with a rich aroma of freshly ground beans to remind them both of their London home. It was an odd train of thought, but each knew the other to be on the same wavelength.

"You're very patient," he said, taking the cup and saucer from her.

"I still love you."

"More than I deserve."

She said nothing, but sipped at her cup, savouring the comforting taste of the hot drink as she allowed it to ease her throat and warm her cold limbs. She stood looking out across the fields at the low lying morning mist that floated across the brightening landscape to reveal the shapes of horses grazing and silently padding near the hedges. A flurry of ducks started up, screeching above the naked trees, to be swallowed into the scurrying clouds.

"How do you feel this morning?" she asked, without turning into the room.

"Stiff and sore. I've got a slight headache. No more than to be expected."

Elizabeth put down her cup and appeared to try to retreat within herself. "Why, Mitch? Why did you get him to do it?"

"I tried to explain last night. Expiation, I suppose."

"Is it always going to be like this?"

He didn't answer, but seemed to concentrate his thoughts on the business of finishing his coffee. It was a trick he had for not responding immediately. "I – I don't know. I really don't know," he said softly.

"I thought it was all over. I thought you'd managed to rise above it and put it all behind you. It's been so long."

"Not really. There was a time during the last Australian tour. I managed to keep it to myself. It happened again when I was in South Africa. You weren't on that one with me."

"I had no idea – "

"You were happy thinking I'd managed to kick the need. I saw no reason to upset you unnecessarily."

"That was kind of you. Now what? Where do we go from here?"

"That's rather up to you. I'll – I'll fall in with whatever you decide. If you feel you want a divorce then I'll – I'll give you grounds. I'll do whatever you want. You've stood by me long enough. You've protected me from myself. You've shielded me from the rest of the world. I can think of at least a dozen occasions when the press could have ruined me through the gossip columns."

"Make no mistake, Mitch. There was a strong element of enlightened self-interest. We both had our careers to consider. We also had the children."

At the mention of the children they both fell into a short silence once again. They both thought about the futility of Robin's death, but each arrived at the same conclusion by different paths.

"Perhaps this isn't really the best time to try to decide what to do. We're both still very tired," said Elizabeth, turning her back upon the window. "Whatever lies ahead of us, it's still the rest of our lives."

"I think I ought to get up. I'll have a bath and a shave and see if I can make myself more presentable. My chin feels as though I've got thousands of pine-cones sticking from it." He laughed. It was a meaningless, inconsequential sound.

"Do you need a hand?"

"No, thanks. I'm sure I can manage." He began to ease himself up, first on to his elbows, and then with his weight resting on the palms of his hands until he finally felt able to pull himself on to the edge of the bed. It was all very effortful. His muscles complained every inch of the way and his bones seemed to grind one against the other.

The morning turned into one of those crisply cold winter days that are designed exclusively for the English countryside. The brilliant April sunshine cast sharply defined shadows, but the air was chill and biting. The grass dripped dew and mist. Spiders' webs in the hedgerows were caught in the watery sunlight and illuminated by strings of tiny particles of moisture in ever decreasing circles. There was the unique smell of freshly damp earth carried on the cool wind that swam across the top of the fields. The air bit deeply into their lungs as they walked around the nearby ruins and listened to the river bubbling below the overhanging willows. The swans billowed their expanse of white wing to catch the breeze and to be propelled away from the intruders. It was all so magically tranquil.

Their long silences spoke more than any words could ever have done, and helped to close the chasm of conflict as surely as any debate. Their joint misfortune was yet another hiatus in their continuing life together. It was a rift that would surely allow them to come together yet again and, yet again, enable them to present a united front to the rest of the world.

The entire day passed in an oasis in time. They saw nobody else, spoke with no one on the telephone. There were no newspapers, and they avoided the radio or television.

By the evening they were both very much more relaxed. They were able to talk about generalities without feeling they were using it as an excuse to avoid what was uppermost in their minds.

"Sleep with me tonight, Liz," Mitch said, quite unexpectedly.

"Are you really sure you want that?"

"More sure than I've been of anything for a long time. I want to feel you close to me. I want to be able to reach out and know you're still there."

"Very well."

The pleasure of finding he still wanted her, despite her recent defection with Victor, was tempered by the knowledge that his was a childlike need to feel her actually at his side, and it roused her old sense of responsibility once more.

Elizabeth cradled Mitch's head in her arms and he wrapped himself close to her warm body. He breathed deeply, expressing his new found security. They lay like that for some time, exchanging more of their thoughts, admitting their regrets about the past, and their hopes for the future. Mitch made love to his wife without the burning passion of a man trying to prove something to himself, or to her. Each was glad that the other experienced full arousal. In a primitive way it endorsed their years of marriage; sex was not yet behind them. There still remained the bond that had been woven and delicately threaded between them over the years of shared problems, and child rearing, and strife. They fell asleep in the warm embrace of each other's arms, smiling through the darkness at each other, knowing they each felt the same togetherness.

They got up quite early next morning, tidied up the cottage and returned to London. As they entered the house they felt the aura of recent events still crouching between the walls. Everything was just as it had been left and had a dulling effect upon their new found closeness. There was a need to exorcise the overlay of tragedy, a need to allow the daylight to return to the corners and establish reassurance.

It was Bruce who had seen to the details of Robin's funeral. He had arranged for the body to be cremated at Golders Green. The service was attended by close family and a few friends. The sermon extolled the boy's virtues, mentioning his talent as an actor of light comedy and his now never to be fufilled promise. It was all so kind, so thoughtful, so very studied, so utterly impersonal.

The organ music rose melodically as the coffin was slowly propelled through a small hatch. It was all so controlled, so very much a production that had been running for a long time. The service lasted no more than a mere twenty minutes. Twenty minutes was hardly long enough in which to dispense with a lifetime, short though the life had been. Elizabeth emerged on to the driveway comforted by Mitch, now dabbing at his own eyes. It was over. All the words had been said, and Robin had made his exit. There was nothing grand about the way his performance had ended; there were no cheers. All that Mitch could think about was a tatty theatre somewhere in the Midlands. A seedy building at which he had been invited to play on the final night of its existence before it was demolished. He remembered making a fatuous speech about the glory that had once reigned within the theatre's walls. There had been a few well chosen words concerning the fine performances that had taken place, and of the brilliant productions that had passed across its stage. He remembered visiting the same town a few years later only to find a modern office block on the site, and no trace of the theatre. There had been nothing erected to commemorate the glory about which he had spoken. Words spoken for the benefit of others seemed so pointless. Expected, but pointless. It was one's very private thoughts that really mattered, the individual commitment that counted. Perhaps it was all akin to justice, something that had to be seen to be done.

Jake had been present at the funeral, but he sat apart, listening with his head bowed and his hand over his face. There were no words exchanged between him and the family. There were none that seemed right for the occasion. As the coffin began to glide away there had been just a chance look from Mitch that said all that was needed. Jake hung back until the family had left the building and then slipped away.

They all went their several ways. Family and friends, and the usual clutch of reporters. There were a few members of the public who had managed to find out about the funeral, but they added nothing to the occasion other than an unwelcome awareness of the public gaze.

They had to wait almost another week before the inquest took place. This was attended by Susanna and Bruce as well as Mitch and Elizabeth. The details of the accident were related from notes. An eye-witness testified that Robin had been seen to weave his way through the heavy traffic at Hyde Park Corner and then to gather speed. There was something said about Robin almost appearing to drive directly into the thick of the traffic as though not caring about the consequences. The coroner passed over this as opinion rather than fact. Mitch and Elizabeth held each other's hands tightly, not looking at each other, not even hearing much of what was said. The boy was dead. Why all the questions? Why the need to probe? Let him rest. Enough! Enough!

The coroner finally pronounced a verdict of misadventure, and the inquest was closed.

Inevitably there were a few reporters milling about outside, hoping for an interview with the family. The small crowd that had gathered appeared to treat the very private matter as though they were outside another stage door. As far as the public were concerned there would always be those who demanded participation in the lives of the Dawlish family as their price for lifting them to eminence and establishing them as minor idols. As Mitch was about to step into Bruce's car a photographer jumped out from the crowd and called to him, hoping for an immediate reaction. Mitch turned, incensed that anyone could be so completely without feeling. He lashed out towards the camera, sending it flying across the road, and its owner flat on his back. There was an outcry from the other reporters and photographers as cameras flashed to capture the single moment of impulse.

By the time they arrived home Mitch was furious with himself for having given way to his emotions.

He poured himself a drink and downed it rapidly, pouring another in quick succession. The others refused.

"I'm sorry. I shouldn't have done it, I know. But for Christ's sake, why don't they just leave us alone?"

"You've encouraged them not to, Mitch. You belong to them," said Elizabeth.

"Every little thing you do is theirs for the taking," said Bruce.

"Not this. Surely not this as well?"

"Everything!" was all Bruce said.

Susanna was at her father's side, trying to quieten him, doing her best to persuade him to sit down. "Forget it. You were entitled to feel as you did. It's all over now. Please, Father, sit down and forget it."

"Yes, I suppose you're right." He finished his second drink and made to refill his glass for a third time within five minutes.

"You haven't eaten much today, Mitch. You'll have a headache in no time. Leave it for now. You've had enough," said Elizabeth. She simply took the glass from his hand and carried it into the kitchen. It was another awkward moment, in which none of them seemed able to find anything to say.

When she returned Elizabeth announced, "I've written to Jake."

"What on earth for?" said Bruce.

"I thanked him for the way he looked after Robby. We might not have understood him as well as we ought to have done, but *he* certainly did. He understood Robby. He knew what he wanted from life."

"Christ! I wish I knew what I wanted," said Mitch.

"Me too, for that matter," added Bruce.

There was a long silence.

"Anything happening for you?" said Mitch. It was something to say, a way of changing the subject.

"Happening?"

"Play? Film? TV? Anything happening?"

"Yes. *The School for Scandal* fell through. Another unfulfilled promise. Alan's on to the casting for a new play about the life of

Sheridan. He seems to have high hopes of getting the lead for me."

"Sheridan?"

"That was my reaction until I read it. He was quite a character. I was truly amazed. It's a fantastic part."

"I wish you all the best for it," said Mitch absently. He was remembering himself at Bruce's age. Mitch had enjoyed the choice of roles in classical drama, modern comedy, films, anything he wanted. He got there quickly. What did it all mean now?

Susanna and Bruce made their excuses and left. There was no point in standing around making small talk. Better to leave their parents to resolve their own problems, and to try to sort out their differences as best they could. There were no real secrets any more. The house suddenly seemed bigger than it had ever felt before. Just the two of them, public figures, envied and adored, rattling around in all those rooms, and with all those memories.

Exits

First Exit

On the morning of the inquest Susanna had contacted Fiona about Kate. There was no doubting Fiona's relief when she knew that the child was safe, but there was certainly anger as well. She strongly resented the fact that Kate had gone to Susanna and looked upon it as unspoken criticism of herself. At the same time she knew there was more than a little justification for Kate's action. There had been countless guarded telephone calls to Kate's friends, and to anyone else to whom the child might have absconded. Finally, at the point of desperation, Fiona had contacted the police, requesting them to be as discreet as possible.

It wasn't until after the inquest that Susanna had taken Kate home.

Inside the house there were signs of packing and things being stacked ready for departure. The company were scheduled to leave at the end of that week. Fiona had decided that if she couldn't find Kate in time, then she would have no hesitation in cancelling the projected tour. The publicity that would have resulted from her present situation would certainly arouse social awareness, but not of the sort that would help her cause in any practical way.

"I know it's nothing to do with me, Fiona, but Kate needs a decent home life. It's unfair of you to expose her to your way of living."

"As you said, it's nothing to do with you. I'm grateful to you for looking after her."

Kate remained standing next to her aunt, still hanging on to her hand and seeming to hide behind her full coat. "I – I didn't mean to upset you, Mummy."

"I'm sure you didn't, darling," said Fiona, reaching down to enfold Kate in her arms.

The living room door opened and Neil appeared clutching a sheaf of typed papers. "Oh! Sorry, I didn't realise – "

"It doesn't matter. Neil, this is Susanna. She's brought Kate back. The silly little girl has been there all the time."

Susanna tried not to look surprised at the sight of Neil, but her face was her fortune and she wasn't very good at hiding her thoughts. "I thought Andrew – "

"He's gone," was all that Fiona volunteered. There was a finality in her voice that didn't invite further comment. "Neil is helping me with the company. He's managing the tour for me. He's been a tower of strength."

"Yes, I'm sure he must be," said Susanna, trying not to sound too po-faced. "What's going to happen to Kate while you're away?"

"I've still got someone living in. Kate's used to me being away for a while. Aren't you, my little pet?" She bent down and kissed the child almost as an exhibition of her maternal feelings. It was an interesting performance.

"Yes, we have lots of fun when Mummy's away. I can sleep in a different bed every night if I want to. Where's Trisha now, Mummy?"

"I think she's in her room. Why don't you go up and surprise her?"

Kate kissed Susanna warmly, throwing her arms around her neck. She didn't exactly hang on, but she did seem less than willing to release her immediately.

"Don't forget to phone me, Kate," said Susanna.

"I won't. Thank you for looking after me, Aunty Sue." She ran from the room, seemingly anxious to find Trisha and to have her giggles. She appeared to be no worse for her adventure, but she was young, and time alone would reveal just how much this sort of life affected her.

"I'd rather you didn't encourage her to contact you," said Fiona, once the child had gone.

"Why not let *her* decide? I didn't encourage her to come

running to me on this occasion, but she found me. You think about it." Susanna turned sharply and left without saying another word. She had made her points, and was satisfied that Kate was home.

No sooner had the front door slammed than Fiona allowed the tip of her fury to emerge. "Bitch! Self-righteous bitch!"

Neil went up to her and put his arms around her shoulders as he kissed her heavily on the mouth. "Come on, let's get the last few bits and pieces sorted out. We've only got a few more days before we hit the road. Tell you what. If we get through in time, I'll take you to bed." He laughed, clutching at her breasts and pushing himself against her thighs.

"I thought Andy was bad enough, but you're worse. You're nothing but a prick on legs."

"I'll accept that as a compliment. Come on." He led her from the room and upstairs to where there were several boxes of props stacked on the landing. There was a feeling of a camp about to break up, except that this one was just about to hit the road.

Second Exit

There was an incessant ringing on the telephone that nagged to be answered. Bruce and Tracy had taken themselves off for an afternoon nap after the inquest and both had fallen into a deep sleep. Tracy was experiencing mid-afternoon sickness as a result of her pregnancy and she found it helped to nap whenever she could. Bruce was feeling the strain of the past few days and had taken the opportunity to lie down with her. They had spent the first half hour talking about Mitch and Elizabeth, about Robin and Jake, about what they hoped for themselves, until the words had simply faded from them as they dozed off.

The telephone continued until Tracy awoke to dig Bruce in the ribs to get him to answer the call. He staggered from the bedroom wearing nothing but socks and underpants and was aware of his unnecessary coyness when answering the telephone.

"Hullo, yes? Hullo, Alan. You sound pleased with yourself."

"So will you when you hear what I've got to tell you."

Bruce was still not quite awake. "I'm listening," he yawned. "I could do with some good news."

"You've got the part."

"Which part? There seem to have been so many bloody parts lately. I've lost track."

"The Sheridan play. You've got the lead."

"Will you repeat that – slowly?"

"You start rehearsals in three weeks' time. There's a six week tour and you open at the Piccadilly Theatre around mid-July. Just in time for the tourist season."

"I don't believe it."

"The timing couldn't be better. The tourists will lap it up, especially the Americans. Look how they went overboard for *A Man for All Seasons*. Scofield played it, went on to make the movie and got an Oscar for it."

"Wow! Wow! Let's not race too far ahead. Tell me, am I on a percentage?"

"Sure you are. Once it's cleared its production costs you get five per cent over and above your salary. There's a six month get-out clause if you want it."

Bruce was now very wide awake, taking in all the details as his mind raced ahead to rehearsals and on to the tour and then the opening night. He knew this could be his big break. He had read the script and had attended three meetings with the management, but he had not dared to think any more about the production. "Bless you, Alan! Thanks a million. I'll be in touch. I'll be in touch. Thanks again!"

Tracy had caught the feeling of excitement. "Bruce, what is it? Tell me what's happening?"

"Sheridan! I've got the part! I've fucking-well got the part!" He picked her up in his arms and swung her round, kissing her between her breasts as he pulled her towards him.

For a moment she was totally lost for words as the breath was squeezed from her lungs by Bruce's tight embrace. "Put me down. I'll chuck up all over you. Put me down, idiot!"

He carried her to an armchair and lowered her into it, continuing to kiss her nose and her cheeks and her eyes. He was smiling and laughing and crying with the sheer joy of the occasion.

Tracy returned his kisses with full eagerness, reaching up to pat his face. She then patted her small stomach. "There, who says little Brucey will have anything to worry about? They all bring their own good fortune with them, you know. I know it sounds old-fashioned. I know I'm superstitious – so what? Oh, Bruce! I'm so happy for you. Congratulations!"

"Thanks."

"Promise me something?"

"What? Anything."

"Try to keep both feet on the ground, won't you?"

"What do you mean?"

"When you've made a big success of this one, stay as you are. I'd hate it if anything happened to – to come between us."

"You are a soppy hap'orth, you really are." He sat down at her feet, his small belly folding over the waistband of his underpants. "You ought to know me better than that."

"You're an actor, Bruce, my love. You come from a family of actors. Success and adulation can do strange things. Just try to remember I said it. That's all I ask."

"Come on, let's get dressed and we'll go out to eat."

"I feel too sick. Even the mention of food makes me want to vomit."

"Charming! Is this going to go on for the whole of the nine months?"

"Come back when it's all over and I'll let you know."

Bruce laughed and stood up, kissing her again. "I know when I'm beat. Tell you what, I'll make a cup of tea. How's that?"

"Perfect. Now that's what I call real understanding."

The room was full to busting with their shared happiness and their faith in whatever the future might hold for them.

Third Exit

At the funeral Jake had wanted to speak to the family, but he couldn't. Only once did his eyes meet Mitch's and it was in mutual regret and sorrow. Jake had allowed a friendly smile to form around his mouth, but there had been no response, no hint of conciliation.

Jake had made his way back to the flat. He was cold and very lonely. Wherever he looked there were Robin's things still lying about. For all its luxury and its warmth, the flat was now cold and desolate, barren of the vital spark that brought them together. The designs for the play were completed and had been given over to the construction company. There had never been any suggestion of Jake being replaced. Whatever had happened between him and Mitch was their private affair. The designs had been warmly approved by all concerned.

All that remained was for the production to be put together and go on the road. Jake knew he had done a good job and he hoped the production would receive good notices during its provincial run. To get any real reaction he would have to await the London opening, and this was not planned to happen for a few months.

Rather than hang around, he decided that the best thing he could do would be to return to New York for a while. He had lots of contacts there. Lots of gay friends who would welcome him back. There was nothing to keep him in London once the play was mounted and on tour. Having made his decision he advertised the flat for a short let, and wrote at least a dozen letters to long neglected friends. As long as he had things to do, business to attend to, that was all that mattered.

Robin was never destined for a life leading to old age. There are some people like that, one knows instinctively. Robin was one such person. He laughed, he brazened it out, he appeared not to care about what others thought of him. He lived life his own way, associating with those with whom he felt safe. Yet deep down, Jake knew that Robin would have changed things if he could – changed everything.

Fourth Exit

When Susanna left Fiona it was with a sense of deep unhappiness. Had she been able to offer the child a place in her own home she would undoubtedly have done so, but she knew better than even to think of such a thing.

It was going to be a long time before she allowed herself to forget that it was to her that Robin had come for help, and she had failed him. She had always understood Robin right from their childhood. She knew the extent to which he often exaggerated a situation. It was almost impossible to know how seriously to take him.

"You've got to stop it, love," said Matthew. "It wasn't your fault."

"I should have contacted my father sooner."

"Come on, sweet. You can't go around talking over the worries of your entire bloody family."

"This time! Last time! Next time!"

He tried to reason with her, unable to hide his impatience. "There'll always be something. If you go on like this you'll make yourself ill. You won't even get to Italy for the movie."

She looked at him, pulling a long face as he tried to make her laugh. "I know you're right, but I still can't help being me."

"It's being you that I find so lovable. Now, come over 'ere and give us a smile." He held out his arms, flicking his fingers towards her.

Susanna ran over to him, throwing her arms around his waist and tugging at him tightly. "I do love you. I'm really quite looking forward to Italy. Why don't you come with me? I'm sure you can find some reason for charging it up as a business expense. You can put it down to studying the Italian film techniques."

"Let me get this production out of the way first. I'm sure Mitch is going to be great."

"Do you really think so?"

"Yes, I do. He's got a nice light touch. He's managing to get just enough pathos below the surface."

"Oh, God! I hope you're right. I do hope you're right. He needs this more than he's ever needed anything else in his entire life. Self respect! Applause! Acceptance! Call it what the hell you like, but he needs it all so badly."

Fifth Exit

For a few days after the inquest neither Elizabeth nor Mitch mentioned Robin's name.

When Mitch left the house to attend rehearsals she would spend her time wandering from room to room. Things would be aimlessly picked up and then put down somewhere else. Vases shifted from one position to another so she could dust around where they had stood. Books were sorted out and placed in size order regardless of content. Elizabeth tried to occupy her time with as many nonsenses as possible. She used the occupation as a means of filling out the day between waking and sleeping. Once she took herself to the hairdresser for a cut and shampoo, going on for lunch somewhere and then on to buy some clothes that she didn't need and, having brought them home, no longer cared for.

Had she not gone away none of the subsequent events might have occurred. Had she agreed to appear in the play with Mitch it might have all been prevented. Had she been more aware of Robin when he was younger, things might have been different. There were so many faults she found to heap upon her back, so many reasons for her to accept the full responsibility.

It had been well over two weeks since the return from Marrakesh and there had been no word from Victor. No letter, no telephone call, nothing at all. She found it strange that he should have remained silent for so long, but with so much trivia to occupy her she was content to brush aside thoughts of his inattentiveness.

It was during one of her shopping expeditions that she met him in a restaurant. She had booked a table at Giovanni's where she and Mitch had occasionally lunched during the rehearsals for *King Lear*. He appeared as if he had been waiting for her since their holiday.

"Hullo, Elizabeth. May I join you?"

"Yes, of course." She moved some of her things so that he could sit opposite her.

"How are you?" he said.

"Coping well enough."

"Good! Your expensive suntan doesn't seem to have lasted very long."

"Sorry." She felt she had to apologise. "It never does with me."

"I've – I've been rather worried about you. I hoped you might have called."

"Oh, really? There's been so much to do."

The conversation was saying nothing. Their words were simply small talk that skirted around issues. It wasn't until they had finished their meal and were drinking coffee that Victor finally said what had been on his mind.

"What's happening, Elizabeth?"

"Happening?" She knew exactly what he meant, but refused to acknowledge the question.

"Between you and Mitch. You've always made the excuse that he needed time to adjust. First one thing and then another. It's been going on for almost two years."

"I couldn't walk out on him now. Not yet, not so soon after – " She couldn't finish the sentence.

"I'm not suggesting now. Not this week. I'm not even suggesting next week, or the week after that. I've a right to know where I stand. I love you very much and I still want to marry you. I *can* make you happy, Elizabeth. I can make up for a lot of the misery you've had forced upon you. Just say the word. I know we could make a go of it."

"What about my career?"

"You've always said you wanted to give it up. Well, you could do just that – "

"And suppose I change my mind? Suppose I decide that spending my time at home wearing fluffy slippers and baking rock-cakes isn't for me. What then?"

"Then you'd find something else to do."

"I might want to go back to the theatre eventually. It takes a lot to get the grease paint out of your system after spending a lifetime of slapping it on to your face. I know I've often complained about the sort of life I've led. About the miserable digs, and the constant trudging around cold railway stations in the middle of winter. I've moaned about the shows that drain you of energy and then close within a couple of weeks. And then there's the public. That great big bloody animal which mentally tears the guts from you and then leaves you bleeding while it walks away in search of another victim. I know all about that. But it's a drug that takes a long time to kick – if ever."

It was a neat little speech, as though previously rehearsed for just such a moment, but it had all been dredged up from the back of her mind. And it was all true, every last word of it. Elizabeth knew, deep in her heart, that whatever she said and however much she complained about the life, she would never quite be able to do without that special backstage smell that was both disgusting and stimulating.

"Have you discussed this with Mitch?" It was as though Victor hadn't really been listening to her.

"Not yet. I've got to wait for the right moment. I can't just throw it at him in cold blood." She stirred her coffee, and then quickly drained the cup.

They were beginning to go around in circles. The same dull circles they had travelled before, so often. Victor called for the bill and settled the account. He helped Elizabeth into her coat as they left the restaurant.

"Tell you what, Elizabeth. I'll wait until I hear from you. You know I'm always there if you want me." He called a cab for her and helped her to sort out the small parcels she was carrying.

As the cab pulled away from the kerb Elizabeth leaned forward and waved back towards the small round figure standing at the kerbside. He waved back to her, neatly dressed, well groomed, and rather dull.

Sixth Exit

Mitch returned to the rehearsals within a few days, throwing himself into the arena like a caged tiger determined to make his presence felt. Matthew had to ask him to slow down. He didn't like his actors to come to rehearsals with such a volume of characterisation and with too many preconceived ideas. Everyone knew that Mitch had played the role before, and it was certainly no secret that he would have liked to have directed this new production. Mitch was courteous to those about him, seemingly trying to hold back his own ideas as well as he was able, but still managing to draw laughs from his colleagues almost immediately. It was truly amazing to listen to the way he used his voice. He played upon it like a musical instrument. First the high notes and then the low, pulling a single word from a long speech and giving it a special meaning through his inflection.

His personality underwent a metamorphosis as he slowly shed the mantle of King Lear in exchange for that of King Magnus. Royal personages suited his temperament and allowed him the stature and command his strong personality could carry.

Maggie didn't appear throughout the entire period of rehearsals or, if she did, Mitch never saw her. She had got what she wanted, her seat on the IEM board and a say in the video division of the company. For the time being that was enough. Whether it would continue to be enough remained to be seen; her personal ambitions were well known within the profession. Her ability to achieve those ambitions by whatever means she chose was equally well known. The Dawlish season at Her Majesty's Theatre may not have been the great financial success they had all hoped for. It may not have put Mitch back on top, but it had served its purpose beyond Maggie's wildest hopes. As far as she was concerned that was reason enough for the entire venture.

Within two weeks the theatrical jungle drums were beginning to tap out reports about Mitch's pending performance. Rumours began circulating within the profession and expectations were running high concerning the success of the production. The sets were delightful, bright yet with a unique quality of their own. They were complemented by a clever use of colour in the costumes. Orinthia's boudoir resembled a richly draped chamber hung in brilliantly toning colours taken straight from Jake's own bedroom. He had decided on this out of hand, and now looked upon it as a small tribute to Robin. It was his private way of paying homage to the fun and good times they had enjoyed together. The concept and the secret made Jake feel just a little bit happier.

The company travelled down to Brighton for the opening performance. Being close to London, a number of the critics had decided to sneak down to give an early reaction. The publicity machine had worked sufficiently well to ensure that the two opening weeks were fully sold out. This alone proved that Mitch still had his band of followers. News of the box office advance made him feel well pleased with himself.

This was the *real* world, not that outside the four walls of the building. Not the stark commercial office blocks that confronted him at every turn, or the dull little people, pinched and pale. These weren't what living and life was all about. They were merely the tools which helped him to distil his own more true world, and so present the essence for others to savour.

Elizabeth had travelled down with Mitch, helping him in any way she could. She sorted out his make-up and arranged his dressing table, brushed his costumes. When she went into his dressing room for a final "good luck" kiss, she couldn't help but notice the Edward Lear open at his side.

"Pour me a drink, Liz," he called to her as she rehung his second act costume. "I've brought in some red wine. Thought it might make a pleasant change."

She poured a small glass of wine and took it across to him, putting it down alongside the book of Edward Lear, glancing at the open page as she did so. A half-smile crossed her face.

> There was an Old Man whose remorse,
> Induced him to drink Caper Sauce;
> For they said, If mixed up
> With some cold claret cup,
> It will certainly soothe your remorse!

"I'm glad you still enjoy reading this. You're certainly not the easiest man to buy presents for," she said, running her hand across the page.

"You usually manage very well."

The five minutes had been called and the final call for beginners was now echoing through the dressing rooms. Elizabeth kissed Mitch's cheek and then stood back to admire how he looked.

"Good luck, my darling. I'll be cheering for you."

"Thanks. You know, this is a bloody sight more difficult than a dozen King Lears."

"You can do it. You've done it before." She slipped out of the dressing room and found her way to the pass door that led to the packed auditorium.

Susanna was sitting next to Matthew alongside Bruce and Tracy, an empty seat between them waiting for Elizabeth.

There was the tell-tale flicker of house lights as music softly filled the auditorium and the glow was taken down to half. The audience burbled a little more vociferously, and then subsided into silence as the house lights slowly faded into soft darkness. This was the moment of uncertainty, the moment that promised success or failure. The front curtain swished up above the proscenium arch as light flooded the stage to reveal the Office in the Royal Palace of King Magnus.

Another production had opened. Another reputation was waiting upon the altar of public fancy and critical acclaim. As had already been proven on countless occasions, each could differ, and either could signify success or failure.

Mitchell Dawlish had commenced yet another season in his long career of seasons.